MRS SPY

ALSO BY M. J. ROBOTHAM

The Scandalous Life of Ruby Devereaux

MRS SPY

M. J. ROBOTHAM

HEAD
of ZEUS

An Aria Book

First published in the UK in 2025 by Head of Zeus,
part of Bloomsbury Publishing Plc

9 7 5 3 1 2 4 6 8

A catalogue record for this book is available from the British Library.

ISBN (HB): 9781035914234; ISBN (XTPB): 9781035914227
ISBN (eBook): 9781035901135; ISBN (ePub): 9781035901166

Cover design: Gemma Gorton | Head of Zeus
Typeset by Siliconchips Services Ltd UK

Printed and bound in Great Britain by Clays Ltd, Elcograf S.p.A.

Bloomsbury Publishing Plc
50 Bedford Square, London, WC1B 3DP, UK
Bloomsbury Publishing Ireland Limited,
29 Earlsfort Terrace, Dublin 2, D02 AY28, Ireland

HEAD OF ZEUS LTD
5–8 Hardwick Street
London EC1R 4RG

To find out more about our authors and books visit www.headofzeus.com
For product safety related questions contact productsafety@bloomsbury.com

To my very own Special Agent Broo – Broo Doherty.
As tenacious and shrewd as any in the Secret Service.
So many thanks.

The life of spies is to know, not to be known
– George Herbert

Prologue

London, August 1962

His urgent footfall echoes on the parched pavement, each step a resounding clip and what seems like a continual clarion bell in his ear, shoes that he's worn for months yet now feel new and clumpy in his attempt to dodge the pursuit. The residential street is almost deserted, save for one elderly woman lifting the lid of her metal dustbin and dropping something heavy in it, but even that doesn't chime like the noise of his own steps. Opposite the sallow light from her hallway, he slides into the gloom of an ivory white portico and listens hard into the relative silence, his soles now static. Where is he, the tracker that's been ghosting him for the past ten minutes? One second, a shadow was there, two lengths behind and doing a good job of being discreet, the next he's vanished into thin air.

Did I imagine it? Have I lost my knack entirely?

Never one to panic normally, now he feels a distinct thrum under his jacket, regretting yet again his choice of a suit over a more casual summer shirt; at nine thirty p.m., the summer skies over West London are darkening, but the day's temperature lingers. The city perspires, as does he.

The old woman opposite retreats and shuts the door, dousing the hallway glow, just as a couple walk by, hand in hand, and he makes a split-second decision to slide from the porch and into their slipstream. It's never good practice to use innocent members of the public as cover, but this doesn't feel normal. Come to think of it, it hasn't felt right all afternoon, some inexplicable but overriding sense of… of what? Oppression? Perhaps dread. They know. What's worse, they know he knows. It changes everything – not only where he'll seek shelter tonight, but where his life trajectory is heading. How will he protect…?

Fuck! The renewed clip-clop from behind is more subtle than his own; the returning shadow is not only a whisper but he must be able to walk through walls, like some ruddy spectre. Plus, the pace is gaining, as the chattering couple in front speed up and round the corner, leaving the street empty and him exposed. Moisture coats the inside of his shirt as he looks for another faux-classical pillar to slide behind, when a voice is suddenly there at his side: 'Hey!'

He slows and twists at the affable tone, a cloud of angst expelled skywards, relief mixed with confusion. 'Oh… what are yo—?' He blinks, absorbs: 'What!'

The blade glints off the partial beam from a streetlight for less than a second before it slides in under his jacket and he feels it make contact with the thrum of his heart. Smooth and slick, as is the coating on his hands as he goes down hard on the kerb, clutching at the breach in his shirt and skin, cold sweat now, and his mind goes instantly to a living room not too far away, the monochrome glow of the television and curtains flapping against the wide-open windows. 'There's a cold beer in the fridge,' Maggie would call out if he walked through the front door right now. 'But go and say goodnight to Libby first, she's just gone to bed.'

Lying on the gritty pavement, he concocts her voice into his ear, picturing every other precious thing contained in that home, and in his now bleeding heart.

One

London, 10 May 1965

For pity's sake, I think I'm brewing a bunion. The soles of my feet ache constantly and my heels sport a layer of hard skin that easily gives me quarter of an inch in height; I'll wager that James Bond is never in need of foot balm. I suppose, though, it is down to the nature of the job, and any chiropodist would have a field day with our department's lower limbs. But this, this... *thing*, sore and throbbing against the side of shoe leather that's just a tad too tight? I'm only forty-five, and even my mother doesn't have a bunion.

Mind on the job, Mags.

With both eyes aimed across the street, I lean in the doorway and peer past the rain coming down in a fine, filmy sheet. Spring showers, the weathermen like to call it, as if it's something beautiful and romantic, and we should all skip gaily through a veil of fine droplets, like Julie Andrews in *The Sound of Music*. The British are determined to categorise rain at every opportunity, making endless talk on the top deck of buses about what type of precipitation we're having: a downpour, a shower, a brief shower or a bloody great deluge. It's wet, that's what it is. It makes you damp and clammy, the pavements slippery, throwing up grime and smells you wish would stay down there. More to the point, rain is not good for people like me. I can do hot and cold without any issue, blustery wind up to gale force, and snow at a push (with the right type of footwear, of course), but rain complicates matters. People have a tendency to disappear under hats, sometimes with intent, losing themselves beneath a canopy of umbrellas, slipping into a sea of black, nylon waves. If you're not careful, it's game over in a matter of minutes.

'*Bane of our lives*,' I imagine Davy would be saying right now. '*A true test of our skill.*'

Enemy agents use it to their advantage. But spies like us – like me – we do not welcome rain at all. Inside my damp shoe, my budding bunion likes it even less.

Oh, here we go. A door opens in the red-brick mansion block opposite, and a man hovers for a second on the threshold, looking skywards in that familiar assessment of the clouds above. Brolly or not? But I know he will, since it's perfect cover and his hesitation is merely an opportunity to sweep his eyes left and right, combing the landscape around Russell Square for a tail. For the likes of me. I slink further back into the doorway, making my own swift appraisal:

Mid-height, dark short hair, clean shaven, gaunt cheeks. Wiry and fit under that sharp, lead grey suit? Slim knitted tie. Shoes seen better days. Heavy eyebrows, hawkish nose. Has the look of a ventriloquist dummy.

The description I set down in my head is in report-speak, logging it for when I'll need to type it up later, having trained myself over the years to retrieve it from a memory index when required. Most likely, it's a consequence of being a working wife and mother, and the need to create a whole series of brain cubbyholes in which to park various bits of your life. In my case, a catalogue that is always packed to capacity.

And he's off. Brolly up, he steps onto the street, striding left towards Holborn. Given it's just before nine a.m., he might well have timed his journey to ease himself into the shoal of office workers bound for London's central district, those in dark suits with black umbrellas, swallowed instantly by the swathe of monochrome moving in the direction of business and industry.

I cut in two bodies behind, my vision in split screen – one eye on the opposing pedestrian traffic, and the other on the pavement yards in front, tracking the worn soles of his brogues, in trying to anticipate a swift change in direction. I've no umbrella, and the heat is rising inside my unfashionable rain mac, the thick plastic hood pulled up over a red crocheted beret. The throng is walking at a pace, perhaps too fast for an elderly woman in thick stockings, wing-tip glasses and a large, embroidered bag slung over her shoulder, but – in the collective intent to reach their place of work – no one pays me any mind as I'm herded along.

One poor sap peels off towards an office block and the day's toil, giving me the chance to skip a body ahead and closer to my target. Normally, we wouldn't track so closely, but I daren't chance losing him in this sea. Something tells me he'll make a move soon – instinct, perhaps, but his gait is just a little too jaunty for my liking. Peering under the back of his umbrella, I see the hair at the nape of his neck shift slightly. It's the tiniest of giveaways. He's surveying. Waiting for a chance. He might not have 'clocked' the little old lady tottering behind, or have looked beyond my thick make-up and drawn-on wrinkles, but if our intelligence is correct, his own impulse will be to assume he has a tail. It's the day-to-day business of 'tradecraft' in the tawdry world of espionage, producing the adrenalin to dampen the sore rasp on my feet as I wait for the elaborate dance to begin.

A few hundred yards on and it's getting uncomfortable. Not just my feet, or the task in hand, but the temperature inside my plastic mac. Hemmed in by bodies, sweat trickles down my back and the nape of my own neck, creating a mobile steam bath. I feel like a greenhouse plant in a heatwave.

Mental note, Mags: ditch the mac.

Mercifully, he makes a move soon after, though I almost miss it as I'm busy wiping steam from my glasses. Never has a so-called pensioner moved so swiftly, darting from the mid-stream of suits and on to the busy thoroughfare next to Holborn tube station. He slaloms towards the station entrance and then swerves to make a right turn, hopping over the zebra crossing at the last minute and narrowly missing a collision with a black taxi. I'm only seconds behind, stooping as befits my pensioner disguise and brazenly stepping out in front of oncoming traffic, hand outstretched and causing a second taxi to screech to a halt. Behind the wheel, the cabbie glowers his contempt and mutters a 'Bloody hell' into his windscreen.

He's good, this Dummy Man. Not once does he glance to his rear, but I drop back a decent distance, conscious that he'll be using the glass-fronted shops along New

Oxford Street as a handy reflection to check who's behind. It's exactly what I would do. He must be feeling a little more confident that he's either shaken a tail or hasn't picked up one in the first place, because he stops by a newspaper stall and hands over change for a daily edition. That's when I take the opportunity to nestle halfway in a convenient nook between buildings, whip off the mac (with an audible sigh), swipe the beret from my head and chafe at my face with its scratchy wool, scrubbing off the worst of the thick Max Factor. Within seconds, both are stuffed into my copious carrier, so recently dubbed the 'Mary Poppins bag' by my mother. Pulling myself up to a full height of five foot six, it's an ordinary woman of forty-five who emerges casually from the nook, one that any passer-by might struggle to describe. 'Just average,' a witness would doubtless comment, scraping to recall. 'Bit taller than most perhaps, maybe. Not thin, not fat. Hair? Mid-brown possibly? Um, I can't quite remember. You know, like any middle-aged woman.'

And that pleases the likes of me, Maggie Flynn. As it would any spy worthy of the label.

Perhaps I spoke too soon, because Dummy Man has picked up his pace again, see-sawing through the office-bound crowds that are now thinning out, crossing left over the road, then right again, doubling back and running for the number 23 east towards Holborn. Now, there's little doubt he's 'dry-cleaning' his route thoroughly, which means he must be on the way to a meet. An important one, maybe? The Czech embassy is in the opposite direction and his cover there as a desk diplomat doesn't hold with this wayward path to work.

Heat is spiralling again as I follow at a run, the bunion

complaining bitterly. He leaps onto the open platform of the double-decker bus as it pulls away and I'm still running. Puffing. Panting, as the conductor hangs onto the pole and looks out with an expression of bewilderment at my frantic efforts to board.

Mental note number 2, Maggie Flynn: get fitter.

'Whoa lady!' The conductor hauls me in following my desperate lunge, as I land knees first on the slippery wet platform like a sack of potatoes. 'You nearly split your difference doing that, missus.'

Scrambling upright with his help, I survey my torn stockings and bloody knees, feeling like a pensioner and a toddler in unison, while passengers on the bottom deck are looking at me with a combined admiration and scorn for my idiocy. Definitely not in the tradecraft manual to attract so much attention. With a sheepish smile, I take a seat near the entrance and focus on the back stairs. At worst, Dummy Man's liaison will already be taking place on the top deck at this very moment, surreptitiously talking in low whispers with his contact stationed on a seat in front. I'll miss a perfect opportunity to earwig on their conversation. Result: assignment failed. Then again, his spontaneous swerve on the street and the timely arrival of a bus – any bus – tells me it's merely part of his routine, and the rendezvous is yet to come. With throbbing knees to match my feet, I've no choice but to sit tight. Three stops later, Dummy Man emerges from the top deck, tightly clutching his newspaper.

While he hops off lithely in the direction of Charterhouse Street, my descent is more of a stumble as the conductor comes at me with a helping hand. 'Look after yourself, love,' he says cheerily, 'and no more heroics, eh?'

Mercifully, it's stopped raining, with a weak sun and blue sky pushing through at last, a warm spring breeze already drying the pavements. Even so, I'm praying we're not on a lengthy cleaning route, given that some have been known to last hours. My legs might not make it, calf muscles seizing up with each step. 'Surely you need a rest, or else a cuppa?' I mutter under my breath, in both hope and desperation.

Dummy Man is walking with purpose, slicing into an alleyway as we run the length of Smithfield meat market and all its associated odours, where I'm forced to hang back more than is comfortable, and then looping towards a small green park in the middle of a square. Sheer relief! This must be it – perfect cover for a man with a newspaper, just passing the time of day and blending into a general tableau of women with prams, plus several children in wellingtons splashing in the leftover puddles.

From a distance, I watch him circle halfway around the lush lawn, passing empty benches dotted at intervals on the path. His ever-so-slight hesitation tells me he's looking for the designated spot. Finally, he sits and opens up his copy of *The Times*, a big spread of newsprint from which to hide behind. I lower myself onto a seat with one empty bench separating us, judging it just close enough for what I need.

Once again, we wait. Delving into my bag of tricks, past the wet mac and several hats, I produce two lengthy needles and a ball of wool, applying a dowdy, cotton cloche hat which ages me ten years in an instant (and one my own mother wouldn't be seen dead in). Click-clack, click-clack.

People smile sweetly as they walk past, and you can see it on their faces: *Ah, bless the old biddy knitting in the park. Perhaps she's lonely?*

Or perhaps this old biddy's eyes are scouring every inch of the perimeter, picking out each person who walks through its black iron gates, with or without a dog or child, barely looking at the wool working its way back and forth. Tick, tack.

James Bond and George Smiley really should learn to knit.

It takes five minutes and several rows of garter stitch until a figure in a similar dark suit enters by the far gate, folded paper in hand, easily identified as a potential target. Dummy Man is planted in the middle of the bench as man two makes a poor play of moving alongside, like a bad American noir film. I wonder if Orson Welles might step out from the shadows at some juncture. Each shuffles a few inches, and within seconds they both are behind two large broadsheets.

Damn it! Their faces are obscured by the day's headlines, and I have to make a play of dropping the wool and leaning forward. Snap goes the shutter of my tiny camera, the lens just peeking out from a bespoke hole in the lining of my bag, relief that the mechanism hasn't been damaged by my spectacular crash-landing on the bus. But it's not enough, since both are making a good job of being obscured, and I'm at the point of considering a risky 'walk-by' when a stiff breeze blows at the newssheet and both men are forced to lower and reposition their cover.

Snap, snap.

I'm too far away to hear their conversation, and annoyingly, a woman has planted herself beside me, bent on a detailed discussion over wool weave. 'Do you prefer worsted or four-ply?' she rambles, while my mouth moves to answer, eyes still fixed on Tweedledee and Tweedledum.

Pound to a penny, this is a KGB or Stasi meet. Too obvious, you might think, in broad daylight and in full view. And yet there's something to be said for hiding in plain sight – no walls, no ears, no proof. They could be discussing a Soviet-style attack on Her Majesty's government, the thieving of nuclear secrets, or a defection among themselves. The weather, even. Who's to know? Just two businessmen passing the time of day. Out of the shadows in their dark and shady world.

The entire episode takes less than five minutes, during which my focus is on both pairs of hands clutching at a newspaper. There's no exchange that I can detect, save for the subtle mumble of words from their lips, as if Dummy Man has found his ventriloquist at last. He leaves first, folding *The Times* and tipping a genial nod to his bench-mate before striding away. Man two gets up several seconds later and heads in the opposite direction. Nothing material has been exchanged, as far as I can see, so it's a simple trade of intelligence. Despite the ache in my lower limbs and a scab forming nicely on my kneecap, I make a prompt decision to follow the second man, and it's soon obvious that he's no seasoned agent. He walks briskly and directly towards his place of work just ten minutes away, which happens to be the seat of a British trade delegation, working to improve links with Eastern Bloc countries. Oh, he's been improving things, all right – principally, his bank balance.

Snap, snap. *Gotcha.*

Job done. Mission accomplished. Isn't that what they say on the television?

Two

10 May 1965

'Morning Mrs F, got a package for me?'
'Hello Terry, just one for today.'

Terry skips from behind the counter littered with merchandise my mother would label 'grubby', flips the shop sign to CLOSED and walks through a curtained doorway. I follow him to a small back room, averting my eyes from the piles of thick, glossy magazines on the floor; I'm no prude but the sexual theatrics on the front covers alone would make anyone's eyes water. Quite why MI5 needs to use a Soho sex shop as a repository for their surveillance films I'll never know, though it's so unbelievable as to be effective. The average citizen would never guess.

Plunging both my bag and his hands into some sort of box, Terry deftly extricates the film from the hidden camera, reloads it, then writes out a chit in receipt and hands it to me.

'Thanks, processing that will keep me busy for an hour or so,' he says chirpily. Beyond another door is a cupboard-like room where, under a dim red light, Terry will happily expose

Dummy Man and co. on glossy ten by eight-inch black and white photographic paper, images that will be forwarded to a desk somewhere in MI5 HQ for 'ongoing investigation'.

Inevitably, there are times when I stop and wonder: how do I feel about that side of it, the fact that each of today's targets is likely to be picked up and subjected to Secret Service questioning? A particular type of grilling that's behind closed doors and hidden from public scrutiny, and so teeters on the fence of legality and morality? Personally, I don't harbour any hatred towards Soviets or communists, and certainly not for our own civil servants that we in MI5 are ordered to tail, those starched, stiff-collared government under-secretaries who are sexually indiscreet, often with other men. This particular Watcher is very much of the 'live and let live' mindset, especially in today's colourful world. But MI5 is not tolerant, not at all. Homosexuality remains illegal on British shores, and while it's an open secret that a good deal of the Establishment breaks this law on a regular basis, being discovered is another matter. Getting caught red-handed is even worse. Which makes those stiff-suit government workers a prime target for blackmailers, the wily and observant KGB agents stationed on English soil, whose job it is to 'turn' those at the heart of Whitehall. In exchange for good information about Britain's defences – the more covert the better – those crafty Soviets will promise not to make an anonymous phone call to the great British press or the police about stiff suit and his antics. As long as they're fed with high-quality intelligence. And that's why MI5 needs to know, why the fine, upstanding men in pin-stripes (when caught *in flagrante*) are summoned to the grand offices of their superiors and gently 'let go', or shuffled off into early retirement. And why I have them in my sights on a daily basis, before their secrets are spilled by the opposing side. The film-makers would have us believe that espionage is a glamorous business, all first-class air travel, caviar and champagne. The reality: missing the last bus home, stale fruit buns and cold tea.

When you examine the world of espionage closely, we're playing a simple game: they watch us, we watch them – they (being the Americans as well as the Eastern Bloc states) pretend they are doing nothing of the sort, while the Brits are indignant at any suggestion of impropriety. Everyone knows everyone else is lying. At various points, I could happily bash the respective British and Soviet heads together, like squabbling boys in the schoolyard. And yet, without this infantile tit-for-tat, I would have neither a job nor a delicious secret to keep close into my chest. Nor would I, technically, draw my wages from the same monetary well as the suave, cinematic Mr Bond, serving to prop up my wayward mother and a fatherless child.

Hence my current shabby demeanour, scabby knees and an urgent craving for a decent cup of tea.

It's a short walk through the narrow warren of Soho that now teems with life; as the sun wins out over the clouds, the streets bloom like a dozen rainbows, bursts of pop music radiating from record shops that have sprouted like dandelions, the air crackling with endless expectation. Thin women with giraffe-like legs walk in multi-coloured shift dresses designed by Quant and her followers, Carnaby Street transformed daily into the catwalk of a cosmopolitan fashion festival. I smile as one man strides out of Lord John boutique in two-tone green trousers and matching velvet jacket, the tom cat that got the cream. 'Look at *me*,' he's saying with an exaggerated swing of his hips and a toss of his dandyish coiffured hair. I mean, what else can you do but admire his vanity and confidence?

I'm a middle-aged parent of one very teenage girl, a widow of almost three years, and the only daughter of a mother undergoing some type of breakdown or renaissance, depending on which day of the week it is. And here I am, smack-bang in what is apparently the world's hippest city.

How on earth did that happen?

Climbing the three flights of rickety stairs above a respectable tailor's shop in Berwick Street doesn't faze me on an average day, since it's necessary exercise. What greets me at the top is a haven of familiarity each time I draw in the comforting, musty smell of dust and church jumble sales. But with my knees now calling a strike, today's ascent is laboured, and I'm grunting with the effort as I push open the door to… uh?

Less palliative is the sight of a near-naked older man pushing his long, wrinkled legs into a pair of bright green tights and over his baggy Y-fronts, struggling to maintain his balance on the worn, wooden boards.

'All right, Magpie?' Frank puffs, without missing a beat. 'Give us a hand, will you? I don't know how you women manage. I feel like a bloody contortionist.'

Stifling my amusement, I ease him backwards into an old armchair nearby, squatting to peel off the offending garment and reapplying the nylon with years of experience in the art of super-stretch hosiery. 'Don't tell me you've landed the drag queen job, Frank?'

He guffaws loudly with his gritty smoker's rasp. 'What

do you think, Mags? Ha! They'd have to be more than desperate to put me on the stage.'

No offence to Frank, but I've a mind to agree. At sixty-three, and with more than forty years of hard-nose policing behind him, there are few disguises capable of convincing an audience that former Detective Inspector Tanner is of the opposite sex, much less a warbling nightclub performer.

'So, why the tights?' I ask.

'I'm on an all-nighter,' he says with resignation. 'Out on the street, more than likely, and it gets bloody cold in the early hours, as you well know. I think those wretched Housekeepers have been in here and tidied up, taken away all my long johns for washing.' He looks down at his hairy legs now clad in green nylon, less Robin Hood and more ageing leprechaun. 'Essential layers for an old codger like me.'

'Rubbish Frank, you'll outlive all of us.' Slapping playfully at his knobbly limb, I wince painfully on hauling myself upright and revealing my own bloodied kneecaps.

'Christ, Maggie, what have you been up to?' It's his turn then to play nursemaid, getting out the antiseptic and bathing my wounds delicately, while I sit back and remember the long-forgotten days when my mother tended to my battered flesh as a child.

As he dabs, I cast an eye over the racks of clothes and props we Watchers have amassed over the years: nurses' uniforms, police and transport livery, all manner of mackintoshes and hats, plus walking sticks and glasses with clear lenses. The garb of a parking attendant is particularly well-used, since it's good cover if you want to loiter, as long as you're prepared for the wrath of slighted motorists.

As the lone female in our motley crew, my own bespoke

collection hangs slightly to one side: the woman about town guise; the elderly but nimble-on-her feet lady (part of which I'm still wearing), and what I loosely refer to as the 'mother-in-law with attitude' look. But Frank is right – the piles and racks are too tidy by half, suggesting the Housekeepers have trespassed upon the Stable, upsetting the Donkeys in the way they poke and sniff about under the pretext of 'organisation'. A visit from the Housekeepers always feels as if we've been spied upon. And that never feels good.

'Hmm,' I murmur, echoing Frank's discomfort. 'It's ages since they paid us a visit. I wonder why now?'

'I'll lay my next win on the gee-gees that it's Grayling's doing.' Frank sniffs disdainfully, in reference to our immediate boss. 'She won't come and poke her large beak in person, so sends her minions to do it.'

I agree it's unsettling, because the Stable is our base, *our* solace away from Leconfield House, the unsavoury MI5 headquarters sitting at the Mayfair end of Curzon Street. It's only a short distance through London's back streets to what Frank has drily dubbed the 'Spy Shack', but, in essence, our Stable is a world away from where high-flying intelligence officers hunker in their secret lair. In MI5's age-old hierarchy, we Watchers stand as the lowest rung of an agency that operates a strict ladder of director-generals and controllers of departments furtively labelled 'S' and 'Z'. The system is set in age-old stone: bona fide officers stationed on the top floors blithely scribble out their requests for a particular Russian diplomat or British under-secretary to be shadowed, and the task meanders its way down through Leconfield House to the office controlling the Watchers, finally making its way to the Stable and the self-titled

'Donkeys', another typically astute Frank-ism. 'We do all the bloody donkey work, don't we?' he pronounced after one particularly long shift. And it stuck.

Proud Donkeys we are.

In writing out their surveillance requests, it's a fair guess that the high-ranking officers give no thought to the exhaustion of all-night observation, hovering outside a nightclub until the early hours, freezing toes in winter or the sweat of summer stake-outs, loitering in cafés and being invisible behind bad coffee. Little do they realise that when they open the buff-coloured dossier stamped 'TOP SECRET' in red ink, to read of the blow-by-blow details of their target and pore over grainy photographs, it's the Donkeys' blood, sweat and aching bunions typed into those pages. That said, I like to think we are a happy enough bunch – Frank and me, Carlo, Pete, Johnny and Ringo. Our tight little Stable of six seems largely content to sit at the bottom of the rung and call ourselves spies.

Spies. Those at lofty Leconfield House baulk at the word, not helped by the popularity of Fleming's handsome Mr Bond looming large on the cinema screens these days and causing a great deal of consternation and mutterings behind the pipe smoke at HQ. The very term 'spy' smacks of duplicity, they grumble. The infamous Cambridge duo of Guy Burgess and Donald Maclean – traitors to the British cause – remains the root of acute embarrassment to the espionage fraternity as a whole: 'Dirty, rotten spies, all of them,' I hear mumbled in the MI5 corridors.

Me? I've never minded being called a spy. It pays the bills. And it is technically true that I 'espy' people for a living (I looked up the meaning in Libby's school dictionary), observing their behaviour and analysing their intent. The analysis isn't part of my job description, but sometimes you just can't help it, being a woman. Only poor old Frank truly wishes himself somewhere else, miles away on the Spanish Costa del Sol, sunning himself in retirement. Sadly, he can only picture his wife on those sun-kissed shores – with her new boyfriend, spending a good portion of his police pension, earned from decades of his toil on the robbery squad. So yes, Frank does have just cause to grumble a bit.

For Maggie Flynn, spying is a job, and one that suits. As it turns out, it's something I seem to be fairly good at, this morning's bus episode notwithstanding. And there are other reasons, too, a solid motivation driving me through those endless hours of waiting.

Frank, the love, brews me a cup of tea while I slump in the musty armchair. He slips a digestive on the saucer.

'You are the man of my dreams,' I joke, 'but I can't stay here all day. Reports to write up.' I limp towards the tiny desk wedged up against the defunct fireplace. In winter, the Stable is freezing, in summer, a veritable sweatbox, with odours to match. In late spring, however, the temperature is just right. I push open a small top window and let the bustle of Berwick Street market float upwards, the traders barking out their wares, settling in front of a portable Olivetti typewriter and rolling in a carbonised sheet.

```
Day 13: Target 3471, 8.55 a.m., target
   leaves Russell Square residence, walks
            in direction of—
```

'Cardinal sin, Magpie,' Frank sings, emerging from behind

the dressing screen, a handy addition to the Stable that he recently 'acquired' from a London theatre. 'You'll get shot if they find you typing it up here instead of the Spy Shack.' There's no evidence now of the emerald tights under his gentlemen's outfit that can, at best, be described as 'beige grandad'.

'Really, do I have to?' I blow out my cheeks like a petulant child. And yet I know Frank is neither nagging nor trying to score points, merely shielding me from the wrath of Hilda Grayling, all-seeing head honcho of the Watchers, and her strict edict on in-house reporting. Before now, statements have gone astray between typing and the logging at HQ, due mainly to a freak gust of wind rather than any dastardly act of espionage. It's caused embarrassment, nevertheless. Hence, all reports to be typed under Grayling's formidable gaze. And while it's a man who, officially, heads up the surveillance section – some old codger from the rapidly defunct colonial service, duly put out to grass on the second floor of Leconfield House – everyone knows that Hilda Grayling runs the show. Trouble is, she knows it too. What's more, she has something of a 'thing' for me.

If only it were a good thing.

'On the ball as always, Frank.' I rip out the paper from the Olivetti with a resigned sigh. 'Suppose I should shuffle over there. You keep warm tonight, and stay awake.'

He gives out a mocking salute. 'Right-o Magpie.'

After a quick change into my own attire, and peeling away the remainder of my old-lady wrinkles (very satisfying), I'm back on Berwick Street and its medley of odours – the slightly overripe cabbages from the vegetable stall, coffee beans from the milk bar next door, and the subtle piquancy of something not quite legal wafting from a window above. Soho amid its variegated bouquet. Fuelled by the sun on my face, I'm soon in Mayfair and at the entrance to Leconfield House, awash with a fresh sense of dread. Squat, square and unassuming, the Spy Shack's six storeys are hardly a grand monolith to Her Majesty's protectorate, and yet the prospect remains intimidating, hence my visits are generally kept to a minimum. Inside the lobby and facing the gloomy stairway, I can't help picturing myself as a child looking upwards at a very steep ski slope, the world looming above, dominating. The slope, in this case, are the noses of the old Etonians and Harrovians squinting downwards at anyone not of the public-school persuasion, MI5 and MI6 being the hotbed of the old boys' network. Women in MI5 are not permitted into the club, and those that do work here tend to be typists, collators and filing clerks, daughters of baronets 'making do' before the marriage market kicks into gear, or debutantes on the look-out for their own man with prospects and a civil service pension.

The ancient, clanking lift is always best avoided and so I trudge up the stairs to the drab and aged décor of the second floor, to corridors that are poorly lit, endlessly partitioned by flimsy walls designed to stymie any form of team spirit, dividing both space and morale. The larger, more ornate offices are several floors higher, and that's where the big boys enter into lofty debates over brandy and good cigars; our espoused director-general, Rufus Garnett, and his fraternity playing their chess games with the nation's security.

Meanwhile, air on the second floor is parched and desiccated, heads studiously bent over desks behind half-glazed cubicles. Above, an ancient miniature train track rattles overhead, transporting files from the bowels of the basement Registry in its tin-box carriages, and I've often wondered if it stands as a major attraction for some of the overgrown schoolboys who occupy the offices.

Finding a vacant cubbyhole, I slide in, hemmed in by thin planks of plywood and glass, where sunshine and fresh air rarely reaches. The peeling paintwork is stained a tobacco yellow, enclosing a stagnant fog of cigarette and pipe smoke. Pulling out a tiny perfume bottle from the Poppin's bag, I give the office cupboard a quick spritz and set to work, typing at speed on several reports, aiming to dot the 'i's and cross the 't's before Hilda Grayling's lengthy and effective nose (which really does resemble a ski slope) sniffs out my presence in the building. If Lady Luck is with me, I might well escape Grayling's notice entirely when I call in to collect the next batch of assignments from the Watchers' office.

Lady Luck is on sabbatical. The distinctive slap of Grayling's flat, sensible shoes is heard over the clatter of my typing only seconds before her prominent nose rounds the cubby's opening.

'You've graced us with your presence then, Mrs Flynn,' Hilda says. It's less of a question, than a sneering declaration. God forbid there should ever be a greeting.

'Morning, Miss Grayling.' I trill, determined to blitz the sarcasm with sweetness and smiles. It comes under 'Effective Counter Measures' in my own tradecraft manual.

'Well, when you've finally finished, please come to my office.' Hilda's beady black eyes shine amid the otherwise dreary surroundings.

'Oh? Anything wrong?' I'm suddenly alarmed. The surveillance tasks are normally dished out via written chits from the Watchers' desk, collected or sent on to the varying bases like the Stable. A summons to Grayling's inner sanctum is never for tea and niceties. Rumour has it that one junior grade entered for a dressing-down and was swallowed into the abyss.

Grayling refocuses the black pearls, while her incongruous red lipstick flattens to a crimson slash against her pale, wrinkled skin. Her monotone voice barely wavers: 'Plenty wrong in this cesspit, Mrs Flynn. Just make sure to come and see me when you're done.'

The typing is necessarily less frantic after that. Finally, though, I can put it off no longer, slipping my pages into a buff folder. I stamp it 'TO BE ACTIONED' and dump it on the appropriate desk. Standing outside Hilda Grayling's see-through sanctum, elevated from a cubby to an office proper by the addition of a semi-solid door, I garner my courage. My only salvation is that, bar a full-blown defection of the Burgess/Maclean variety, it's almost impossible to be fired from HM Security Services. Ghosted away, or sent to the depths of the deepest filing department, perhaps, but a sacking is rare. It's just not cricket, according to the chaps upstairs. And by virtue of the job, ex-employees know too much. Hence the old colonial soaks and drunks taking up desk space on the third and fourth floors of Leconfield House, their long, boozy lunch 'meetings' and woeful work rate leading them slowly into retirement.

But if it's not that, then what can Hilda Grayling possibly want?

Deep breath, Maggie.

'Ah, Flynn, there you are.' Grayling barely lifts her dyed black head of hair from the document on her desk.

Her roots need attention, I think uncharitably. 'You wanted to see me?' My eyes sweep over the regulation desk and stark surroundings. A single picture of the Queen hangs on the solid back wall, but no knick-knacks, aside from a gaudy, half-filled ashtray of Venetian Murano glass. The glare of strip lighting overhead does Hilda Grayling no favours at all.

Mid-height, painfully lean. Wiry blue-black hair has the effect of ageing her, indeterminate years – estimates among the Donkeys only conclude: 'ancient'. Long pointed nose and thin, puckered lips, fingers stained by nicotine. Typical school mistress/Evil Queen in Sleeping Beauty.

When she does cast her face upwards, Hilda's expression says desire or want has nothing to do with her summons. 'I have a task for you,' she announces.

'Of course. Should I collect it from the desk?' I'm already half-turning, desperate to escape the room that smacks of interrogation. In fact, Grayling would make a master inquisitor, hardened enemy agents sure to quake at a single flash of her stare.

'No.' Grayling shuffles some paper and tenders a single A4 sheet. 'You've been requested.'

'Requested? By whom?'

'Never mind by whom, Flynn,' she snaps back. 'It's a job, that's all you need to know.' Irritation is layered over her general dislike; Grayling disapproves of everyone, but reserves special contempt for those she considers 'unworthy' of Service employment. Namely, me.

Resisting any reflex to say, 'Yes, ma'am,' I turn my eyes

towards the sheet and recognise the address as an MI5 safe house in central London, near to where I once squatted for six hours in a shop doorway in tailing a suspected communist. The brief instruction is to report by eight thirty a.m. the following morning, day's end at five p.m., it states. It's not an average Donkey assignment, and I'm already awash with curiosity.

'I'm not happy about it,' Grayling prattles on, 'but the order comes from above. They want a woman. Needless to say, you're not my first choice,' – she says this with unabashed candour – 'but you are available, and who am I to argue? It's a babysitting job, pure and simple. You go, you make tea, you do whatever's required.' She dials up the interrogation stare to another level. 'But most importantly, Flynn, you keep your mouth shut. Understand?'

Hilda lights a cigarette, sucks the life from its stem and pokes the fiery end at me, at which point I assume the interview is over, turn and flee through the door. Outside Grayling's office, a debutante with pale pink lipstick and a halo of blonde hair glances up from her typewriter with a look of faint astonishment. *You survived!* her expression says.

Buoyed by my escape from a hot grilling, I bend into the deb's ear as I sweep by. 'Me and Hilda – best friends, you know,' I whisper.

I'm only following protocol: spies tell lies all the time, don't they?

Within minutes, I'm beating a hasty path away from the dingy, oppressive Spy Shack and back towards Soho, stopping in the Express Café on Curzon Street for a decent sandwich, a much-needed cappuccino and a helping of gossip from Maria, the café owner's Italian wife, who keeps her ears open for interesting titbits when she's serving the Leconfield lunch crowd.

'That bald one, from the third floor, is trying to *engage* his filing clerk,' she tells me, with effusive hand gestures that leave no one in doubt as to the intent. 'And his wife is six months pregnant!' Seems the comings and goings of the nation's secret-keepers are not as covert as they like to think. Or terribly interesting. 'Pah!' she adds disdainfully, 'and so he must think he is Paul Newman.'

I leave Maria to her acute disapproval and sit at an outside table, leafing through an abandoned copy of today's *Daily Mirror*: American fighters targeting the red threat in Vietnam, and Soviets parading their latest missiles, feeding the nation's paranoia. Alongside, I'm strangely comforted by the adverts for anti-dandruff shampoo and lawnmowers, telling me the world is near normal for someone, somewhere. I should head back to the Stable, but I'm lingering, telling myself that I was on Donkey duty from eight a.m., and that people-watching for the likes of me is technically classed as work, my eyes drawn to a woman striding along Curzon Street with purpose.

Female, approx. twenties, blonde, dyed (roots just showing), long limbs, short but staid pinafore – hates her bust and trying to hide it. Embarrassed by her own beauty. Serious. Student perhaps?

The woman marches by, slicing a look at me as she does so, as if aware of being under the microscope. Licking away a thin moustache of coffee froth, I cast about for a further subject for scrutiny.

Male, forties, mid-brown hair, face jowly, body once toned but now running to fat, little disguised by suit slightly too small. One gold bracelet, tan mark where wedding ring once was. Once-successful businessman feeling the pinch, alimony from recent divorce? Ingrained, determined scowl.

'*How sure can you be, Mags?*' Davy's voice worms its way into my ear canal, crystal clear, as if he's sitting right next to me and I can smell his aftershave on the sudden breeze. '*He might be a film director,*' he goes on, '*an unscrupulous landlord, or an impresario on the look-out for the next big boy band. A pimp, even. Always second-guess yourself, Maggie. Always. It's survival.*'

Irritatingly, he's right. *I'm just practising, Davy*, I snipe back. These days, it seems nothing is out of bounds in the capital that's spawned pop stars and cheeky-chappy photographers, models pulled from the suburban gutter to be splashed across the front page of *Vogue*. And in this world of nuclear arsenals and rife suspicion, we can't afford to get it wrong: don't I know for a fact that people aren't always who they say they are?

Open up the papers on any given day and you'd be forgiven for thinking that the man next to you in the bus queue is an East German sleeper agent, or the woman offering change at the corner shop is loyal to the Kremlin. When Cambridge Spies Burgess and Maclean defected to their utopian USSR in the early 1950s it caused panic in offices up and down Whitehall, ministers scrabbling for leaks and asking themselves: *how can we not have known?* To their horror, it merely opened the floodgates: the Portland

Spy Ring in the early 60s (proving that the old suburban couple next door really *could* be Russian agents); turncoat George Blake in '61; naval attaché John Vassall jailed for spying the following year; the Profumo triangle of call-girl, political minister and Russian spy, which sparked a media frenzy and brought down a government in '64, and – just today, in fact – MI6 man Frank Bossard in the dock for spying. It's only a matter of time before the public discovers the closest secret of the espionage world – Kim Philby as the 'third man' in the Cambridge ring, already defected to Moscow but the news miraculously kept out of the papers so far. When that breaks, Fleet Street will have a field day.

Each time a new scandal unfolds, MI5 and MI6 squabble over where the blame lies – the homeland security service or the overseas intelligence agency – but the average Briton doesn't quibble over job descriptions: 'A spy is a spy and Her Majesty's Secret Services simply aren't up to it,' you can almost hear the average man on the street complain.

Public opinion, goaded by the press, says the spook fraternity needs to open its eyes a lot more. That's why I, and the rest of the Donkeys, plus the entirety of MI5, are on permanent alert, looking for grey shadows amid this dazzling city of possibilities. Anyone could be an infiltrator or a snitch. Lord knows, it could even be those nearest to you.

As if by magic, Davy has suddenly gone AWOL from my ear canal.

Downing my coffee dregs, I pluck tomorrow's job order from my bag (having conveniently forgotten to slip it into the shredding bin on my way out), and stare at the page. Grayling has tagged it a 'babysitting' job, which means it's unlikely I'll spend tomorrow scanning the street through a pair of binoculars. Still, it's a notch up from street roaming, since the 'Static' Watchers are a level above us 'Mobiles' in the MI5 hierarchy. Even so, there's the boredom to contend with, and the incessant eating that goes with it. Donkey work is hard on your feet, but good for the figure, especially these days, when 'thin is in' and my waistline seems intent on getting thicker by the day. I resolve to buy lettuce for sandwiches on my way home.

It's only two o'clock, and there's been no mention of further work this afternoon. Frank has already left on his job, and the other stablemates will be out too, no doubt. I really should head home, to greet my daughter from school, and to give the underemployed Hoover an outing. It makes my heart sag. Why are domestic duties so damned tedious? It's a good job Davy never expected me to be a stay-at-home spouse, since I'm undoubtedly a better worker than a housewife. And now that my sixty-four-year-old mother has apparently woken up to the innate slavery of Western women in the home, declaring herself 'free of all those shackles', there's little chance the Hoover will be liberated from the cupboard under the stairs in my absence. If only the dirt would liberate itself from my carpet.

Oh, hell. The dust can languish a little longer, especially when Selfridges has a sale on good bedding this week. While the rest of London is apparently out seeking 'hip gear' from Carnaby Street and the King's Road, I set my sights on a goose-down pillow and a new eiderdown.

Even spooks need a good night's sleep.

Three

10 May 1965

Despite my fondness for the vibe of the streets around the Stable, I do love riding the bus from central London towards home, especially now that we've climbed out of that long, post-war fog of the 50s that only ever felt black and white. True, life through the upstairs window becomes noticeably less of a prism as we lurch towards the city's outskirts, but I like its relative roughness. Walking across Trafalgar Square these days, you're practically falling over leggy models with Bambi eyes, draping themselves around Nelson's column in posing for an East-End-boy-made-good of a photographer. But as the number 30 nears Highbury Corner, fairytale London turns to reality beyond the glass. The streets are not dowdy, but it's where women shop for cauliflowers instead of Quant, and the air gives off a muted hum, rather than a high-pitched buzz of 'happening'. After a day's covert lurking, I crave normality, the principal worry being whether it's calm or chaos beyond my own front door.

As I round the corner on foot and number 54 Calabria Road comes into view, the spring chorus of birds overtakes the traffic bustle of Highbury I've left behind. Tree-lined and bordering on suburban, it's been my childhood home since the age of five, prompting alternate feelings of angst, nostalgia and love. That the terraces of Edwardian red-brick mansions survived the war without too much damage is an enduring relief to the older residents, my darling mother included, as well as the swathe of younger 'knock 'em through' couples bringing prosperity and new blood to the area.

The second my key turns in the lock, I smell something's afoot, and it's not good cuisine.

'I'm home,' I sing into the hallway, instantly tripping over two enormous pots of emulsion, one black, one white, on my way into the front parlour. 'What the bloody hell are you...?'

'Oh, Mags,' Gilda says casually from the top step of a paint-splattered ladder, brush in hand. 'I wasn't expecting you back until much later.'

'Evidently.' There's little need to ask what my mother is doing, because the proof is right there, bashing at my retinas. Op Art, they call it – a swirling, twirling, two-tone patterning of Gilda's current hero, artist Bridget Riley, mimicked on one entire wall of the living room in stark monochrome, just behind the television and the chair she recently upholstered in flaming orange. I feel a headache coming on.

'Are my lines even?' Gilda muses, descending the ladder and cocking her grey head of curls at the optical illusion of waves that spans from door to the bay window. 'It's more difficult than I thought keeping between my pencil marks.'

'It's lovely,' I mutter. 'Very restful.'

A well-practised look of disdain shoots my way. But really, what have I to complain about? Gilda's house is a haven for Libby and me, and although we are more than mere lodgers, neither of us has any claim on the bricks and mortar of number 54. After forty years of marriage, and the last five as a widow, it's an understatement to say that my mother has undergone a rebirth of biblical proportions in recent years – her array of art classes and literary discussion groups taking up space in the living room, the running-up of outrageous fashion items from second-hand curtains, and her abject refusal to bow down to old age, which includes shedding the labels of 'Mum' and 'Granny' and the insistence on being just 'Gilda'.

When I'm not awash with tiredness or beleaguered by life in general, her spontaneity amuses me. And perhaps I'm a little bit jealous, too, of the responsibility she's managed to cast off. Beyond that, I am certain Gilda deserves her freedom, much like all women of that era, those expected to stay at home through the prime of their lives, like it or not. When I look at my mother now, bursting with energy and ideas, I think how painful it must have been, for her creativity to be quashed, charged with caring for two small children and putting food on the table each and every day. I never thought of my father as a bad man, but he was no different to any other husband in his expectations back in the 40s and 50s, plus he was a little too fond of the horses, leaving Gilda's purse permanently short. So, yes, if my mother wants to plaster Bridget Riley across her living room, then she should do it, even if it's me that's left to Hoover the stairs and nag at a fifteen-year-old to do her homework. I rarely forget that it's preferable to squeezing into some poky flat with Libby, waging war with a music-mad teenager who thinks her mother is anything other than 'hip' or 'smashing'.

'There's no dinner, I'm afraid,' Gilda says, flopping on the sofa and turning to the *Guardian* Women's Page. 'I thought we might get fish and chips?'

I hold my tongue and keep a large sigh captive. Much as I loathe cooking, I'm also weary of food on the hop, and I need to eat a decent meal at my own table. 'It's all right, I'll think of something. Is Libby upstairs?'

'In her room, with her friend, Sally.' Gilda peers wide-eyed over the printed page. 'But I warn you, she's been on about those Beatles tickets again.'

I stifle another groan. The demands of the washing basket, the pile of household bills and the unveiling of Soviet espionage is nothing compared with Libby's enduring obsession with the Fab Four: records, posters and ephemera plaster the walls of her bedroom, alongside The Rolling Stones and The Who. Actually, I don't dislike any of it – I'm really rather taken with the music – but it's John-this, and Ringo-that, Mick, Keith and Roger. Often, it feels as if a whole host of long-haired minstrels have also taken up residence at number 54.

With a new set of concerts planned for the end of the year and the world still gripped by Beatlemania, tickets are already gold at the end of an elusive rainbow. 'That's all I want for Christmas *and* my birthday,' Libby keened when the dates were announced. 'Please, *pleeasse*. You of all people can find some, Mum, I know you can.'

Am I buoyed by my daughter's utterly misguided faith

in me? Do I spoil my only child? Yes, and yes. But Libby lost her father less than three years ago, and life since has been spent trying to make up for the enormous hole in our existence. Libby was a daddy's girl, and Davy would have gone to the ends of the earth for his beloved daughter. He would have sourced those tickets, front row more than likely. A backstage pass at a push.

Only he's not here, is he?

The tinny transistor sound of Radio Caroline snakes down the stairs from Libby's room, two shrill, pubescent voices at full pitch to 'My Generation'. '*Hope I die before I get old*,' they shriek. My gut churns again, more from anguish than hunger. It's the likes of me that they're singing about. How is it that being forty-five is suddenly ancient? *Feels* so damned ancient.

Leaving Gilda in her studio of Op Art, I mope into the kitchen and, as with each day, put two fingers to my lips and place them gently on the framed photograph sitting atop the fridge. It's the one of Davy and me on a Cornish beach, four-year-old Libby between us, all three beaming around the sandcastles father and daughter had spent hours building under a hot summer sun. We looked so happy together. We *were* happy. But together?

Peering hard into Davy's open, joyful expression now, I'm left to wonder: how can I have been so blind? Mr and Mrs David Flynn shared a daughter, a home and a life. A future, too. But not, apparently, everything. My beloved husband was in possession of a secret. A colossal one.

And one you damn well took to your grave, Davy Flynn.

His death was shock enough. A car accident, so the police said – hit by a drunk driver on a quiet street in

West London, on the same, momentous day that word of Marilyn Monroe's own demise hit the news, 5 August 1962. He hadn't stood a chance, they said. But the gaps in the official account were more concerning for me. Davy was a salesman for a large stationery firm, and his job that day included a trip to York, more than two hundred miles north, with an overnight stay. So, what was he doing in West London at ten p.m. on a dark night? Like any wife in the same situation, my suspicions veered instantly towards another woman, a fling or full-blown affair. And yet... it was entirely naïve, but I just couldn't believe it of him. Not *my* Davy.

Against my better judgement, I requested to see his body, and that's when further doubts surfaced, as the excuses came thick and fast. 'Not a pretty sight, Mrs Flynn,' the police cautioned. 'We're still completing our enquiries,' or 'The pathologist hasn't finished yet.'

Despite my overarching grief, I refused to be stonewalled. No wife welcomes the distress of facing a lifeless husband on a slab, but I had witnessed a good deal of death and mutilation in my time as an ambulance driver during the London Blitz. I wasn't immune, but I had to see him for it to be real. Without proof, it was merely a bad dream playing out on an endless loop.

Eventually, the police agreed, leaving me alone with him only when I insisted. It was real all right; Davy's face lay serene and unmarked, but when I lifted the shroud pulled up to his chin, I saw his body was relatively free of fatal bruising that violent contact with metal and concrete would surely create. One or two deep purple welts on his stomach caused me to wince, and that he must have died instantly was my only comfort. I had no chance to scrutinise any further because the mortuary attendant returned unexpectedly. Still, something didn't feel right.

By then, I'd worked for several years as a store detective following the war, returning to work after Libby's birth. My eyes were trained to spot the quiet slip of criminality by seasoned shoplifters, plus the subsequent indignation when I tapped them on the shoulder: 'Who you calling a thief, lady?'

Emerging from the morgue, I was broken, only just held together with a firm resolve. 'So, constable, is someone going to tell me what's really going on?'

It was at that point the police beat a swift retreat, to be replaced by two unsmiling men in identical grey suits, who perched opposite on Gilda's living room sofa and lied by degrees – about their names, where they worked, and Davy's role in their 'organisation'. He'd been doing some freelancing for them, they revealed. Nothing underhand, but it meant some 'pretexts' were necessary as a safety measure. His death was 'unfortunate and tragic'. The obvious deceit poured liberally from their lips.

'What kind of work?' I pressed.

'Nothing to concern you, Mrs Flynn. You and your family will be generously compensated, of course.'

'But what kind of work warrants my husband losing his life?' It took every effort to swallow back my sorrow and turn a professional, stony expression on the foolish men trying to pull the wool over my eyes. 'Perhaps I should ask my local Member of Parliament about it? Or even the press?' I growled at them.

They mumbled some more and swiftly left. An hour later,

a third man in a dark jacket arrived. He came with a driver and his suit was of a better quality, his aftershave patently expensive. Refusing tea, this one looked me straight in the eye. 'For the past sixteen years, your husband has worked for MI5,' he said without a shred of emotion.

When I'd recovered myself, he told me Davy had been sought out to join MI5 in 1946, having worked as a courier for the Special Operations Executive until the German surrender in '45. In fact, the SOE work was no surprise, something I'd long suspected about Davy's war, but never knew for certain. Neither of us talked much about those years – we met soon after VE Day, and it slotted into our past, when we were hellbent on planning a future.

'He worked as a spy, you mean?' I queried. For me, it was one hell of a leap from war games.

'He was in surveillance,' the unnamed man explained. 'And we prefer "intelligence officer" rather than "spy". The latter seems a little duplicitous.'

'Clearly, he's been lying to me,' I replied flatly. 'For years. I consider that fairly duplicitous.'

'It comes with the job,' he qualified, with a sycophantic smile. 'Had you known, we would have had to let him go, as it were. But your husband was a very good surveillance officer and, I'm told, he loved his job.' Sharp Suit adjusted his tie and coughed uncomfortably. 'His death, however, was an accident – a tragic result of his tailing someone rather important. I am sorry, Mrs Flynn, but he died in the service of his country. I hope that is of some comfort.'

It wasn't. Bombshell didn't begin to cover it. I was blindsided, first by a swell of grief and then a tidal wave of anger. I'd loved Davy with all my heart. I *trusted* him. And look how he repaid me. All those years when I believed him to be in Edinburgh or Manchester peddling paperclips to retailers, he'd been running around playing at spies. When the fury subsided, I was ashamed to learn that I actually felt jealous – of the subterfuge, his working for a clandestine organisation. Perhaps even the thought of holding a secret close inside (though that was tricky to admit, given Davy's mammoth betrayal). I enjoyed my job as a store detective, loved feeling useful, and – despite the so-called freedoms of the early 60s – there weren't too many husbands like Davy who encouraged their wives to work, simply because they wanted to. And yet there were days when business was slow and the hours on the shop floor dragged. I longed for something more. Some excitement. Just a year or so before, I'd toyed with joining the police force, but a mother past forty made a poor candidate in their eyes.

Several days after delivering his hammer blow, Sharp Suit returned. Once again, he offered no introductions, presenting me with a single sheet of paper instead. 'Given what's been revealed, we need you to sign the Official Secrets Act,' he said.

'And what if I don't want to?' My belligerence had been festering as I tossed and turned in bed at night, processing the heavy treachery of my own husband. One conversation in particular swished around my head, like a washing machine on a slow cycle. It was the day after Libby's birth, as Davy and I decided on a name for our child with a thick cap of dark hair and impossibly large hazel eyes.

'You know, Maggie, there's no freedom without liberty in this world,' he said, gazing at his newborn. 'That's what I want for her – always.' So, she was Liberty, Libby for short.

Perhaps that was his motivation, and why he felt the need to lead a double life? For his daughter. For us all. Knowing that, could I stay angry at him for eternity?

However, I was in no mood to be pushed around by a man from the Establishment.

For the first time in our two exchanges, Sharp Suit baulked visibly at my near refusal to sign; shock overtook the faux sympathy on his face. Swiftly, his expression reverted to a steely hardness. 'Your husband's monthly pension is dependent on, let's say... certain provisos.'

I deliberated for all of three seconds. 'I'll sign it. But on one condition.'

Hence the Stable and the Donkeys, indoctrinated into the Watchers, and the training – which, at times, felt like dressing up in school drama classes – and the necessary purchasing of comfortable shoes. Since that day, I've learnt that families and children of Watchers are sometimes innocently employed to act as decoys or make up the numbers during an operation, and so following in Davy's footsteps wasn't so much of a jump for me.

Yes, it is sometimes dull, I'll admit – the endless hours stalking minor civil servants as a way of satisfying the Service paranoia since Burgess and Maclean, or days spent tailing street sellers of the left-leaning *Daily Worker* newspaper. It's hardly 'defence of the realm' stuff.

But there have been periods of excitement, too. In late 1962, the world was brought to the brink of nuclear conflict when the United States and Soviet Union locked horns over missiles stationed in Cuba, Britain as the benign piggy-in-the-middle as keepers of US weapons on home soil. While the world held its breath, and premiers Kennedy and Khrushchev traded threats across oceans, the Watchers' feet barely touched the ground, tracking every Russian diplomat to set foot outside the Soviet embassy complex in Kensington. I had little time to absorb the nation's dread, or the prospect of annihilation, between long shifts and offering comfort to my terrified daughter and bewildered mother. Even now, I find it hard to admit that the thrill was intoxicating, my being a part of it. Of something. It was at that point I began to fully understand Davy and his need to work towards a better world, the germ that had been firmly planted in his war years. Skulking in a doorway outside the Soviet citadel and stamping my feet against the cold, I could finally share his secret, hugging it closer to my heart. It brought him back, if only for a fleeting second. Were he alive, Davy would have been doing the same, blowing on his hands and thrusting them deep into his pockets, with that devilish smile of his. Oddly, I felt closer to my dead husband then than at any other time since his death.

And it's why I can transfer a kiss to the photograph on the fridge, without a scowl. Today, like all days, I miss him madly. With time, I've also come to forgive him. Not quickly, and not fully, perhaps, but I'm getting there.

Opening the larder door and peering in, I struggle on what delicacy can be created with one onion and two carrots that have seen better days, plus a block of near mouldy cheese. There's a heavy clump of footsteps overhead as a herd of elephants – in the form of two sylph-like adolescents – descend the stairs.

Libby appears in the doorway, those impossibly big eyes lined black with kohl and her heavy fringe made blunt by a recent trim, courtesy of Sally, I've no doubt. 'Hey, Mum, can Sally stay for tea?' she punts breathlessly. 'Only Gilda says she'll help us make a new dress afterwards. It's a new pattern and we want to be the first to wear it.'

There's no fudging the answer since Sally hovers awkwardly in the background.

'Um, yes, of course,' I say, giving up on the fridge and the larder, resigning myself to running out to the corner shop before it shuts.

'Thanks, Mum.' Libby swivels, then pokes her head back through the doorway. 'Oh, have you got anywhere with those Beatles tickets? Brenda at school says her dad has already got some.'

Bully for Brenda's dad. 'Not yet.' I force a pained smile. 'I'm working on it, my love.'

Working on it. That's a laugh. I might as well be asking for an audience with the Queen or a dinner date with Sean Connery. But work on it I will; if it means rising in my daughter's estimation as anything but an 'unhip' mother, then – like Davy would – Maggie Flynn will move heaven and earth.

After dinner and when Sally has gone, Libby sidles into the darkened living room and wordlessly squeezes in to lie with me on the sofa, just like she used to as a baby, her head pushed into my chin and her back spooned tightly into my abdomen. My breasts tingle with heady smell of her hair, her youth in my nostrils. Gilda is snoring gently in the opposite chair, her paint-spattered face lit only by the monochrome glow from the television set, where a run-of-the-mill sitcom is causing my eyelids to droop.

Libby giggles at the screen, sending a shiver through her body, and prodding me awake. 'Huh, Dad loved this sort of programme, didn't he?' she murmurs, though it's without any regret or sadness, as if he's just popped out to the pub for a quick beer, and he'll walk back through that door any minute with a slightly lopsided grin.

'Hmm, he did,' I reply, stilling my body so she doesn't sense the momentous torque within, the gut spasm that never dies at the thought of him forever absent. 'He really did have a silly sense of humour.'

'Yeah.' She laughs again. 'Good old Dad.'

And I love her for making him suddenly dance into the living room like those characters on the screen, and I want to stay here forever, with my daughter pulled in close, and forget there are spies and peril and betrayal anywhere in this world. Least of all on our doorstep.

Four

11 May 1965

The safe house is tucked in a tiny pedestrian mews behind Tottenham Court Road, the thoroughfare into central London that's already bustling with pre-office workers at eight thirty a.m. As I look at the terrace of scaled-up doll's houses, all very well-to-do, I reason that whoever needs babysitting must be valuable to MI5. It's a far cry from other refuges I've glimpsed, those in the rundown suburbs of London's East End, where low-level defectors are sometimes kept for weeks in near squalor until they are bled dry of every useful piece of information, after which they are ghosted away to Lord knows where.

An empty milk bottle rests on the front windowsill, my signal that all is well, and I rap twice on the heavy door, followed by four more in quick succession. It opens a crack with two eyes just visible, scanning left and right, before allowing me into a small, low-ceilinged living room. Inside, there's a night-shift Watcher I vaguely recognise, who peers and then nods at my Service card.

'Our Russian is still asleep upstairs,' the man yawns, scratching at his unshaven chin and rubbing his red eyes. 'Probably won't be up for another half hour. You just need to make his tea and toast, and sort the bedroom out when he's vacated. When the relief comes at five, you can go out and get fish and chips for his dinner.'

Since when am I employed as a household skivvy? I huff inside, though I say nothing. A job is a job and, hopefully, this one will be short-lived.

'Is he a defector?' I ask in a low whisper.

The night Watcher shrugs. 'No one has said, and I didn't ask, but I presume so. Strict instructions not to discuss anything. The interrogation boys will be here by ten, and they'll all disappear upstairs. Our man is not to be left unguarded, so you have to wait for them to arrive before you go out and get fresh milk and the like.'

Peering into the room behind, I see a small galley kitchen that is screaming for attention, dirty cups and plates piled high. A smell of stale grease wafts into the small living room. While house drudgery is one of my least favourite pastimes, it's better than twiddling my thumbs. I set down my overstuffed bag, glad to have crammed in several knitting projects and a good book for the hours ahead.

'Off you go, then, get some sleep,' I say. 'Are you back on tonight?'

'All week,' he sighs. 'Until they ship him off somewhere else. But he's all right, for a Ruskie, he won't give you any trouble.'

Within minutes, I'm at the kitchen sink, battling with the spluttering hot water geyser, when I hear movement overhead. A short time later, the 'Ruskie' appears in the doorway. He has the manners to try hiding his surprise at seeing a new face in situ, but I note the flick of his eyes and the swift resetting of his expression.

'Good morning,' he says in English, heavy with a Slavic lilt.

Early forties. Clean-shaven, wavy mop of dark hair flecked with grey, bright blue eyes. Smile is weak. Looks weary. Forehead lined like one of those dogs with too much skin. A Soviet diplomat who's turned?

Most notably, he looks anything but furtive, too friendly to be cast as the filthy commie in a Bond film, or an episode of *The Man from U.N.C.L.E.* But then, if all enemy agents looked the same, espionage wouldn't be much of a challenge, would it?

'Morning,' I reply. While my instructions state no talking, manners cost nothing (as I drum into Libby almost daily), and it's hardly spilling state secrets to be polite. 'Would you like some breakfast?'

'Please, yes. If it's not too much trouble,' he says.

The contents of the fridge are sparse, but workable. 'Do you like eggs? I'm not much of a cook, but I can do scrambled on toast.' I pull out a plate of bacon and sniff it tentatively. 'Bacon, too, if you'd like.'

He cocks his head in surprise. 'The full British experience, that sounds very good. Thank you.' Behind the Slavic drawl, his English is practised and accomplished.

Placing the eggs and black tea on the small dining table, I turn toward the kitchen to sip at my own mug with a grimace. Seems the MI5 budget doesn't run to a decent brand of tea leaves.

'Please, stay.' He gestures to the chair opposite his.

'I... erm... not supposed...'

He smiles, widely this time, the skin around his eyes crinkling. 'I pledge faithfully that I do not bite. Or that I'll tell you anything.' He grins boyishly. 'No big secrets, in any case.'

Ah, a Soviet spy with a sense of humour.

The hooded blue eyes stay on me, perhaps signalling that he's hungry for company, likely starved of normal conversation. How long has he been in this limbo? Until recently, he might have been this nation's adversary, and may still be, but I sense an odd, sudden spark of empathy. In my days as a store detective, I'd always been keen to weed out the real thieves – the professionals who stole for money – against those in dire need, the older women whose only desire was for essential underwear, or the want of a winter coat. More than once, and very much against company policy, I found myself turning a blind eye.

So, I take the chair opposite, ever mindful of my training. Watchers in my intake were treated to advanced, theoretical spycraft more as an afterthought; being the lowest rung, there was little chance of us being captured on home ground and interrogated by KGB agents. But a civil service box had to be ticked somewhere and we recruits dutifully sat through the lectures warning of the friendly interrogation approach, of drawing you in slowly with amiable conversation. 'They will be pumping you for any snippet of personal information to twist the knife at a later date,' the tutor cautioned. 'Be conscious of every word you utter.'

Reveal nothing to this man, I remind myself as I sip at the frankly foul tea.

He must sense my reticence (*of course he does, Maggie, you idiot – he's a spy!*), because he looks up from his plate of eggs.

'Let's say I am Yuri,' he begins. 'That's not my real name, of course, but it's easier to talk with an identity, even if it's just for today, don't you think? It might prove to be a long day.'

I nod. Tentatively. Almost three years in, and this is my first close encounter with a real-life spook, very possibly KGB. I wonder, how much can he detect with a simple tip of the head?

'So, I am Yuri, and you are…?' he nudges.

'Oh, um,' I hesitate, unsure why this man has so quickly put me on the back foot with his… well, his normality. 'Nova,' I blurt, plucking the name of Gilda's favoured magazine, the one with serious-looking women on the covers, asserting views and opinions on subjects of gravity. Equally, it sounds cosmopolitan to me, perhaps a sultry agent Mr Bond might encounter on a foreign assignment.

'Ah, good. So, now you and I can have a conversation, Nova.'

It's less of a two-way exchange, than Yuri airing his frustrations. He doesn't talk *at* me, so much as ramble gently and quietly as he eats. His questions are not personal, but rhetorical and universal: 'What's to become of this world, Nova?' he says, before relaying the wise words of his father, as if I'm some type of sounding board for his meandering, nostalgic thoughts. 'We all have to put things right, for our children, don't we?'

I nod again, like an idiotic rag doll. But after two world wars, Hiroshima, Nagasaki and the Cuban Missile Crisis, it hardly seems controversial to agree with a man extolling peace.

'Do you have children, Nova?' he muses absently, and then – when I stiffen – corrects himself. 'No, of course you can't tell me that. Well, it is no longer a secret that I have, and your people know this. I'm not certain when I will see my babies again, but I hope what I do here makes them safer.'

His pause doesn't feel deliberate, but it does beg for an answer.

'That is honourable,' I say, using my mug to cover my mouth and the indiscretion. I'll bet a pair of Beatle boots that the room is bugged. Will it result in another dressing-down from Hilda Grayling?

'Not honourable, so much as necessary,' he replies, 'and worth the sacrifice.' For a few seconds, he seems elsewhere, perhaps on another continent entirely. He scrapes up the last of his food and brings himself back to reality, patting at his stomach. 'Well, Nova, that was the best breakfast I've had for a long time,' – and, leaning in conspiratorially – 'certainly since I came to this house.'

It may only be a convincing lie, but I can't help feeling a little pleased, despite the training. Gilda and Libby rarely comment about the meals I put on the table. Little that's positive, anyway. Yuri's sentiment is either genuine, or he's simply a bloody good liar, and it's this flair for charm and mendacity that will doubtless make him valuable to the top floors at Leconfield House.

A succession of raps on the front door cuts into our affable mood across the table. Again, I note the tiniest of changes in Yuri, the way his little finger twitches, and the visible throb of a pulse on his neck, a reflex that's not easily controlled. Is this something of the real Yuri, I wonder. Fear rippling under the surface of his laissez-faire manner?

Two po-faced men barely speak as they flash their Service

cards, shuffle in and move upstairs, issuing an order as they climb up. 'Two teas, love. Milk, three sugars apiece.'

Delighted to be at your beck and call, boys.

Yuri follows in their wake, casting a look of jaded resignation as he goes. 'I hope to see you later, Nova,' he mutters.

Delivering mugs of tea without a word (and with no thanks from either of the interrogators), I raid the kitchen tin for the cash float and seize the opportunity to step out into the spring sunshine. I buy a better quality of tea, decent coffee, fresh bread and eggs, and – guessing the MI5 grilling will go on for some time – walk briskly through the back streets to Covent Garden and the vast vegetable market that's just closing up. In among the odour of rotting greens, I find a bagful of cut-price fresh goods, and top it up with ingredients from a nearby butcher's shop. I have a plan, albeit a small, domestic one.

On the way back, I run a visual sweep of the streets while walking at a pace, using the reflections in successive shop windows to flush out any possible tail. There's nothing to alarm. I'm no catch for the KGB, and there's little evidence to suspect the Russian Secret Service are onto Yuri's deception – yet.

Once a spy, they say…

There's something else that prompts me to go one step further, and I wonder if it's a desire to protect Yuri more than the safe house itself. Despite the weight of the grocery bag, I hop on a bus down Charing Cross Road (the act being positively balletic in comparison with the previous day's athletics), leap off two stops later and catch another in the opposite direction. Only when I feel confident of dry-cleaning the journey sufficiently do I stride back towards Colville Place.

The downstairs room remains empty, murmurings from the floor above just audible. There will be an array of recording equipment set up in one of the bedrooms, plus the bugs set into the skirting boards or nestled in varying lampshades downstairs, each filling hours upon hours of tape, the transcripts to be typed up and pored over later by successive departments – counter-intelligence and the Soviet office – deciphering every scrap of Russian intent. For his promised asylum and protection from a vengeful KGB, Yuri will be forced to scrape out every operation he's ever known or heard a whisper about: names, dates and contacts, double agents and traitors like Kim Philby. Rehoming a defector doesn't come cheap and MI5 will demand their money's worth, down to the last penny.

Unpacking my wares, I busy myself with chopping and peeling, setting a saucepan to bubble on the gas ring. There's no radio to switch on (a known ploy to interfere with bugging devices) and so I hum as I cook, a Dusty Springfield tune, or the jaunty 'You Really Got Me' from the Kinks, a Libby anthem of late. While I'm under no instruction to feed the 'asset', and have absolutely no desire to play the servile female in this arrangement, I do feel Yuri deserves more than shop-bought fish and chips on every day of his stay at HM's hotel.

By three p.m., the aroma of a large shepherd's pie baking in the oven is wafting up through the house, masking the acrid fumes snaking their way down the stairs from the upper floor. I can picture the ashtrays already piled high, the air thick with smoke and suspicion. Twice through the afternoon, a head bobs at the top of the stairs and demands tea. Twice, I mutter expletives under my breath and boil the kettle.

By four, the two MI5 men descend the stairs, mumble a belated 'Ta' for the tea, and drive home the insult by asking: 'You will stay until the relief arrives, won't you love?'

'Does a library have sodding books?' is what I want to shout back at them, but don't, of course. Not if I'm to avoid another flailing by Grayling.

Yuri comes down several minutes later, reeking not of cigarettes, but a faint tinge of Pears soap. His hairline is wet, and I muse on whether he's been sponging off the cloying taint of tabacco or the stench of betrayal. Both, probably.

He smiles and comments on the pleasant smell of home cooking, but looks even more drained. Wrung out. As far as I know, he's eaten no lunch, and I've not seen him light up a cigarette, so it's been a diet of tea and second-hand fag fumes since breakfast.

'It's a little early for dinner, but would you like yours now?' I ask.

'You made this, for me?' Yuri's troubled face lights up as he bends towards a good portion of shepherd's pie served onto his plate. 'Nova, I think you must be the perfect British woman. Smart, good looking and you can cook!'

Now, he is flattering, but I'm wise to it, and so what's the harm?

'Hmm, before you convince yourself I am some kind of goddess in the kitchen, you should know that it is the only thing my grandmother taught me to cook properly.'

'And your mother?' he asks.

'She just about runs to a decent fried egg.'

He eats hungrily, clearing one portion and accepting seconds. Once finished, he sets his knife and fork together with a sigh of satisfaction, and – for a briefest of seconds – appears like a man having his last meal. From my bag, I pull out the morning's edition of the *Daily Mirror* and offer it to him without a word. It's likely against protocol, but what possible harm can it do, if Britain is set to be his home now?

While I clear away, Yuri devours the newsprint, squinting, nodding and muttering to himself as he turns the pages. Setting two mugs of tea on the table, I sit opposite.

Yuri gestures at the day's news and the front-page headline: 'BIGGEST SPY PROBE ORDERED', details of the twenty-one-year sentence handed down to Frank Bossard, his penance for selling secrets to the Russians. Government ministers are demanding explanations from the security services. Again.

I can't help but squirm inwardly, careful that my face betrays nothing. Last month's directive from MI5's top floor had gone Service-wide, serious enough to reach the Stable: No More Scandal, had been the gist from Rufus Garnett's office. Work harder, spy better, or the spook fraternity might not survive another traitor. But No More Cock-Ups. And now, calls for an enquiry are on the front pages, meaning that heads will roll. The mood at the Spy Shack is likely to be morose and edgy for months to come.

'It seems to me, Nova, that everyone is looking for their little piece of freedom,' Yuri says. 'Whether it's steeped in politics or ideology, or money to buy one of these new holidays abroad.' He points to an advert. 'Even a new washing machine.'

I laugh into my tea. 'And unless you are a woman with

a family and a large linen pile, you have no idea what joy that hunk of metal can bring. I would say that's a freedom of a sort.'

'It's a poor example,' he concedes, 'and I think you might be right. My wife has been a committed communist all her life, and yet she would possibly trade me in for a washing machine. I promise I will buy her one, when... well, soon.'

Acutely aware of our conversation being fed back to MI5 ears, I sip silently. Does innocent chit-chat count as breaking the rules?

Yuri sits back, seemingly relaxed, our previous affability returned to the table. 'I have had a lot of time to think over the past days,' he says wistfully. 'To reflect on my life so far. And today I recalled a conversation I once had with a man in Berlin.' His eyes flick towards the lightshade and the hidden microphone. 'Two spies together, sharing a drink in a hotel bar, and a certain life, I suppose. In between trying to wheedle secrets from me, we had a long, frank exchange on the differences between our worlds – he was from your country – and I remember something he said, that stays with me to this day. He told me: "You can't have freedom without liberty."' Yuri nods several times at the memory. 'He announced it with such conviction that I took it as truth. I still do, but in my country, even after Stalin's death, there is little of both. That, Nova, is what I hope to gain for my children by being here.'

He glances up, smiling, though his expression is soon altered. Puzzled perhaps, because I'm staring – gawping at him. My mug is aloft, partway between the table and my mouth. The tea inside is making tiny waves, prompted by trembling fingers. *What did he just say?*

You can't have freedom without liberty.

It's Davy's sentiment. His words. The exact sentence. Is it a quote? Did Davy steal it, appropriate it from some philosophical writings? I've never thought so, either then or now. Not in the way he said it, looking at our daughter with such love and conviction on the day after her birth.

'Nova? Are you well? You look very pale all of a sudden.' Yuri leans into the table.

'No... I... was just thinking about what you said,' I stutter, lowering my mouth into the table, and my voice to barely a whisper. 'What he said. Did you know him...'

Blasted door! The practised rap resonates through the room, and a swift glance at the wall clock says it's five p.m. The sodding relief is right on time.

Yuri sits up sharply, all evidence of familiarity swept away.

The night Watcher from this morning shuffles in, clutching a pack of home-packed sandwiches.

'Ooh, something smells good,' he says, the grey bags around his eyes suddenly animated.

Stunned and confused, I gather up my things and stumble towards the door. 'Help yourself, there's plenty left,' I manage.

Yuri is silent in the Watcher's presence, not even a murmur of goodbye, though I feel his eyes on my back as I step out into the freedom he doesn't yet have. Except my head is throbbing, insides roiling.

Safe house? That's a joke. In the last ten minutes, my life has become a trapeze act teetering over a pond of hungry piranha. And someone has just cut the wire.

Five

11 May 1965

Christ, I need a drink.

C I don't indulge very often, but right now alcohol is essential before the journey home. To think. To run over Yuri's words again. To banish the possibility from my mind that it's Davy he was talking about. Davy that he'd met, in a hotel in Berlin. A coincidence, surely. But then, hasn't my husband already sprung a gargantuan surprise over his past life? Who's to say there isn't more?

The door to the nearby Wheatsheaf pub is closed until six p.m., so I'm forced to wait it out in a nearby coffee bar, squeezing myself onto a corner table. It's noisy with office crowds waiting for clubs to come alive, chatter rising over the jukebox pushing out top ten hits. *'I'm in love with her and I feel fine…'*

Glad you are, boys, because I am not fine. Not at all. Yuri's words ricochet around my head, as I grow increasingly suspicious that they were uttered by my own husband. In Berlin? The Sharp Suit who faced me across Gilda's coffee table after the funeral said Davy had been a surveillance officer, a Watcher. But if MI5 lied about his death from the outset, what other type of fakery could they have spun? A fine web of filthy deception, something I now know that every nation is capable of. Could Davy have been – as Yuri says – a fellow agent, a bona fide spy, steeped in secrets and espionage? Worse, could it have something to do with his death?

Oh Davy.

My head is no clearer after coffee, followed by a large brandy at the Wheatsheaf. And it's definitely no comfort that the pub was once a favoured haunt of the late George Orwell, his picture hanging above the bar, a reminder of the oppressive worlds he wrote about so eloquently, just streets away from the candy-floss life of Carnaby Street.

There's no question I need to talk to Yuri again, privately. I've received no instruction from the night Watcher to return in the morning, but I have to. By supplying a simple description of his spy-mate in the Berlin bar, the Russian defector can allay all my suspicions instantly, my life returning to its near normality. A life where Davy's past sits like a dirty sediment, but is no longer allowed to multiply. He was of average height and build, fair to brown hair, but he had distinct grey eyes, and a small, irregular birthmark below his left ear – bad for subterfuge, but in this case, an advantage. With his knowledge as an agent, Yuri can resolve my angst swiftly. And then I can evict that herd of wildebeest running amok in my belly.

The bus journey home goes by in a blur, largely down to the headache that's taken hold, confusion, and that double brandy. Arriving home to an empty house, I'm initially glad, then alternately guilty. *Gone to cinema with Libby*, a note from Gilda says. *Don't wait up X.*

Switching on the television, I flop onto the sofa, my throbbing temples not helped by Gilda's artistic endeavours on the facing wall, plus another inane comedy show on screen. I want to sleep, and for all of it to go away. For the man I loved and married not to be clandestine and furtive, for him not to have had illicit meetings in shady foreign capitals, and be someone I no longer recognise.

Is that really too much to ask?

Six

12 May 1965

The phone trills at just gone seven a.m., and – like it does most mornings – it rings until I pad wearily into the hallway and lift the receiver, since it's only ever likely to be for me at that time of day. Gilda is no fool, and the two of us have long since given up on the pretence of my work; I no longer fabricate fictitious days as a store detective, and Gilda doesn't demand details about her daughter's true profession, content that it involves the 'civil service'. The bills are paid and Libby is happy. Beyond that, we respect each other's privacy.

'Hey ho, Mags,' Frank's voice chirps down the line. 'Sorry to ring so early. Did I get you up?'

'No, you're fine,' I say, rubbing at my sore, dry eyes. I'd glimpsed the bedside clock touching on three a.m. and almost every hour after that. 'What's the score?'

'It's you and me, today – the super squad,' Frank goes on. 'Routine stuff, cabbage and commies all day.'

The Communist Party of Great Britain (CPGB in MI5

speak) has its headquarters not far from the Covent Garden veg and flower market, hence another of Frank's glib nicknames. I'm consumed with tiredness and resignation, and desperate to be recalled to the safe house, but that's clearly too much to hope for.

'What time?' I ask.

'Ten onwards. Fancy a bite beforehand?'

My foggy brain calculates swiftly. I daren't risk Yuri being moved before the chance to question him further, and yet it's essential to present a normal front, even to the likes of the solid, trusted Frank. My suspicions may yet be an elaborate figment of my imagination, though the twist in my core says otherwise, the same uneasy feeling during nights in the Blitz when the Luftwaffe took London to task, and all of us in the ambulance station sat in silence, listening to the bombs falling and waiting to face the unspeakable. I recognise that particular form of dread all too well.

'OK, I'll see you at nine thirty in the Egg on Old Compton Street,' I say.

'I'll line you up two poached on toast,' he pledges and rings off.

My stomach flips again. The thought of facing such fare right now is unthinkable, but by then, my world could well have righted itself after a brief conversation with Yuri.

'Mags? Have you got time for tea?' Gilda calls down the hallway, against the strains of the BBC Home Service chuntering on with the day's news.

'Erm yes, perhaps half a cup.' Gilda has her nose into the morning paper as I sit opposite at the kitchen table, pouring strong, brown liquid from the pot. 'Good film last night?' I ask.

'It was all right,' Gilda murmurs. '*The Ipcress File*. Not my thing, really, all that running about with spies and guns, but Libby was keen to see it.'

'Oh really?' A fresh gut twist makes my skin prick with sweat. Can it be a mere coincidence that my daughter chooses to watch a spy film, set in communist East Berlin, on the fate of agents who fall foul of their controllers?

'She likes that Michael Caine chap,' Gilda adds, her focus on the paper. 'He doesn't do much for me, but it was faintly amusing.' Finally, she looks up, eyes large behind her reading glasses. 'Christ, Maggie! You look terrible. I thought you had an early night?'

'Well, thanks for your honesty, *Mother*,' I bite back. 'I'll go and layer on some more Max Factor, shall I, and make myself look dashingly beautiful for a day at the office?'

'Don't be so tetchy,' Gilda says. 'I'm allowed to be honest with my own daughter, aren't I? Or maybe not.'

'Perhaps it's the way you say it.' I get up from the table sharply and head towards the door. 'I shouldn't be late tonight.'

'That'll make a change,' Gilda snipes. But I'm already halfway up the stairs and out of sparring distance. That's one war I don't need right now.

By eight fifteen, I'm seated at a convenient bench near the entrance to Colville Place, peering over the broadsheet pages of the *Guardian*. Today's Service babysitter is easily spotted a good hundred yards down the road, tottering on a pair of kitten heels towards the safe house, her lacquered, back-combed hair just about yielding to the stiff morning breeze. I recognise her from the second floor of Leconfield House, one of the Deb typists rather than a trained Watcher. For all their pretence of secrecy, MI5 are strangely lax about staff 'filling in' when they are short of bodies to go round. Presumably, if this woman has signed the Official Secrets Act and can make tea, she's considered an able candidate.

'Morning.' I fold my paper and stand to greet her.

'Oh! Good morning.' She startles, her heavily mascaraed eyes sporting surprise, then alarm.

Without missing a beat, I pull out my ID card and flash it rapidly. 'Message from the house,' I say and gesture knowingly towards the mews. 'You're not needed for an hour or so. I think they're busy in there, and need some privacy. That's why I'm out here, keeping an eye.'

'Oh,' Bouffant Girl says. Several cogs look to be turning in her brain, but unless she's a typist with specific tradecraft schooling, she could be fooled by my flannel. 'Oh, all right. An hour you say?'

'Yes, there's a good coffee bar just up the road. I did yesterday's shift, and believe me, it's a long day. So, I'd grab at the opportunity if I were you.'

'Well, if that's the case...' She seems almost convinced.

'Say, nine thirty then?' I press. 'I'll cover for you if they need someone else before then.'

'Oh right, thanks. I'll be back at nine thirty,' and she trips up the road towards solace in a coffee cup.

The night Watcher opens the door with an extra layer to the dark bags under his eyes. 'Oh, it's you,' he says wearily. 'Thought it was a new one today.'

'She's going to be late,' I lie. 'I'm just filling in.' My inner turmoil steps up a gear as I enter, the stale fug of cigarette smoke and instant coffee catching at the back of my throat. 'Is he still asleep?' *Keep it casual, Maggie. Mild disinterest.*

'Yeah, though he was up at about three, said he couldn't sleep. We had a cuppa and talked about the football.' He picks up his pack of uneaten sandwiches, and makes to go. 'Oh, nice shepherd's pie, by the way. Just how my missus makes it.'

'Thanks,' I reply, ushering him towards the door. 'Sleep well.'

When he's safely out, I set water on to boil. It's just gone eight thirty, and I've limited time for my interrogation, but if he's anything like me, Yuri will need tea to lubricate his memory.

He must hear the whistle of the kettle, because his steps are soon on the stairs and entering the kitchen.

'Nova!' His rumpled features spread to what looks like a genuine smile. 'I thought I heard your voice. How nice.'

'I'm just filling in for an hour or so.' There's no fooling the electronic ears embedded in the walls, and I will have to explain away my presence eventually, but that's a lie for another day. Right now, my need is more pressing. 'Tea?'

'Yes, please.'

Noisily and directly under the lampshade microphone, I draw out a pack of Players from my bag and offer the packet. 'Cigarette?'

Yuri goes to shake his head, but my stare is intent, steely enough that he must grasp the international language of spy-speak. 'Hmm, just this once,' he says. 'Perhaps, in the garden, though. I need some fresh air.'

Good man, Yuri.

Being non-smokers, neither of us lights up a cigarette,

but we stand on the postage-stamp lawn and look out over the backs of buildings, which muffle the snarling city to a low traffic hum. A crow caws noisily from the branch of a small tree, and suddenly I am in the midst of that Michael Caine film.

'Nova?' Yuri's breath puffs white in the early morning air, his gaze straight ahead.

My throat is constricted as I swallow. What he tells me in the next thirty seconds – if it's the truth – could alter my life entirely, both past, present and future. Everything, in fact. I wish I weren't here, forced to ask these questions. Part of me doesn't want to know. But the essence of Maggie Flynn, especially in the last three years... I can't *not* know. Having been ignorant about Davy for sixteen years, it doesn't feel like a choice any more.

'What you said yesterday,' I begin. 'The man in Berlin, all that talk of liberty. Did you know him well?'

He swipes his face sideways. Clearly, this line of questioning is not what he expected of the woman who came to cook, and his nostrils flare as he draws heavily on the morning smog. 'He and I worked together for a few years,' he says quietly.

'So, you met him more than once? In Berlin?'

'Many times,' Yuri reveals. 'In various places.'

I swallow again. Dry sawdust. The ripples are running wild, sparking painful pins and needles as far as my toes. 'Can you describe him?'

'Hmm, tall, fair hair...' Yuri reaches with one hand for the flesh below his left ear '... a small birthmark here.'

I can barely move, let alone breathe. But I've come this far, risking a bollocking, or worse, from Grayling, and so it has to be worth it. 'And was he your handler?' My eyes swipe to focus on Yuri as he speaks, needing to read his features for certainty.

He nods once. 'He recruited me, after the war.' His already wrinkled brow knits with confusion, fleshy lines set closer together. 'Nova, these are the questions I'm used to answering upstairs, from very forthright men who scowl at me. Tell me, did *you* know him?'

'He was a friend.' It's an answer I've rehearsed over and over into the early hours, while blinking at the sunrise peeking through my bedroom curtains. And now, it's the most I can admit to without emotion betraying me entirely.

But Yuri is too good an agent, and his eyes solicit for more.

'A good friend,' I qualify.

'Then being such a good friend, you will know he's dead? Several years ago.'

'Yes,' I say. It's only my intense curiosity that beats back the tide of unease. 'An accident, they said.'

Yuri scoffs audibly, and even though we are a distance from the back door of the house, his eyes flick left and right. 'And I thought it was only the Stasi and the KGB who were expert at *those* kinds of accidents.'

Bile pitches violently in my throat. 'How do you know it wasn't…?' No amount of tradecraft can mask my reaction of shock and disgust.

'It's rarely an accident when someone falls onto a knife that's conveniently lying in the street, wouldn't you say?' In that moment, the sadness in his eyes says it all – the duplicity of that life, the outcome. His outcome maybe, his future. And perhaps a similar fate.

It's time to stop playing games and come clean. Already, I'm out of my depth. Floundering. I'm a Watcher, for God's sake, lowest of the low. Donkey in the field.

'Yuri, this is all new to me, but I need to know everything that you do.' Now it's me that scans the air full circle, paranoia at fever pitch. 'And I haven't got much time. Please.'

He sighs into the breeze. 'I suppose there's little harm now? He's dead. And his good friends should know the truth.' Pause. 'His family, especially.'

I waver, like wheat in a breeze, worried that I might bend too far and fall – me, who's never fainted in my entire life.

He sucks in more of London's early-morning ether. 'I knew him as John Stapleton, codename "Standard", and his cover was as a visiting business attaché in West Berlin, which meant he could travel into the eastern sector of the city.'

'But I thought MI6 generally dealt with agents abroad?' I've rallied, enough to lodge the shock at the back of my brain, allowing it space to calculate. MI5 remains strictly home-turf security, and the distrust between the services is well entrenched; from the canteen talk, it's not hard to glean that Five regards the overseas intelligence boys as conceited, overimportant prima donnas, and Six looks down on Leconfield House as uneducated dullards. It's not exactly harmonious. The Philby defection in '63 cleaved a further breach, MI5 accusing MI6 of 'going easy on their own man', and effectively allowing him to abscond to Moscow, scot-free. Two years on, the gaping fissure is nowhere near repair.

'I first met John two years after the war, in London,'

Yuri goes on, his eyes set skywards. 'I was on a year-long sabbatical for an East German engineering firm, but he knew instantly I was KGB.' A weak smile crosses his face. 'There was no fooling John. He spotted fairly quickly that I was jaded with the whole East–West... what do you call it? Tittle-tattle, I think. Anyhow, over a drink and several weeks, he recruited me. When I moved back to East Berlin, John kept me on – he insisted he wouldn't let MI5 "hand me over", and I assumed he meant to MI6, rather than anything sinister.'

Yuri turns into my face, as if he's inviting me to read his honesty, that the time for lies in his life is over now. 'Because, you see, I trusted John, which is odd, since we were both spies, trading in secrets. We never spoke about our families, but I always felt he had one, in the way he talked about a future.'

That sour tide rises again. 'Was he ever—?' Again, I have to know.

'A double agent?' Yuri pre-empts. 'No, not that I detected. He never revealed anything to me. I gave him details about the KGB, for my own sanity, and he gave me money, I don't mind admitting. Money for my family. But meeting with John always gave me something more. A sense of worth.'

'And when was the last time you saw him?

'Oh, it was late July in 1962. I remember it was a week or so before Marilyn Monroe died.'

'In East Berlin?'

'Yes.'

'And how was he?'

'Troubled,' Yuri says plainly. 'We met at the Berolina Hotel, we did our business, but he lingered for another drink. We sat for a full ten minutes in silence until I asked him plainly what was wrong.'

'And?' I glance at my watch, aware that nine thirty is fast approaching. The bouffant babysitter will soon be rapping on the door, followed by Yuri's interrogators.

'He played with the ice in his drink and said: "What would you do, if you thought everything you believed in turned out to be a lie?" I'm afraid I laughed then. I said, "John, it's already happened for me. I'm sitting here now, with you, aren't I?" He laughed too, but underneath I felt he was deeply unhappy.'

'Did he say what he was troubled about?' I pump, with my thirst for detail. I've no idea what I'll do with it, and much like the shock of Davy's death, it's all for later, to chew over in private. But I need the facts first.

'He said they had betrayed everything.'

'They?'

'I took it to mean either MI5, or the British government.'

'But you don't know for sure?'

Yuri's wavy brow crimps again. 'What's sure in our business, Nova? There are shadows, and only occasionally, people or things come into the light. Very rarely does anyone speak the real truth.'

We both turn to the inevitable rat-tat-tat from behind, rhythmic and determined, snaking through the house and into the garden.

'What will you do?' he asks, stepping towards the back door.

'I don't know, but his family deserves some answers,' I say.

For the first time, Yuri pushes out a hand and clasps

my forearm. The act startles me, and yet there's no threat, only concern on his face. 'Be careful, Nova. Be very careful. John was anxious and conflicted, certainly, but he was also afraid. It takes a very big man to hide that, but I saw it in him. He was afraid for himself and others, I'm sure.'

'I will be careful,' I assure him. The door knocker resounds again, impatiently this time. 'One more thing – what did he know you as, in your business dealings?'

He smiles, a small hint of conspiracy on his lips. 'Yuri, of course.'

Silently, we move back through the kitchen and into the living room, Yuri sitting himself at the table and staring into a cold cup of tea, as if nothing at all has happened, that his revelations have not caused another's world to implode. I hesitate at the front door, hand on the latch, turn and mouth a silent 'Thank you' at him.

The Ruskie blinks twice and nods, like a man who has nothing – and everything – left to lose.

'All right?' Bouffant Girl says as she pushes past with a bag of shopping. 'Has he had breakfast? They said I should make him something.'

'No, he's only just up,' I lie again. 'There's been some delay and the quiz team haven't arrived yet.'

'But I thought you said—' The woman spies Yuri sitting at the table and drops her voice to a whisper. 'Is he, you know, all right, to be left alone with?'

'He's fine,' I attest. 'A true gentleman.'

Seven

12 May 1965

What now?

The route towards Soho goes by in a blur, streets
that I've pounded over and over, tattooed on my brain
like a *London A-Z*. Head down, the grey pavement looms
as my mind spirals inwards like a bloody Bridget Riley
masterpiece.

*How in the hell do I prove what Yuri has said? And can
I? Where to go first?*

There's no question of accepting the grenade that's been
laid at my feet, ignoring a fuse that's primed and ready to
explode. Yuri is a spy, and a traitor to his country – he'd
be the first to admit that – but my old store detective
nose senses that our exchange was genuine. Besides,
why would he say those things about Davy, except to
toy with me, like a mean cat with a mouse? It may be
naïve to rest my future so squarely on instinct, but I feel
certain he wouldn't be so cruel. A Soviet spy is still a man
with mother and father, with the hopes and fears of his

generation. Behind his intense stare, I glimpsed a good man at heart.

So, if Davy was much more than a Watcher, I simply can't let it lie, sliding back into my life like the goodly wife and widow. Not if I want to sleep properly ever again.

The question is: what now?

The bright, illuminated sign of the Golden Egg on Old Compton Street comes into view, and with it, the first, small comfort of the day. Frank is already seated in his favourite booth, very much at home with a mug of tea in hand, going over the day's racing pages and marking off his best bets. I see why the Egg is his happy place, or his 'hatch-patch', as he calls it. Under the golden glow of lighting and décor that is all things ovoid, it's like coddling in a warm incubator beyond Soho's bustle. I slide across the vinyl benchseat and sit opposite.

'Morning Magpie, ready for another day in search of truth and justice?' Frank chirrups, looking up with his gaunt, grandad face and nicotine yellow smile.

'What? Yes, ready as I'll ever be.' I pretend to look at the menu laid out on the wipe-clean place mat that is, of course, egg-shaped. 'Have you ordered?'

'Not been here long,' he says. 'Poached or omelette for you today?'

'Just coffee and toast, thanks.'

He lays down his paper and pen. 'Something up, Mags? You look like you've seen a ghost.'

Spot on, Frank. Detective Inspector Tanner wasn't a crack villain catcher for nothing.

'Bad night's sleep,' I lie. 'Yowling cats outside my window.'

This silences Frank, since the joy in his life – aside from

racing, the Egg and the pub – are his two cats, Blofeld and Bond, newly acquired when his wife skipped off with her latest beau and Frank's life savings. He won't have a word said against his or any other feline friend.

The coffee and toast I manage to force down, though I'm surprised when my stomach feels more settled for it. My mind, however, struggles to keep track of Frank's chatter, on football, and the day's depressing news over the country's failing steel industry.

'Better get going,' he says finally, draining what must be his fourth cup of tea. 'The shady world of communism awaits.'

In nearby King Street, we settle ourselves on a wooden bench facing the Communist Party headquarters. Frank, in his flat cap and faded, slightly worn suit, pulls out the *Sun*, while I leaf through an issue of *Woman's Own*, always careful to have purchased the latest copy (because one day there will be an eagle-eyed spook who spots the anomaly). Before leaving the Egg, I'd dragged out a crocheted beret and tucked my hair into its folds. With another pair of wing-tip glasses and lipstick badly applied in the ladies' toilets, it puts a good twenty years on me. Frank has furnished himself with a walking stick from the Stable's stock and, side by side, we mould into each other with the familiarity of an old married couple, in among the constant traffic of Covent Garden porters and barrows brimming with fruit and vegetables. Between casual chat, our eyes focus sharply just above the printed page, with my hidden camera lens pointed towards the main entrance. Click, click, snap, snap goes the shutter at each body passing in and out of the party's front door. Frank's camera, neatly poking through the aperture of a grubby shopping bag, does the same.

Along with general toing and froing of Communist Party supporters, our targets have been identified as two men, grainy black and white images of whom Frank pulls out of his jacket. If either emerges, the instruction is to follow both men. Easy enough for two, experienced Donkeys.

Through sheer will, I force myself to concentrate, driving back Yuri's words that are loud and constant in one ear, trying to look absorbed by an article on how to make courgettes more appealing, coupled with Frank's banter in the other ear.

It's no good. Questions spark like fireworks: after today, how can I believe anything Davy ever said? Why would he deceive me so thoroughly? It was no simple untruth, or a poor alibi for an affair, but an elaborate tissue of lies that he maintained for almost two decades. Why? Believing him to be a Watcher had been bad enough at the time, amid the shock of his death. In almost three years, I've just about come to terms with his subterfuge on home soil, grasping Davy's attraction to undercover work after his time in the SOE. That was before. Before Yuri. This treachery feels more profound. Ergo: was Davy's love for me *ever* real?

'Mags, I think we're on.' The rustle of Frank's newspaper as he closes and folds it forces me round. It's timely, since my buttocks are heading towards numb.

Instantly, I'm on point, squinting at two men descending the steps of the headquarters, then glancing at the pictures squashed in between us. 'Am I seeing things, Frank, or is that both of them together?' It seems almost too good to be true.

'I think you could be right. Time to fly, Magpie.'

One is easily identified by his ragged salt and pepper

beard and large, round glasses, the other less distinct in dark, scruffy jacket and worker's cap, but certainly matching the grainy profile we've been given.

'A stroll, my good lady wife?' Frank says, rising from the bench and offering his hand.

I make swift but casual work of getting up and hoisting the bag over my shoulder, slipping an arm into Frank's. 'If they split, you take the one with the beard,' I mutter behind a loving smile.

'Roger that, squadron leader.'

The two men talk animatedly as they stroll down Garrick Street and dodge the traffic on Charing Cross Road, and into the maze of lanes which make up Soho. Because they are so absorbed, it's easy for an elderly couple to blend in behind. Only the really observant would notice the old man walking at a confident lick and his wife shuffling along at a pace not quite befitting a pensioner.

Our targets zig-zag north, past the bustling Oxford Circus – where Frank and I have to slalom around clutches of tourists – and in the direction of BBC headquarters. When both men stop suddenly at a street corner, I slide into a shop doorway and rifle through my bag as a ploy.

'They're getting ready to split,' Frank relays through set lips. 'I'll see you back at the Stable, eh?'

'Fine. Be safe.'

After a firm handshake, the two part company. Frank peels away towards Regent Street, while my 'mark' heads off to the side of Broadcasting House, the BBC's ocean liner of a building. Now, he picks up speed and I'm forced to match it, pulling off the beret and glasses as I go. My affected stoop disappears in a slightly comical live-action replay of the

Missing Link – early man evolving to modern civilisation in three seconds flat – and I'm soon upright and bouncing along in his wake through a warren of streets around Marylebone. It's entirely presumptuous, but I wonder where he can be going in a well-to-do part of London? Is it wrong to assume a communist doesn't have money enough to live around these parts? Having said that, it's not my concern. I'm a Donkey, plain and simple. Watch, track, report, and leave the why's and where-for's to the higher-ups.

The angle of his body and the force of his stride tell me this man is now in a hurry as he rounds into Duchess Mews, with its cutesy and expensive little townhouses that are home to London's moneyed, plus an up-and-coming film star or two. He forges ahead, not looking back as he makes a swift left and then right into Weymouth Mews, and towards the Jackalope public house. Ah! That's it. A simple pub assignation and, as such, easy for me to move in close.

But no. Our man sweeps past the Jackalope and into a small cul-de-sac, where he pulls out a key and lets himself into a smart, two-storey mews house. Still walking, I angle the Poppins bag camera. Click, click.

The mews is deserted, except for one pub punter weaving unsteadily in the opposite direction. It's still only midday, and something about this target's demeanour signals to me that he's on a mission, possibly on the move again soon. I hover, tucked behind a garage awning, bothered only by a passing Siamese cat, which eyes me with acute suspicion and meows loudly. 'And you can be quiet, too,' I scold.

Ten minutes feels like twenty when you're exposed, without any greenery or trees to hide behind. I'll give it another ten before it's prudent to abandon ship. On second thoughts, it might be sooner, because from the end of the mews I spy the distinct outline of a London bobby with his domed helmet and dark blue uniform strolling in my direction. He looks to be casually patrolling the patch, hands clasped behind him, eyes roaming rather than scouring. I could make up some cock and bull story to explain 'loitering with intent', or flash him my Service card, but revealing yourself even to the constabulary is considered bad form at Leconfield House. This target's address will have to be enough for the investigation team to follow up in due course.

I'm just about to move as the front door opens. Out steps my man, though I'd be hard pressed to recognise him in any other scenario. Gone is the workman's cap and shabby jacket, replaced with a smart, three-piece suit and shiny, black brogues. His dark hair is combed flat, giving off an oiled sheen. To my irritation, he doesn't stride out again, but steps towards the garage door facing onto the street. He opens it, disappearing into the gloom. With one eye on the approaching bobby, a hand guiding the camera, and the other eye on the target, I hear the soft purr of an engine start up. In seconds, a shiny metal grill pokes out into the light, my man at the wheel of a very sleek navy blue Bentley.

Now that is interesting. He's no chauffeur, not in the way his elbow rests confidently on the edge of the rolled-down window, and the slight lifting of his nose. So, what is a man rich enough to own a Bentley doing at Communist Party HQ, hobnobbing with the workers and so-called dissidents of this capitalist realm?

Snap, snap, snap.

The policeman reaches me just as I spin and walk with

confidence across his path. 'Good day, constable. Lovely morning.'

I sound assured, but inside I'm running with anxiety and indecision, as I scream inside myself: *Is there anyone in this ruddy city who doesn't harbour a secret?*

Eight

12 May 1965

There's no choice but to return to Soho, dropping my film into Terry's porn emporium on the way back to the Stable and catching him sneaking a peek at the 'high-end' stock as I walk in. *Gotcha Terry.*

In Berwick Street, a faint noise leaches through the flimsy Stable door, and I wonder who is doing a quick change or taking a nap before an assignment. It turns out to be Carlo, snoring lightly in the easy chair, feet up, in his vest and underpants. It's fortunate that I'm not easily affronted, because the sight of his thick, muscular legs and squat, hairy torso squashed into a small amount of stretch fabric might alarm others of a delicate disposition.

He stirs when I fill the small electric kettle and set it to boil. 'Tea?' I offer.

'You, Mrs Flynn, are a mermaid from heavenly waters.' Carlo yawns widely and scratches his rounded belly.

'Cheers, Carlo. But I'm wondering, have you been on a long shift, or are you trying out for a new career modelling the latest in underwear? I hear Jean Shrimpton is looking for a stooge.'

'I wish,' Carlo bemoans in his flat, East London drawl. 'Was out most of last night on a job, and then I gets home and the baby decides he's going to scream all morning without drawing breath. This is the only place I can get any kip. I'm back on at seven tonight, outside some posh-knob casino in Kensington.'

'Well, then I'm sorry if I disturbed you.'

He shifts himself upright and takes the mug of tea I hold out. 'S'alright Mags. I got used to it in the war. They say the army makes a man of you, but all I learnt was how to fall asleep at the drop of a hat, pegged to a washing line if need be.'

As with most of the Donkeys, I like Carlo – he's solid (literally), straight-talking and comes with no frills. He loves his wife and two children, and his ambition goes as far as Arsenal winning the football league and FA Cup double in his lifetime. Beyond that, he works hard and always has your back on the street. Today, however, this Donkey is in need of his beauty sleep.

'I'll leave you to it, Carlo,' I say. 'Frank might come back any time now, so I'll wait downstairs and steer him towards the Blue Post.'

'You sure, Mags?'

'Since when has Frank ever refused a pint at the Post?'

'True,' Carlo agrees. 'I owe you one.'

He's already dozing by the time I leave five minutes later, having picked up a chit from the Spy Shack that says they need relief at an address behind the Caledonian Road, by two p.m. if possible. I'm still running with adrenalin, desperate to sit, run, scream, and think, in unison. All of it mixed with a feeling that I don't want to come in to land. Ever. Because if I do, I will have to search, ferret and dig some more into my dead husband's life, and then who knows what horrors I might find.

Hovering outside a café just by the Blue Post pub on the corner of Berwick Street, I waylay Frank when he stomps by twenty minutes later, looking very cross. His old man's jacket is ripped on the arm, though there's no blood in sight.

'What on earth happened to you?' I pilot him to a corner seat in the Blue Post and order a pint, plus a tonic water for me.

'Dogs,' he grumbles with true disdain. 'Give me cats any day, Magpie.'

'He set his dogs on you?'

Frank takes a large gulp of his bitter beer and sighs into the amber liquid. 'No, but he might as well have. I trailed him on the tube to a house near Finsbury Park. All good so far, and then he comes out a few minutes later with this fluffy terrier thing – like a rat on a string – and takes it into the park. It looks to me like he's on another meet, with the dog as his sidekick. But then he greets this woman, and they're all lovely-dovey, and I realise it's a date, a proper one, in the way they're getting schmoozy sitting on a bench. Only she has a bloody great hound with her, and as I do a walk-by, the creature takes a distinct dislike to me.' He offers up the ragged sleeve as proof. 'Lucky to escape with my life, Mags, let alone an arm.'

Despite what my day has brought so far, I can't help laughing, and I'm grateful for the respite it brings. I thank my lucky stars for people like Frank, and that he sees the funny side of it.

'I feel sure that mutt is in counter-intelligence,' he mumbles, glass to his lips.

'Well, you take an early day,' I say. 'I'll head over to the afternoon job.'

'Oh thanks, Mags.'

'But hey – home, eh Frank? It's not a licence to stay in here all afternoon. Or the betting shop.'

'If you say so, Mama Magpie.'

'I do, Frank.'

Time is marching on, so I endure the stale air of the tube and rendezvous with the current Watcher on duty, who trudges away with relief. I'm already swilling with fluid, but I sit nursing a large mug of tea in the window of a café just off the Caledonian Road and make it last a full hour, my camera pointed towards a women's hairdressing salon opposite. Granted, 'Cathy's Coiffure' is not your average MI5 stake-out, but anything is considered good cover for illicit activities these days. The instructions are to log and photograph any men moving in and out, particularly those dropping off and picking up women from their appointments. Out comes my *Daily Mirror* crossword, always good for staring into the distance over those tricky clues as I sip at my very tepid tea. Around me, the café is a haven for odd-bods and lonesome souls, old men chatting up the waitress as someone to talk to, buzzing with tradesmen picking up bacon sandwiches, and it's no effort to blend in well.

Opposite, female customers move in and out of the hairdresser's, in with a dowdy, flattened mop, emerging half an hour later with a stylish, puffed-up, back-combed pagoda, or a chic, gamine cut. I finger my own dry locks and consider making an appointment, minded of my daughter's constant comments about my lack of style, while she pushes magazine pictures under my nose, professing 'This would suit you, Mum.' *Thanks, darling.*

I can do this type of surveillance with my eyes shut. Not technically, perhaps, but my gaze is soon on automatic pilot, primed for any male form at the doorway. Which means the rest of my concentration – ninety-nine per cent of it – veers inevitably towards Yuri and his words. The conundrum of how to prove or disprove almost twenty years of a lie will not be quashed – nagging, nudging, poking, jabbing and stabbing. Amid the irritation, it hurts.

Where, Mags? Where would anyone go looking for information about an agent, current or previous? The Spy Shack, obviously. I almost laugh out loud at the scenario of me striding into Hilda Grayling's stuffy office and requesting to look at my late husband's file. *A quick peek, Hilda. Please? Just so as I might breathe again.*

The question hangs heavily: how do I access a file from the bowels of the Secret Services – secretly?

My little brain compartments must be doing their stuff because, out of nowhere, a name pops into my head. Vivien. While my good friend Mrs Remmers doesn't have a direct path to MI5 personnel files, she'll know the process, and how to request a document without inviting suspicion. I ponder on how much I need to tell her. And can she keep a secret? The latter answer is a resounding yes, but this is no tittle-tattle, Vivien's usual stock in trade. It's more like life and death if Yuri is to be believed. Still, I have a starting point, something to stop my nerves clanging like Big Ben on the hour.

'A top-up, love?' The waitress eyes the distasteful scum that's formed on the surface of my tea. 'Must be stone cold by now.' She smiles, but it's a heavy hint at my lengthy occupation of the table.

'Oh yes, another thanks,' I say. 'And a scone with butter.' There goes the waistline again.

The hairdresser closes at five thirty p.m., and like so many Donkey outings, there's little to show, only that Cathy and her staff can pull off a decent hairdo. But no men, in or out. A woman who I take to be Cathy emerges from the shop on the dot of closing, locks the door and totters towards King's Cross in a pair of stiletto heels, at which point I feel my bunion wince in sympathy for her poor toes. I can't decide which end of me needs attention first – my swollen feet or a deflated head of hair.

In a nearby phone box, I dial a number from memory.

'Ministry office.' Vivien's voice is prim and business-like in response, until I reveal who's on the line. 'Maggie! Lovely to hear from you. How's life?'

'Fine. Listen, it's been ages since we had a drink. I don't suppose you're free after work today?'

There's a flicking of diary pages down the line. 'I am actually, and yes, I could murder a G & T.' She lowers her voice into the receiver. 'His Right Honourable has been particularly testy today, so I feel I deserve it. I finish at six.'

'A large one, then. My treat. Shall we say the Langham Bar at six thirty?'

'Perfect. Bye, Mags.'

I'm not too far from home, but I daren't risk Gilda's glacial mood if I race into the house, change and run out again, mindful of my promise not to be late. Instead, I hop on the tube again, which at rush hour is packed like a sardine can, and make it back to the Stable, where I do a mix and match of my own clothes, embellished with something from my dressing-up box and use half a tin of lacquer in sprucing up the flat locks, plus a dash of lipstick and mascara. There's no hope of equalling Vivien for glamour, but I can try to appear less like a bag lady.

Nine

12 May 1965

I've always liked the Langham Hotel, sitting directly opposite BBC Broadcasting House, with the bar that fizzes with media talk. It's not posh enough to make me feel uncomfortable, but definitely a step up from a smoky pub. Plus, Vivien is one for the good life and so the general atmosphere, along with a double gin and tonic, will be in my favour. I try to forget that the traitorous Guy Burgess once propped up the bar here (along with so many other hostelries across London), but given that Arthur Conan Doyle and Noel Coward were former patrons, there is a lot to recommend it.

The drinks are lined up when Vivien blows in, oozing sophistication and attracting several admiring glances. Even at the end of her working day, her auburn hair is pinned and twisted into a perfect French pleat, her make-up flawless, and the two-piece suit skimming those slender hips without a crease. I'm in awe.

'Darling,' she pronounces, kissing me on both cheeks. 'You look lovely.'

She's lying, of course, but we go through the motions while there are several pairs of roving eyes upon her. What's so refreshing about Vivien is that we each know what's behind the façade. She's aware of my true employer, and I know of her past – the fact that she started life as a tailor's daughter who lived two doors down in Calabria Avenue until they had to sell up and move beyond London when her father's business went bust. Vivien quickly decided she didn't like the humdrum life, and set about changing it. Out went the distinct Essex accent, and in came the rounded vowels of the well-to-do. She knew the cut of good cloth, which is how we became reacquainted in adulthood, her in my sights as she expertly 'lifted' a Chanel suit from the rails of Selfridges. One of those moments when I turned a blind eye as a store detective, after she'd returned the suit to its rightful place on the rack.

It was a mere hiccup in Vivien's determined trajectory. Within months, she'd expertly snared her catch and flounced down the aisle with an up-and-coming lawyer. Fifteen years later, he upped and left her for a younger model. As a former wife without children, alimony, or experience in the job market, she was entirely stranded and with few prospects. Undeterred, what Vivien did have was a good memory and a little black book, which she'd filled over a long career of being the perfect wife and sidekick to her ex-husband's glittering role as a defence barrister to the great and good, when they weren't being so great, and far from good. Vivien was an excellent listener and keeper of secrets – discreet until it was necessary not to be. Necessary for her, that is. When the divorce papers came through, she opened up her little notebook of scribbled indiscretions.

Now, while Vivien is busy keeping the diary and typing up top secret reports as personal assistant to the man in charge of Britain's atomic capabilities at the Ministry of Defence, he is assured she will not spill the beans about his long-term mistress, or his proclivity for using fruits in the bedroom. Fruits not always of the soft variety. In turn, Vivien is guaranteed solid employment. Smart woman.

In living this new, independent life, Vivien's principal goal is in proving to her ex-husband ('The Bastard') that she remains appealing to the opposite sex as a forty-something woman. To this end, she attacks the challenge with gusto. Blessed with the bone structure of an actress, and with her advanced training in flirtatious chit-chat, Vivien is often on the arm of a diplomat, an under-secretary to this or that, or her favourite beau – the foreign attaché.

'So much more interesting when English isn't their first language and they don't know how much you're bluffing,' she once told me. 'Sign language in the bedroom can be so much fun.'

Such as it is, my contribution to the friendship is ensuring Vivien doesn't end up as the patsy in a Profumo-type love triangle; more than once I've had to steer her away from the loving, incendiary arms of an Eastern Bloc diplomat that I've had under my professional, beady eye.

Safe to say, we make an unlikely pairing. But Vivien has sources, and resources. And she is, above all that, a good friend, particularly since Davy's death. Given that she's also signed the Official Secrets Act, I've felt safe in confessing my complex, unorthodox situation. Besides, she's fun, and I can be myself with her. Mostly.

'How's tricks then?' She takes a large gulp of gin in a most lady-like manner, after we slide into a corner booth.

'Fine, fine.' I'm getting almost blasé about lying in the space of a day.

'And Libby? Your mum?'

'Well, Libby is a teenager, need I say more? And Gilda is on a mission to act like one.' I have a sudden notion. 'Oh, I don't suppose you know how to get hold of any Beatles tickets?'

Vivien gulps again. 'Sorry, no. Tickets for the opera maybe, but everyone is my office is so bloody strait-laced, they wouldn't know a Beatle from a Stone, let alone George from Ringo.'

'And how are you?' I ask. 'Any men in play currently?'

She wrinkles her nose and shuffles closer towards me. 'Well, he's very nice, and just a tad younger than me, though I think I might have been a little conservative when he angled for my age.'

'Nationality?' My look is just a little bit stern and maternal.

'You needn't worry, Mags. He's Italian. And a businessman, though he comes from Venetian nobility. His grandfather was a count, you know.'

Pigs might fly, Vivien, and Italians do have a spy network, too. 'Just be careful, eh?' I can't help saying. 'Unless you are going to marry him and be whisked off to a palazzo in Venice – in which case, you *are* my best friend – you should be wary.'

'Oh Maggie!' she nudges her delicate shoulder into mine. 'Always so suspicious, though I suppose that does come with the job.'

Both of us sip at our drinks and gaze at the bar's clientele in silence, drinking in the lively post-work chatter. Working at the BBC across the way does seem to inspire a lot more mirth than MI5.

'Come on, then, tell me what's really wrong,' Vivien says at last.

'What? No, nothing.' But my stock of lies fails in the face of Mrs Remmers' shrewd expression. She can dig out a confidence ten feet under with a teaspoon, and now she will not let my eyes leave hers.

'Maggie, it's lovely to see you, and we're way overdue a catch-up, but I'm neither blind nor decrepit, not yet anyway. I can tell something's up.'

In truth, I'm almost relieved she's prodding at me to spill, because if I don't tell someone I'll either explode or drown pathetically in a bucket of gin. Securing Vivien's help is by far the better option. And isn't that what I really came for?

'I found out something today,' I start. 'About Davy.'

Vivien's sculpted eyebrows arch dramatically. 'Oh Mags, he wouldn't be the first husband to have had an affair...' she starts.

'It wasn't an affair – at least I don't think so.' *Oh, that a woman was the extent of his betrayal.* 'I can't tell you all of it,' I go on. 'I mean, I will when I discover more, but for now, I need to find out what Davy was doing before he died.'

Vivien puts her mouth in close to my ear, and to the

crowd it must look as if we are sharing giggles and gossip. 'You mean something other than working for MI5?' she murmurs.

I nod.

'Oh. More than being a Watcher?'

I tip my head again.

'Christ, Mags.' She scrabbles in her handbag and lights up a cigarette, blowing out smoke in an alluring, film-star way. 'Are we talking top secret stuff?'

I shrug. 'I honestly don't know. It didn't come from my bosses, or anyone on the inside,' I say. 'I found out by accident, and it's something he – and they – deliberately kept from me. Which means I have to go looking on my own, to be certain.'

'And do you really *have* to?' Vivien's face is ashen – this from a woman who types up covert content on a daily basis. 'Are you sure about that? Look, Maggie, I know how you felt when Davy died, and what you discovered then, the shock it gave you. But isn't it better to let it lie? I hate to be blunt, but it won't bring your husband back, and... well... there are some good things to emerge from it. You have a new job, and I can testify it's a damn sight more exciting than typing up letters for an oversexed secretary of state.'

'I can't,' I manage between set teeth. 'I can't let it go.' For the first time today, I think I might cry. She's right, of course. It won't bring Davy back, but Vivien doesn't know the full story and I can't risk her safety until I know more. Knowledge is power – it's what the security services worldwide are built on – but it's also a heavy burden, and a cosh that can be turned back on the user. Equally, in uncovering Davy's motive, I may truly understand his duplicity. Finally, I might be able to forgive him.

'I just have to,' I say, the bottom lip not quite under control. 'Will you help me?'

She downs the last of her gin, and moves to get up. 'Of course I will. But first we each need another large one.'

'So, if I request any information from either MI5 or MI6, I need the minister's signature to action it,' Vivien explains over a second gin. 'That's easy enough – he'll sign anything I put in front of him. The problem is, any request creates a paper trail that leads right back to his office.'

'It puts paid to that plan,' I say defiantly. I knew it wouldn't be simple, but in my shock and confusion, and my zeal to lurch forward, my reasoning is that of a bull in a china shop. 'It's ironic that I damn well work in the place, and yet I can't get access to things inside.'

'Hmm, that's the Secret Service for you,' she sighs. 'It's the Registry you need to get into. If Davy's details are anywhere, that's the place. Are you friendly with any porters or desk clerks?'

I shake my head. 'Surveillance staff have no reason to be down there, so it would raise a few eyebrows. And it's very well policed.'

That's an understatement, since the gates of heaven or hell are more easily breached than the MI5 Registry. Vital decisions may take place on the upper floors, but without the hundreds of thousands of files, card indexes and cuttings logged in the basement, there would be no top level. 'Everything is in those files if you look hard enough,' intelligence officers say again and again, in deference to the archives. Without the Registry, there is no MI5. And without the ear of the 'Registry Queens', there is no access.

Like varying departments within Leconfield House, the

overseer is a man, but the real work is done by a tight team of women who hold court over the racks of filing cabinets and rows upon rows of cross-referenced card indexes, information at their valuable fingertips, and who inspire fear in the hardiest of agents. No one crosses the Queens.

Worse, Queen Bee is a woman with a reputation to match Hilda Grayling's.

'Maggie, what on earth are you thinking?' Vivien says. 'You've gone a very odd shade of green.'

'I'm just wondering how on earth I charm, fool or get past Bea Baglan.' The prospect makes me drain the last of a very strong G & T.

Vivien sucks thoughtfully on her leftover lemon slice. 'Well, that's one area I might be able to help you with.'

Ten

12 May 1965

My intention is to revisit Colville Place on my way home and engineer a few minutes alone with Yuri, to pump him for a lead, some tiny nugget to guide my search. Anything, at this point. But two large gins and the day's adrenalin makes for a dodgy cocktail. I am shaken *and* stirred, Mr Bond. Tomorrow morning will have to do and, in mind of Gilda's nose that has the acuity of a badger's, I down a very quick espresso and suck on several slightly dusty mints lodging in the crevice of my jacket pocket. I really don't need my mother suspecting that I'm turning to drink.

Landing at number 54, I feel overcome with tiredness and would happily head straight to bed. Libby, though, is downstairs and without a friend in situ, plus she's in a good mood and unusually chatty. Gilda has cooked, too, an indeterminate mix of vegetables and Middle Eastern spices, but it's hot and edible, and we sit at the kitchen table together. At peace.

Have I landed in an alternate universe?

'Mum—?' Libby starts.

'No, no word on The Beatles tickets yet,' I intercept. 'But I am working on it.'

'Good, but I was actually going to say… erm… it's the school dance soon, and I was wonderi…' She forks more food into her mouth.

'What she means is, will you take her shopping?' Gilda butts in impatiently.

'When?'

'This weekend?' Libby pitches. The thick kohl under her innocent eyes makes her look like a model from one of those teen magazines she reads, and suddenly I'm afraid for her beauty. 'Mum?' She's normally more forthright in her demands, and never shy of reminding me of what I lack in the maternal department. Which means she must really want it.

I hesitate, wishing I could tell my only child that yes, I will take you shopping, precious girl, but there's just a little matter to resolve first, of finding out why your father was a spy who associated with the insidious KGB.

Gilda aims a severe, loaded look over a plate of aubergines: *You need to do this. For your daughter.*

'Yes, of course.' I force my mouth to form the right words. 'But what exactly are we shopping for?'

'A dress. And some shoes maybe?' Libby says hopefully. 'There's Bazaar, and I'd like to look in Countdown, plus Carrot on Wheels.' And she's off, quoting every bizarrely named boutique the length and breadth of the King's Road. 'And maybe some tea at Derry and Tom's after?'

'I'll get my chequebook out then, shall I?' Whatever the

dent in my finances, it will be worth it. It's entirely worth it for this moment, of not being the old and tired enemy for once. After all, isn't that what Davy was working for, in his own very strange way?

For the first time in an age, all three of us spend the evening together in one room, loafing on the sofa and watching an episode of *The Fugitive*. The plot strikes me as so fantastical that, for a full hour, I forget how much of a mess my life has become in the last two days, and even Gilda's shocking efforts with the paint pot seem less alarming by comparison.

I must have dozed because I wake with a start at the familiar sound of the news coming on. Suddenly alert, reality returns with brute force. As Gilda stirs and heads off to make tea, and I chivvy Libby up to bed, the questions circulate like an eddy of dirty bathwater that refuses to go down the plughole: why would Davy be a full-blown MI5 agent? And what did he discover that was so important, so awful that he just might have been killed for it?

'I might head up too,' I call out to Gilda in the kitchen.

'All right, love,' she yawns. 'Sleep well.'

Except 'sleep' and 'well' have no dominion in my bedroom, or my head, lying there staring at the strobes of streetlight on the ceiling. I might as well get up and do something. Rifling in the back of my wardrobe, I dig out the large circular hat box that's taped with a label, scrawled in his block handwriting: 'OUR THINGIES'. Tipping its contents onto the bed, there's a temptation to spend hours in the comfort of nostalgia – the pebble with a hole in it that we found on a beach in Devon, and that Davy put on the end of my finger with great aplomb, kneeling down in the sand and proposing marriage; Libby's first blonde curl that we cut, her first tooth, too. All the paraphernalia of a normal life. But I've no time to reminisce, or cry, or lament, though I do slip that pebble on and off several times, until the lump in my throat begins to feel harder than the stone, and I drop it back in the box. To my disappointment, there's nothing new in there, harbouring a secret pocket or compartment to help calm my aching insides.

'Davy, give me something, will you?' I press aloud, head tipped back toward the ceiling. 'Aren't spies supposed to leave a few breadcrumbs?'

The ceiling. Above which is the attic – largely Davy's domain, and where he used to store boxes even after we'd moved into our own flat with Libby. Gilda rarely ventures up there, down to the rickety wooden ladder needed to access it.

Deathly ascent or not, my zeal for any kind of clue wins out. Creeping onto the landing, and sensing Gilda and Libby are safely tucked up in their rooms, I pull down the steps and gingerly begin the climb. Each rung creaks under my socked feet, but in truth it feels a good deal more solid than my life right now, serving to spurring me on. I'm grunting slightly as I reach the lip, haul myself through the small square hole and pull on the light cable that Davy had installed. The bulb swings its dim glow over a surprisingly tidy array of cardboard boxes and a good deal of dust. Despite the heat of the house, I shiver in my thin nightdress. The last time I'd been up here was a month or so after Davy's death, shoving a bag of his clothes I couldn't bear to part with into the corner. Now, it's his own stores I head for, pulling at the tape carefully so as to quell any noise. The first box is filled with old photographs; I sort through quickly, forcing myself to skate over those in which we're pictured together. It's too cold and late for sentimentality. Nothing stands out. The second is what I would term his 'man chest' – full of old bits and bobs, metal washers, nails and screws, the hammer he cherished and pretended to be good at DIY with. I punch the heel of it into my palm. 'Hell, Davy!' I hiss. 'What am I supposed to look for?'

'Mum?' The ladder creaks below, and Libby's tousled head appears through the opening like a jack-in-a-box, her wider eyes coming into view. 'Who are you talking to?'

'No one,' I say. 'I just caught my finger on a nail.' I suck it for good effect. 'Did I wake you?'

'No, I was reading,' she says. 'I thought it was a rat scrabbling about until I saw the light.'

I scan quickly, hoping to God there is none of the latter. Sinister Soviets don't hold a candle to scurrying vermin when it comes to my own terror. 'I'll be down in a minute,' I say. 'You go back to bed.'

But she's already pulled her lean nimble body up into the space and is peering into the first opened container. 'What are you looking for?'

'Just a picture of Dad.' Another lie to my daughter, though I reason it's a protective one. 'Some archive his old firm is putting together. I said I'd try and help.'

'There's plenty in here,' she says, stooping to pick up a sheaf of old black and white photographs. I find myself stopping to watch her expression as she leafs through them, her lips spreading into a smile at some of us on the beach, then frowning at the silly faces she pulled into the lens. I remember with clarity how Davy goaded her into misbehaving that day, simply by telling her to 'be serious,

Libs'. Now, she pouts at one of her in a school fancy dress costume which Davy had helped make – nay construct, with the passion of an architect. 'Dad was up until all hours making that,' I say.

Libby laughs. 'And I was so embarrassed, because it was obvious he'd done it and not me.'

'He loved you so much,' I say. 'He just wanted you to be proud parading in front of the class.'

'Huh, funny how I'd give anything for him to embarrass me now.' She's silent again, eyes bored into the grainy black and white paper, then murmurs: 'Do you miss Dad, think about him much?'

Tonight, of all nights, I'm almost sent skittering back across the flimsy floorboards and into the dusty eaves by her casual inquiry. 'What sort of question is that?' I reply, perhaps too defensively.

She looks at me across the yellow gloom, innocent instead of accusing. 'You don't talk about him, about the things we used to do, or when we were all happy together.'

'Well, it's just…' How can I tell her that the hole – the gaping abyss – has not diminished over time, that I loathe the space next to me in the bed, that some days I hear his voice so clearly I think I might be going mad. All of it, quite apart from Yuri confessional today, stretches my grief chasm to a whole new level. 'Sometimes, I think it might upset you, Libby.'

She pushes her head up, eyes glassy in the parched attic air. 'But I want…' she wipes the tear that goes rogue down her cheek '… Yes, I know I'm upset now, but it's because I miss him and I want him close. Even if it's just in a memory between us.'

I wonder how my own daughter, at the tender age of fifteen, can speak so eloquently and trump her mother for maturity. 'Oh Libs,' I say, pulling her close, my own tears into the cotton of her skimpy nightie. 'I miss him like you wouldn't believe, and think about him every single day. And yes, we can talk about him as much as you like.'

As befits a teenager in receipt of maternal emotion, she untangles herself quickly, sniffs and goes back to the box. Meantime, I'm stymied from my real search, poking about pretending to look for old photo albums.

'Hey, look!' Libby says, this time with a smile. 'Is this your wedding picture?'

It is. Not the official one, but a snap someone took of us on the steps of the registry office, Davy in his demob suit with that mischievous smile, and me in something dark and tailored that I must have borrowed. We look so delighted with one another. The lump in my throat turns to granite again.

'What on earth is Gilda wearing?' Libby asks.

I bend over her shoulder, at the sight of my mother in all her glory, some fur wrap around her shoulders, looking every inch a dowager cum mother-of-the-bride. Whether it was faux or real animal skin I can't remember, though her new bohemian self would probably shudder at the very thought of it adorning a live creature.

'Shall I take it downstairs and show her tomorrow?' Libby says, her smile returned.

'Not if you want her in a mood good enough to run you up a few dresses,' I warn her. 'That part of Gilda's past is best kept in a box as far she she's concerned.'

'Oh.' Still, she can't put it back. 'What are you wearing around your neck?'

I peer again. 'It's Granny Flynn's locket – a sort of family heirloom. Dad gave it to me just a few months before we were married. One day you'll have...'

I'm halted mid-sentence by an arrow of thought piercing my brain, for the second time in as many days. The locket! 'Libby, you're a genius.'

'What? Why?'

'Come on, it's getting very late and you've got school in the morning.' I shuffle her toward the hole in the floor. 'Take that picture if you like and keep it in your bedroom.'

She seems placated by her little jewel and shimmies down the ladder with far more grace than I can claim, the wooden rungs complaining again under my weight. She allows me a brief kiss on the landing and disappears into her room, clutching the photograph. My fingers are dusty and dry as I leap toward the small jewellery box on my bedroom dressing table, which has little of value in it bar my collection of earrings and bauble necklaces. The locket is buried under some trinkets, a little tarnished and neglected, the pattern etched on the oval facing dulled by age. On the back, the engraving that always tweaks at my heart, Davy's father to his beloved wife: *To Ida, my only love – Stanley.*

I take a breath before opening the clasp, since I know what will face me – and I have to face it. It's that picture of Davy I took the same day he proposed, sun-kissed and smiling, the wind pushing back a flop of sandy hair. God, he looks so alive, and handsome. In love, too, with the lens and – dare I think it – the person behind it. Me. It was almost a year after the war and he might not have been leading his double life by then. I like to think it, keeping the delusion alive a little longer.

Gingerly, I pull out Davy's image from the metal surround. On the back, I've written *Torquay 1946* in pencil. Still trapped in the locket, though, is something I've not seen before, a minute square of ivory paper. It feels like gossamer as I tease it out carefully and unfold a square on which is simply written: *Love you, Mags. X.*

So, he did, at the time he wrote it. Except that my heart and gut flip in unison. It can't simply be a love missive. I calculate the timings: it wasn't there five years ago, because I distinctly remember pulling the locket out on Libby's tenth birthday and wondering if she was ready to be entrusted with it. Back then, I took out the picture in readiness, then thought better of it, replacing the photo in its slot. Sometime between then and his death, Davy had gone into my jewellery box. For what reason?

My senses piqued, I pull the paper close and scrutinise every fibre under the bedside lamp. It's either a faint discolouration in patches, or wishful thinking, and basic tradecraft is needed to confirm which. Creeping down the stairs on tiptoe, I retrieve a box of matches from the shelf over the stove and sit nervously at the kitchen table. My mind see-saws – I need a lead badly, but if there is something here, then it puts Davy's duplicity beyond any doubt. And yet, I went looking, and now there's only one way to go. Forward.

The match flares and illuminates the tissue paper like an old-fashioned peep-show behind a veil. Is that writing? I squint closer. Jesus! The match catches the paper's edge and suddenly I'm flapping at what could be precious evidence going up in flames and praying Gilda's badger nose doesn't sniff out burning from her upstairs room. *Calm down, Maggie!*

Finally, I get to grips with the basics of schoolboy spying, the revealing of invisible ink messages fashioned from lemon juice and – I've learnt from eavesdropping at Leconfield – bird excrement, too. Who cares if I'm holding ink made from avian poo in my hand, because there it is. Meant for me, surely.

In faint brown, the letters emerge, blurred at the edges but clear enough to read:

TMBE XPMQ. USVTU BC

Any reader of penny spy novels would recognise it as code and, ordinarily, such gibberish would make my heart sink, it being so inaccessible. But I knew my husband and vice versa. One of the few conversations we had about our respective wars was about code, on a lazy Sunday afternoon picnic in Regent's Park if I remember, side by side on a blanket and staring at a clear blue sky. It was a rare moment where he touched on his war years as a covert operator. Davy told me about codes and the simplest of them, where the coder takes the next letter of the alphabet, writing B for A, and so on. He'd have guessed that any seasoned spy could spot it instantly, and yet gambled that no one but me had any reason to be rifling in the jewellery box. Plus, he knew of my innate curiosity, my love of the notes he subsequently left peppered around the house for me to discover after that picnic day – in the fruit bowl, under my pillow and, once, in the cereal box: *J MPWF ZPV.*

I LOVE YOU.

On a scrap of paper, I decode the short message. *SLAD WOLP. TRUST AB*

Damn it! Still a load of bunkum. I check the paper again and run the flame dangerously close to the surface, in case I've missed something vital. But nothing. Clearly, it meant something to Davy. 'But, my darling husband, what the bloody hell am I supposed to make of it?' I huff, snuffing out the match glow.

I need a point of reference, anything to tie this puzzle to what Yuri revealed, and then to Davy. As I memorise and then toss both scraps of paper into the embers of the living room fire and watch them dissolve into ashes, there's a path emerging. It's foggy, and without a firm destination, but it's a start. Yuri first and then the Registry. And luck. Lots of that.

Back in bed, I blink my sore eyes that, oddly, can't now raise a tear, even when I'm alone. Instead, every artery and vein, top to toe, scuttles with a new army of minute creatures, pricking at my idiotic need to move forward into territory that's at best alien, and at worst, potentially dangerous. As the crawlies reach the blasted bunion, I'm furious at myself – for being driven to discover the truth about my dead and never to return husband (to the detriment of my living family), and all when I have no hope of changing the past, let alone the future.

For God's sake, Maggie, how can you love him and still be so bloody angry at him?

'To sleep, perchance to dream' skitters around my head. I know enough schoolgirl Shakespeare to sympathise with poor, tortured Hamlet. Like him, I crave only a few hours of boring, black shut-eye without flights of fancy or fleeing the devil.

Eleven

13 May 1965

Sleep must have come eventually, but it felt sporadic. Even so, I'm awake at seven and out by eight, met by cursory grunts from Gilda and Libby. It's fair to say that none of us are good in the mornings.

Reaching the safe house by eight thirty, I walk down the mews refining my cover story to gain entry – I'd left something important in the kitchen and need to retrieve it. Straightaway, I sense something isn't right. The milk bottle is absent, but so is everything else. Facing the door, it feels abandoned, and peering through a slit in the front curtains just confirms it; nothing left lying around, no signs of habitation on the table, ashtrays clean. Through into the kitchen, what I can see looks tidy. As if no one has ever been there.

SHIT! No access to Yuri. Then a second thought comes chasing on the heels of the first: has he been ghosted away because of me? What would MI5 eavesdroppers have heard as we sat at the table talking? Perhaps Yuri was saying something in code that I was too naïve to pick up on, a thought that prompts several waves of nausea.

It means the Registry has to come good, and by virtue, my performance within it. And all before a day's work. Before heading to Leconfield House, I make a stop at a café within spitting distance of the Ministry of Defence, where – with a strong cappuccino to fortify us both – Vivien shares last month's issue of *Harper's Bazaar*. I casually flip through the glossy pages pretending to admire a baby-faced Paul McCartney, while pocketing a small envelope tucked next to 'Outer Space' fashions.

'It's just a written request, but it should get you into the Registry,' she explains between puffs of her cigarette. 'I'd still be as quick as you can, in and out before anyone senior checks your credentials.'

'I'll try. Thanks Vivien. I owe you.'

'I'll hold you to a double date one of these days,' she smiles, slipping off her stool. 'No spies and no attachés, just a nice man to make you feel special, Mrs Flynn.'

Oh, what a lovely prospect to mull over, something akin to a normal life.

Just a small matter of infiltrating MI5 first.

Dread has been my usual response on approaching the dowdy exterior of the Spy Shack. Today, it's bolstered by nerves, manifest in the tremble of my fingers, not helped by that last caffeine dose. Getting past the porter's lodge is not a problem, as I'm often in and out to type up reports, but I wait until the old sentry's back is turned before descending into the gloom of the basement, running through the practised lies that Vivien and I have concocted. It doesn't escape my notice that on reaching the bottom step, I'm crossing a very firm Service line.

'Request?' The woman at the desk barely looks up as I approach. When she does, it's to reveal an aged, pallid face etched with deep lines, untouched by daylight and empathy.

Coarse, permed grey hair, red, thready veins on her dry-skin cheeks, faint smell of sandalwood under the cigarette smoke.

For a second, I wonder if she possesses any lips worthy of description. *She's as 'ard as nails*, would be Frank's acute take on her. It's my first professional encounter with a Registry Queen, and her rigid expression upholds every stereotype. My one consolation is that she's unlikely to recognise a lowly Watcher.

'Request,' she repeats impatiently, twitching her bony fingers at me.

'Actually, I need access to a number of files,' I say, confidently pulling out Vivien's authorisation from a small handbag. Today, I am in my Professional Woman guise – two-piece grey suit, white shirt, flattened hair and minimal make-up, plus block heels that clip-clop efficiently but prove a bugger on the bunion. I feel naked without my trusty shoulder bag, safely lodged with Maria in the Express Café.

She squints at the letter for an age, my heart leaping upwards to plug my airway. Vivien has been circumspect about the wording. *'Please allow the bearer access to security files...'* it reads. No name, and I'll only pull out my Service ID if forced.

'Hmmm,' she murmurs, looking hard at the ornate, embossed letterhead.

'I am on a time scale,' I say haughtily, wondering if it's unwise to get shirty this early into the exchange. 'The minister is waiting on my return.'

She narrows her eyes through magnified lenses. Unimpressed. 'You would normally need two signatures,' she remarks flatly, and looks around for colleague confirmation. Behind her in the cavernous, windowless rooms, there are no signs of life in the racks of files or dotted around the desks. Above us, the mini train track rattles away industriously, with an occasional sucking and whooshing noise as the Lamson's elaborate pipe network whisks small tubes of documents upwards and into the belly of the building.

I sigh heavily at her officiousness, while below the desk my knees are jelly. Bluffing is required. 'You can ring the office and they'll confirm for you, though don't blame me if you get an earful. Here's the number.' I hold out another piece of typed fakery, courtesy of Vivien. The Queen looks at it with disdain but doesn't take it. It's a war of attrition, and I wonder for a minute if she wasn't with the Gestapo in a previous life. I'm fairly certain that, nowadays, the Stasi would welcome her with open arms should she ever wish to hop to the other side.

'All right, but I'll need to check it with Miss Baglan when she comes in,' she says at last. 'Which files do you need?'

'That's classified.'

If looks could kill I would have been six feet under, except that she does open the gate to allow me access. 'Obviously, it's eyes only, and your bag will be searched on the way out,' she adds. 'Procedure, you understand.'

'Of course,' I smile sweetly. 'And thank you so much.'

Amid the looming metal racks and ladders reaching up to shelves a good ten to twelve feet high, I have to work fast, either before Stasi Queen has second thoughts or the formidable Bea Baglan comes on the scene; I met her once before at a function, and she might well recognise me as a Watcher. She struck me then as a woman who never forgets a face, among many other things.

Just as I imagined, there's nothing in the 'F' section, and it was always optimistic to expect a file marked 'Flynn'. Wary of the clack of my heels, I move with stealth on the balls of my feet to 'S', denoting 'Stapleton' or 'Standard'.

I blink in the gloom: relief mixed with disbelief. There it is at eye level, the label on the spine marked 'Standard'. Davy's codename, according to Yuri. My shaky fingers reach up, making a mental note that it seems hemmed in tightly by neighbouring files and sharing identical layers of dust. No one's been here recently.

Don't ask me why, but I feel in my pockets for a pair of Marigolds and snap on the bright yellow washing-up gloves before drawing the file out. Overcautious, perhaps, but that's how my mind is functioning right now. Heart nudging at my gullet, I venture inside the buff cardboard, the one containing my husband's alternate life. The one marked in red: 'MOST SECRET'.

His mugshot stares back at me, a black and white photograph paper-clipped to the inside. My Davy – no disguises, no false moustache. Just what I still consider to be his handsome face. But the details on the opposing page are stark and regimented:

David James Flynn, born 29.5.1919, Oxford
City. Mother and father deceased. Spouse:
Margaret Flynn, nee Richmond, married
14.1.1947. One daughter, born 1950.
Siblings: brother Douglas (deceased
France 1944).
Relatives: Gilda Richmond,
mother-in-law.
Codename: Standard.
Aliases (to date): John Stapleton.
Robert Brayling. Thomas Needham.

Three aliases. 'Three! How much ruddy spying were you doing?' I scream at him silently.

Across the black and white type, one word stamped in favoured MI5 red: 'DECEASED'.

The atmosphere between the racks is dense and clammy, and I'm suddenly hot, broiling inside my suit, feeling faint and wishing there was one of those funny little library stools to sit on. A woman marches by the end of the row, soles smacking on the linoleum, though doesn't look my way. It's only a matter of time before someone does, and I have to act rather than just gawp. As expected, the file is physically too large for me to hide under my jacket (with the added threat of Stasi woman's inspection) and there are around twenty pages, too many to memorise. But Terry – caretaker of the porn supermarket – has come good, always keen for his customers to test some up-to-the-minute tech that he's trialling. I pull out a pencil-slim Minox camera secreted in the cleft of my breasts (*'just four inches long, Mrs F!'*) and somehow hold the file between elbow and chin, while flipping pages with one hand and aiming the camera, praying Terry's assurances that it's a 'bloody marvel' are well-founded. Between each near-silent click of the shutter, I pause to listen out for encroaching footsteps or voices. Between fumbling, hesitation and the Marigolds, it takes well over five minutes; my rubber-clad fingers scratch on the dry, cracked paper while my tongue rasps against my parched throat. I pledge there and then never to bemoan drinking too much tea ever again.

Finally, I'm able to return the camera to my bra and embed the file back in its place. I can't replace the dust, so brush at the surrounding folders thoroughly, sending up a filthy, dense cloud. Bad decision, I realise far too late. There's a determined fizzing in my nostrils and what feels like an unholy sneeze brewing. I'm not allergic to anything, and practised at suppressing coughs and splutters in the field, but this one has taken hold and it won't be quashed. It will spill, like an overdue eruption of Mount Etna by the feel of it. Another conundrum: stay and muffle it poorly, or come out with guns blazing and brazen it out?

I opt for the latter, thinking Stasi woman may not want to get close to potential germs of a cold, certainly not close enough to my breast, where the Minox is slipping and sliding against the perspiration of my B-cup.

AITCHOOO! Noise ricochets around the metal racks as I step out from the end of the aisle, burying the bright yellow gloves alongside the camera and ready to lament my oncoming cold with a resigned smile and a quick exit.

Only I freeze. Something else shudders through me, top to toe. I think it's fear, but it could be anger at my own stupidity, staring as I am into the face of Beattie Baglan.

'Mrs Flynn,' she says, with no hint of a welcome or a smile.

Busted.

'Oh, er, hello…' I play dumb and squint at her name badge '… Mrs Baglan.'

'*Miss* Baglan.'

'Sorry, Miss Baglan. Have we met?'

'Just the once.' She fixes me with a stare that would freeze the depths of Hades, her pinched white cheeks sallow under the gloomy lighting.

Tall, thin and gaunt, salt and pepper hair coiled and pinned like an exotic pagoda, no stray wisps. Age: early fifties? Crow's feet kept at bay around piercing blue eyes, mid-range suit, department store perfume. Does not suffer fools: Queen Elizabeth I in modern-day Marks & Spencer.

'To what does the Registry owe this pleasure?' says Miss Baglan, with not a single hint of emotion. 'I'm not aware the surveillance section has access to our files.'

For 'our' read 'my'. My files. Her fiefdom. Which means I'm either a guest or the enemy, and I think I know which one it is. The grapevine says her and Grayling share a long-running antipathy to each other but, evidently, they were comrades in the same Stasi prep school.

'No, normally we wouldn't,' I fudge. I did have a rehearsed reason/excuse/story, only it seems trapped in one of those famous cubicles of my brain tissue, unwilling to come forth. 'But they are short-handed in the courier section, and you know us Watchers, all hands to the pump when it matters.' Blah, blah. *Shut up, Maggie.*

'I do,' she says calmly, her eyes flicking towards my small handbag. 'Very admirable. And have you finished? Do you require anything else?'

Her words are plain enough: *Get off my patch.*

'No, no. It was merely to check a detail and report back,' I say, smiling to cover my vagueness.

'Well, I won't detain you any longer, Mrs Flynn. From your important work.'

Her words penetrate like poison darts, those pin-prick pupils bearing down on me. Definitely an elite form of training. She stands, planted like a sentinel, and I'm forced to sidle by and hot-foot it towards the exit, where the desk sentry makes her promised search of my bag and seems just about to pat me down when I force another sneeze and mutter about 'my entire department coming down with flu'. She backs off, herding me towards the door with her death stare. As I head for the exit, I glance back in time to see Bea Baglan emerging from the very same aisle where I may well have just committed my first act of high treason.

Twelve

13 May 1965

It's just past ten when I reach Soho, having stopped by the porn shop and slipped the Minox to Terry for processing, along with a £5 note. It's a huge hole in my purse but then this is a large void in my life, and I'm buying his silence along with his expertise.

'Be ready by lunchtime tomorrow, Mrs F,' he chirps.

It feels like an age away, and I wonder how many interrogations from Grayling I might have to face before I actually see whether today's idiotic caper – compromising my job and losing years off my life – has been worth it. Davy's reasoning just *has* to be in that file, or what else am I left with?

Spilling out of the porn shop, I'm exhausted, craving tea and familiarity. And someone to make me laugh.

It's no surprise to find Frank at the Egg on Old Compton Street, in situ at his favourite booth. The good news is that his hand is unaffected and well able to hover his pen above the racing pages.

'Magpie! An unexpected surprise,' he says with a characteristic grin. Bathed in the glow of Egg lighting, he looks almost saintly. 'Blimey, you look posh, you been on a job?'

'Morning Frank. No, I had an early appointment at Libby's school,' I lie. To Frank of all people. 'How's the arm?'

'Mustn't grumble,' he sniffs, 'though I might if Grayling comes snooping. I could always put in a request for danger money.'

'Good luck with that one, Frank.'

'You mean getting money out of those tight old bastards at the Spy Shack?'

'No, eliciting any kind of emotion from Grayling.'

We order more tea, and go through the chits that Frank has picked up from the Stable on his way in. 'Quiet day for once,' he says. 'Listen, you covered for me yesterday, so why don't you take the day off? I can sign you in at the Stable. 'Cos, if you don't mind me saying, Mags, you look really tired.'

I'm not affronted – in fact, I could kiss him, though it might raise a few eyebrows over by the till. 'Frank, you're a star. Are you sure?'

'Of course. Besides which, you might want to check this out.' He plunders his pocket for a scrap of paper and lays it in front of me. 'Those Beatles tickets you're looking for. I overheard a bloke in the pub talking about them yesterday, and he's going to be here this morning' – he points at the scribbled address – 'so, perhaps you could muscle in there, sharpish.'

The Beatles tickets! Had they slipped my mind? Yes and

no. The enduring image of Libby's disappointed face is with me each and every day, but it hasn't been top priority in the last twenty-four hours. And it will help to occupy my mind while I await Terry's magic in the darkroom.

'Frank, you are a superstar.' Now, I do lean over to plant a kiss on his cheek, and I think he might actually blush a little, this man who has spent decades locking up fearsome villains.

Over breakfast, I try hard to focus on Frank's engaging babble, principally the date he's secured with a woman he met in the betting shop. I'm not entirely sure about a coupling of two gamblers, but I sense that, underneath his chirpiness, Frank is essentially lonely, despite the companionship of Blofeld and Bond.

'Perhaps you should take her somewhere other than the pub, Frank? You want to impress her.'

'Yes, you're right, Mags. What about The Trat?'

'Perfect,' I say, thinking a meal at Soho's celebrated Terrazza would impress any woman. 'I'd go for the pasta alone, and she'll love it. But won't you bump into half the mob that you once tried to lock up?'

'Maybe,' he says, scraping up the last of his fried egg, 'but it's all water under the bridge now. Those boys know I'm not in the Met any more, and so it's all gentleman's rules. They might even stand me a glass of champagne.'

I find it quite astonishing that Detective Inspector Tanner would have pursued those London mobsters – 'tooled up' with guns and crowbars – like a bloodhound in his years on the force, sometimes with a violent, bloody climax to the chase, and yet they can nod with deference to each other nowadays and reminisce over a drink. His lot might not have gone to public school like those at MI5, but is it really so different to the old boys' network? With thoughts of Davy bashing at my temples, I'm suddenly struck by what might be considered betrayal, and what is passed off as 'just the job' – the filthy undercurrent of espionage and criminality combined.

'Frank, in all your time on the force, what would have been the worst your lot could have done, enough to make you turn on your own?' I crunch on my toast in a vain attempt at nonchalance.

Frank peers hard into the sunny glow of the overhead lighting. 'What's up, Mags? Are you all right?'

'Fine,' I lie again. 'I don't know, it's just all this stuff about Frank Bossard's betrayal in the papers, and wondering what would actually cause someone to work against their own colleagues like that. Apart from money.' I couldn't care a fig about Bossard, of course – he deserves all the years of jail-time thrown at him. It's Davy's motive that sits with me morning, noon and night. Nagging.

Draining his tea, Frank chews it over. 'Well, I tell you, Mags, I nearly did it once – turned in my own bosses.'

'Really?' I thought the blue blood of the Met moved through Frank's veins even now.

'Yeah,' he rattles on. 'I was working a case, ooh, fifteen years ago – some smooth bloke who was shafting old ladies of their life savings, and not averse to doing it with violence. He went too far with one of them and killed her, beating her black and blue in the process.'

I arch my eyebrows, appalled.

'Well, we caught him, and the snide bastard didn't even try to hide it,' Frank continues. 'He called for the chief constable, who actually came to the cell and met our culprit in private, no witnesses, no tapes. The two of them made a deal, that the murdering shite would be released in return for being our snitch. The chief said it would bring "great returns of intel", but we all knew he had some dodgy secret to hide. It was clear that our murderer had the chief by the balls.' Frank shakes his head in disgust. 'Well, I wasn't having it, Mags. I saw that poor old dear's body in the morgue and it made me sick. Letting that bastard back on the streets would be like arming one of our own missiles and aiming it at an old people's home. We would have been... what's the word? Complicit. In murder.'

'So, what did you do?'

'I got the chief constable in the blokes' toilets – alone – and told him that whatever that grotesque monster in the cells had on him, I would find out much worse, and take it straight to the papers, that I didn't care what happened to me, my job or my pension. He looked scared then, though I did have him by the balls – quite literally.'

'What happened to the murderer?'

'Doing a life stretch in Wormwood Scrubs,' Frank says with satisfaction. 'Plus, the chief took early retirement soon after that.'

'Blimey, Frank.'

'Yeah,' he sighs, 'I was shitting it, of course, for my job. But sometimes you have to disarm your own missile, don't you? One more tea for the road?'

I skip the tea, and make a quick stop at the Stable for a change of clothes, back to being me, though I do slip a hat and some sunglasses into my supply bag. After the encounter with Baglan, paranoia is worming its way under my skin, ready to take root. My target of the nearest library seems quite innocent, but you never know who's on your tail, do you? The alarm bells might already be ringing at Leconfield House.

'Our maps of the British Isles are on the left,' the elderly librarian says, peering hard through the dark lenses of my glasses, and perhaps wondering why I might need them in the gloom of the sunless space. 'Where is it you want to find? I might be able to help.'

'Slad,' I say, though I hold out little hope. Since discovering Davy's note, my mind has been beavering away at the meaning of SLAD WOLP: place, person, codename, abbreviation or acronym? It could be anything, and it's a case of trawling through the list. Vivien is already going through her index of government organisations and employees, but in a distant part of my memory a tiny bell has tinkled that Slad might be a place.

'Oh, do you mean Laurie Lee country?' Behind her glasses, her magnified eyes sparkle with recognition and she looks almost excited to put down her stamper. 'Have you read *Cider with Rosie*?'

'Er, no,' I stammer. I'm not entirely sure if it's where I mean, but it is a starting point.

'Lovely part of the country,' the librarian mutters in hushed tones as she walks, leading me between tall shelves heaving with texts. 'The Cotswolds. Very hilly, but a lot of nice pubs. Slad is a bit of a pilgrimage site for fans of Mr Lee's work.'

'I was just thinking of a few days away, assuming it's not too far,' I say.

'It's not that long a journey,' she replies. 'There's a train, to Stroud, if my memory serves me. Then it's one of those country buses to Slad, but there is a lovely pub when you get there, where I believe Laurie Lee is quite a regular still. Very quaint.'

Helpful Librarian leaves me with a large map and a glossy book on the English countryside. Somewhere between Gloucester and Cheltenham, and a few miles from the market town of Stroud, Slad looks indeed very picturesque. So, what on earth could it have to do with Davy and his death? I'm convinced, however, that I have to go there in order to be sure of its rose-trellis doorways not hiding a secret of national import. It's the sole lead I have until Terry comes good in the darkroom and, if nothing else, it might be an escape from the city and my paranoia that now seems wrapped up in every thoroughfare.

I glance at my watch – barely midday. The train timetable furnished by the front desk tells me there's a train at twelve thirty from Paddington, and I calculate on just making it. For a second, I think about hopping home and picking up my trusty Mini from outside the house, but the danger is not in being spotted by MI5 so much as my own mother. The Spanish Inquisition is child's play alongside Gilda.

Mistrust peaks again as I step outside the safe balm of the library. I've no idea if my recorded conversations with Yuri over the kitchen table have been reported to Hilda Grayling yet, or whether Bea Baglan has put aside the feud with her sworn enemy and taken her concerns upstairs to Grayling's office. Given that the left hand of MI5 rarely knows what the right hand is doing, there's a chance they've yet to connect the dots on my off-piste activities. But paranoia is illogical by nature, and so mine clings firm, wheedling its way inside nicely.

Limited time means I have no chance to dry-clean the route, hopping in a black cab and telling the driver: 'Paddington, as fast as you can.'

Once again, I'm immersed in my own terrible script.

Thirteen

13 May 1965

The guard's shrill whistle resonates as I beat a hasty path down the platform, along with several others rushing for the nearest open door. Puffing with the steam of the engine, I'm too focused on catching the train, along with fighting the whinnying complaint of the bunion, to slow up and test out if any of the late arrivals are tracking me step for step.

Falling into a compartment, hot and sticky, I choose a corner seat and squint behind my sunglasses at three other passengers who follow in behind, red with the effort. We trade weak smiles of relief: *phew! We made it.* Two men and one woman: which of them could potentially be a Watcher? None, as far as I can tell.

Woman in her twenties, a skimpy handbag across her shoulder and kitten heels, highly impractical. Both men: pristine shoes that have yet to see plenty of pavement, soles intact. Both young, crimson-faced one looks as if running for the train set him back ten years, smokes incessantly. Unlikely spooks.

It makes me hopeful that MI5's bush telegraph hasn't yet begun transmitting. And, anyway, what am I doing on the face of it? Merely taking advantage of a spring day and time off to visit the countryside.

Pull the other one, Maggie.

Careful observation tells me I'm untrailed, but I move carriages to be on the safe side. All three sets of eyes follow with curiosity as I rise out of my seat, and their natural reflex is a further comfort, since a Watcher may be tempted to purposely ignore the movement, another tiny 'tell' to look out for. Hunkered into another seat, I begin to question my own antics, and my sanity.

What am I looking for? So far, I have reference to a chocolate-box village that neither have I been to, nor heard my husband ever mention. 'Wild goose chase' springs to mind. But I'm driven this time by more than my own nosy nature, a real need to understand Davy and his demise. What he might have sacrificed himself for. And been killed for.

It's early afternoon by the time we pull into Stroud, a tiny, quiet station with one track in, and one out, a single railman lazily brushing the platform down. I hang back until the train leaves, but aside from a very elderly woman with a walking stick, I'm the only one who alights.

'Excuse me, how can I get to Slad village?' I ask the station guard.

He looks at his watch, and makes that pained 'ooh' shape with his mouth that civic workers and plumbers specialise in. 'The bus went half an hour ago,' he drawls. 'Next one is hour and half.'

Say what you like about London buses, chugging, growling and clogging up the capital's streets, but they are frequent. 'How far is it?'

'Two mile,' he says. 'Or thereabouts.'

Too far to walk, I gauge, with my time constraints. 'Taxi?' I pitch.

He points. 'To the left of the entrance.'

Beyond the ticket office is a world away from the bustle of Paddington, quiet enough to hear the constant twitter of nature and the low-level hum of small-town living. From what I can see, 'hip' hasn't reached this far west yet. I do like it, but the inactivity compared to London prompts fresh nerves inside. What the hell is here, and how do I find it? Into the distant hills, I spy one or two haystacks dotted around the green fields. Needles or nothing in there?

'Visiting, are you?' the taxi driver asks.

'An aunt.' He's probably being friendly, but in my mood, I'm wary, and a bit short.

'Anyone I know?' he chirps. 'I tend to know most, around and abouts.'

'I doubt it, she's only just moved here.'

'Oh, right. Have you the address?'

'Just drop me in the village centre please.'

He pulls up in Slad at the pub, and I hand over the fare under a sign swaying in the breeze, my eyes instantly drawn to the name: The Woolpack. I check back behind my eyelids, Davy's note scratched into the back of them.

WOLP. Woolpack? Could I be so fortunate, and so quickly? Or Davy so overt?

It turns out that the library picture book was spot on; this country hostelry does have roses in a perfect arc hugging the doorway, a prime example of Ye Olde England, sitting opposite the church and nestled between two rolling valleys, one glowing under the afternoon sunshine, and the other in a deep shade of emerald green. A single cow moos and sheep bleat in response, a sort of countryside repartee. Quintessential, you might say. No wonder people are inspired enough to write, I think, breathing in the heady smell of freshly cut grass. It's a million miles from subversive.

It's then I realise how thirsty and hungry I am after my dash across London, and I move inside to the cool, dark wood of the pub's interior and the few late-lunch drinkers standing around the bar. Alongside is an empty chair, a photograph of an older man above it, and I guess it's reserved for their renowned customer, though Mr Laurie Lee appears not to be in residence at this very moment.

'Aft' noon,' the man behind the bar says.

Round, red face, greying beard, built like a barn door, stomach girth bursting buttons on thin checked shirt. Instant suspicion in fleshy, furrowed brow.

Several pairs of eyes switch from their pints to comb over the newcomer. I feel watched.

'A half pint, please,' I say. I'm no connoisseur of British ale, but I can drink it without wincing, and I feel it's the best way of sparking conversation. 'And do you serve sandwiches?'

'Cheese and pickle, ham and pickle, ham and cheese,'

the veteran barman reels off. Despite the initial scowl, his address is neither rude, nor off-putting, merely bored and clearly wanting to get back to conversation of the regulars clustered around the counter.

'Ham and cheese, please. Thank you.'

While I'm itching to pull out my photograph of Davy and ask anyone about his possible presence, I sit instead, sipping at my half of – as it turns out – very good cloudy beer, and bide my time. When my sandwich is brought over, a mountain of thick white bread either side of great chunks of filling, I seize the opportunity.

'Erm, I'm new here,' I say to the barman.

'You don't say.'

'... looking for someone.'

'Oh, yes?' Now he is wary, narrowing his eyes. Evidently, I'm one of those London Types.

I might as well play up the stereotype, figuring the long-lost relative story probably won't stand up. 'On behalf of a firm of solicitors,' – I flash a business card plucked at random from my handy supply – 'trying to track down some lucky individual who's in receipt of decent inheritance.'

His eyes widen, but still he surveys me, looks me up and down, at my outfit which doesn't shout solicitor.

'It beats doing the bailiff work,' I say by way of explanation. 'And it's a nice day out as far as I'm concerned.' I pick up my glass of amber liquid. 'Good beer, too.'

'Local,' he says.

'My client? No.'

'The ale,' he says flatly. 'From a local brewer.'

'Oh.' Hell, he may actually be a tougher nut to crack than Hilda Grayling. And yet I reason there's nothing to lose, pulling out Davy's photograph and handing it to him. 'We've some information the recipient of the will had been staying locally. I wonder if he's been in here?'

Since there is no gaggle of customers clamouring for attention, the bartender has no option but to scan the picture. In turn, I comb his face for signs of his own tell, which he fails to hide – a fleeting but distinct twitch of his large nostrils. Before he has a chance to confirm or deny, I leap in. 'Do you remember when?'

'Hmm,' he grunts, 'not exactly, but must be a few years ago – two or three at least. We get a decent amount of tourists around here, holidaymakers and the like. He's probably long gone.' He tries to hand back the photograph, but the rottweiler in me won't let go.

'Did you see him more than once?'

He sighs, as if with true boredom. Darned Londoners. 'As I remember, he came in a few days in a row, then back again sometime later. Maybe once more.'

'Would your regulars have seen him?' I nod towards the small clutch of pensioners and ruddy farmer types around the bar. With the picture still in hand, and possibly as a way of coaxing me firmly from his premises, he takes it over. The heads go together, then a combined murmur. I've never understood the term 'bated breath' in its truest form, but now I do.

Grumpy Barman beckons me over. 'George here says he remembers him.'

George is seventy if he's a day, body stooped and hands gnarled, but his eyes are a sharp, sparkling blue.

'Did you talk to him at all?' I ask. Perhaps a little too keenly.

'Oh aye,' says George. 'We shared a pint and conversation more than once. Nice chap, as I remember.'

'When was that?' Given his age, and the barman's already vague recollection, I'm not hopeful.

'Three and half years ago,' he says with precision. 'Almost to the month.'

'Oh, you're that sure?'

'Certainly,' he says. 'I'm not known to forget a face. My Gracie died in the November, and we had several chats about life and what it throws up. Like I say, nice bloke.'

And now he's gone the way of your Gracie.

So, Davy was here for sure. But why? The next reaction is vital for taking me forward, and while I'm aware of breaking cover, there's little choice. 'Did he say why he was here, or where he was staying?'

Now, the blue sparkles turn steely. They're a guarded lot, these country folk.

'It's all background,' I rattle on lightly. 'You know how it is – no result, no fee from those bloody solicitors. I do all the legwork, but it's all money, money, money with them.' *Best sweet smile, Maggie.*

They all grunt a combined derision for professional city types, and that seems to earn me a reprieve.

'I do know he was lodging down the road with Mrs Ellis,' George reveals. 'She does bed and breakfast. And he mentioned doing some work up at Congleton House. I presumed that's why he was here.'

'Congleton House?'

'Up on the hill, beyond the wood,' another chips in. 'But you won't get past the gate there.'

'Why's that?' I ask. Interest definitely aroused. Radar fizzing.

'It's all locked up,' the bartender says. 'Loony bin for the criminally insane, electric fences and all that. Used to be a big old family house, then it was requisitioned by the army in the war, and after that the men in white coats.'

Inside, I'm running with suspicion, a veneer of surprise on the outside. 'That sounds a bit dodgy. What if they escape?'

'Never known it,' George says. 'I mean, there was a few villagers who protested when it first opened, but since we've never had cause to moan, we've almost forgotten it's there.'

'And the staff, do they drink here?' Now, I'm affecting the conversational tone of the downright nosy.

'No, not them.' Grumpy Barman is back to polishing glasses behind his counter. 'I think perhaps we're a bit too ordinary for them, aren't we lads? A bit too sane.'

A peal of laughter goes up, and one slams his empty glass noisily on the counter. 'My granddaughter reckons it's just like a book she's read recently – some chocolate factory where no one goes in or out. Full of Oompa Loompas, she says, whatever they are. Except I'm not sure she's far wrong.'

I buy a round as a true mark of thanks and step out into this alien world beyond the rose-clad doorway. Something with hooves brays noisily in the distance. 'Exactly,' I mutter to myself. Sunshine and possible subversion in the Gloucestershire countryside.

What was Davy onto?

Fourteen

13 May 1965

M r Connery springs to mind again as I rumble along the beautiful Slad Valley, a gentle quiver to my cheeks, echoed in the rump of my bottom; 007 gets a sleek and coveted Aston Martin, and I'm left with hitching a lift on an open-topped tractor, courtesy of Bill, one of the Woolpack drinkers who said he was 'going my way'.

He leaves me at the end of a drive with a cheery farewell and a look that says, *Watch yourself*. In truth, I've no idea what my purpose is, other than sighting this mysterious Congleton House, and a 'bloody good recce', as Frank would say. Plus, trying to look through my dead husband's eyes as to what he might have detected. Briefly, it occurs to me that Davy might have been visiting an old relative as a patient, someone never spoken of in the family. But then why wouldn't he have mentioned them? Plus, there's his need to create a cover for the Woolpack crowd. Dismissing the idea, I realise that I'm fumbling for excuses, desperate to make things right again and not feel endlessly duped by the man I shared a life with, and was supposed to know inside out. The truth is, I'm terrified of what I might find – about Congleton House, and Davy – and yet compelled to go on, like picking at a scab that's best left to heal. Only fools will scratch away until it bleeds.

Whichever way I look at it, there's something else beyond that electric fence, something that could have made my husband both sad and fearful in the later months of his life, enough that Yuri detected it. Possibly enough to get him killed, and yet so important that Davy wanted me to discover it.

It's gone three p.m. as I reach the end of a long drive, keeping just off the tree-lined path and shielded from the late sun that's more fairytale golden by the minute. The house finally comes into view, one half bathed in the glow.

Blow me down, Mr Darcy! It's a solid and square Georgian pile, all white columns and verandas, though the paint is faded and unloved, ivy snaking with abandon around the pillars and the surrounding grounds peppered with weeds. Even with the stark wire electric fencing, it's still magnificent and far too well appointed to be a National Health facility. A private asylum would be better cared for, I reason, leaving me almost certain the 'loony bin' façade is an effective front.

Rarely do I think of my Donkey work as skulking, but for the next half an hour I lurk amid the trees. At first glance, there are no patients or staff milling about the gardens, and that's strange in itself. Within ten minutes, two young women appear on the veranda carrying buckets, hurling dirty water onto the grass in front of the heavy wooden doors. Job done, they each light a cigarette and lean against a stone pillar, heads back and blowing smoke rings. They are both tall, lean, and young. While I know very little about the inmates of an asylum, something about their demeanour suggests they are neither patient nor staff, merely enjoying a much-needed break. From what, I wonder. And who are they? After a short time, both heads snap up and swivel towards the door; they throw the butts on the ground, snatch up the buckets and move inside, leaving me with only birdsong for company.

Mindful of the journey back to London and my pledge to Gilda to spend more time at home, I'm just about to find my way back to the station when the grind of an engine overwhelms the gentle sounds of the countryside. A white Bedford van barrels up the main path and towards the wire fencing at speed, spitting gravel on the drive as it comes to a stop. Seconds later, the gate opens and the van drives in, parking just shy of the front steps. The vehicle itself could belong to any butcher, baker or candlestick maker, but not the two men who step out, dressed in dark boiler suits. With more than two years as a Donkey and my former years as a store detective, I'm adept at reading people's posture: the slouch, the seemingly innocent move of a thief towards a designer handbag in her sights, or a dead drop site for vital intelligence in a London park, against the truly innocuous gait of a tradesman making deliveries. This is none of those.

Shit.

Without a doubt, this is military.

★

Even before I board the train back to London, my objective is clear. I have to get in there. *How* I do it remains a mystery, and one that will take a good deal of thought and a greater amount of courage. A fair slice of audacity and creativity too, since being a Watcher means that we always remain aloof, keep our distance, and – Grayling's rules dictate – we don't get involved. That's left to MI5's fully fledged officers, the real spies, whether they like the term or not. I could observe the activities outside Congleton House until the Stroud cows come home, but it's likely to reveal very little. I need to get beyond those heavy, ornate doors and see what their security defences are trying to hide from prying eyes. More precisely, who those women are.

It's gone seven by the time I make it back to Calabria Road, slotting my key in and bracing myself for Gilda's glib riposte on another late arrival.

Instead, there's a tinkle of laughter from the living room and it sounds like my mother, albeit twenty years younger. For the umpteenth time in one day, I'm stopped in my tracks. Too good to be true. What's up? I steel myself for more paint pots, the construction of an entire faux jungle, or the front room transformed into a space age cavity. From bitter experience, I know anything is possible when Gilda has one of her 'brilliant' ideas.

Tentatively, I put my head around the living room door, to see her on the sofa, a strange expression on her face. Serene, perhaps even a little child-like. One step further and I take in the full picture, of Frank sitting opposite, a cuppa in hand.

'Oh Maggie, there you are,' Gilda says in a voice several notes higher than her usual timbre. 'Your colleague Mr Tanner came around to see how you were.'

'All right, Mags?' Frank beams from the chair. 'Your lovely mother has made me feel very at home.'

In that split second, I feel – I am – a large, overripe gooseberry. 'I'm fine.' It's another fat lie, of course, but I'm not about to spill the beans on my day in the country before a good deal more chewing of the facts, in private. Certainly not within range of my mother's acute sensors. 'You didn't need to come out here to check on me, Frank.'

'Maggie!' Gilda remonstrates as if I'm a small child. 'Don't be so rude.'

'Oh, don't you worry, Mrs—' Frank starts.

'Gilda,' she jumps in. 'Let's not stand on ceremony, Mr Tanner.'

'Gilda, sorry. But only if you call me Frank. Your daughter and me, we're good work mates. Know each other inside out, don't we Magpie?' His skin crinkles around eyes that look right into mine.

He knows. Not what, perhaps, but he knows something is up. That's why he was a good DI, and now a damn fine Watcher.

'I was just wanting feedback on that job you did this afternoon,' Frank prods. 'Where was it?'

'The south London office,' I lie. 'Bermondsey. I filed my report already.'

'Of course you have.' He turns towards the sofa and takes a slurp of tea. 'She's one of our best, Gilda. We're very lucky to have her.'

'I couldn't agree more,' Gilda sings.

I'm now certain to have stepped into an alien cosmos, one where Frank and I talk in indistinct code, and my mother has become another being entirely.

'Another tea, Frank, or something stronger?'

'Don't mind if I do, Gilda. Never say no to a sherry.'

'And why don't you stay and eat with us, Frank? Now Maggie's home, I'm sure she can rustle up something, can't you love?'

'Of course,' I push through set teeth. *I just live to rustle.* Ordinarily, I relish spending time with my favourite Watcher, but not right now. Tonight, I want to lie in bed and process what I've seen and heard today, to make sense of a large puzzle with an array of missing pieces. That's quite apart from having to witness my mother flirting like an overgrown schoolgirl.

On cue, the real schoolgirl descends from her teenage lair and meets me in the kitchen. 'Oh, you're in,' Libby huffs, making her ritual perusal of the fridge contents.

That's all I need – mortification from my mother and disdain from my beloved daughter.

In the end, having to fashion a meal from our paltry larder proves a welcome distraction, and Frank holds court at the table with his usual charm. Even Libby is drawn out of her shell, laughing at his jokes with true amusement.

'Lovely grub, Mags,' he effuses, even when there are no eggs involved. 'Your daughter is full of talent, Gilda, can turn her hand to anything, though I never knew she was a dab hand in the kitchen. A dark horse, I'd say.'

The look he gives me is swift and unseen by Gilda and Libby. 'We all have our secrets, Frank,' I laugh it off with a lightning glare back at him.

Dinner over, Frank insists he must go. 'Do come again,' Gilda titters, in her newest guise of a coquette. 'You're welcome anytime.'

'Thank you for such delightful company, Gilda. And Libby, of course.'

Oh Lord, the old charmer.

'See me out, will you, Mags?' he punts as I go to clear up in the kitchen. In a heartbeat, the old charmer has switched to old spook.

His voice at the door is the Donkey I know, back to business but heavy with concern. 'What's up, Mags. Anything you want to tell me?' He grabs at my hand and squeezes down tight. 'You're not yourself. I'm worried, that's all.'

'I'm fine,' I lie spectacularly, as the granite stone in my throat turns to hot coals. But I'm too weary and conflicted to spill my heart and secrets on the doorstep, even to my best confidante. 'In the morning, Frank,' I pledge. 'I'll see you tomorrow, eh?'

'All right, Magpie. Sleep well.'

Sleep well. Who is he kidding?

Fifteen

14 May 1965

'Ugh.' I've learnt not to look too closely in my own bathroom mirror at the dawn of each day, given that my face often needs transforming with some form of disguise at the Stable, and so there's little point. This morning, however, the reflection draws me towards the sorry sight, like a fly to pile of, well... you know. The only saving grace being that the spindly red lines radiating like a sunburst on the whites of my eyes mimic the thready map of veins on my cheeks. I match.

Star of the show, however, is a single but spectacular white spot pulsing on the very tip of my nose, nicely cultured overnight and screaming to all of London society: *LOOK AT ME!*

In the mirror, I am bilious, despite a single half pint of cloudy ale at the Woolpack. What's more, I feel hungover. Yesterday's multiple stops, trains, tractors and automobiles and my beloved mattress did render me unconscious within seconds of hitting its springs. But the brain cubbyholes had other ideas, hosting a noisy conference when I roused at two a.m., with questions and theories winging across my brain matter until the birds began to sing. When I finally sank into sleep again, those wretched dreams came visiting. Enough said.

Unsurprisingly, and to my relief, Gilda doesn't surface as I mull over coffee, cornflakes, and the slightly sad front-page pictures of a widowed Jackie Kennedy sightseeing in London with her young, fatherless children. I try to think less of my own absent husband and concentrate instead on formulating a plan.

With a grudging acceptance, it's patently obvious I cannot do this single-handed. Even the Lone Ranger has his Tonto. Intelligence officers go out in the field solo, but they have the support of a whole web of field agents, plus the Spy Shack to bail them out when the going gets tough. Shit-hits-the-fan type of stuff. So far, I have the Poppins bag as back-up. As to who I trust, there's only three. I remove Gilda from the equation, not because I don't have faith in her, but because her loyalty is maternal – she *would* lay down her life for me, but might be quite noisy about it. Besides, someone has to look after Libby if I'm in jail. Equally, Vivien will go to the ends of the earth to help me, but she's desk-bound and far better at using her charms over the phone to winkle out information. And she wouldn't get far in the stilettos welded to her feet. Frank *is* the only one qualified to help. I swallow down scalding Nescafé. Even though he clearly suspects something, do I have the right to ask him, knowing he will say yes to whatever hairbrained plan I lay down? Two more years and he might be able to afford a proper, well-earned retirement.

I look over at the photograph on the fridge, Davy's enduring smile staring back at me. *'What choice do you have, Mags?'* he says, clear as day. It locks heads with my conscience, nagging endlessly at my temple. Annoyingly, though, he's right, even from beyond the grave. What alternative is there, other than stumbling like an amateur sleuth into what I believe is a government facility hiding state secrets and heaven knows what else? Fakery on this scale demands a team effort.

Frank has been and gone at the Egg, and so I head straight to the Stable, where my thighs tell me I'm scaling the north face of the Eiger instead of three flights of wooden stairs. To my relief, he's at the desk of makeshift pallets, sitting opposite Ringo and Carl.

'Morning, Magpie,' Frank chimes, with nods from Carl and Ringo. In between a quick hand of cards, they are divvying up the day's assignments. He takes one look at me, the badly dispatched nose situation and my poor attempts with the pancake stick, and offers up the chit observing a regular *Daily Worker* newspaper seller outside Holborn station. By far, it's the easiest mark of the day. Good ol' Frank. Guilt churns inside me like the dirty swell of the Thames, and I ponder on whether I really could go it alone. I sit with a sigh – of relief or exasperation, hard to tell.

'Heavy night at the pub?' Ringo squeezes out the words between lips holding onto his roll-up ciggie, the long ash finally tipping onto his knees. Except he says it without humour or affection, more like accusation.

'No,' I say. 'Tired, that's all. Lots going on.'

'Even in housewife suburbia?' he bats again, followed by a sly grin.

This time, I merely narrow my eyes. For all his youth and enthusiasm, I'm finding it hard to warm to Ringo, the Stable's newest recruit. Aside from the thickish lips of one Mr Starr, he looks nothing like his Fab Four namesake. And while claiming to be a true Liverpudlian, I suspect he hails from a sleepy village several miles out and hams up the scouse accent to full effect, attracting plenty of female attention in the process. Rather ungenerously, I feel sure he awarded himself the nickname. I wager his real name is Clive.

'Come on, you two, hop it,' Frank chivvies, like a factory foreman. 'Or we'll have Grayling making a royal visit to check up on us. Worse still, His Highness Garnett.'

They shuffle out, donning hats and picking up newspapers as they go.

Frank sidles alongside, giving me that paternal look I glimpsed in my father during his minimal moments of sobriety. Inspector Tanner would have made a fabulous grandfather, I think, though I don't say it, knowing the hurt it would induce. Frank's one and only son was lost at Dunkirk, and his daughter in the Blitz. Lord knows how he's kept going, what with the unfaithful wife skipping off with his heart and everything else held dear. What would I do without the solid, dependable Frank? No, I resolve firmly: despite his suspicions, I can't involve him. I'll fly solo, me and my limited experience.

'Are you going to tell me now, Mags?' he says, dropping onto the chair opposite and looking hard into my eyes. Unlike a Gilda glare, it creases me inside. 'If it's man trouble, you don't have to spill, but I think it's something else.'

My lip ripples. I could claim 'time of the month', but not with Frank. He deserves more. And yet I'm drowning. In quicksand. I know the sensation of fear creeping upwards, licking at my insides and threatening to overwhelm, identical to the weeks after Davy's death. Helpless, and yet desperate to keep my head above water for Libby and the future. Now, I'm paddling furiously for I don't know what, with the same urgency and resolve. To make something right, perhaps for Davy and – from the little I've discovered so far – possibly for others out there in the world.

Frank cocks his head with concern. I resolve there and then to tell him something, seek his advice, but nothing more. As he protects me, I will do my best to shield him from whatever government or military filth is out there. But 'a problem shared is a problem halved', isn't that the saying?

'How about a pint after work?' I say, and while his face brightens, it says he's caught my meaning.

'Fine, the Blue Post?'

'No, somewhere else.' *With no ears and eyes.*

'All right,' he concedes. 'I've bagged the watch opposite the Soviet embassy for my sins, and my relief takes over at five thirty. Exmouth Arms at six?'

'Perfect.' I reach out for his hand. 'And thanks, Frank.'

'Anything for you, Magpie.'

That's exactly what I'm afraid of, Frank.

He heads for the door in beige grandad guise, and turns as he's halfway out. 'Oh, how did you get on with the bloke and those Beatles tickets?'

Dammit! Running around the Cotswolds had totally consumed me, and I'm filled with remorse at sidelining my daughter. Again. 'Oh, er, yes, he's going to look into it,'

I stutter. 'Says it's hopeful.' But even lying to spare Frank's feelings is nauseating.

'Good stuff, see you later then.'

If I'm to keep my job, I've no time to drop by the MI5 sex shop and pick up the contents of Davy's file from Terry. Probably a good thing, since my mind needs to focus on the surveillance, rather than be distracted by secrets loitering at the edges of my brain.

Today's assignment proves to be a straightforward Donkey job. I go for the lonely old lady guise and lodge myself on a bench opposite Holborn underground entrance, where a balding middle-aged man in shirtsleeves stands patiently with a sheaf of today's *Daily Worker* draped over one arm. 'Read the truth about Britain's industry,' he barks at intervals to streams of commuters going in and out. The bunion throbs in a rhythm and I look with sympathy at his feet and wonder how they are faring.

The day is dull and lengthy, but the seller quits well before five, giving me time to hot-foot it over to Soho and Terry's porn palace, my heart beginning race at the prospect of what I might find.

Be careful what you wish for, Maggie Flynn.

'All good, Mrs F?' Terry reaches under the counter for a large brown envelope, and for a brief second, I feel very mucky.

'Thanks Terry. Did they come out all right?'

'Needed a bit of skill in the darkroom, but I think what you have is readable.'

'And did you read it?' My heart flips a full, uncomfortable somersault.

He shakes his head. 'Me? Nah. I'm the proverbial wise monkey, Mrs F. See no evil, hear no evil, speak no evil. It's safer that way, and good for my life expectancy.'

Another heart stop. Is that a flippant turn of phrase, or does he know of people – agents – bumped off because of getting too close? But he's gone back to fiddling with other brown envelopes under the counter, those with content far grubbier but much less incendiary, I shouldn't wonder. I tip him another pound, borrowing heavily from Gilda's Library of Disapproving Looks as I hand it over. *Between me and you, eh Terry?*

He grins with understanding. 'Thanks, Mrs F. See you next week.'

I'm already swilling in tea, so I walk the streets back to the Stable for some peace and quiet, ignoring for once the circus of colour criss-crossing the Soho thoroughfares. Terry's envelope is relatively light, but my load feels instantly heavier over my shoulder, bashing against my side as I walk at a pace towards Berwick Street. The question is: pregnant with promise, or leaden with a heavy toxic canker?

Today, I tackle the stairs like a rat up a drainpipe, passing Johnny on the way out, fully decked out in the traffic warden garb. 'Good luck,' I say.

'Thanks, I might need it,' he calls back. 'Subversives we can deal with, it's the British motoring public I worry about most.'

My fingers are trembling as I settle in the musty armchair and pull out the envelope, tempted to retrieve Frank's brandy bottle from the bottom drawer of the filing cabinet

– 'for emergencies', he insists. But right now, pinpoint vision and a clear head are vital.

With the sun casting shadows through the tiny windows, I squint at the twenty or so file sheets photographed only yesterday morning, though that already seems like a lifetime ago. A few are clearly Davy's written reports, and although they are not in his handwriting, I somehow recognise the blueprint of his language, his gravelly voice in my ear. The first name to leap from the page is 'Yuri', followed by details of the meet between Yuri and 'Standard' in 'WB' and 'EB', which I assume to be East and West Berlin. It hammers home Yuri's honesty, not only in knowing Davy, but also by entrusting me with his Service codename. According to the report, Yuri provided details of suspected KGB infiltrators within the fabric of British society, the so-called 'sleeper' spies that MI5 fears the most, those spooks who don't drawl with a Slavic accent or drink vodka like it's water. Instead, they shun the stealth of spies and live in plain sight, that person sitting next to you on the bus or in the corner shop. The insidious invisibles.

What catches my eye next also sticks in my throat: Yuri's mention of a sleeper potentially working in a military outpost: 'CH.G', Davy had typed. I don't need much encouragement to join my own dots. Congleton House. Gloucestershire. Was it Yuri's revelation that led him there in the first place?

Standard's travel record shows him as visiting CH.G in December 1961, a rail chit to Stroud and a taxi receipt pinned to the page that I'd thankfully not had time to detach in my haste to snap all the pages, his cover that day listed as 'workplace safety officer'. It ties in with what Woolpack George confirmed about Davy's visit. But what of his second and third trips to the Slad Valley? Hurriedly, I flick through the pages and the travel record, right up to what I assume was one of his last trips to see Yuri in Berlin, in late July '62. Not a single mention of a train to Stroud, taxis or subsequent reports.

Why?

If the Woolpack barflies are reliable, Davy did return to Slad, though perhaps under his own steam – he had a car, and sometimes borrowed my Mini too. Why he didn't submit a report or expense claims for those other trips is the key question. Was he there without the backing – or the knowledge – of the security services?

'Did you find something in that first trip, Davy?' I find myself muttering. 'Did you go back to be sure, to make certain of what you'd found?' I slam the photographs down by my feet in frustration. 'Christ, man! Why can't you – didn't you – tell me?'

Crucially, why didn't you report back to your employers? Annoyingly, there's no Davy worming in my ear when I need him most.

Focus, Maggie Flynn. Focus. I have Congleton House, but what I also crave are threads, those that connect or lead to anyone else who might have had similar suspicions. Sadly (both for him and my quest), Yuri is beyond my reach now, so any other stray fibre is vital.

At the bottom of the penultimate page is a name, as a sign-off for what seems like an unrelated assignment: 'J. Quinn'. I scrape at my memory. Of course, Davy didn't talk about *that* work, but I wonder if I've heard it in passing, at Leconfield House or muttered in disdain by the Donkeys.

Even scratching in my deepest corners, J Quinn is nowhere to be found.

Until I can get back to Slad, though, the name is my only strand to follow. The sheets I will pore over again at home, but more urgent is what I will or won't reveal to Frank. At least there's a bus ride on which to chew over my quandary once again: share the entire load, or keep a trusted friend safe?

'I got you one in, Mags,' Frank says from his corner table at the pub on Exmouth Market. 'Gin and tonic. End of the day – thought you might need it.'

'Thanks, Frank, you know me too well.'

We sip, watching the office crowds spilling through the open doors and onto the road outside, basking in the longer days and the May sunshine, the pungent but strangely comforting smell of onion skins and carrot tops underfoot.

'And how were our delightful Russian diplomats today, Frank?'

'Busy,' he says, taking a large gulp of his pint. 'Bodies in and out like a fiddler's elbow. I ran out of film twice and had to run around the corner to reload the camera in a bush. One of the cheeky bastards even waved at me as he swept away in his chauffeur-driven Mercedes. I sometimes wonder why we bother.'

'Well, you know what they say, don't you Frank?'

'Ours is not to reason why...' we chime together, with a ceremonial clink of glasses.

'So, I guess your *Daily Worker* man didn't turn out to be the spy of the century, either?' he asks.

'No, poor bloke,' I say. 'Four sales all day. The only thing he's guilty of is dedication.'

We both know why we're here, but Frank does allow a decent pause before he tackles the real issue, enough that I've got a single measure of gin inside me.

He sets his glass down firmly. 'Come on, Mags. Spill.'

I don't mean to tell him everything. On the bus journey over, I pledged to reveal that I've discovered an 'irregularity' which needs checking out. I would be asking his advice, plain and simple. Who am I kidding? Certainly not Frank. He would – and does – see through my pathetic attempt at fiction in a heartbeat. A simple look (and it's not even one of his best interrogation glares) unlocks what is clearly a pressurised dam and suddenly I'm spilling everything – Davy's true self as a spy rather than a Watcher, Yuri, my treason at the Registry and the recent day trip to Slad. My entire chaotic life. The tears I just about rein back.

'Bloody hell, are you telling me you stared down Beattie Baglan?' He whistles respect.

'To what end, Frank? I'll likely be hauled before her and Grayling any day now to explain myself. And I'm still none the wiser.'

'Then we have to work fast, don't we?'

'What do you mean?'

'It's obvious, Mags. We have to get inside this so-called loony bin as soon as possible, and find out if there's something within those walls that we shouldn't be seeing.'

'But it's my problem, Frank,' I say, fairly pathetically. 'Look what happened to Davy…'

I'd go as far as to say Frank slams his pint glass on the table then, inviting several heads at the bar to turn. His voice turns to a hoarse whisper. 'And how, Mrs Flynn, do you propose to penetrate this establishment with its wire fences and security? Go on, tell me.'

'Well, I hadn't quite got that far.'

'Two is definitely better than one on a job like this,' he says knowingly. 'I've worked undercover before – not just surveillance, but infiltration. In this sort of case, people are less suspicious of couples. That's a fact.'

I slump back into the worn leather, gin glass to my chest. I'm exhausted and winded, with absolutely no fight inside me. Certainly not against Frank's sensible reasoning.

'All right,' I concede. 'But if there's any whiff of danger, we get out. And you first. If there's one of us left to face the music, it will be me. Agreed?'

He frowns through the bottom of his glass.

'Frank? That is the only way we're doing it.'

'Oh all right.' He sniffs. 'But I get to choose the disguises.'

'You're on, DI Tanner. Same again?'

A second gin is ill-advised, but I want one all the same. 'Cheers, Magpie. Here's to our Donkey day trip,' Frank says.

I'm tempted to frown at his flippancy, but we all have ways of dealing with the hurdles that life throws at us. Frank prefers alliteration.

'There is one name I did find in Davy's file,' I venture.

'Oh yeah?'

'J Quinn.'

It must mean something because Frank freezes with the glass on his lips.

'Do you know him?'

'Of him,' Frank mutters. The instant tic-tack of his eyes around the busy pub speaks volumes. 'He's an intelligence officer, one of the new brooms that swept in during the late 50s, maybe early 60s. Ambitious, is the word around the Spy Shack.'

'So, he might have been working with Davy?'

'It's possible. I've heard he's already running his own band of agents across the south – Czechs, Poles, Soviets and Hungarians. It's rumoured he's gunning for the top floor, for Garnett's desk, though he's biding his time for now.'

'Have you met him?'

'In passing,' Frank says, and this time, his disdain is undisguised. 'Once or twice, he's turned up at the Stable asking for our surveillance logs.'

'At the Stable!' I'm aghast. For one, our space is sacrosanct, and two, it's an unspoken rule that officers do not interfere with Watchers. That's Grayling's job, and she's only ever appeared once in Berwick Street to turn up her long nose at Donkey basecamp.

'Yes, for a minute, I thought he was simply new to the job and wet behind the ears. Then I detected the real reason.'

'Which was?'

'Arrogance,' Frank says firmly. 'That tiny but distinct sneer on his top lip. I've seen it in the Met, and on villains too. Like we're the dog-doo on his shoe. He simply thought he had the right to go wherever he pleased.'

'Hmm.'

'I know what you're thinking, Mags. And I can't stop you, but if you seek out Quinn, you'd better be careful. He's self-important but smart with it. Just watch yourself.'

Frank's right again, and I should be careful. But much like the pursuit of Davy's truth, I won't be held back. Not now there's a thread to tease out.

Sixteen

15 May 1965

We agreed on a Monday mission, Frank and I. We'll both call in sick and make haste for Gloucestershire in the Mini. Which means I have two whole days (and sleepless nights) to tussle with my conscience, dread and expectation – and go shopping.

With constant reminders about my pledge to Libby, Gilda pushes us out of the door early on Saturday morning, with hissed instructions at me not to come back until teatime. My daughter is just fifteen, but in that moment, I am all of eight years old and being shuffled out onto the street with my precious ha'penny for sweets.

'Yes, *Mother*,' I glower at her. 'See you later.'

For a time, I am able to forget what lies before me, and whether I might land up in a police cell, or worse – an MI5 safe house that is anything but reassuring. Cloaked and ghosted away. It happens, clearly. What I've also forgotten is how much I miss an entire day with my daughter and what a delight she can be, when not playing up her role of sulky teenager versus irritating mother. On the bus, she rattles on about school friends and music, the latest fashion for hemlines, shops she wants to visit today (all of them, by the sounds of it) and 'What do you think The Beatles might do next?' as if I have an insight into the mindset of John, Paul, George and Ringo, which of course would be helpful in tracking down a ruddy ticket for a live concert. That said, Libby's joyful innocence helps to distract from Russian sleeper spies, MI5 skullduggery and the devilish leer of the Janus face leering at me around five a.m. – half Grayling, half Baglan, which put an end to the few hours of slumber I'd managed.

Libby is only too glad when I suggest a coffee at the impossibly hip Guys 'n' Dolls before we begin our pilgrimage down the King's Road, she for the opportunity to gaze at the beautiful people gliding along the city's public catwalk, and me for the caffeine that the glorious hiss of a Gaggia machine provides. Finally, we get to the serious business of shopping.

How many outlets does a teenager need to visit in one excursion? A lot, apparently. I'd basted the bunion and cushioned it with a plaster in advance, but it's not enough against Libby's endless trawl of the most vital shops. We hit Mary Quant's Bazaar first, with all its vibrancy, colour and the carefree chatter of females with money in their pockets. Picking over the rails, I'm almost jealous. Were I a lot younger, I'd be purchasing quite a few of those straight-down shift dresses for myself; the lack of curves seems positively liberating for women with a thickening waist. A few doors down we're reduced to window-browsing in the pricey Top Gear, though Libby insists we go in, the boutique being a known haunt of The Beatles, The Stones and other pop royalty. For a second, I think I spot Mick Jagger among the racks, but when the figure turns those skinny shoulders, it's obvious he doesn't have the lips for it. Plus, this lad is far too handsome.

'No, Libby! Absolutely not!' I find myself saying when she emerges from the dressing room in Countdown, already famous for its rising hemlines and skimping on skirt material.

'Oh, *Mum*,' she laments. 'Don't be such a fuddy-duddy!' I win the day, but only by enticing her towards Kensington and the Biba boutique, where it's like shopping in some old Victorian boudoir, all palm fronds and swirling wallpaper. We spend an age in there, among the vibe that is 'totally wild', according to Libby. Being a fuddy-duddy, who am I to argue? Any minute now, I think Gilda might pop out from behind a potted plant, complete with her paint brush and sewing machine.

'Are we finally finished?' I'm rubbing one foot against the other as we land in my familiar stomping ground of Soho, having thrown caution to the wind and hopped in a taxi. Given the number of shopping bags at our feet, my purse has already taken a battering, so what the hell? Derry & Tom's is closed, and so Libby opts for a plate of ravioli at Moka in Frith Street, where I'm revived by a double espresso, good pasta and thoughts of my sofa.

'Your Dad and I used to come here,' I tell her, mindful of my pledge in the attic. 'You were quite small and Gilda would babysit for a few hours while we had a break, because it had the first proper Italian coffee machine.'

'Really?' Libby's eyes are like saucers. 'Did you sit here, in these seats?' Her hand goes to the faux leather counter stool on which she's perching, as if it maintains part of Davy's fabric.

'Very probably, since we came quite a lot. Your Dad actually preferred it to the pub, and I was grateful for the caffeine, I can tell you.'

'I like it in here,' she says into her milkshake. 'You and Dad had good taste.'

'Had? What about now, madam?' I gesture at our shopping bags.

'Yeah, well,' she concedes. 'Sometimes, you do.'

She pumps me for more memories, and I oblige quite happily, because talking about Davy the family man – my husband – still seems a world away from David Flynn, the MI5 spook. Warmth and love versus deceit.

But it's been good. We've talked, sparred like mothers and daughters are supposed to, and I've spent time with my child, finding out what makes her tick, something that's long overdue. At least I've tried, because who does know the insides of teenager's mind in this crazy world? Plus, I've put aside the filthy world of espionage for a whole afternoon.

Libby waits for me to sink a second coffee before turning her wide eyes and engaging smile on me. 'I know Gilda says I shouldn't nag at you, but have you got any further with those tickets?'

Oh hell. 'Like I say, I'm working on it, love.' I utter it with conviction that's a total fabrication. Worse, I get carried away by the afternoon and just how nice it is not being at loggerheads with my child. I should have learnt by now, but clearly not. 'I promise, Libby, I will get them. You will go to a Beatles concert.'

Yes, Cinderella, you will go to the ball.

There, I did it. Launched myself into a deep, dark hole of my own digging.

'You're the best,' she beams at me, sucking up the last of her drink. 'No one else has a mum like you.'

No, they don't. And it's probably just as well.

Seventeen

17 May 1965

Frank is ready and waiting outside Acton tube station at eight a.m. sharp, though I barely recognise him in the chosen guise of a crisp dark grey suit, complete with waistcoat and sober tie, his hair neatly cut and oiled back, his chin 'smooth as a baby's bottom, Mags. A proper barber shop shave,' he reports, climbing into the Mini's front seat.

My utter love for him in that moment fights to override the nerves that have been running amok for, oh, only the past forty-eight hours. 'Very dapper, Mr Tanner.'

'You don't look so bad yourself, Mrs Flynn.'

Truth is, my own woollen blue suit itches and the white nylon blouse buttoned almost to my neck is already fermenting sweat as I drive westwards, windows open wide to blow away the heat of another sunny day. Would that nerves could be gusted away so easily.

'All right, let's go over it again,' Frank says. He doesn't seem edgy as such, though I detect some angst in making sure we get this right. We have one chance to convince the gatekeepers at Congleton House that we are professional surveyors come to make a spot check on the building, requiring a comprehensive tour. No fluffing of the lines or slipping of the mask, and hope to God our faux personas hold out.

We've done as much preparation as two days of a weekend will allow. Frank has 'acquired' two convincing identity cards for a spurious firm (I don't ask about his source and he doesn't offer any details), plus we have Vivien sitting tight at her desk, for when we need her.

Obviously, I'm the assistant, a Miss Parker, to Frank's Robert Treach, lead assessor of 'Treach & Lamb', contract surveyors to government property. Sadly, my trusty bag has been labelled as 'too bohemian' in Mr Treach's opinion, and so replaced with a staid grey leather handbag, which I spent the previous evening adapting to the lens of my camera.

'We have to be officious,' Frank instructs as I dry-clean the route in a zig-zag direction towards Oxford. 'I might come across as a bit bullish to begin with, but believe me, people bow down to that show of authority.' So says a man who spent decades kicking down the doors of known thugs, with a battering ram and a clutch of constables in tow. I can only hope that his approach is a little more sensitive today.

'If they start questioning, our reaction has to be belligerent,' he goes on, 'and we may need to use a good deal of bluff.'

'That's exactly what I'm afraid of, Frank.' I turn my head sideways and catch the faint smile on his lips. I do believe he's enjoying this. 'You know the old nursery rhyme about the three little pigs, and all that huff and puff?'

'Yeah?' Frank looks perplexed.

'Well, if they call our bluff, we haven't got a cover that's made of bricks and mortar. It's straw at best.'

'It'll be fine, Mags. Life is all a front. We'll probably use up our quota for today, that's all.'

'Might be a bit more than our daily allowance, Frank.'

With all the looping back, stopping and starting to check we have no tail, it takes until midday to reach Stroud, where we stop for lunch in a small café. The waitress and the two women at the next table smile and talk to us as strangers, perhaps deducing that we're father and daughter. At first, I'm alarmed by the interest, scouting for anyone who might just be a Watcher, casually buttering a scone in the corner. Gradually I begin to itch less in my suit and realise no one is trying to extract anything from us. They're simply passing the time of day and being nice. Apparently, it can happen.

Over eggs (what else?), Frank and I have a debate about whether to motor up in the Mini, or leave it in Stroud and take a taxi, which will appear more professional. In the end, we both decide the means of a speedy escape takes priority. While Frank engages the waitress for any further intelligence about the nearby 'loony bin', I slip into the toilet and attempt to morph myself further into Miss Parker, adding a touch of understated lipstick – not too red, but not pale, like those flighty models on the cover of popular magazines – and powdering the film of sweat around my brow. 'Good morning, I'm Miss Parker,' I mumble into my reflection.

'That's good – clipped, but not too uppity,' Davy comes in, from somewhere over my left shoulder.

'Glad you could make it,' I reply tartly.

Outside, a tinny transistor perched on the café counter

pushes out a disco-jockey's unrelenting zeal, '… and here are those bad, mod boys, The Who…' followed by a jangling of guitars and the opening bars of 'I Can't Explain', at which point I release a sudden bleat of hysterical laughter into the mirror.

'You said it was all for Libby, for her future,' I huff into the air. 'I really do hope you're right, Davy Flynn.'

Bumbling along the sun-kissed Slad Valley, we park up in a quiet lane about a mile from Congleton House, get out and stretch our legs, brushing off the stray crumbs of fruit cake from Frank's jacket that he insisted was his 'pudding'. Just as with my previous trip, there's a cool breeze, and the birds are in good voice; I can't help feeling that to see a looming grey cloud overhead would be more appropriate, since the thrum of my heart dictates this is anything but a jolly day out in the countryside. Maybe Frank feels it too. Facing me, he breathes deeply. 'All right, Magpie?'

I nod, because it's not technically lying if I don't speak.

'In and out in thirty minutes, tops,' he adds. 'Keep checking your watch, as if you're used to hurrying your boss along.' He pulls out a builder's measuring rule and a heavy-bladed chisel from a bag in the car's footwell.

My eyes widen. 'Jesus Frank, you're not going to use—?'

'No! What do you think I am? It's for poking at the walls. I saw a real surveyor on television do it.'

While he gets to wield a sharp instrument, I'm furnished with a clipboard, though I'm grateful for it, since it will prevent my hands from a nervous flapping. On goes my wig, a thick, bluntly cut bob that prompts further prickling at my temples, plus a pair of wing-tipped glasses. Ready as we'll ever be. And yet in the next breath, I feel utterly vulnerable, stupid and downright foolish, a kid playing with the dressing-up box. All my determination drains away. This is a world – a universe – away from Donkey work. Maggie Flynn – 008? It's laughable.

'Frank,' I begin weakly, 'should we really be...?'

He silences me with a paternal stare, as if he half expected courage to desert me. 'Do you want to right the wrong that your husband may have discovered? Isn't that why we're here?'

'Yes, I suppose.' Right now, I need him to prop up the bravado that is threatening to collapse at the crucial moment, the skill that I imagine separates a true spy from the pretenders.

'Come on, then, Miss Parker. Let's cast a beady eye over what this glorious government of ours is doing behind closed doors, shall we?'

If it wasn't certain to crease his corporate suit, I would have hugged Frank Tanner to within an inch of his life in that leafy country lane.

Slowly, we drive up to the barbed wire gate and the tiny wooden booth alongside, from which a bored-looking guard emerges, sweating under his heavy serge jacket emblazoned with 'SECURITY'.

He lowers his reddened face towards my open window. 'Yes?'

Frank leans across and thrusts out his business card. 'Government surveyors,' he says. 'Spot check.' And it is *very* officious, from the king of glib, the master of Stable wisecracks. Even I'm convinced.

'I'll need to ring inside to check,' the guard says, making to turn.

'Just let us in, will you, man?' Frank growls impatiently. 'I have several other appointments today and I can't afford to waste any time. I'll speak to your superiors inside.'

Blimey.

The man takes a step backwards in the face of Frank's sergeant-major address, and for a minute, I think he might actually salute. 'Well, er, all right. But you'll have to check at reception,' he concedes limply.

'Thank you, my man.'

My role at this point is to stare blankly, since I'm merely the assistant, and not to panic, or send the gravel flying under the Mini's wheels as we drive through the now open gate. I manage to bumble in slowly, parking next to several other cars alongside the house. Still, no one in sight, either patients or staff.

'Step one,' Frank mutters under his breath. 'Now the real test.'

I think my face must be the classic rabbit-in-the-headlights.

'Come on, Mags – this is what you do every day. Only with the talking bit added.'

Perhaps the subterfuge, too, and the trespass, in strictly legal terms. And I'm not entirely sure if today's endeavour constitutes treason. But yes, he is right, and his words help to inject a frisson of courage at this crucial moment. I push back my shoulders and clutch the clipboard to my chest.

I *am* Miss Parker.

In answer to Frank's firm rap on the door, a receptionist

opens one of two large double doors and leads us into the lobby, empty of bodies. Instantly, I feel justified in my suspicions: be it medical, maternal, physical or mental, every health facility oozes the odour of disinfectant, the cheap chemical bulldozing of disease. My nose twitches. There isn't even a higher grade of bleach, as per a private sanatorium. Instead, a familiar, thin vapour of stale tobacco rises towards the high ornate ceiling, with an undercurrent of dust and wax polish in the wood heavy foyer. It smells like Leconfield House.

The receptionist guides us towards the desk, and it's the first real test of Frank's fake ID's under her beady eye. She hooks on a pair of glasses from the chain around her neck and peers. Five seconds, then ten. A second perusal of each one.

I begin to itch again and make a show of looking at my watch. 'Mr Treach is very busy today,' I say, shifting the clipboard from side to side. Officiously. 'If the government requires his skills then...'

She looks up, her mascara-crusted eyes huge through thick lenses, lips crimped in a pout. Clearly, she has studied my own mother's manual of condescending scowls. 'I'll just have to verify it,' she says. Firmly.

'If you must,' I huff, as per an irritated assistant, handing over a printed card containing a phone number, and watching her reaction intently; she doesn't baulk at the words 'Ministry of Defence'. Very telling.

Frank flashes me the speediest of looks and I spy concern deep behind his eyes as she dials the number. Is this where we stumble? We hear the receptionist speak to the switchboard operator and ask for personnel. I picture the phone ringing not in the MoD's personnel department, but in Vivien's office, she having had a quiet word with the switchboard supervisor that very morning (someone who might well have a dedicated page or two in V's famous black book). I imagine my good friend gasping for a cigarette and with an overblown bladder, because Vivien would have welded herself to the desk all morning, waiting for this call to come.

'I have a Mr Treach and Miss Parker here from contract surveyors,' the receptionist says, reeling off details. 'Security confirmation required.'

Vivien's efficient voice is only just audible. 'Just a moment, please,' then silence as she pretends to go away and check a file, while she's probably just sitting there with her hand over the phone and crossing her legs tightly in desperation for the toilet.

The seconds crawl. Two men pass through the lobby, one in a suit, and the other looking like a PE teacher; both throw a disinterested glance in our direction. Frank coughs with impatience once or twice, but the receptionist ups the ante on her frown. *Come on Vivien*. Finally, I hear her clipped voice again. 'Yes, they have security clearance,' she chirps. 'And may I take your name please?'

The prospect of her name being on a file somewhere in Whitehall throws our receptionist, who spits it through the receiver and hangs up with a loud clunk of the phone. Hastily, she picks it up again and dials an internal line, asks for a Mr Simpkins, and scribbles out two temporary passes with our names on.

I see the relief wash across Frank's face when Ken Simpkins turns out to be the building's caretaker rather than a defence official. As such, he's less likely to question our presence. The downside is that he undoubtedly knows more about buildings than Frank.

'Where do you want to see, Mr Treach?' says a very keen Ken.

'Everywhere,' Frank barks. 'I'm told the structure is questionable in these old buildings, and given the purpose, we don't need any collapsed ceilings, do we?'

'No, sir. Though we can't actually gain access to some of the rooms at a moment's notice, not when they're in use.' Ken makes a face, an expression that reflects what goes in on within is 'dodgy' to say the least.

'Well, we'll just have to make the best of it, won't we Simpkins?' Frank blusters. 'Oh, and because this is a spot check, we're keeping a low profile, all right? Strict instructions from the top brass.' He taps the side of his nose twice and Simpkins puffs out his chest with self-importance, smiling his complicity.

'Come on, Miss Parker. Keep up,' Mr Treach orders.

Despite his deeply patronising tone towards Miss Parker, Frank is playing a blinder.

The house has four storeys, Simpkins tells us, and we climb the winding central staircase to the top floor, working our way downwards. Floors four and three appear to be offices, although most are vacuous and empty, with creaking floorboards and a musty smell. Those employees we do intrude upon largely ignore our presence, as Simpkins does a grand job of being our unwitting stooge, announcing us as 'government inspectors – nothing to worry about, we'll be in and out in a jiffy, Miss Low.'

Frank moves about each room with impunity, his tape measure giving him licence to make a full tour, barking measurements that I scribble down on a non-existent chart, and poking into corners behind a secretary's chair – 'I do beg your pardon, miss' – while I see his eyes skate over the papers on her desk. At intervals, he prods at the skirting boards and cornices and mutters about the 'integrity' of the brickwork.

It's what I don't see which alarms me most. I'd fully expected not to see patients or the ubiquitous men in white coats, as it's been clear from the outset this is no asylum, municipal or otherwise. More startling is the lack of anything personal in each office; no pamphlets or newsletters pinned to the noticeboards, no photographs of loved ones on the desks and a distinct lack of signage on each door. There are no indicators, and I realise it's the sort of place that could be evacuated – nay abandoned – at a moment's notice, a whole department ghosted away.

But what type of department? The lack of anything descriptive means I'm no wiser yet, and I have a distinct feeling there are far more people here than the scant staff we've seen so far. If so, where are they, these 'Oompa Loompas' that the Woolpack regular spoke of?

Descending to the second floor, the atmosphere changes dramatically. We go from a tired old building to something altogether more organised, with corridor walls painted a fresh, uniform green, and half a dozen semi-solid doors, behind which I can hear commanding voices. It has the feel of country house turned minor public school. But one with a security guard, wire fencing, and run by the MoD?

Where there's glass in each door's top half, it's covered on the inside with blinds; as Simpkins leads us along, I note a few inches of light and sight at the bottom. Frank must see it, too, because he has a sudden, convenient attack of arthritic knee and stumbles, enough to distract the caretaker and for me to angle my covert camera at the glass and snap several times into the gap.

'All right, Mr Treach?' Simpkins bends and fusses with genuine concern.

'Perfectly fine,' Frank pulls himself up slowly. 'Catches me unawares, that's all. Caught a bit of shrapnel on the German front, nothing to worry about. Onwards Simpkins, where next?'

'Well, we can go into the classroom office, if you really need to check in there.'

'Always does to be thorough, I say. Motto of the forces, isn't that right? What were you, Simpkins, a sergeant?'

'Not quite, sir. Lance-corporal. But yes, the same principle. Follow me, sir.'

At this point, I'm beginning to think Frank has missed his calling to the stage.

From the minute we step into the office, my faith is restored. We're onto something. It's equally stark – one filing cabinet and an empty desk, on which sits a white telephone, the type that has just two buttons instead of a dial and a light that might well flash red, the perfect prop in a TV show. As well as Frank doing his Olivier impression, I'm now thrust into a scene straight out of *The Avengers*.

Here, one wall is topped by a plate-glass window at waist height that looks onto a large hall, perhaps a former ballroom of this grand house. Now, it's more of a gymnasium, with a selection of benches and what I recognise from my own schooldays as a vaulting horse to one side. Several large objects hang at the far end, but even squinting I can't quite see what they are.

Frank makes a meal out of prodding into corners, enticing the gullible Simpkins to help with complex measurements. I'm attendant with the clipboard, my back to the wall and bag aimed at the hall, when the door sweeps open suddenly. It's enough to nearly knock Frank off his feet for real.

'Ooh, steady on Mr Lambert!' Simpkins is instantly protective of his new forces comrade.

'Huh, didn't see you there,' the man says gruffly, before his eyes comb the room and narrow, a scowl to his mouth. 'And who are these people?'

Frank ignores the request and pokes expertly with chisel, leaving his new best friend to explain. 'Government surveyors,' Simpkins pipes up. 'Integrity of the building, apparently. We'll be in and out in no time, Mr Lambert.'

'Well, I need the space – and privacy,' Lambert grunts. 'Quick as you can.' He barely glances at the inconsequential note-taker and her clipboard, and so doesn't spot my own eyes squinting at the papers now laid on his desk. We're all startled by a single trill of the phone, and the light blinking an urgent red, as if something vital is about to occur. Or that we've been rumbled.

Lambert snatches up the receiver. 'Yes, what?' Much like the woman on reception, his telephone talk needs work. 'Now? I'm in the middle of something.' Huff. 'Oh, all right, I'll be down.' He grunts again with exasperation, and barges out of the room, stopping only to bark at Simpkins, 'Don't be here when I come back.'

'No, Mr Lambert,' the caretaker mumbles, and it's evident what he thinks of his testy overseer.

'He's a barrel of laughs, isn't he?' Frank says when the door is closed.

'You could say that,' Simpkins agrees. 'Though he's head of development, so he's got a lot on his plate.'

'Oh, these engineers are always the same,' Frank suggests, fishing subtly.

'I only wish he was an engineer,' Simpkins grumbles. 'That's what my dad was. Lambert is the big cheese in this place. Rumour has it that he's a medical man, too, though who knows what his bedside manner would have been like.'

During this exchange, I am more than eyeing the papers left by Lambert in his bad-tempered haste. My back to the window, and Simpkins focused on one corner with Frank, I creep towards the typewritten top sheet and aim the loaded corner of my bag, as Frank hacks again with his chisel noisily. But there's more than one page; with a visibly shaking hand and my nerves strapped into a rollercoaster, I reach out and gingerly move the top one aside. In time with Frank's rhythmic destruction, I capture pages two, three and four. Chip, chip, chip. Snap, snap, snap. In seconds, I've restored the pile to its original state. Inside my jacket, there's a full-on sweat.

'Mr Treach,' I cut into their builders' banter, tapping at my watch. 'We should be aware of the time.'

'Yes, Miss Parker,' Frank clips back, rolling his eyes in masculine collusion with Simpkins. 'It's just like being at home with my wife, always moving me on somewhere else. But yes, perhaps we should forge on.'

We speed through floor one, which appears to be more classrooms and an empty corridor, until Simpkins asks if we need to look in the old stables, 'as there's been talk of converting them into more accommodation. Though you probably know more about that than I would, Mr Treach?'

'Sadly not. We don't get wheeled in until the decision's been made,' Frank comes back. 'A pre-emptive strike today would seem extra efficient, don't you think?'

I glance at my watch again, for real this time. It's creeping towards thirty minutes. Frank's still in full flow, but our cover might not hold much longer, particularly if the irascible Lambert begins asking questions about our presence, and my nerves are stretched like a traitor's spine on a mediaeval rack. I need to bring down the curtain on Mr Olivier.

Catching his attention as we walk towards the stables, I glower a distinct message. He presses three fingers into the leg of his suit. *Three minutes.*

Simpkins opens the battered wooden door of the stables; Frank and I can't help stealing a look at each other. It was a gamble worth taking. Several of the old stalls are filled with rectangular boxes, a straw-like padding spewing from one or two that have been opened. It could be my imagination – that is becoming wilder by the minute – but each looks to be the size and shape of a weapons carrier, at least those that I've seen in war films and spy thrillers. More alarming is the skull and crossbones that stands prominent on a few square cartons, and the stencilled warnings: 'DANGER!' and 'EXPLOSIVE'.

There's something more sinister here than kids smoking behind the bike sheds. Frank wields his trusty chisel once more at the walls, and I saunter close to the containers. Click, click.

'Well, my good man, you've been an enormous help.'

Frank is effusive in his praise for Simpkins as we make to leave, and with very good reason. For a minute, I think they might part with a salute, or even a brotherly hug.

'Don't you need to leave via the reception, sir?' Simpkins asks.

We've rounded the back of the building and the Mini is easily within sight. So, too, our escape. I hear the approach of voices and rhythmic chanting, like a military marching song. My tongue feels leathery as I scour the immediate landscape, wanting to glimpse what's around the corner, but dreading the security guard getting a call in his little sentry box and barricading the gates shut – with us inside. *Get a move on, Mr Treach.*

'We need to press on,' Frank says, though I note he doesn't hand back our visitor passes. Fingerprint-heavy, he'll be thinking. 'Perhaps you'd be so good as to say thank you, and tell them my report will arrive in due course.'

'Of course, sir,' Simpkins nods. 'Glad to be of help.'

How I exit without a racetrack-style spin of the wheels, I'll never know, but even the beleaguered guard issues a cheery wave as we drive through.

Once we're down the driveway and well out of sight, I pull into a lay-by and swipe the wig off, discard the glasses and run one hand through my hair, my fingers instantly wet with perspiration. In the seat next to me, Frank is grinning from ear to ear.

'Jesus, Frank! When was it you said you were undercover? And you never told me you'd been in the army.'

'That's because I wasn't.' He smiles like the Cheshire Cat. 'Like I said, Mags – sometimes all you need is bluff.'

Eighteen

17 May 1965

'So, what do you think?' I turn towards Frank, the tornado ripping through each of my lungs gradually calming to gale force. 'Did we just break all manner of laws for absolutely no reason?' *And am I losing my mind entirely?*

Frank loosens his tie and sparks up a cigarette, fiddles with the buttons on his waistcoat. All without a word. Why won't he say something?

'Well, Magpie,' he huffs at last, into the still air. 'I don't know about you, but it doesn't take a genius – or a detective – to see there's something dubious going on in there. Downright deadly, too.'

The gale threatens to swirl again, though it's a small amount of relief that – according to Frank – I didn't just compromise the both of us on a fool's errand. 'Did you get a look at any papers close up?'

'Nothing that made any sense,' he says. 'It was all typed directives.'

'Same here. A couple of the pages I managed to photograph had a few drawings, too, though we won't see the detail until I get them to Terry.'

The both of us stare through the windscreen, clearly trying to piece all the elements of the afternoon together. The air is still and the birdsong seems louder and even more surreal.

'Where was everyone, and who are they?' I think aloud. 'And why do they need a head of development in what feels like some type of correctional school?'

'Bloody strange type of education with guns,' Frank mutters.

Whatever it is that we've just left, it's not what the Ministry of Defence purports it to be, the creepy old asylum in a rural idyll. In my mind, such an effort to hide the true purpose smacks of moral discomfort. They don't want anyone to come close, let alone find out what's inside.

Equally, I think Davy must have discovered more than Frank and me, something to have sparked his moral outrage. I'd seen it stoked in him before, principally over flashpoints about each nation's nuclear research, living through the jittery post-war years of the US, Britain and the Soviets threatening atomic testing in far-flung oceans and deserts, boasting about their ability to blow one another to kingdom come, yet again. He was against it, I knew, saw the futility and the ridiculous showboating of weapons that could only result in sorrow, more so since becoming a father. But The Bomb was, and still is, an open secret. What we've seen today feels... I don't know, more personal to Davy.

Frank shakes his head slowly. 'Whatever's being taught in there, Mags, I'm not convinced it's improving anyone's mind. It feels a lot dirtier, don't you think?'

'Downright filthy.'

I'm not minded to agree with his next suggestion, since I'm drained, itchy with dried sweat and desperate to head back to the familiarity of London. For heaven's sake, even Gilda's psychedelic wall might afford some solace right now. But I concede, because he's right.

'Might as well, while we're here and dressed for the part,' Frank states sensibly.

Slad village is basking in its late afternoon glow, and I have to applaud Frank's willpower as we motor past The Woolpack and stop instead outside another chocolate-box dwelling sporting an aged 'Bed and Breakfast' sign. With his tongue practically hanging out for a pint, Frank reknots his tie and combs the Brylcreemed hair. 'Come on Constable Parker, put your wig on, and stand too.'

An evidently short-sighted Mrs Ellis is easily duped by a quick flash of Frank's very out-of-date police warrant card and leads us down her dim hallway towards a living room with not one but three cages of budgerigars in the window. It's hellishly hot, smelling of birdseed and lemons.

'You want to see what?' The landlady cups a hand to her ear. Quite deaf, too.

'Your visitors' book for 1961 and '62,' Frank repeats, enunciating each sound.

'And why do you need to see that?' She's squinting close to Frank, and getting far too good a look at him for my liking.

He pulls himself up, as per his last performance. Enter Mr Olivier, stage right. 'Because it's a police matter, Mrs Ellis,' he says with loud clarity. 'We have reason to believe a man we're currently looking for stayed here once, possibly twice. So, your visitors' books, if you please.'

'Well, I don't know why you couldn't just send the local bobby,' she grumbles, shuffling towards a gargantuan mahogany sideboard and ferreting inside for several large notebooks. A budgie tweets loudly in my ear, more of a concerted squawk. A suspicious one.

'Here,' she says, finally. 'I suppose you'll want tea, while you're looking?'

Since my throat is like the deserts of Africa, and what with inhaling an eddy of dust-motes twirling in the sunlight, I could sink a reservoir. But in line with Frank, I shake my head; fingerprints on the cups, not to mention a lip impression. Just in case.

She leaves us to go over the books, but only as far as the next-door kitchen, where she clatters about, leaving the budgies as her eyes and ears.

'You take '61, from June perhaps,' I tell Frank, 'and I'll do '62.'

We leaf through the pages of guests – despite the dowdy surroundings, plenty of people evidently want the Cotswold B&B experience.

'Got something,' Frank whispers in seconds. 'December '61. John Stapleton.'

'I wonder if that's the first time he came?' I pull out a small notebook from Miss Parker's handbag, and consult the dates of Davy's travel receipts logged with MI5. 'Yes, that ties in with his first official visit.'

Both of us comb over the pages from '62, until we spot one from February and then March, another in April, as per his conversations with Woolpack George. All John

Stapleton, 'Though he could hardly sign in as another person here, could he?' Frank punts.

'Mrs Ellis?' Frank projects his inspector's voice towards the kitchen. Nothing but a chorus of bird cheeps. 'MRS ELLIS?'

'Yes? Yes, no need to shout, dear.' She comes in, wiping both hands on her apron.

'Are you the only person offering bed and breakfast in the village?' he asks.

'Yes, dear. Ever since Mrs Maxwell passed away in 1960, though everyone says I was always the best.' She puffs her chest out proudly and, in the background, I notice one of the birds affecting the same stance. It does explain why Davy stayed here on several occasions, officially or otherwise, since there was no alternative close by.

Frank points at the visitors' book, at the signature of my husband, as another man entirely. 'Mrs Ellis, do you remember this gentleman, a Mr John Stapleton?'

She peers for what feels like an age at the writing, as if she's expecting it to speak to her. Loudly. With each passing second, my hope dwindles, and I find myself almost wishing she won't remember, that it won't be him at all.

Her bird-like head pops up suddenly, pupils beady black and alert as Frank holds up a small black and white headshot of Davy Flynn. 'Mr Stapleton, yes, that's him! Ooh, is that who you're on the look-out for? I wouldn't have guessed in a month of Sundays that he was a wrong 'un – lovely man, so polite, and always complimented my breakfasts, poached eggs rather than fried egg as I remember.'

Davy didn't care much for eggs, let alone fried. My heart cranks at a stranger's recollection of the man I shared my life with. And yet, I have to remember this is another persona. It's not my Davy, but the shadow he played.

My head is swirling, with heat, the day and too many emotions, so it's a good job Inspector Tanner is on the ball. 'And what was the intention of his visit, did he ever say?'

'Business, he told me. A health inspector up at Congleton Hall, I seem to remember.' Arms folded, Mrs Ellis is enjoying this now, logging every syllable for her gossip bank. 'Of course, I was able to tell him all about the place, what happened in the war, and when it was taken over as an asylum.'

'Did he ever stay here with anyone else?' Frank pumps. 'A colleague, perhaps?'

Now she does scratch around her brain, as a flurry of birdseed is ejected from one of the cages. 'Hmm, let me think.' The pupils spark again. 'Yes, I'm fairly sure it was the first time, because I remember it was cold and we had to set a fire in each room. Another man, perhaps a bit younger.' She runs a gnarled finger over the signatures. 'Here he is. Peter Quill.'

Sloppy, I think immediately. John Quinn. Peter Quill. Not exactly sophisticated tradecraft.

'Can you describe him?' Frank asks. He's not leaving anything to chance or supposition.

'Tall, young, dark hair, slicked-back, looked a bit like that Tony Curtis bloke, oh you know, the one that was in the film about the circus and the trapeze people. I do like him. Though Mr Quill wasn't as nice, a bit snooty I thought, certainly not as polite as Mr Stapleton. He stayed once or twice on his own.'

Frank's eyes flick towards me. *Bingo*, they say.

As Frank is wrapping up his thespian turn and assuring Mrs Ellis that the constabulary *will* be in touch in due course, and yes, she might be required to testify in court, I pull out the Minox and snap the relevant pages. Above all, we need proof, and right now, any tiny piece of thread is valuable.

'So, what do you think?' I almost fall into the driver's seat of the Mini, brush birdseed from my jacket and breathe in the age-old leather for comfort.

Beside me, Frank has taken off his jacket and moulded into the passenger seat. Now, he does look tired. 'I think,' he breathes, 'that I need a pie and a pint.'

In a pub somewhere in Oxfordshire, I stick to ginger beer while Frank licks his lips at the amber glow of ale in front of him.

'I'm not sure that's the going rate for an A-list actor of your calibre,' I question, 'but will it do?'

'Consider it due payment, Mrs Flynn, with a nice steak and kidney to follow,' he says.

'So?' I venture. My gut says we're onto something, but I need Frank's shrewd nose and his years of experience to confirm it again, having heard Mrs Ellis' contribution.

'Well, it's a bloody cesspit, isn't it, Mags?' he says, after his first long draught. 'And your Davy smelt it, the fetid shit of something very wrong.'

I'm relieved. And not. It means we – I – have to go on, to finish what Davy didn't manage to put a stop to, whatever it is. Wasn't allowed to. Was actively prevented from doing so.

Can I really succeed where he didn't?

★

Frank forks a chunk of pie into his mouth and chews thoughtfully, while I can only look at mine. I simply can't shift the echo beating at my brain and making my stomach churn: *There's no freedom without liberty.*

We're both agreed there's little to do until Terry develops what we have on camera, planning to regroup when I collect the processed pictures. Head lolling, Frank sleeps all the way back to London, though I'm glad as it leaves me to see-saw the route home and dry-clean my own mind in the peace, the tinny sounds of Radio Caroline in the background and the poppy, upbeat tunes of Britain's *Top Ten Hits.* Ironically, I begin assembling a full roast dinner in my head, working out my shopping list and picturing Gilda, Libby and I around the table, eating like normal families do. Anything, rather than mull over what we saw today, and the resonant feeling that it was nothing like liberty.

Frank stirs only when I draw up at his flat in Hornsey. 'Ugh, sorry, Mags, it must have been the early start, and that pint.' He gathers up his bag and chisel, and looks me straight in the eye, seriously. 'You know what you have to do, don't you?'

'Yes, unfortunately.' It's something else we agreed at the pub; for me to infiltrate the Registry once again and discover everything I can on a Mr J Quinn, intelligence officer. I have to do it openly, and yet without raising suspicion. I have to be a better snoop than a fully paid-up MI5 spy, and the darling of the top floors at Leconfield House.

All in a day's work, surely. Though I would like a decent night's sleep first.

Before reaching home, I stop in a call box and dial the number for Vivien's flat, intent on letting her know Frank and I are both safe. At least that we're not languishing in jail. The phone rings and rings, but I'm not surprised, since she's often out, being courted by some wealthy or stealthy man, her Italian count, no doubt. I'll catch her tomorrow at the café she drops into each morning before work. Before that, I want my bed, and time. Better still, I need to sort out my bloody life.

'All right, love?' Gilda's voice pushes from the sofa as I walk into the darkened living room. Libby is sound asleep, spooned in beside my mother, who is glued to an episode of *Perry Mason*, strains pushing out from the illuminated box in the corner. 'Good day? Productive?' Gilda murmurs.

Good? Perhaps not. Productive more so. There's a hint as to why my husband might have fallen foul of the people he worked for. Those he previously trusted. Does that count?

'So-so, I suppose,' I reply. 'And you?'

Nineteen

18 May 1965

The look of relief on Vivien's face as she spies me sitting at the café counter is evident, especially as I have her favoured cappuccino ready and waiting.

'Heavenly,' she sighs, practically falling into the foam. 'Thanks, Maggie, I really need this. And I'm so glad to see you.'

'I did try to call you last night and let you know we got out in one piece,' I explain.

For a half-second, she stares at me blankly, the perfect bow of her lipstick tainted only by a small milky deposit. 'Yes, oh yes,' she splutters.

However much she cares for me, it's then that I realise Mrs Remmers' relief isn't about me or Frank, or anything to do with yesterday. 'Vivien, are you all right?'

The painted lips quiver, and her rock-solid confidence appears to crumble into her half-empty cup. 'Oh Maggie, I think I've done something stupid. And very possibly illegal. Treasonous even.'

Despite her efforts to explain, I'm struggling to get to grips with what she's telling me about dinner with her newest beau the previous evening. 'What's so alarming about this... what's his name?'

'Phillipe. Phillipe Giroux.'

'I thought he was an Italian count?'

She swats away the suggestion like an annoying fly. 'No, the Italian has been and gone. This one I met at a party at the French embassy, so of course I assumed he was the real thing. Plus, he has the sort of Parisian accent that makes your knees wobble,' she explains. 'And you know what I'm like for a foreign diplomat.'

I do. Vivien has done for international relations what countless governments have yet to achieve.

'What's changed your mind and got you into such a flap?'

'Well, that's it, Mags. I can't quite put my finger on it, except that he was very interested in my work. I suppose I'm used to that, but when we were alone and we got to... you know, *dessert*... he kept steering the conversation around to what I did, and what I saw in the office.'

'You of all people know how to handle that.' And yet, she looks sheepish, not the Mrs Remmers in control of her little black book. 'Vivien?'

'God knows I'm good at holding my liquor, Maggie – years of practice, you know – but last night I felt very woozy, and oddly confused. I don't really know how I got to his hotel room.'

'And?'

She sips, with a subsequent grimace. 'And I might have told him... things.'

'*Things?*'

'About work. Though I can't quite remember. Looking back, it's possible he slipped something in my champagne. I've had a fair few hangovers in my time, and this doesn't feel like a normal one. My head is in a vice this morning.'

'Oh Vivien.' It's merely what comes out of my mouth first, but in all honesty, it's all I can think to say. Inside, my mind is racing. If he's French intelligence, I have no idea what they are doing operating undercover in London, gleaning information about British defences. Aren't they supposed to be our allies?

Vivien drains her coffee in one gulp. 'There's one other thing,' she says.

'What?'

'As he left, I sort of roused, and then pretended to be asleep. He must have let his cover drop, because I heard him mutter a few words.'

'Oh yes?'

'I couldn't tell exactly what it meant, but I'm fairly sure he said something derogatory.' Now she looks very forlorn. 'In Russian.'

Leaving Vivien to nurse her splitting head, I'm not even sure which disaster to tackle first. The dilemma about holding anything back from Frank has long passed, and my path towards the Compton Street Egg is necessarily speedy. My surrogate father, confidante, fixer and therapist is mercifully in situ already, a yellow halo of egg lighting neatly placed directly above his head.

'Morning partner, sleep well?' He's in a worker's garb of collarless shirt and a navy zip-up jacket, a tweed flat cap on the table beside his paper, a guise he inhabits with natural aplomb.

'So-so.' It's fast becoming my stock in trade as an assessment between downright awful and grim. I spill the latest about Vivien before our poached egg on toast has even arrived. 'If this gets out, Frank, she'll be in the midst of something that makes the Profumo affair seem just innocent tittle-tattle. Christine Keeler looks positively angelic in comparison.'

Frank barely bats an eyelid. 'Well, it's obvious you need to sting him before he does the dirty on your friend.'

I look at him quizzically, with a forkful of eggy toast.

'A honeytrap,' he clarifies. 'Catch the killer bee in his own ointment, and make sure he goes away knowing he has more to lose than your friend by revealing their pillow talk. But perhaps a little surveillance first, to check the best way of laying the trap. What do you say?'

I say I'll add it to my list of already near-impossible tasks, but really I'm beginning to wonder if Frank should be allowed to retire, ever. Instead, he could rightly march into Rufus Garnett's office, perch behind his desk and take up the mantle of running MI5.

The honey caper will have to wait, because I have an errand to run before running the gamut of MI5 royalty at the Registry. On the way, I duck into the Soho emporium of salacious products, where a face pops up from under the grubby counter. Except it's not Terry's, but that of a man who seems both sheepish and surprised a middle-aged woman has breached such an establishment.

'Oh, is Terry not here?' I ask casually.

He looks around furtively, as if Terry might be hiding amid the shelves. 'He's on a day off. Can I help?'

If there's one place to lend an air of shiftiness, it's a porn shop with high-end material that doubles as a dodgy MI5 den. Only something about this chap gives off moral and physical 'seediness' in abundance, and I'm not of a mind to entrust the potential grenade of my camera film to a squalid stranger.

'I'll catch him another time,' I sing, and exit promptly.

Who to go to? Still mindful of the potential mutterings over at the Spy Shack concerning a wayward employee – namely me – I need that film processed fast. So, it's a swift walk just three streets away, to another on my list of Darkroom Masters.

'All right, my sweetness, what can I do for you?' Bob has never yet called me by my name, and for all I know, he was christened Archibald in real life, except to everyone in Soho he is 'Slimy Bob'. For good reason, since three – or is it four? – strands of greasy hair lie over his pink, perspiring bald head, and the looming belly of flesh spills over his soiled trousers in all its unctuous glory. I can trust him not to look at the frames of my Kodak film in detail, simply because they do not feature a near-naked woman with the shapely measurements of Brigitte Bardot.

'Give me a few hours,' Bob says, at the flash of another five-pound note.

'Perfect.' I'm almost bankrupt, but it will be speedy at least.

There's no putting it off any longer. With aching legs and my courage fuelled by egg and a fresh chit from Vivien, I enter my illustrious place of employment. Descending the stairs in the Spy Shack basement, the Stasi princess is nowhere to be seen, but it's of little relief. In front of me

– meaning it's too late for a U-turn – is the chief sentinel herself.

'Mrs Flynn, back again so soon?' Bea Baglan looks down her nose and over the rim of her glasses. If I had any air left in me, it would be seeping from all pores, and it's only Frank's croaky voice in my inner ear which keeps me upright: *Bluff, Mags. Huff and puff, and plenty of it.*

'Well, isn't it always the way? You do one person a good turn, and then you're first on the list to be asked again,' I twitter at Baglan, rifling in my bag for the chit which says that, once again, I'm on a fact-finding mission for the Ministry of Defence. 'I should learn to say no, shouldn't I?' Smiling broadly, I offer up my pass-key of paper.

'We should all learn a lot more than we do, Mrs Flynn,' she replies through lips that barely move. Her glacial tone in that moment could douse the Great Fire of London.

Disappearing into the stacks of shelves, I know my limited time has to be worthwhile. If Baglan hasn't felt inclined to report my presence to Hilda Grayling before, she will certainly be ringing upstairs now, perhaps as I'm scouring the files on John Quinn. Which means speed and efficiency are paramount.

With my bright yellow Marigolds in place, I've learnt my lesson and hold a tissue over my nose to offset the inevitable dust and prevent another almighty sneeze. Little need, because there's no layer of grey filth when I locate his file under Q. His and the alongside folders have been disturbed only too recently. Coincidence? Or has someone else got an interest in our Mr Quinn?

I read nothing, only flick and snap at his biography page, and then at as many sheets as my rising pulse rate will allow. Beyond the shelves, I swear I hear Baglan's leather court shoes prowling on the other side, like a tiger circling the bottom of a tree, sure their prey will have to descend eventually. And as a fellow woman of a certain age, she knows all too well my bladder is likely to give out before my courage. Slotting Quinn's file back in place, I stop to listen – the pacing has ceased. Is she a mere step away, ready to pounce on my camera? Caught red-handed. Certainly a sackable offence, even for MI5, one that inevitably involves jail time too. I'll be in the papers, like John Vassall and Frank Bossard. 'MOTHER TRAITOR', the headlines will scream. Gilda might well bask in the notoriety, but what about Libby?

Get a bloody grip, woman.

Unbelievably, the coast is clear as I emerge from the stacks, the Minox warm in my trusty bra pouch. I can't quite believe it, but Baglan is nowhere to be seen. Already up on the second floor, whispering in the ear of Hilda Grayling, maybe?

'Oh, it's you again,' Stasi princess says from her post behind the reception desk. The frosty voice and prison-guard expression convince me she is ill-suited for a job in hospitality.

'Yes, for my sins,' I tinkle as she throws her beady gaze inside my handbag like a laser beam. 'All done, though. And thank you so much.'

'Hmm.' That's a dismissal – I think – but I don't wait for the accompanying death glare, climbing the steps at a pace. Upstairs, I retrieve my bag from a locker and dive into the first cubicle of the ladies' toilets, noting that my breathing is now on a par with my galloping heart. *This is not good for you, Maggie Flynn,* I tell myself. *At this rate, you will not have a skin to save.*

There's Quinn, and the mysterious purpose of Congleton House, plus MI5's potentially murky involvement. Now Vivien and her indiscretions. Reaching to the bottom of my bag for a handkerchief to wipe away the sweat and tears pricking at my lids, I come out with a crumpled cloth, plus the slip of paper with Frank's scrawl on it from several days ago. Oh hell, and The Beatles tickets, too.

Are there enough pieces of Margaret Mary Flynn to go around?

It's not Davy's voice, but Gilda's popping into my head right now, a memory from schooldays when I was apt to burn the candle at both ends – studies and too much of a social life: *Something's got to give, my girl.* I'm not sure if the image of her wagging finger is real or a figment, but it serves to drive the solution home.

Annoyingly, my mother was right then, as is her sentiment now.

Desperate to exit the Spy Shack, I nonetheless pay one more visit to the personnel department on the first floor, where I put in a written request for two weeks' urgent leave, starting immediately, citing 'a family crisis' as the reason. It's no lie; I'm part of a family, and I *am* the crisis.

'Mrs Flynn! Stop!'

I'm two steps from the door when the stark cry hits me in the back like a sniper's bullet. Is this it, the firm grasp on the shoulder that I exercised so many times as a store detective? The cold sweat dread of capture? A half-second calculation: do I cut and run, meaning I'm a fugitive from here on in – on MI5's wanted list – or brazen it out, like

Kim Philby did for years, the ultimate in the old boys' school bluster?

Libby's face flashes up in glorious technicolour, the obvious distress of her sole parent as an outlaw. At times, she thinks little enough of me now, but what would that do to her faith in motherhood? I swallow a sour taste and swivel on one heel to the shock of the duty porter striding towards me. One glance left and one right – no one else in sight. No burly security staff, no police. What the...? Surely Hilda Grayling would not miss this prize opportunity of seeing me brought down, reserving a ringside seat for herself?

'Mrs Flynn,' Mr Pike, the porter, says again, waving a folded piece of paper in his outstretched hand. His crooked smile looks anything but threatening. 'There's a message for you. I just noticed it in the F pigeonhole. Best take it now, eh?'

'Yes, yes.' How the words make it out of my mouth I'll never know. 'Thank you,' I say, accepting it gingerly.

A trap? Will the MI5 mob be lying in wait on the street, making certain that I'm intent on removing sensitive material from government premises? Awkward as it promises to be for all concerned, the bra pocket won't hold up to a rigorous search.

What choice do I have but to sally forth? There are no windows large enough in the ladies' loo to squeeze my expanding waistline through – I've already checked. Only fate awaits me.

I don't know what it is, but something makes me open up the folded sheet there and then. It could easily be a routine message about my wages or shifts, but I flip it open all the same.

Look closely at John Quinn.
Look beyond the man.

My heart rate spikes again. I recognise the font as in-house, from any one of hundreds of typewriters throughout the building. Nothing else, and I backtrack towards the porter's desk. If the capture squad are lurking beyond the doors, they can damn well wait.

'Mr Pike, did you see who delivered this to your desk?'

He shakes his head. 'I emptied the pigeonhole this morning, as per usual. I only noticed it when I came back from my tea break, so it must have come in the last half hour or so. Is there a problem, Mrs Flynn?'

'No, no it's fine.' I tuck it into a pocket and step towards the door, into the sunshine and an uncertain future.

Twenty

18 May 1965

The midday glare makes me blink and wince on the steps down to Curzon Street, with no clear view of either side. With each tread, I expect another audible bullet, a rush of footsteps from behind or the laying on of hands, in anything but a biblical fashion. And yet the rushing of blood in my ears merely gives way to London's daily soundtrack, a taxi's toot and the throaty rumble of a nearby double-decker. No heavy hand of the law, or my employers. I can't pretend to skip down the remaining steps but I'm across the street and into sunless shadows tout-suite.

The thick, strong espresso of Maria's café draws like a magnet, desperate for some friendly chatter, but it's too close to contemplate a lengthy stop and I forge back to the relative safety of Berwick Street, careful to clean my route. I don't trust Grayling and co. not to put me under a Watcher's stare before they go for an arrest.

I've still got time to kill before picking up from Slimy Bob, preferably out of sight, and then more until I can hook up with Frank at day's end to go over the results of our trespass on government property. I need Frank and his common-sense assessment, but if I'm really honest, part of me is terrified, at what I'll be forced to view, and what I might have to do in righting what feels like a very big wrong. It's just what level of wrong this is.

Practically, it means leaving a message for Frank on where to liaise. Oddly, I'm wary of approaching the Stable; for such a place that's felt like a second home for almost three years, the prospect makes me nervy, even without MI5's version of the Keystone Cops chasing behind me. They know exactly where I reside between jobs, and given that they pay the Stable rent, they're entitled to visit without notice.

At street level, the early-bird market traders are winding down as I arrive. Making a circuit of the stalls, I buy an apple and stand in a doorway that's less than fragrant, munch at the tart flesh with my eyes fixed on the Stable door. After several minutes, Carlo emerges in full tourist regalia, bad shorts and inappropriate shoes, plus a camera slung around his neck. I can't help smiling – he looks every inch the part.

After ten more minutes, I'm nibbling at the core, having scanned the street several times for loiterers and those that would stand out, even against the eclectic mix of Berwick Street. No one individual has done a casual walk-by of the door, or is lingering opposite with an open newspaper. I'm relieved and yet confused at the same time at MI5's inability to snuffle out a rogue employee. No wonder that Cambridge lot got away with it for so long.

I reason that our cosy Stable may still be safe. For now.

'Oh, didn't think we'd see you today.' Ringo's head whips

up as I push through the top door, catching him lacing up a pair of running shoes.

'Why would you say that?' My paranoia peaks early. Has he heard something? Received a message from Leconfield House to report any sighting of me?

'Dunno, just something Frank said,' he mutters casually.

Too casually? I've never warmed to Ringo, but now my suspicions are amplified beyond reason. 'I'm on leave, just here picking up a few things,' I explain.

'Uh, as of when?' He looks up from his laces with, I think, genuine curiosity.

'As of now.' Firm, direct. 'Family stuff. At home.'

'Well, I hope it gets better.'

He exits the Stable in the next breath, and I'm left with a shard of warm sunlight cutting across the boards, plus the kettle to tempt me. Sod it, a cuppa might be my undoing, but I'm gasping for tea and space to lay out my thoughts. For once, the bunion sits in abeyance.

Cup in hand, I pull out this morning's enigmatic typed note. *Look closely at John Quinn.*

Haven't I just attempted to do that, and risked my job at the same time? Does it mean closer than merely the files?

The more immediate question is: who knows of my interest in Quinn? Perhaps not even Bea Baglan, since – without X-ray vision – she couldn't have possibly seen which files I accessed this morning. That leaves the landlady back in Slad, and Frank. Both I dismiss immediately; Frank because, well he's Frank. In a madcap TV storyline of *The Avengers*, the birdseed and lemons landlady might turn out to be the dastardly sleeper spy, but in what's left of my real life, I just can't see it. The budgie has a better chance of being a spook.

There are no answers, but the fact remains that I have an ally, or at least someone who knows. Trouble is, they may not be the same things.

Twenty-One

18 May 1965

Come on, Mags. Despite its lumps and wayward springs, the Stable armchair is too comfortable and the sunlight spreads a drowsy cloak over me. I might even have dozed off. *Get up!* I need to be busy until my meet with Frank, to offset the trepidation of those photographs, plus use the time I have left – time before MI5 finally puts two and two together and makes the requisite five.

It's almost one p.m. when I haul myself from the comfort of the Stable and head out into the bustle of London's streets, slipping into Slimy Bob's on the way. I exchange the Quinn film for a buff envelope that he hands over with scant interest, eating a fried-egg sandwich and smoking a large cigar, all in unison. He is, I think, a man of many talents. Safely deposited in the Poppins bag, the evidence sits heavy on my shoulder once again, far weightier than a few photographs have any right to be.

As the hours tick by, I'm becoming less paranoid about an MI5 tail, but even so, I take a circuitous bus route towards Kensington and the sprawling complex of the Soviets' official embassy. By that, I mean the Russians' own Spy Shack – the Rezidentura – because it's estimated that more than half the so-called diplomatic staff stationed here are KGB, or GRU, Soviet military intelligence. Doubtless, the same is true of the British embassy in Moscow, such is the enduring spit-spat of the espionage game.

Here, I need to be doubly canny, in order to be nigh on invisible to the suspicious Soviets, plus the MI5 Watcher doing the usual shift logging traffic in and out of the heavy wrought-iron gates. On approach, I note it must be our turn today, since Stablemate Pete is parked on a bench opposite the embassy, his ever-present copy of the *News Chronicle* open at the sport pages.

Mid-height, mid-build, with mid-brown hair and not a single feature that you could accurately describe (other than 'average'), Pete came straight from the womb ready for a life in surveillance. He's that man at a bus stop, on the football terraces, walking in the park and keen for a friendly chat, not that you'll ever manage to recall him or his monotone voice ten minutes later. The perfect ghost. Except he'll remember you, because his mid-brown eyes mask a deft, hawkish focus. All of which means I need to plant myself out of his gaze and a decent distance from the main entrance, hoping my middle-aged eyesight is up to scratch.

Vivien has given me a small black and white picture of her French friend, snapped by one of the British staff at their first diplomatic gathering. It's a side view of a strong jaw and an aquiline nose, a good profile but not much else, and not the best for reference, 'But he seemed very reluctant to pose for any of the official party photographs,' Vivien reported.

I'll bet he was.

The first hour drags, and I've made my way through today's *Mirror*, plus *Woman's Weekly*, then on to a dog-eared paperback. My scrutiny is split between the large entrance admitting a stream of sleek black-sedan types, and the smaller side gate discharging a flow of people on foot. From what I can see, Pete is focused on the array of cars coming in and out, capturing each image from the tiny porthole in the bottom of his sports bag. My fixation on one individual means there is less to do and yet it's equally taxing, lending an anxiety of one target slipping from my sight in a tiny lapse of concentration.

Of course, this could be a spectacular waste of time; Vivien's man might not have been speaking Russian at all. She was drugged, woozy and not at her best intuitive self, she'd be the first to admit. But above everything, Vivien knows men and her radar is tuned to work through the thickest of fogs. And, so I wait, that envelope slowly burning through layers of bag and clothes to create a hot ache in my side.

At two thirty precisely, and page twenty-four of my frankly terrible romance novel, there's a breakthrough. A black-suited man steps through the pedestrian gate, the right height and build, according to Vivien's recollection. He scans left and right, which is when I get to squint at his profile: it's the nose to a tee. It's a stroke of luck... up until the point where fortune runs out.

Dammit! I had hoped he'd stride across towards Hyde Park for a surreptitious meet, something to give us a little extra leverage, but instead he hails and bends into a black taxi. I've given over my last fiver to Slimy Bob, and there's mere change jangling in my pocket. Undeterred, I launch myself towards the road, scrabbling in the unseen depths of my bag as I run, my fingers hitting something old and moist, and then the crinkle of paper. Aside from the fake Monsieur Giroux, my target is a suited and booted skinny lad on a stationary Vespa, preening his mod-cut hair in one of many wing-mirrors. He looks horrified as I race up to him, settling to minor relief when I push a ten-shilling note in his face.

'All yours if you follow that cab,' I huff, giving him no time to refuse, since I've already heaved one leg over the wide seat, waiting impatiently to ride pillion.

'Oh, er...'

'Well, come on, are you game or not?'

Stunned, and perhaps a little afraid of the mad woman currently tugging at his bespoke suit tails, the engine pops noisily as he pulls away. I realise soon enough that Lady Luck has returned, because Boy Vespa proves himself an adept rider, weaving in and out of the traffic as I remember (just) in time to lean with him into each turn, a flash memory of the days when Davy had his own motorcycle, the wind whipping through my long hair as he pushed the speed along country lanes. Now, London's polluted ether settles like grit on my hairspray as I hold fast and hang on for dear life. The cab steers north-east through Piccadilly, with us rounding Eros at speed in its wake, and on towards Tottenham Court Road and beyond.

'Cheers, missus,' Boy Vespa says, as our phony Gallic friend exits the cab and he pockets the note. 'That was a lot of fun.'

Meantime, I'm windswept, totally broke and feel like I've done several hours on a runaway horse. I am in time, however, to log Monsieur Giroux's destination.

'So where did he go?' Vivien's whispered voice is classic cloak and dagger, despite being in a coffee bar where the jukebox is blaring out something jangly by a new boy band at a volume that only teenagers appreciate.

'To a flat in Bloomsbury, on the second floor of one of those Edwardian red-brick blocks,' I say. 'I followed him up the stairwell, and he let himself in with a key.'

Vivien ponders. Her lips waver. 'He told me he lived in Chelsea,' she says. 'That's miles away.'

'It could well be a safe house,' I suggest limply. 'Though I waited an hour and he didn't emerge.'

'Hmm.' She looks unconvinced. 'And a safe house for whom, the Russians or the French? Either way he's lied to me.'

I can't disagree. The vital point is what our Monsieur Giroux does next. And how we extricate Mrs Remmers from being the star turn in a national scandal before it becomes one. 'If he is a Soviet spy, it's likely he'll confront you with some photographic evidence soon, as blackmail,' I tell her. 'We just have to beat him at his own game.'

Unusually for Vivien, she looks crestfallen – at being the subject in someone else's little black book. Even her make-up looks slightly awry today. 'What can I do, Maggie?'

'Has he suggested another date?'

'Yes, dinner tomorrow night, at a restaurant not far from my flat. He's promised to pick me up.'

It doesn't give us much time for planning, but it's too good an opportunity to pass up. My guess is that the restaurant reservation doesn't exist, and our French toad will love her and leave her clutching a batch of compromising pictures, plus an ultimatum about information he needs from the British ministry. My job will be to engage Slimy Bob again, and the box of electronic trickery I know he keeps for 'special customers', plus one other essential component.

'We'll sort this, Vivien,' I pledge. Rashly. In truth, I don't know exactly how, but doing nothing seems much less of an option.

Huff and puff and we'll blow your house down.

There's no avoiding it any longer, and five p.m. approaches too fast. I make my way to a particularly rough pub near the Arsenal football ground – Frank's choice obviously – noting my soles sticking to the tiled flooring as I enter the gloom of what feels like the Victorian era, all dim wall lamps and dusty flock wallpaper. A man resembling Bill Sikes props up the bar, with a squat, square dog that seems strangely close to Dickens' portrayal of Bulls-Eye in *Oliver Twist*. Luckily, Frank has already bagged a corner seat, under a bulb that offers a few watts of illumination.

'Cheers, Mags,' he says, as I place a pint on the tacky table that's evidently been rinsed in beer.

'Lovely spot, Frank.'

He laughs. 'Ah, but it's so bloody awful that no one wants to come here. Not even the spy fraternity. Perfect for us.'

'Have you heard anything, from base camp?' I take a larger than average gulp of my gin and tonic, relaying the morning's encounter with Bea Baglan, holding back on the spiral of paranoia and my near tears in the ladies' loo. 'Any whispers about me?'

Frank shakes his head. 'Nothing. I purposely dropped by the Shack this afternoon and made sure Hilda Grayling saw me, thinking she might grab me for an interrogation about you. If she had, I could have gleaned something of what they know, or suspect. But she looked straight through me.'

'That's so normal it's almost worrying. Something's not right, Frank.'

'There's a lot that's not right, but yes, the fact there *isn't* a leak inside MI5 concerns me more. For once, people are keeping their traps shut. The question is: why?'

He takes a gulp of ale. 'Anyway, let's get this over with, shall we? At least we might discover what we're facing before they haul us away for execution.'

I'm not sure I appreciate Frank's gallows humour in that moment, but there's no postponing it now.

It takes us a while to put Slimy Bob's twenty or so prints in order, and identify where and what rooms of Congleton House they depict. The first few are of the offices, of nothing in particular, in line with what we recall first-hand. It's when we reach the second-floor corridor and the office itself that things become clearer, in more ways than one.

Frank actually sets down his pint. 'Blimey, Mags, I was beginning to think our imaginations had gone into overdrive. But perhaps not.'

I have to agree, and it turns my heart to lead, thinking of Davy's eye on the same content, maybe in a photograph, maybe in real life, and his faith plummeting at what he saw. His trust in *our* humanity, as a nation. Humanity as a whole.

Heads together, we peer at the scene I captured in what

looked like classrooms when I blindly pointed the camera into a tiny gap. They *are* classrooms, the camera just focused enough to show up adolescent boys and girls in identical T-shirts at desks. The two we can see, and a partial view of a third, tells us they are sitting straight-backed and facing one way, military-style. Like chess pieces. Or pawns.

Frank squints at something slightly fuzzy on each desk. 'What's that?'

I pull the image closer and angle it towards the dim bulb, icicles shooting through me as the light catches it. The sharp, pointy kind. 'I hate to say it, but I think that's a revolver.'

Frank will have gone through it in his police drills, and although it didn't feature in my Watcher training, I know exactly what I'm seeing. We're both dumbstruck, horrified at the thought of a lesson in stripping and arming an object whose only purpose is to kill and maim. With pupils that can only be described as children, all under eighteen, judging by their intent, innocent faces. It's so unbelievable as to be farcical, and yet here is the proof, in our hands. I peer again to be doubly sure, think of Libby and feel physically sick. Exactly as Davy would have.

Flicking to the pictures of the large vacuous ballroom behind the office, the strange objects hanging at the back have been pulled into focus. Now, there's no mistaking the stuffed sandbags made to look like crude torsos; every wartime soldier going into battle would have been coached in where the human body is most vulnerable to knife attack, to extinguish life or merely injure. Again, I can't help conjuring an image of these children holding knives in their previously unbloodied hands. Trained to kill, almost from the cradle.

'Jee-sus,' Frank whistles through his teeth.

We both take another gulp of alcohol in unison, hardly needing to look at the pictures I snapped in the outhouse, of the weaponry and explosive material. The few pages I captured in the office look to be some sort of psychological analysis, with chilling phrases such as: 'has adapted well to intense training', and 'top marks in sniper skills'. There's no doubt: MI5's grubby secret is a small but filthy 'school' in the idyllic Cotswolds, where they produce insidious, furtive weapons to kill the enemy. Human weapons, made from little more than juveniles. Those of Libby's age.

'Christ, Mags. I mean I know this is a Cold War and all that,' Frank exhales, 'but is this what we fought a war for? *Who* we work for?'

He sounds exactly like Davy. Or what my husband would have said if he hadn't been prevented from doing so. I might have been blind to his alternate life, but I knew Davy's morality inside out: he would have been appalled beyond measure. It's a badly kept secret in the spy world that our Soviet adversaries run similar schools in Moscow, bent on training agents from an early age – in ideology, spycraft and the fine art of killing. Now, it's as if some inside Whitehall have come to view it as part and parcel of the espionage game, the tit-for-tat of the Soviets versus the Western world, a kind of self-preservation for each side, and the accepted rules of the game. Only not Davy. What was it he asked of Yuri? *What would you do, if you thought everything you believed in turned out to be a lie?*

Up until then, I imagine Davy would have had faith in the security services – in MI5 – to keep us all safe, Libby included. He must have, or he wouldn't have maintained such a concrete lie for sixteen years. And while Davy proved to be no angel, he was a man of principle. Possibly a little naïve, but that's no crime, and certainly not deserving of a death sentence.

Instead, he discovered that the British are nurturing children for use as spies, as weapons. Possibly to rid the world of enemy spies like Yuri, with a family, and his own principles. To Davy that would not have amounted to war.

'*It's murder, Maggie, plain and simple,*' his voice worms into my ear.

It's not the objective either of us signed up for and, to quote the head honchos on the top floors of Leconfield House: 'It's just not cricket.'

Frank is already at the bottom of his pint, sunk in gulps. While we're running around playing at dressing up it's never occurred to either of us that we're gainfully employed by an organisation of assassins.

'Where do they get these kids from?' Frank asks. 'I mean, it's absurd to imagine any parent, however desperate, would offer up a child.'

I think of the teeming streets of Soho. 'There's plenty of runaways in London, come to find their fortune, and ending up on the streets. If the only other choices are slinking back home in shame, or prostitution, what might they opt for? And I dare say borstal is another prime recruiting ground for the boys.'

The image of children's homes being scoured by MI5 recruits for rootless orphans is unthinkable. But after what we've witnessed, anything is possible. Some things you can't unsee, and now it feels as if Frank and I are both equally tainted with this knowledge, even if we went looking for it. Never mind the practical dangers of owning such intelligence.

'So, Magpie, this is a bit of a to-do, isn't it?' Another of Frank's spectacular understatements.

'The question is, what do we do, Frank? What *can* we do?'

'I need another pint,' he says.

Furnished with more beer, and a second G & T for me, we lock heads – literally, voices low. The way we're feeling, even flickering mock-Victorian wall lights might have ears.

'Are we agreed that we want to – have to – stop this?' Frank begins.

I nod. I'm scared stiff, of course, but it's Davy's legacy, and more than ever, I can't let it go. Besides, we've come this far, breaking all sorts of protocols and laws. 'Frank, this is my battle, you don't have to go any further.'

'Bloody nonsense,' he insists. 'In for a penny, in for a pound, I say.'

Once again, I could hug him, and I do this time, horrified at the thought of either of us facing real jeopardy, but hugely relieved not to be tackling the next steps alone.

'To me, it's clear that we can't stop it physically,' Frank goes on. 'Not unless we attack Congleton House with a flame thrower, and with all that explosive about, there will be dire consequences. Besides which, they'll simply set up elsewhere.'

I nod again, trying to tear my mind away from an image that I can't now expunge: Libby sitting at one of those desks.

'What do you think MI5 fears the most?' Frank thinks aloud, oiled by his second pint.

Rufus Garnett's recent directive flashes up instantly: *NO MORE SCANDAL.* And it would be a scandal all right, hitting at the core of our fine, upstanding British

Establishment. While the great British public don't relish Soviet spies in their midst, *knowing* about any methods of disposal counts as far too squalid.

'They fear the news getting out,' I say.

'Exactly!' Frank throws down a soggy beer mat to show his accord. 'So, our best weapon is nothing destructive, but a convincing threat – to spill the beans. After the Cambridge shower, and then Profumo, they'll do anything to avoid embarrassment.'

'You're right, Frank, but do you think that's why Davy was dealt with?' I point out. 'Because he found out. Possibly, he threatened exposure too.'

Frank narrows his eyes and fingers the rim of his glass, always a good sign that he's totting up the odds, using the well-exercised part of his brain that deals with his daily flutter on the horses. 'Ah, but we'll have an insurance policy, Mags. We'll play MI5 at their own dirty game.'

'How?'

'Some old-fashioned blackmail. But first, I need to talk to a mate of mine from my time on the force.'

'What can I do?' I feel like Frank is taking all the risks on my behalf. I'd never forgive myself if he didn't get to that retirement.

'Keep your head down, Magpie. Stay out of the Spy Shack, play at being a doting mother and daughter. Meantime, let's draw up a safety plan for both of us. We can be ghosts, given we're the experts.' He gives me a full-toothed grin, made all the more yellowy by the dim and dismal lighting. 'Let's toss a grenade into the Spy Shack and threaten to pull out the pin.'

Twenty-Two

18 May 1965

Tomorrow, I pledge. Tomorrow, without work to soak up the hours, I will get organised, head out to the café Frank gave me as a starting point for those Beatles tickets and ask around for likely spots where I'll find the touts and the pot of gold at the end of the rainbow. My bank balance is sorely depleted, but I'm prepared to throw money at securing a slice of the Fab Four, if only for the problem to go away and make Libby happy. Next to ridding this country of an assassins' factory, it seems insignificant, but to tick at least one conundrum off my list will seem like a major step forward.

There's a glow and a distinct hum coming from number 54 as I walk up the path and slot my key in the door. Voices, chatter and laughter spill into the hallway, and rather than feeling deflated at facing one of Gilda's infamous gatherings, I'm quite glad. It means normal people, doing normal things, and right now that's very welcome.

The fact that my own daughter is centre-stage in the living

room, standing upright on a stool and surrounded by a gaggle
of women, seems fairly par for the course. 'Oh, there you
are,' Gilda mumbles through a mouthful of dressmaking pins.

Libby beams from her pedestal, cloaked from shoulder to
shin in bright yellow PVC. 'Hello Mum. Look at this! I'm
going to have a Mary Quant cape, and a dress to match.
Well, one that looks exactly like hers, and it costs hardly
anything. Don't you think Brenda will be *so* jealous?'

Several women of varying ages and ilks turn and grin at
me, sewing needles in hand. 'Wonderful,' I say. 'Aren't you
lucky?'

'Deborah here works in a factory, and they were throwing
out yards of this PVC,' Gilda punts with such enthusiasm
that I wonder which of our rooms will soon be adorned
with shiny curtains the colour of a sunrise. Or the interior
of the Egg. If it's alongside the Bridget Riley swirls and the
fluorescent orange chair, I may well object, or else get a
migraine. At the very least, some better sunglasses.

'There's a dish of moussaka in the kitchen,' Gilda adds.
'Dimitra made it. It's very good.' Dark-haired Dimitra gives
a wave and flashes a broad smile between stitches. I fetch
myself a plate of food from the kitchen and settle myself
in the armchair, an observer to the cape taking shape, the
industry and the love playing out in my living room.
The food is delicious, but Libby's broad beam is the only
nourishment I need in that moment.

If a sharp, acrid sensation stabs at me from time to time –
of the uphill task ahead – I push it back with all the energy
I have left. Because this is what I'll be doing it for, what
Davy would have been striving to ensure: happiness and
humanity rolled into one.

'*All for her*,' Davy reminds me.

'I know,' I mutter between bites. 'Now be quiet.'

19 May 1965

It's with a certain shade of guilt that I slip out of the house the next morning, just as if I were going to work. What Gilda doesn't know can't hurt her, and will save me from all manner of ear-bashing if she suspects I'm officially on leave and not spending time at home.

My first stop is the bank, and onwards to Slimy Bob in Soho, where I press another crisp fiver into his palm as he slurps tea from a cup the size of an urn. He hands me another envelope from the Registry roll of film, spending a further ten minutes relaying simple but detailed instructions (between bites of a sausage sandwich) about the additional small package that I slide into my bag of tricks, noting its now bulging seams, the once hardy stitching protesting against the weight. Perhaps I've filled it a little too much with supplies from the Stable – the odd wig, scarves and glasses – for my short sabbatical. And yet, you never know when it's necessary to throw on a quick disguise, do you? But the seams are under stress; Lord forbid, if that receptable should give up on me now, I might easily take it as an omen, and I vow to borrow Gilda's sewing kit at the day's end. It will be akin to shoring up my life.

Having already discovered the worst about MI5 (or what my imagination will stretch to), I feel braver breaching the inside of this envelope, but even so, I'll need privacy and good dose of caffeine to help. That task will have to wait, because this morning, I'm on the most vital of missions.

★

'Have you seen Benny today?' I shout above the jukebox and hiss and spit of the Gaggia machine at Bar Italia in Frith Street. Bodies mill around like chickens at a poultry farm.

'BEN-NEE!' the woman behind the counter hollers. Since I've no idea what Benny looks like, it's the best way of garnering his attention, if only he were here. One look at the bobbing heads signals that no one is owning up to being Benny.

I try a different tack. 'He said he had some tickets for me,' I tell the woman, who is frothing milk at a rate of knots. 'Suggested I should meet him in here.'

'I haven't seen him for days,' she says. 'Sometimes he goes up north, Manchester, I think.' Through the cloud of steam between us, she must see my face visibly sag. 'If it's tickets you're after, you could do worse than have a word with Gianni over there.' She gestures to a clutch of men standing around a high counter, four or five espresso cups between them. 'He's the one with the blue hat.'

She doesn't say 'enormous nose', because that would be unkind, but it is wholly more accurate. *A spectacular probiscis like a Roman general*, I'd have typed, had he been under my Watcher's eye. *Small and neat, Italian blue suit, bespoke shoes, olive skin on the way to being leathery.*

'Gianni?'

He spins to reveal piercing blue eyes and caterpillar eyebrows that hover between questioning and suspicion, though they seem to relax a little on catching sight of an apparently innocuous middle-aged woman. 'Yeah, and who wants to know?'

When I explain my quest, air is sucked in through the gaps in his tiny teeth. On shaking his head, the pork-pie hat doesn't move. 'Like cow's eggs,' he says, in a thick Italian accent. 'You could try Lorenzo. I heard he had a few last week. But, lady – not cheap.'

At this point, I might cash in my pension for a seat in the back row: the Liverpool lads insist you 'Can't Buy Me Love', but I wholly disagree where my daughter is concerned.

Lorenzo apparently 'hangs out' in a café in Pimlico, and so I've no choice but to hop on a bus and sail past Downing Street and the opulent Houses of Parliament, mindful that the chief pilot of our great nation squats somewhere in those hallowed chambers. How much does he or the current Home Secretary know about MI5's little countryside venture? Realistically, do they even want to know?

The Regency Café sits on a corner amid residential streets in varying states of shabby, wafting a steady odour of frying bacon and eggs into the street. It's after the breakfast rush and before it fills up with the lunch crowds, and I seat myself in the window, lifted by the sunshine reflected off the yellow Formica table, though it hasn't the cosy feel of the Egg. The café is half-full and I scan the other tables, finding no one that looks much like a ticket tout.

'Morning love,' chirps a ghostly waitress with pale lipstick, eyeshadow and pallor to match. I'm gobsmacked mostly by the size of her beehive, the tallest and most voluminous I've ever set eyes on, a scaffolded extravaganza of hairspray excess kept in check with a bright pink Alice band. How does she sleep? Upright? What about a hat?

'Tea? Coffee?' she prompts, in a bored voice. Her huge eyelashes wave at me like two friendly spiders. 'Something to eat?'

'Mushrooms and tomatoes on toast, please, and a tea.' My waistline notwithstanding, chatting up the waitress with a decent order takes priority. 'And has Lorenzo been in?'

She sighs heavily and turns towards the telephone table, points towards the broad back bent over it. 'That's Lorenzo. I'll send him over.'

'Thank you.' Her elongated head moves away, just catching the hanging lightshade as she shimmies towards the phone table. I note the shade wavers in response. The hair, by contrast, is less movable than Stonehenge.

My tea is in hand by the time Lorenzo lumbers over and squeezes his wide girth into the booth seating. 'I hear you're looking for me?'

No, not when you put it like that.

> Bear-like, rounded face, black button eyes set in like currants in a doughy bun. Hair unkempt, dark unshaven whiskers, soiled shirt and scruffy bomber jacket. Faint smell of BO and whisky. An easy mark to follow if I were on duty.

Unlike the dapper Gianni, Lorenzo looks like a street tout, and talks like one too.

'Beatles tickets. For December. Do you have any?' I say in staccato, having decided on being forthright. Regrettably, the words come out as simply needy.

He lights a cigarette and leers, not with lust, but almost

certainly with the idea of my desperation and his profit margin. 'Possibly,' he says. 'But it will cost you.'

'How much?'

'Twenty.'

'Twenty pounds for two?' I splutter. It's extortionate, over a week's wages. Who would pay that? *Me*, I think. *Stupid, idiotic me.*

'For one,' he puffs.

My face must reflect a renewed horror, because he merely shrugs. 'Depends on how much you want them. People will pay double that nearer the time. It's The Beatles.'

It's four once scruffy lads from Liverpool, but has he met my only child and her overriding obsession? Or my mother, egging her on from the sidelines?

'Um, can you hold two tickets, for a week or so?' I ask, wracking my brains for any forgotten baubles secreted around the house that I might be able to sell or pawn. What with fivers handed out liberally of late, plus bankrolling my own investigation, I'm heading into penury.

He draws in a lungful of chip-fat air through his large, hairy nostrils, and a reluctant smile creeps across his lips. 'All right, just for you, missus. A week. But after that, they're back on the open market.'

Seven days gives me enough time to beg or borrow the money. Or rob a bank, which at this juncture doesn't seem such a bad idea. I could add it to my list of felonies stacking up. Lorenzo slopes off with a promise to meet me back at the Regency Café in exactly one week, and when I query aloud if he'll remember, he raises one eyebrow in contempt. 'Till then,' I backpedal. Pathetically. 'I'll be here.'

I'm smiling to myself as I leave the Regency, celebrating

a minor success. Cinderella *shall* go to the ball. Her mother might be in the poorhouse after the event, but my darling daughter will not be overshadowed by Brenda and her all too efficient dad.

In fact, I'm far too pleased with myself, bouncing along as if I haven't a care in the world, steeped in that delicious fantasy that something has come right in Maggie's world. *Daft woman.*

I've almost reached the Tate Gallery, overlooking the river, by the time I notice it. Him. The tail. Just a glimmer at first of a reflection in a newsagent window as I sail by. But it punctures my good mood and injects instant discomfort. I slow up very slightly and sidle into the next open shop doorway, hit by the chaos and mustiness of second-hand clothes in abundance. The burgeoning racks are, however, a perfect cover to observe through the front window, peering between tightly packed winter coats, watching him stop, tie his shoelace and make a play of looking in several shop windows. Everything we were taught in training.

> *Young, suited in grey, a black felt trilby pulled low to obscure his face. The gait of a younger, lithe man, not the heavy trudge of a veteran with years of pub pies and bacon sandwiches around his waist. Too young for Special Branch. MI5 definitely.*

What's more worrying is that he seems familiar. At least I think so, though I'm beginning not to trust my own judgement any more, even when he does turn his face towards the second-hand shop, forcing me to duck behind a red velvet trouser suit. He's a professional, that much is obvious, so there's nothing in my supplies that will help, as he'll have assessed my shape, size and walk. I would have done so, if the tables were turned. I'll have to employ what Frank dubs the 'slice and dice', the use of speed and stealth, plus a convenient alleyway or two to shake the tail. I check my shoes – low heel, decent sole, and wriggle my toes. Mercifully, the bunion is having a sleeper day. Someone up there likes me.

Here goes, Mags. Role reversal.

Making a point of sauntering casually out of the shop, I cut left along the street and meander in front of several glass plate windows, the reflections of which tell me he's affecting nonchalance, and asking a passer-by for a light. *Carpe diem*, as lovers of Latin are apt to say. I'll seize whatever I can.

While his head is dipped downwards, I move, swerve left into the next street and up my speed to 'hurrying for an appointment' pace, a rapid skip rather than run. Behind, I hear the flap of his coat, and a faint pant of his breath – ruffled, perhaps, but still on track. The white stone monolith of the Tate looms up ahead, conveniently, since a vast gallery is the perfect place to lose yourself, and others. Rounding the building that sits squarely on the banks of the Thames, I trip up the main steps and hit the grand, echoey atrium, my ears tuned to his tread several yards behind.

But oh, he's good, this one – up and down staircases I go, sliding between the austere darkened Renaissance rooms, and the light and airy décor of the young guns of British art, slowing at some exhibits, but moving at a lick between each one. He's sensibly picked up a pamphlet guide, faking an interest in the words, and it helps maintain the pretence nicely. Typically, it's at this point the bunion decides to wake from its hibernation, a developing ache turning to a sharp stab on the inside of my foot. It takes all my effort not to limp towards the exit, where I stand atop the grand sweep of steps and rapidly assess the options. My senses tell me he's alone, with no capture squad waiting in the wings, but even so, I can't keep this up for hours; he's clearly younger, fitter, and without the baggage of afflicted feet. The river offers up a vast expanse in which to disappear, but I might choose a nasty interrogation over the polluted brown soup of the mighty yet filthy Thames. Left and right there's a wide, open thoroughfare where traffic flows up and down between western Whitehall and the eastern side of the city.

I hover, feeling his presence just behind and rooting in my bag, as women of a certain age are apt to do. He'll know I'm stalling, choosing the right moment. The question is, which one of us will gain the upper hand? I feel like a fox hiding out in the undergrowth, ready to spring to freedom, knowing the rabid teeth of a pursuer is just behind. How big are his Service teeth, and will he kill, capture or maim?

Hallelujah! My saviour arrives in the form of a gaggle of noisy schoolchildren being herded upwards by beleaguered teachers. Small bodies swarm either side of me, at which point I leap forward, pushing myself down the steps, two at a time, like the bow of a snowplough, to carve a path. I hear his voice behind, 'Excuse me, EXCUSE ME!' as he struggles to negotiate the throng of excited pupils, by which point I'm on the pavement, watching two double-deckers sweep in from opposite directions. What's that saying? 'You wait an age for a bus and then two come at once.' I thank the gods and London's transport system for this timely arrival of two red monoliths on wheels coming from opposite directions; as my tail reaches the pavement, I've already cheated death with one van and see-sawed behind the nearest bus, inciting one long, angry toot of a taxi horn, leaping to the other side of the road and launching myself at the bus platform. Mercifully, I land on my feet, instead of my knees, though it's no less painful with the bunion on fire. The driver pulls away, and I glimpse the man blow out his cheeks in frustration, the same expression I've worn several times in my short career as a Watcher. *Lost the bugger!*

On the top deck, it takes several minutes to catch my breath and quell the thrum of nerves. I don't like it, this being the mark, the prey, running from I don't know what. What was his purpose, and if he's tracking me – presumably aware of my visits to the Registry – why isn't the might of MI5 descending on me even now? Where are the unmarked cars screeching to a halt and dragging me from the top deck? It's not what I welcome but, equally, this simply doesn't add up.

Alighting from the bus three stops later and only yards from a tube station, I nip smartly into the underground, the tube being a good place to sit tight and keep moving in unison. At this point, my feet dictate taking a good half hour journey further east, before swapping platforms and retracing my steps. I'm at sea in my own city, time on my hands but needing to get a message to Frank, pronto. Then there's Vivien to attend to.

I'm on the return journey by the time I remember Slimy Bob's untouched brown envelope. With the morning's endeavours, I've almost forgotten about the unseen images of J Quinn's file still to be pored over. The carriage is almost empty, and so it's as good a place as any. The first print makes everything clearer, and a good deal murkier at the same time. Quinn's profile page has the requisite headshot of our man in black and white, pinned to the page. The expressive face that stares out is not new to me, at least not since an hour or so ago when I left him outside the Tate nursing the sharp stab of failure. It seems familiar now, that dark, slicked-back hair, 'like that Tony Curtis bloke', the description that frank had garnered from the landlady in Slad. It begs a more immediate question: why, oh, why is an MI5 man like Quinn, a hotshot who runs an expanding network of agents, doing his own Donkey work in tailing me? If I were a woman prone to suspicion (my tendency increasing hour by hour) I'd wager he doesn't want his own employers to discover what he's doing, has done in the past, or is about to do.

Who are you, Agent Quinn?

While the train hurtles into central London, I scan details of the file: born in Peterborough to teacher parents, James Sebastian Quinn attended grammar school before winning a place at Oxford, another of the security services' favoured hatching spots for new recruits. Being Davy's junior by almost twenty years, he'd have been too young for war service, but ripe for the picking when the Cold War established itself as the world's new peril in the late forties. The next page lists two aliases, and a number of associates, 'DF' among them. So, it's official, from two sources – he and Davy worked together.

Next, I go to Quinn's travel record; from memory, he looks to have journeyed with Davy to Stroud on that first official visit. Much like Davy's file, there are no further journeys listed to either Stroud or Slad, and yet the bird-lady confirmed he stayed with her on several occasions. There's no doubt in my mind that Quinn knows exactly what goes on behind those grandiose doors of Congleton House. The difference is, he's still breathing, and my husband isn't. What does that tell me?

I ponder over the next step. Principally, to keep my head down, and run it by Frank.

Vivien's need, however, is the most pressing this evening, creating much the same quiver as being on MI5's watchlist. Quinn's actions tell me he's got something to hide from the top floors at Leconfield House, and that makes us if not equal, at least on an even footing. We're both potentially up shit creek without a paddle.

With Vivien, however, I'm running my own op. A Donkey flying solo.

Twenty-Three

19 May 1965

As per usual, I ascend from the smoky bowels of the London Underground a least a stop early, clean my way around the block and then hop on a bus towards Vivien's. It's just gone four by the time I ring the bell at her smart Clerkenwell flat, the one she wrestled out of the ex-husband's property portfolio in lieu of financial recompense for him being – and I quote – 'the worst bastard on the planet'.

Vivien is already there, having feigned a toothache and left work early. She's just emerged from the bath and, I hate to say it, looks like she's been through trauma in the dentist's chair. She's without her make-up, the pan-stick that hides a multitude of sins and pesky wrinkles. But it's more than that: Vivien looks worried. Stricken, in fact.

'What's up?' I say.

'Phillipe called me at work today,' she says. 'To confirm our date.'

'Well, that's good, isn't it? We need him to be here.'

'I suppose so,' she says, sounding unconvinced. 'He says he's got something important to tell me.'

I place both my hands on her svelte dainty shoulders, which are sagging in a way I've never seen before.

'That's also good,' I encourage. 'The sooner we get this over with the better. Go and make yourself doubly alluring while I get ready, and then we'll snare the sneaky rat in our clever little trap. Yes?'

'Thanks, Mags,' she says, in a small, very un-Vivien voice. 'I'm not sure I could do the time in prison.' I see in her eyes the image of Christine Keeler – a beautiful but broken victim of the Profumo affair – being led away from the dock to begin her prison sentence for perjury. The mere thought clearly terrifies the normally serene Mrs Remmers.

'Of course, you can't,' I reply with the briskness of a formidable matron. 'They don't have champagne in there, or a decent G & T, and so it's just unthinkable. We won't let it happen.'

She nods and turns towards the bedroom, unable to see my fingers crossed firmly behind my back.

I've almost finished the preparation when, fifteen minutes before Monsieur Giroux's arrival, there's another knock on the door. 'Oh good, you're here early,' I say and open it fully in welcome.

When Vivien emerges from her boudoir, she's more like the woman I know – made up to perfection, her simple but sparkly shift dress clinging in all the right places, the pendant earrings swinging around a swan-like neck and below the coiled ice-cream sundae of her hair. *How the bloody hell does she do it?*

'You'll be fine,' I assure, grasping her trembling hands.

She nods, with no words, the angst still evident beneath her perfect façade. It's easy for me to say, since I'm not the one centre-stage in the performance that's about to unfold. In the time we have left, I go through last-minute directions before curtain-up – where she should lead him to stand and the locations for maximum effect. I retreat into the bedroom with the door just ajar, and we wait.

He's a few minutes late, causing Vivien to pace in circles around her small living room, and I hear the flick of her cigarette lighter at least twice. Finally, a knock at the door, three confident raps which toll like a doomsday bell in my brain. God only knows what Vivien must be feeling.

'Phillipe! Oh, how lovely. For me?' Vivien turns on her star light at precisely the right moment, the confidence of the Mrs Remmers I know and love. He must hand her a bunch of flowers and I wince at the sound of the paper wrapping, wondering how my various listening bugs will cope with the rustle of interference.

'Come in, come in, I'm nearly ready,' she tinkles. Good woman that she is, Vivien deposits the flowers on a surface out of earshot, and draws our man in – as is her speciality. 'I'll get my coat.'

'Perhaps a drink, first?' he suggests. 'There's no rush.'

There's the stall. Predictable. Through the tiny gap in the bedroom door, I glimpse him walk past, with nothing clearly in his hands, and I wonder where he has the evidence secreted, followed by a short but firm stab of doubt in my breast: have we got this spectacularly wrong?

But no. Followed by the clink and chink of whisky and ice, he is handed a glass, yet there's no squeak of her leather sofa to signal that he sits.

'Phillipe? What's wrong?' With a slightly nervous edge to her voice, Vivien leads him like a pro.

'Oh, Vivien,' he oozes in a silken Gallic tone. 'I'm afraid I have something to show you.'

'Show me? What do you mean?' Her voice affects just the right amount of surprise.

He must pull it from his person somewhere and present the tangible evidence to her, photographs of her drugged and drunk. 'You were a little indiscreet, my darling,' he prattles on in a patronising tone of affection. 'I'm afraid you said some things you shouldn't have. And that means I might have to ask for more.'

'More?'

'Yes, darling. Quite a lot more.'

I hear Vivien's convincing tears. 'Phillipe, you wouldn't, would you? I can't, I would lose my job and—'

'—and your freedom,' he threatens. 'The British courts don't take too kindly to treason, do they? We know this already.'

From behind the door, my stomach knots. The cold, calculating bastard. This is not spycraft, it's sordid and grubby, exerting the power he arrogantly believes he has. That he has a right to possess.

'What sort of things?' she sniffs. Vivien knows we have to elicit a clear and full threat before revealing our own hand.

'Well, there are many things of interest within the ministry that we would want to know. You have access to documents and opportunity, if I supplied you with a small device for copying.'

'But... but I'm just a secretary,' Vivien baits. 'How can I—?'

'You'll find a way, I'm sure,' he says, the threat firmly implied.

'Or what?' she comes back, just enough irritation in her voice. 'What will you do?'

'You know what, Vivien darling. Your boss may well get these pictures through the post, and a very clear little tape recording of our last conversation.'

'Oh Phillipe, how *could* you?' Vivien the victim plays out beautifully. What the smooth faux Frenchman doesn't know is that her words are our precise cue to pull down the curtain on his sleazy little game.

It's a two-pronged ambush, as I leap from the bedroom at the same time as our bit-part player springs from his hiding place in the bathroom. Vivien steps back nimbly as we each dart towards Phillipe in a pincer movement. Alongside me, the slim, muscular – and buck-naked – Fabio is on the French man within seconds, utilising the shock in Phillipe to move in very close, grabbing his hand and placing it high on his own nude thigh. Before Phillipe's stricken face can fully swivel towards me, Fabio leans in and plants a determined kiss towards his mouth, while I aim my Minox and press the shutter multiple times. That distinct Roman nose is everything we need for a firm ID, and the whole sting has lasted all of ten seconds.

Gotcha. You slippery Soviet snake.

I'll give it to Phillipe, or Sergio, or whatever his real name might be – he knows when he's been outfoxed. His expression moves from disbelief to resignation in the blink of an eye, and he pushes Fabio away roughly, his action heavy with disgust. Ignoring me, he turns to face Vivien.

'I'm not sure what the British police might say about these particular out-of-hours activities, monsieur,' she purrs, in a voice like velvet. 'It is still illegal, after all.'

His fake smile comes into play, though it's far from alluring now. 'Vivien, darling, I'm sure we can come to some arrangement, hmm?'

'What can you be suggesting?' she says, the flightiness in her voice replaced with a steely tone.

'Your photographs for mine, and that tape recording, of course.'

The earrings jangle as she shakes her head resolutely. 'Oddly enough Phillipe, I don't trust you not to have several copies squirrelled away. Despite my being female, and you not being in the least bit honourable, we'll simply have to work with a gentleman's agreement, if in fact you know the meaning of the words. Because while I suspect the KGB is very fond of using this type of masculine honeytrap for its own purposes, I'm also certain the Soviet security service is equally intolerant of its own officers leaning towards that particular sexual orientation.'

He scowls. She smiles. Triumphantly. 'Perhaps I'm not just a secretary after all.'

One look at Phillipe and it's clear he doesn't suspect his own handlers are intolerant of homosexuality among the ranks. He knows it. His comfortable assignment in London, with its free access to Western commodities, would be severed, possibly along with other valuable assets that Phillipe currently possesses. His eyes scan the three of us with contempt, Fabio having conveniently found a cushion to shield his manhood.

'I can keep a secret,' Phillipe concedes.

'Then you'll just have to do that,' Vivien says. 'A form of insurance on both our parts. And don't be in any doubt that I will log your visual misdemeanour somewhere very safe, should anything happen to any of us present. Plus, the tapes we've made tonight.'

He swallows, settling on a mean smile. 'As the French say, "Touché." Believe it or not, it was nice knowing you, Vivien.'

'If only I could say the same, Phillipe.'

Bravado and colour drain from her the second the door closes behind him, Vivien slumping into the nearest chair. 'She needs a stiff brandy,' Fabio suggests, scampering off to the bathroom to get dressed.

She takes a large gulp of the medicinal alcohol. 'Did I do all right, Mags?'

'A rival for Liz Taylor, if ever I saw one. You were superb.'

'Do you think it worked?' Her fingers wrap tightly around the glass, though the liquid trembles. 'Will he keep his side of the bargain?'

'I think so,' I say. Out of Vivien's eyeline, my fingers are still crossed, but I've seen rats cornered before, and – despite his innate swagger – this particular vermin had that look of defeat, only too glad to scurry back into his hole. 'The KGB back in Moscow wouldn't look too kindly on this fiasco. He has more to lose than you.'

'I bloody well hope so,' she sighs. 'I'm not sure I could do that again. How about a glass of champagne to celebrate?'

Fabio joins us in a tipple before he needs to leave for his evening performance, part of a troupe in some dark and dingy 'theatre' off Dean Street. It won't be the first time this evening that he's required to shed all his clothes.

'You were wonderful, Fabio,' I say, pressing a fiver into his hand as he leaves, another gaping hole in my bank balance.

'Always glad to help you, Maggie.' He kisses me theatrically on both cheeks. 'It was a lot better than some jobs I'm offered, and I must say, I adored his aftershave. Toodle-oo.'

I ponder on the fact that working in Soho does have its advantages.

I shouldn't, and it's very unwise, given everything else that's going on in my life, but I join Vivien in draining the bottle of fizz, and perhaps a second. On an empty stomach too. Pretty soon we've regressed a good thirty years and flopped to the floor, giggling uncontrollably like the schoolgirls we once were.

'You should have seen his face when you and Fabio appeared!' Vivien hoots, tears making tracks in her make-up. 'I thought he might actually dirty his underwear.'

'Do you think it would make a good scene in the next James Bond film?' I ask, at which Vivien laughs so much she loses the dregs of her champagne on the carpet.

Coffee, and even cheese on toast (drunkenly made with the sole ingredients of Vivien's larder), do little to sober us up. The room spins and I'm forced to concede that I cannot be trusted to board a bus safely, while a taxi feels like a luxury after tonight's expenses. Some small part of me, a tiny slice of logic still intact, imagines facing Gilda as I fall in the door, an absent, wayward and now drunken mother to her granddaughter. Perhaps not.

'Stay on the sofa,' Vivien slurs as she tosses me a blanket and moves to her bedroom. 'Please. I will feel safer if you're here tonight.' She hesitates in the doorway, looking very child-like in my haze. 'I love you, Mags – you know that, don't you?'

I do. I just can't articulate it in that moment, paralysed and wondering why she has need of not one but three light fittings on her ceiling.

Twenty-Four

20 May 1965

It's gone ten the next morning when I sneak into my own house, like an intruder or an MI5 search squad, though tripping over my own feet on the stoop doesn't exactly lend itself to covertness. How long does alcohol take to clear from your system?

'Maggie, is that you?'

Blast! Nabbed red-handed. On the bus over from Vivien's I'd been wracking my brain for Gilda's weekly diary of happenings. Is Thursday morning her macrame or portrait class? The over-fifties book club perhaps? Then again, I doubt it's even Thursday, given the jackhammer doing its worst from behind my eyebrows.

'Hmm, yeah, just me.'

Unusually, she comes out to greet me from the living room, a duster in hand and an apron over her clothes.

'What are you doing?' I ask. My imagination stretches to some kind of new paint technique, the likes of which will probably not complement the Bridget swirl, and so aggravate the fracas playing out inside my head.

'Dusting,' she says. 'What on earth do you think I'm doing?'

'Oh.'

'Someone's got to do it, haven't they?' she carps back, trailing me into the kitchen. 'Hey, are you all right? You sounded quite odd last night.'

'Last night?' Now my brain cells are forced into action, dragging the memory cubicle with it. The one that sits empty, vacuous and echoey.

'You rang, remember?' she nudges. 'About nine o'clock, said you wouldn't be home.'

'Oh yes, yes, that.' If I wasn't so hungover, I might manage a convincing story. But I'm still sodden with alcohol, and this is Gilda Richmond, my mother, mind reader and all-round soothsayer.

She takes a closer look at me. 'Oh, like that, is it?'

'Like what?'

'Out drinking.'

'I may have had one or two,' I concede.

'And you stayed the night, fully engaged, I expect. With him.' For all my mother's bohemian leanings, she can still purse her lips like a champion fishwife, awash with judgement. Her arms fold and rest on her breast with a shiver of disdain.

'*Him*? Who's him?' I dump my bag and round on her. Humdinger of a headache or not, I square up to argue my case. 'I was with Vivien and we had one too many. Stupid but simple. It's hardly a crime, *Mother*. I have not been "engaged" with any man, and – if you averted your eyes long enough from all your worthy causes – you would know I could not do that, not yet. It's too soon, after…' The rage dies and my voice cracks.

Eye to eye, the stand-off lasts less than a second before she pulls me into her arms and I sob into her matronly chest, she mopping my tears with the duster. 'I'm just concerned for you, love, that's all,' she murmurs into my ear, sounding like Mum of old instead of Gilda the Great. 'All this running about at all hours. I worry for you.'

I'm on the brink, made vulnerable by a hellish hangover and her sudden softness, knowing it's still there. I almost tell her, just as I blubbed to Frank in a weak moment not so long ago. Mercifully, I stop myself in time, because what's at stake is far more than my crumpled core, which has some chance of recovery after a good weep. Our earthly bodies do not have that luxury if life is extinguished. So, there are futures at stake – mine and Frank's, but hers and Libby's too. Unlike my teenage self, I *do* want to confess all to my remaining parent, and for it all to go away. But I can't and it won't.

'I'm all right,' I lie, reaching for a tissue that doesn't reek of polish. 'You caught me at a bad moment, that's all. I'll be fine with some aspirin and a good bath.'

She unfolds her arms. 'Go on then, I'll make you breakfast while you sort yourself.' She reaches into the bread bin. 'But you're not wrong about the bath. You smell like a brewery.'

Good old Gilda – she's back in the room again.

I'm dispatched from the house after eleven, held together with toast and aspirin, with my own promise to be back for dinner, and intent on spending a decent evening with mother and daughter, even if the television and good ol' Bridget are invited to the party.

'Bring in a large bar of chocolate, will you?' Gilda says on parting. 'The biggest you can find.'

My destination is a meet with Frank in a pub on Fleet Street, but only after checking the way is clear. On the way to Vivien's the previous afternoon, I'd sauntered by the gated greenery of Russell Square and slipped behind the statue of the fifth Duke of Bedford, chalking a single mark on the plinth that faces the wrought-iron fencing. It hasn't rained overnight and so when I return and make a full circle of the statue with my cloche hat in situ, I see my own mark, crossed with another. Pale blue. Frank's way of saying, 'Come on down.'

In mind of my still delicate head, I've strapped the bunion to within an inch of its life, and it's now strangulated by Elastoplast and unable to move, let alone complain. I can endure one or the other, but not both poles of my body causing havoc in unison. Stepping into the dank interior of Ye Olde Cheshire Cheese pub, I'm hit by the heavy sediment of liquor. My middle section suddenly takes issue, rolling and pitching like a dinghy in a sea storm.

'Morning Mags.' Frank is tucked inside the front door and already in the company of a pint. He looks up keenly. 'Oh hell, you seem a bit green around the gills, if you don't mind me saying. Here, you sit down before you fall down. Tonic water?'

'Thanks, Frank.' I feel grateful, though I'm not sure how much sympathy a single person can take in one day. I might just get used to it.

He returns with my drink and slides back into the window seat, which is – I grant you – not your ideal spot for two renegades trying to melt into society's darkest corners, except the glass to our rear is so caked in London grime, it barely warrants a description of transparent. Ergo, a window. The woody, cavernous confines of the hostelry offer up the perfect refuge, the seats around us filling with fellow rebels of Fleet Street's press fraternity, crowding the bar for an early liquid lunch.

'He'll be here any minute,' Frank says.

'And so, who is this chap?' I realise I may be about to entrust my future with a stranger, not least a hard-talking, hard-drinking newspaper man, without knowing a thing about him.

'Eddie Markham. Known him since I was in the force,' Frank says. 'He was on the *Chronicle*'s crime desk then, and we did each other a few favours, if you know what I mean. Tit-for-tit. He had his ear to the ground, we made the arrests, and the paper got a few front-page scoops. Everyone was happy.'

I raise my eyebrows, quickly realising that it still hurts. 'And you trust this Eddie?' It's not an unreasonable question, since the good men and women of the press don't have the best reputation for discretion, it being their job to break stories into the open. Embarrassing the government of the day comes as a bonus.

'Absolutely, Mags,' Frank insists. 'If I tell him to keep this under wraps, he will. Unless it becomes necessary for us to do the opposite. For now, he is our insurance policy.'

'But surely it's too much of a temptation for a journalist to sit on?' I lower my voice, leaning into Frank. 'If this gets out, it seems to me that heads will roll. Big heads. That's a pretty big scoop for any paper.'

'And that's why Eddie will keep it to himself. He's smart but, unlike a lot of other journos, he's also patient. He'll get the story in the end, and when he does present it to an editor, they'll take him very seriously. Front-page stuff.'

I've no chance to quiz Frank any further, because the man himself pushes his way through the lunchtime crowd. He's wasted no time, with a whisky and soda already in hand.

'Good to see you, Frank,' he says, sitting opposite us.

As we make the introductions, I feel sure I've seen this Eddie Markham somewhere before.

Salt 'n' pepper hair badly in need of a cut, tie askew and suit jacket dusted with cigarette ash. Finger pads tattooed with nicotine and blue Biro, crooked, stained teeth. Unkempt. Ink running through his veins.

Perusing as he lights a cigarette (in what must count as his lunchtime dessert), I remember why he's so familiar – not Mr Markham as such, but the archetypal image of a press hack from countless films and television shows. He needs only a felt trilby with a 'press ticket' lodged in the brim to complete the cartoonish stereotype. I don't doubt Fleet Street takes him seriously, but personally I think he needs to take a bath.

'So, what's the story?' Eddie says, leaning in and disseminating his particular *parfum* of stale living across the table.

In a huddled whisper, Frank explains while I watch Eddie's reactions as we go through our suspicions about Congleton House. The press man merely nods once or twice, sniffing at intervals. He seems unperturbed, his face blank. Unimpressed? I worry he won't think it warrants either his time or the risk. Bang goes our life insurance.

'So, what do you say, Eddie?' Frank wraps up.

Markham nods, turns and signals to the barman for a whisky top-up. 'So, I sit on this while you present your findings to MI5, as some sort of lever for shutting this caper down?'

The weathered but kindly Frank face is suddenly granite. 'Our plan is to issue them with a threat, Eddie, plain and simple. Blackmail. They shut it down, and *prove* they've done so, or it's splashed over yours, and then every front page from Land's End to John O'Groats. If the cat is out of the bag, it's a fair bet the Americans will want to publicly distance themselves from such underhand dealings. A real threat to international relations, and they won't want to risk that.'

Markham nods, his tired eyes a little wider.

'But, if they do as we ask,' Frank goes on, 'you hold off presenting this to your news desk – for now. Instead, you get every piece of evidence we have, meaning that you can dig deep into this grotesque operation at your leisure. A few months down the line, or however long is safe enough in not implicating us, you get to be the investigative hack who "independently" breaks a stonker of a story about the historical use of children as spies by the upstanding British government.' Having made his pitch, Frank sits back. 'Think about it, Eddie – you might even make *Time* magazine.'

Markham's nicotine fingers twitch at Frank's last suggestion, likely visualising his name in big, bold letters, his byline on a global publication, on every newsstand, and entry into the press annals of history. Eddie Markham is a hack all right; to him, the story is all.

But that's all Frank and I need – for him to take it on and

hold tight on our legacy, an explosive buff file of coercion. It might just be enough for MI5 to think twice about killing us.

'Deal?' Frank says, extending a hand.

Markham sniffs. 'Deal. Now, how about you get your hand in your pocket, Frank, and buy me a proper drink. I've got to go back and write tomorrow's lead story.'

When Markham leaves, I suggest we follow several minutes later, since I need Frank with a clear head, and strictly speaking he's still at work.

'Ah, don't worry Mags, Ringo's offered to cover for me,' he says.

'You didn't tell him where you were going?' I'm all eyes as we step out into the lunchtime shoal streaming to and fro, proving good cover when we splice into it and move with the flow of bodies.

'No, course not. But Ringo's OK. He's one of us.'

At this moment, I wish I had Frank's faith.

'Anyway, he's not expecting me back until after lunch,' he adds, 'and I'm starving.'

We end up at the Egg, of course, since it's like a second home, and so obvious as to be a perfect foil for anyone seeking us out. And let's face it, Frank is always better with an egg inside him. I stick to coffee, strong and black.

'You look tense, Mags,' he says, bathed in his customary halo and chewing on buttered toast.

It's another understatement of Frank proportions, given what we're proposing to do, but I manage a weak smile. 'Do we *really* know what we're getting into?' I can't help asking.

'Once we poke at Her Majesty's nest of vipers, who knows how they'll bite back.'

With venom, obviously.

'And yet, do we have a choice?' He gestures at the two copied files I have tucked in my bag, having handed over the original dossier to Markham. We've agreed it's best to have back-up life insurance.

'No,' I sigh. The evidence still burns a hole through my heart, the reality that kids of Libby's age are being trained to kill. It's that monstrous. So, no – we don't have an option.

Frank hesitates before spearing his egg yolk. 'Though it is probably a good idea to move your mother and daughter out for a bit, somewhere safe, until this is all cleared up.'

He's got a point, but where? My depleted funds won't stretch to a hotel, or even a holiday let somewhere, for what will easily be a week.

'My sister's got a small cottage near Brighton,' he adds, neatly as if reading my mind. 'I could ring her and check it's free. It'll be easy enough to get them down there tonight.'

'Oh Frank, could you?' He's a lifesaver, and I tell him so.

'Well, we can't have anything happening to your girls, can we?' he says. 'Lovely woman, Gilda. Good looking and smart. In fact...' He hesitates with unaccustomed reticence.

'Yes?'

'I was wondering, Mags, when this is all over, whether I might ask her out for dinner. Whether you'd mind. A proper restaurant and all that. What do you say?'

I think the pairing would be utterly bizarre, but who am I judge in the current mire of my life?

'Gilda is her own woman, Frank,' – and that *is* an understatement of epic magnitude – 'so you go ahead and ask.'

His smile reflects the sunny side of his breakfast. 'Perfect. Then let's get this bloody debacle over with.'

When he sweeps up the yellow residue on his plate with his toast and pops it in his mouth, it feels somehow pivotal. A finality. Will we be doing this again? Both of us are certain to be personae non gratae at Leconfield House after the next few days. That's the best-case scenario. And then what?

'Frank, what will you do after all this?'

He looks at me, his crinkly face seemingly unworried. 'Oh, don't you worry, Mags. I never thought of Donkey work as the end game for me. You never know, I might move down with my sister and take up sea fishing.'

My return expression says we both know that's unlikely.

'Failing that,' he adds, signalling for the bill. 'How do you think I'd fare as a store detective?'

The very image elicits the best and loudest laugh I've had in days, even if it sparks a fresh throbbing in my temple.

Frank has to bow to my parting suggestion, since it's non-negotiable. It's me alone and not us who will confront Hilda Grayling with the evidence and ultimatum, presenting a copy of travel documents and photographs to prove our threat is not just a balloon of hot air. I tell him about Quinn's tail the day before, proving without a doubt that they – our venerable employers – are onto us. Certainly, me. So far, Frank is not under the spotlight, though we both know it's merely a matter of time before he's pinpointed.

He protests, of course, but I'm immovable: 'I need you on

the outside, Frank. Grayling is bound to go straight upstairs to Garnett with the evidence, and I'll be lucky to walk out of there.' My mouth dries to a desert wadi as I say it.

Reluctantly, he agrees: I will ring the Spy Shack and make a seemingly innocuous appointment to see Grayling in the morning, hoping her suspicion alone means she will agree to it. Frank rings his sister from the Egg and arranges the cottage, agreeing that I will drive Libby and Gilda in the Mini tonight, out of harm's way. Goodness knows how I'll stand up to the full-on interrogation from Gilda who will demand to know why she's being asked to up sticks and go into hiding. How and what I tell her needs careful consideration, something akin to staging an East–West peace negotiation.

Frank must hear the wobble in my voice, because he aims his bristles and pecks me on the cheek. 'Stay safe, Magpie.'

'Right-o, Frank. You too.'

It's early afternoon, and I've a couple of brief stops to make before home, by which time Libby will hopefully have returned from school and – after the inevitable verbal tussle with Gilda – we can set out on the A23 to Brighton. With all the route-cleaning needed, it's bound to take some hours. Just before hopping on a bus, I slide into a phone box and dial the number for my own employer, requesting a meeting with Hilda Grayling for ten a.m. the next morning.

'And can I ask what it's regarding?' her secretary queries. 'Miss Grayling will want to know.'

'It's personal,' I snap into the receiver, before replacing it with a resounding clunk.

All set. No going back now.

I catch my reflection in the glass, grim-faced and weary. 'Davy, please tell me this will be worth it,' I ask of him. Again.

'The real question is, do you have any alternative?' he comes back.

Alighting from the bus at Archway tube, I feel the strain in my calves as I hike up towards my final objective before home. While Frank maintains his normal working façade, it's up to me to stash the third copy of our insurance policy, since we both agree you can never be too careful.

The black gothic gates of Highgate's age-old cemetery loom large, and if it wasn't such a pleasant May afternoon, I might shiver at the scene: think a prime site for a production of *Frankenstein, Dracula* or the tales of Edgar Allen Poe. The entranceway is a grand folly of stone, leading into the tumbledown of high mausoleums and family tombs, vines and ivy weaving a dense blanket over the dead. While the lush parkland is pleasant enough in daytime, I wouldn't relish being lost in its labyrinthian walkways as the sun goes down. With a hat pulled low and sunglasses in situ, I head up the steep path into the centre, skirting the semi-circular arena of catacombs, and onwards. Part of me would love to tuck our booty on or near the imposing grave of one Karl Marx, on the opposite side of the road – such a delicious irony, given what our file contains – but that's too obvious, even for MI5's detection. Besides which, the stone effigy of Mr Marx is under constant surveillance from eagle-eyed tourists, not least the busload of Japanese pilgrims disembarking as I arrived.

It's perhaps a second irony that as I'm moved inwards,

a feeling comes over me. The 'Watcher's curse', as we call it, of suspecting the tables have turned and you're the one under the spotlight. Déjà vu. It's beyond description, but much like the cold dread of a spectre hovering nearby. Or, given our current location, like someone walking over your own grave.

A quick glance over my shoulder confirms my suspicions. My shadow is clutching a bunch of cheap tulips, easily bought from a vendor at the gates, but this individual has either lost some poor relative in the multitudes of headstones listing at half-mast, or he knows a lot of dead people, such is his hovering/grieving around a variety of graves in the distance. The third, and most likely, option: he's my tail.

A second glance tells me it's not Quinn, and that incites further shivers. I can only assume Agent Quinn is no longer acting alone, and that perhaps it's official – MI5 have decided now is the time to close in and cut me down, though I'm not sure I like my own phrasing there.

Halting in front of the sad, lichen-covered resting place of one Ebenezer Cox (1840–1889), I sidle between two sets of visitors, giving myself time to ponder.

Think Maggie. Bloody well THINK.

It would be easy enough to go on autopilot in ditching my tail, but juggling priorities inside a distinctly fuzzy brain is far more demanding. My heart tells me I need to reach the phone box just outside the gates, ring home and instruct Gilda to get out. Bluntly and with vigour: go anywhere with Libby. Check into The Ritz if you have to. My head, however, says that without a watertight insurance policy, there's little point in them fleeing anywhere, since I'll have zero leverage to save my own family. Against my own better judgement (and the raw emotion of a mother hen protecting her chick), I realise that finding a safe refuge for the last file copy is paramount. Increasingly, it's unlikely I'll get as far as presenting Grayling with the second copy, currently stuffed in my bag.

Sod's law, but this is the moment when the bunion decides to 'act up'. Cocooned in a near cast of Elastoplast until now, it determines on staging a breakout, pulsing and pounding inside my shoe. I slip it off, shocked to be faced with raw flesh poking through the binding.

Ouch! Losing my tail might have been clear-cut up until this point, but a limping middle-aged woman in a cloche hat? A billboard on Piccadilly Circus counts as more discreet.

This demands stealth over speed, digging deep for the spy within me. Turning away from Ebenezer's resting place, I head towards the exit gates on the looping path, desperately trying to conceal the agony inside my shoe, while each step feels as if a hot nail is being ground into my bone, and it's only thoughts of my mother and daughter that drive one foot in front of the other. My shadow is walking on a parallel path and making little effort now to conceal his purpose, having discarded the flowers; his confidence in the face of my physical affliction is evident.

By virtue of this being a cemetery, there are occasional funerals being conducted – irony number three is that the sad passing of one life might just save my own. I bumble towards the crowd gathered around an open grave and plant myself amid the bodies like a latecomer. I'm not in black, but today's clothes are muted enough to blend in.

'Desperately sad,' I mutter to one woman giving me the

eagle-eye, while my own pupils stalk the MI5 man, edging his way to the left of the grieving huddle. His stance suddenly appears less assured, perhaps wondering if he's lost me, and I just catch the slight ripple of his lips cursing at himself.

The vicar drones on, as the bunion beats out a frantic rhythm of pure pain. Eventually, the immediate family step forward and toss their handfuls of dirt onto the poor blighter down below. The black mass of mourners shuffles off, me still in the midst, and it's as we reach the waiting cars that I seize on good fortune and chance my move, slipping behind the large, high-sided hearse and out of the shadow's sight. The undertaker gets in, and within seconds, it motors off at a snail's pace, as I crouch down and walk crab-like in pace with the car. Never mind the bloody bunion, my thighs are now flushed with an intense muscle burn, but I chance one glimpse at my tail and see his head bobbing, whipping from side to side, the curse more evident on his lips. *Keep going, Mags.*

Fate has placed a large oak tree beside the concrete path, so that when the hearse picks up speed, my legs are finally relieved as I'm able to seek refuge behind the wide trunk. Then, it's a matter of finding the nearest appropriate grave in which to secrete the file, under a layer of grey shingle and a pot of begonias. I mumble an apology to Florence Beecham (1887–1953, beloved wife and mother), 'But your services are very much needed in the afterlife,' I tell her.

With limited speed and a strange, lopsided gait of a hop and a skip, I reach the cemetery gates and throw myself into the phone box. In spite of all my training, my hands are shaking while delving into my pockets for coins, emerging with a shilling and two-pence – just enough for the limited explanation that Gilda will demand. Watching the phone dial spin again and again is painful, then the slow click of a connection at the other end and I picture it trilling on the hall table. Ring, ring. Ring, ring. Four, five times. Is she painting on top of that ruddy ladder again?

'Come on, Gilda,' I breathe fear into the stale-smelling receiver. 'Where the hell are you?'

'Richmond residence,' she says at last, in her best plummy phone voice.

Thank God! I slam the coins into the slot. 'Gilda, it's me. Listen, I'm in a phone box, and I haven't got much time.'

'You sound flustered,' she says.

'I am. Is Libby there with you?'

'Yes, she's just got in. What's wrong?'

'Please listen and don't for pity's sake object. I need you to pack a small bag each and go somewhere.'

'Where?'

'Anywhere. Pick a hotel, or one of your slightly obscure friends. Just get out of the house. Please, Gilda.'

There's a brief silence during which I can literally hear one of her Arctic expressions aimed into the phone. 'Maggie, you're not making any sense,' she says, in that tone of hers.

'Just DO it, *Mother*.' Her tenacity as a woman is all very admirable, but why do I have *the* most pedantic of parents?

'But I can't,' she says flatly. 'Not right now.'

'Why not?' If it's one of her bizarre groups making pyjamas for orphans out of dishcloths I may just self-combust – not easy or pleasant in a phone box stinking of cat pee.

'Because there's someone here, and he's waiting for you,' Gilda asserts.

'Who's there?' I almost shout into the receiver, over the blasted pips signalling my coins have run out.

'Nice chap, name of Quinn,' she manages, before her voice is severed and the line goes completely dead.

Twenty-Five

20 May 1965

I'm left staring into the receiver, with a myriad of dread shooting top to toe at speed, a burning black sludge running through my veins and settling like lava in my stomach. Retching towards the filthy floor, I just about hold onto Gilda's breakfast.

There's no point ringing back: Quinn is there, likely drinking tea at 54 Calabria Road and evidently turning on the charm for my mother. It speaks volumes about his intent, turning the screw. Tightly. Running away to Brighton, or anywhere else, is now futile because of what his presence signals: *We will find your loved ones. We have the power.*

And the truth is, they do. What in the hell was I thinking, in proposing to take on the might of Her Majesty's security services, a portion of which is clearly not even answerable to Parliament, let alone its people? And me, not even a bona fide spy in their eyes. All triggered by some imagined and idiotic duty to the legacy of my dead husband who

– whatever I do – is not coming back. *How can you be so naïve, Maggie Flynn?*

Foolish or not, I can't stay in this phone box for eternity, staring at a grubby card taped to the wall extolling 'Wanda's rubber hosiery, made-to-measure'. I have to do something. Warning Frank is not possible, as he's out on the job, but I feel sure his radar will be switched on, and he'll dodge them for as long as possible. Instead, I scribble a quick note, fold and stick it with some hastily chewed gum on the underside of the phone table.

I could go home and confront Quinn, but to what purpose? For him and his heavies to lead me away in front of Gilda and Libby? My daughter is already fatherless, and for her mother to be hauled away by faceless men, to God knows where – I just can't do that to her, or Gilda.

There's only one path open, and that causes another spasm in my gut, sour bile leaping into my gullet. I'll give them what they want: me and my intent, and by doing so, hope to minimise the collateral damage. If I look on the bright side (and Lord knows I'm trying), it's merely bringing forward the appointment with Grayling and cutting out the middle man. Sooner or later, I was going to have to face Quinn, though I had banked on having more of an upper hand in the confrontation. David and Goliath? Right now, this David measures about two inches tall.

From behind the small, smeared windows of my red-box sanctuary, I spy Quinn's Watcher, sauntering through the cemetery gates, his steps heavy with defeat. I can guess he's thinking how to confess losing his mark, and the ridicule that goes with it – a fellow Watcher, and worse, a woman! He'll never live it down.

I'm still in possession of the last copy of our damning file, the one I planned to present to Grayling. It's our golden ticket but, in a split-second decision, I reason that to have any bargaining power in facing Quinn, it's better he doesn't know quite how much evidence Frank and I have. Damn it! There's nowhere to conceal it convincingly, either under the phone shelf or behind. I scrabble the depths of my bag again; of any one occasion, now is the time for it to live up to the Poppins reputation.

'Come on, come on,' I hiss. 'Yes!' My fingers hit on the rubber of a large elastic band and a crumpled but thick paper bag. Shoving the file in the paper, I roll both as tightly as I can, securing it with the elastic. Stepping outside the box, Watcher man is to my right and hovering on the pavement, gazing at his feet. Eyes fixed firmly on him, I drop what now looks like a rolled-up magazine into a nearby waste bin. That's one third of our insurance policy on its way to the municipal dump.

'I hear you're looking for me,' I say, striding towards the Watcher, both palms in sight and splayed outwards.

'What? What?' He steps backwards, startled, then hurriedly scans the horizon for any potential ambush. The training drills us to take nothing at face value. Except this is exactly what it looks like: a simple surrender.

'You'd better take me to Quinn,' I say. 'I believe he wants to talk to me.'

He doesn't bother to deny it. Spotting a clutch of Japanese pilgrims emerging from Mr Marx's resting place, he loops one arm into mine, appearing as if we are a couple, but with his elbow set firmly against my ribcage. 'This way,' he grunts.

Back to the phone box we go, and for a second the pungent ammonia wafting out is almost like an old friend.

Not so welcoming when we squash into the tiny confines, like two teenagers on a farcical first date. He dials a number that needs no payment in coins, mutters our location and a code – 'sparrow' – and then replaces the receiver.

'Perhaps we could wait in the fresh air?' I ask, at which his eyes narrow with suspicion. 'Listen, I've given myself up to you, and so why would I plan to scarper now?' I argue. He doesn't need to know the precise details of my errant bunion currently making any escape impossible.

'Hmm, suppose so,' he concedes, but utters not a word as we wait on the pavement for the sizable black Zephyr that rockets up minutes later and comes to an abrupt halt. Not quite the screech of a TV cop show, but near enough. 'In,' he commands, his big hand pushing my shoulder down.

Up until that point, I'd been keeping my nerves under control. Just. Now, Quinn's men up the ante; there's a second suit in the back seat, who shuffles in close and snatches at my bag, producing a black scarf. Instantly, I freeze, picturing my lifeless body discovered on the banks of the Thames, tongue protruding and eyes bulging from strangulation, torso bloated and rigor set in the contortion of my limbs as I'd taken my last, fighting breath. Gilda viewing my body on a slab as I'd seen Davy's. Spirits slump to somewhere near the earth's core.

This man must see the fear, because his staunch face softens just a little. 'Blindfold,' he utters, and loops it over my eyes.

In the front seat, the transistor radio is low, but behind the soot black of my vision, I hear the words with pinpoint clarity. '*She's got a ticket to ride...*' John Lennon sings to a jangly guitar, with his sad, nasally lament.

Christ. Can we please just stop with all the ironies now?

Twenty-Six

20 May 1965

We drive, in silence save for the radio, which is turned up, maybe as a way of derailing my sense of direction. And it works, to a large extent. I sense the Zephyr's big engine gunning up Highgate Hill and away from the Spy Shack, but after several left and right turns, I'm already disorientated. Besides which, I'm concentrating far too much on suppressing the fear from spewing out of my mouth, instructing myself in the art of breathing, wedged tightly between the grumpy Watcher man and blindfold boy, one with a decent aftershave and the other not friendly with a bar of soap.

They say nothing, though the driver hums along to the songs played in succession and, despite the fear keeping me rigid, I find my mind beginning to wander, eyelids heavy behind the black weave. Last night's overindulgence with Vivien is catching up fast, and I have to shake my head several times to stop it from lolling, thinking that perhaps it's not a good look for the prisoner to wake, head slumped on her captor and with a slack, drooling mouth.

We drive for long enough that, eventually, I can't fight it, drifting in and out, just conscious of registering the void of sounds I know so well: the throaty exhaust of a bus, growling taxi engines or the general hum of a city hub. We're heading out of the metropolis, but I can't focus enough to think where. Or perhaps the brain cubbyholes are doing me a favour in not allowing the connections. It's sure to be somewhere quiet and discreet, possibly remote.

Any of those scenarios counts as Officially Bad.

Amid my drowsiness, there's no telling how long we drive, only that when I finely rouse myself the sun is still high enough to warm my face through the windscreen. It's not dusk, I calculate, and if the sun is directly ahead we must be heading west. I feel sure we haven't come as far as the Slad Valley; even Quinn wouldn't be so obtuse as to take me there. In minutes, the car makes a sharp left turn onto what sounds like a rutted path, the pungency of cow dung pushing through the open front windows.

'Jeez!' the man next to me says. 'That's pure shit.'

Plenty else about this moment that's pure effluent, I think, now that I'm suddenly alert. Not least that we are clearly heading to a farmstead, which in my mind computes to a barn, surrounded by fields, and animals that produce a lot of said waste matter but, equally, won't give a shit if a bullet were to ring out in their midst.

Against every will I can muster, my body begins to tremble independently. Is this where they brought Davy before they dumped him?

'Hey,' the man with the scarf says in my ear, in tone that sounds – if not reassuring – then conciliatory. He puts a hand on my arm, I imagine to quell the shiver now going from top to toe. Perhaps it means I won't be killed yet, not until after the interrogation. What a relief.

The car comes to a stop, with two doors opening and slamming, muffled voices and groaning as they stretch their legs after the journey. Unlike the city, the noise doesn't bounce back, and I gauge the landscape as being open and flat. The half-human bullyboy next to me gets out, dragging on my elbow. 'We're here,' he says.

I've felt the knotted scarf loosening in past minutes, and I move my head up and down so that it finally slips below one eye as I stumble from the car, noting a large and solid but dilapidated two-storey house in front of me, a barn and varying outhouses to the right. Beyond, there are fields as far as I can see.

'Fuck!' my keeper hisses under his breath, hoiking up the scarf quickly, in such a way that makes me think no one else has seen his folly, and he wants to keep it that way. But I have. I've glimpsed the scene and snapped it to my memory in a single blink of one eye. Does it aid my situation to have an image of where I might take my last breath? Physically, no. Mentally, perhaps. I have knowledge they clearly don't want me to possess and – bar the keeper who let it happen – they don't know I have it. It stands as a minor victory to me, if miniscule in the circumstances. Right now, I'll take what I can get.

I'm shuffled not into the barn, but up one step and inside a musty hallway, our shoes clumping on the bare boards and what feels like an unlived-in space, then pressed to sit in a badly sprung chair that puffs up dust and makes me sneeze.

'Where do we put her?' the cemetery Watcher says.

'Upstairs, second on the right,' a new voice says, one of Quinn's little tribe, I don't doubt.

'I'm going to need the ladies' before you put me anywhere,' I pipe up, to a grunt of derision somewhere to my left.

'Uh, if you must.' An arm loops under mine and hefts me up towards a set of stairs – I count ten steps on thin carpet before we make a right half-turn and climb a further ten to a landing. 'Here,' the voice says, and then hesitates.

'Well, you're not coming in with me.' Turning squarely towards his cigarette breath, I voice it firmly, and without compromise, Frank's advice crowding in at just the right time: the belligerence that worked so well in browbeating our way into Congleton House. 'Unless you happen to get a thrill from gawping at middle-aged women in their underwear,' I add.

I hear him suck in air, out of embarrassment or my audacity perhaps, but it has the desired effect. 'Be quick about it,' he grumbles.

Of course, I rip off the blindfold the second I'm inside, and test the small window of heavily frosted glass, closed and padlocked. I relieve my bladder in double-quick time, and then scout for something to use as a defence. The bathroom is bare, stripped of anything homely, but there is a toilet brush left on the floor. I'm utterly certain James Bond has never had to stoop this low, that even the cunning Q would never furnish 007 with a high-calibre weapon disguised as a cleaning receptable, but beggars cannot be choosers. Stepping on the offensive bristles with my good foot, I snap off the wooden spindle, muffling the crack with a flush of the cistern in tandem. It leaves me with a short, heavily splintered spike, good for brandishing, but tricky to conceal.

'Oi! What are you doing in there?' my gaoler barks through the door.

'Only what nature demands,' I snap back. 'Come in if you like, though I don't recommend it.'

'Well, hurry up.'

I am making haste, but it takes time to lay the spike along the inside of my left thighbone and pull up my tights, without the potential for splitting my difference on sitting. I squat once or twice to ensure I can bend without grimacing, as the bunion sends a sting upwards, reminding me it's still very much in play.

He bangs on the door angrily, patience running thin.

'I'm coming!' I shout, replacing the blindfold and opening the door. 'You try being snatched and blindfolded and see how *your* guts cope.'

He doesn't seem to have any riposte for that.

Boards creak under the carpet and I'm shoved along on the upper floor, propelled into a room and the door banged shut. Taking off the scarf, I see a sparsely furnished room with one bedstead, a thin mattress and steel bars on the windows; a strange interpretation of an MI5 safe house. Behind the bars, the windows are whitewashed with emulsion on the inside, obscuring the view entirely, with catches that are welded shut, making it hot and stuffy. More and more, this appears to be an endeavour very much 'off the books'.

Increasingly, I suspect that Quinn has gone rogue, taking a small band with him. Not for the first time, it dawns on me that the only way he can hope to keep this under wraps is by disposing of both Frank and me. And Eddie Markham, if Quinn has eyes everywhere.

'Oh Magpie,' I hear Frank's voice chime in my ear. 'What a bloody pickle.'

Stripped of my watch, I don't know how long I sit on the bed, head in hands, stewing in a swill of my own making. Tears prick the backs of my eyes, but I do not – will not – allow them to spring forth. *This is all your fault, Maggie Flynn, so just deal with it!* It's my own self-imposed rebuke, made tougher by Gilda's voice beating into my conscience, and it's enough to yank me from this state of self-pity and prompt me to think laterally. I cannot escape from this room, and so I have to wait for them to come to me. What can I offer Quinn in return for my life? The documents, clearly, but I need to discover if he already knows about Frank, Markham and the spare files out in the field. And who he's working for. Where, for example, are those teenage trainees destined when they graduate from spy school? For MI5 use, as we originally predicted, or sold to the highest bidder – Czechs, Hungarians or the Soviets? Both are unthinkable, but the latter seems all the more heinous.

Mired in thought, I barely notice a scratching in one corner of the room until its consistent rhythm cuts through my dread. Another heart sink. Mice? Or worse. Please, not rats. I've viewed some sights in the war, but nothing gives me the heebie-jeebies more than the prospect of creatures the size of small cats scuttling over my feet. Much like Orwell's anti-hero in Winston, my resolve will collapse instantly if they employ large, grey vermin as a weapon.

After the scratching, though, comes a faint knocking. Rats are clever creatures, but not that smart. Bending my ear to the torn wallpaper and crumbling plaster, I tune in.

There's a pattern, repeated over and over. For some

inexplicable reason I'd taught myself Morse code in the war, in a misguided belief I might be recruited to some code-breaking elite of women. It didn't happen, of course, but Frank and I kept up our skills on long, dull stake-outs, rapping out stupid messages to each other: 'i'm as cold as a witch's bed' (Frank), or 'more tea, you old codger?'

I close my eyes and tune in. 'who are you? who are you?' the message echoes.

Is it a trap? A way to draw me in, and give false hope? It's a well-known fact that both sides used such deception in the war, planting fake prisoners in among the POWs as an effective method of wheedling out secrets. But Quinn & co. already know my name, so what have I to lose?

The bullyboy housekeepers have left a tin cup with a pitcher of water alongside, and I crouch down on the floor, using the beaker to tap out: 'm-a-g-g-i-e f-l-y-n-n', leaving a second or two, before following up with: 'who are you?'

Silence, save for the mumble of conversation from the floor below. Did I dream it? Am I going mad already? I imagined myself holding out a little longer before the hallucinations took over.

Nothing but a faint shuffling beyond the wall, so I score at the old plaster with the cup handle until I reveal red brickwork – shit! Not a flimsy stud wall, and no hope of digging through it.

The beat comes again. 'i am... u... o.' The last part is swallowed by dense bricks.

'say again,' I tap out.

'i am yuri.'

I almost fall backwards. Not for the first time, the charming Soviet has the ability to suck air from my lungs.

What the hell is Yuri doing here? Though, on reflection of MI5's current moral compass, it's not too much of a shock.

I'm tempted to bash out a joyful greeting, but hold back. It may not be my friendly Russian defector after all, given that I'm deeply embedded in the world of lies and liars. Yuri could be cold in his grave, and this a stooge intent on gaining my trust. Methodically, I comb my memory for what Yuri and I talked about in the kitchen and living room of that tiny safe house, where the microphones were concealed. Then, for what we discussed in the garden, away from electronic ears.

'i am nova,' I reveal in Morse.

'nova.' The reply comes quickly. 'my god, nova.'

'what talk in the garden?' I question.

Again, it's not foolproof – such information could have been beaten out of Yuri, but I recall the trust I felt on that day as we both cast our eye towards the London skyline, the fondness he seemed to have for Davy and the odd affinity they had as spies across the Cold War divide. Also, the quiet acceptance of his fate in the way he spoke, that defecting from the Soviets was a huge gamble, one that he could so easily lose.

I believed him then, as I'm forced to now. Let's face it, with my arse on splintery floorboards and no chance of using a charm offensive as an escape strategy, I have little option.

'the garden,' I prod.

'standard.'

I suck in a mouthful of dust motes and pick up the tin cup again. 'how long you been here?'

'five days. why you here?'

'standard,' I reply.

'ah.'

Silence from beyond the wall, as we must both hear the growl of an engine draw nearer, spitting gravel on the drive outside. It comes to a halt, doors slamming, and I move to the window, one ear on the bar and my eye on a milky blur of the now setting sun, struggling to pinpoint any words. What I hear is indeterminate, but surprising all the same. A gruffness but undoubtedly the higher pitch of a female voice. Older. Could it be... Grayling? Bloody hell. How many insiders are embroiled in this grotesque operation?

A tapping brings me back down to the floor. 'are you hurt?' my co-captee asks.

'no.' I swallow. 'not yet. how you?'

'am ok.'

It doesn't tell me much, or fill me with confidence, other than he's alive. 'how many here?' I entreat.

'too many.'

Plenty of bullyboys, then, so it's all down to the charm offensive. Bugger.

I hear the heavy steps on the stairs with just enough time to scrabble upright and dart to the water jug, replacing the blindfold. The door sweeps open with a waft of colder air.

'Take the scarf off,' the cemetery Watcher's voice commands. 'You won't need it now.'

Shit. My ignorance of some faces has, so far, afforded a smallest hope of survival, of not identifying the key players after the event. Now, I'm apparently entirely dispensable. Even the bunion is struck numb.

'Downstairs,' he grunts.

Momentarily, I consider telling him I've alerted a

colleague about my visit to the cemetery (true) and how he could be tracking me right now (very untrue), but such pathetic prattling is better suited to a bad gangster B-movie. Better to save my weak leverage for later.

Down one floor, he leads me into what might have once been a den or a library, lined with empty bookshelves and a shabby sofa, covered with a crocheted throw which, if it weren't so moth-eaten, would definitely appeal to Gilda's taste in soft furnishings. It's chilled, since the windows are boarded up to banish every chink of light, with a single bare bulb hanging over a pocked wooden table, a dining chair on one side, and two on the other. Those clever MI5 set dressers have been in again, upping the intimidation nicely.

They've done an excellent job.

'Sit,' Watcher man gestures and leaves.

I shiver in this sunless room that's been stripped of anything I might utilise as a weapon, while eyeing the camera that's lodged in the corner of the room, its red light winking. There's no need to check on my toilet truncheon, as the splinters are pinpointing nicely where it sits – and stabs – at my inside thigh. Maybe it ought to team up with the bunion and scupper my chances of a future completely.

They make me wait, as per the opening chapters of the inquisition handbook: allow the captive to steep in their own paranoia, encouraging that innate tendency to Think The Worst. And yes, I'm percolating nicely over the catastrophe to come. Out of left field comes the realisation that I've failed dismally as a parent, my only child to be an orphan at age fifteen. And without getting her to a Beatles concert. By the time the door handle turns, I've whipped myself into a depressive frenzy, if such a thing even exists.

For goodness sake, Maggie, calm down.

By sheer will, I force my eyes to focus hard on the lone body stepping through the door.

Late twenties, slim, tailored suit, dark brown hair, clipped and parted. Sneer of supreme confidence below a sharp nose, narrowed and steely blue eyes. Service to the core. Rattlesnake comes to mind.

James Quinn slithers into the chair opposite, and unbuttons his jacket, as if we're at some jolly corporate get-together. 'Afternoon, Mrs Flynn,' he says, eyes immediately on me, 'good to meet you at…'

'Again,' I launch in. For obvious reasons, I really shouldn't set out to rile him, but I can't resist, and it leaps off my tongue too soon.

'Yes, again. How could I forget?' He makes a play of smiling, much like a rabid dog shows its pearly whites to impress. 'So, to the formal introductions. I'm Johnny Quinn, but you probably already know that.'

I stifle a laugh. Who does James 'Johnny' Quinn think he is? Some film star cowboy, or is he trying to emulate the casual 'Jack' of John F Kennedy? I'd love Frank to be sitting alongside me right now, delivering his best jibe to cut this little squib down to size. Aside from the incarcerated and under-threat-of-death part, I'd love Frank to be here full stop.

It takes everything I have to look intently across the table, blinking only when my eyelids are giving out, lips pinched and my teeth set together, helping to quash the tremble that threatens to make a vibrato of my voice. At the same time, I pull out tendrils of my training from a pocket deep in my brain. 'Let them talk, tell them nothing,' they drummed into us.

Johnny Q can lead the charge, with pleasure.

Amid the ensuing silence, he takes a pack of cigarettes from his jacket pocket and lights one, using the carton as his ashtray. His actions make the stagnant air instantly thick, and the staring contest harder to maintain.

'I believe you have seen something you shouldn't have,' he begins. 'What's more, you've actively gone looking for it, and that's a bad thing, Maggie. Very unwise. Can I call you, Maggie?'

'You can address me as Queen Elizabeth for all I care.'

The resulting smirk across his face makes me want to slap him. If his mother were here, I feel sure she'd want too as well.

'All right,' he says, pulling back his shoulders in that 'well, if you want to waste our time' fashion. 'I'll set out what I desire, and you tell me if it's worth making sure your family is safe for. Charming woman, your mother. She offered me tea, and some delicious homemade cake. We had rather a good chat about you.'

The little shit knows he's got me, but equally I now see he's lying: Gilda can't bake a cake to save her life. So, what else is our Johnny bluffing about? Crucially, he hasn't mentioned Frank.

'I've put plans in place,' I say bluntly. 'Because a slimy little toad like you, one without morals, would always target the obvious.'

'Careful, Maggie, or I might take offence.' He stubs out his cigarette and leans forward, a brief flick to lick at his bottom lip, revealing his tongue as reptilian pink. 'Let's face it, you've acted well above your pay grade, and it's time for that to stop.'

'But my husband wasn't above his station, was he?' I spit. Yet again, it's against all the advice to expose my weakest side, but in that moment my brain is out of control. If I'm facing death, I need to know about Davy. Not only who wielded the knife which killed him, but who gave the order to extinguish one of their own.

'David,' he muses, reaching for another cigarette. 'Yes, David Flynn. I could – and did – learn a lot from him, I will admit that, Maggie. Vitally, I also learnt how *not* to be, when you need to see the bigger picture rather than lose your nerve at the smaller details.'

Under the table, two fingers find the splinters under my skirt and next to my thigh. Pushing through my tights and ramming my flesh hard into the spikes is the only thing to stop me from launching myself at this turd of inhumanity.

'Smaller details? Is that what you call children learning to be assassins?' I feel sick even saying it.

'The bigger picture, Maggie. That's what MI5 has lacked for years, not seeing the Soviets as people we can learn from, because we're so busy being appalled at the ingenuity.'

Ingenuity. Is he serious?

'So, what was my husband's reaction?' We're clearly into an all-out confessional now and the agent handbook has been duly tossed into the fire.

'It wasn't my choice to bring him in, but he stumbled on it via one of his agents,' Quinn says flatly. 'Sadly, he was as disgusted as you clearly are now.'

'Then I'm proud of him.'

'He also threatened the future of the operation, as you have also tried – and failed – to do.'

'Is that why you killed him?'

James Quinn, agent of Her Majesty's government and man who seems to be modelling himself (badly) on a fictional film spy, appears – for the briefest of seconds – unseated by such a forthright accusation from a middle-aged woman who occasionally looks like a bag lady. If my Watcher skills serve me well, he visibly wobbles. A mere millimetre, but he needs to drag on his cigarette to cover it.

'Murder,' I say. 'Cold-blooded murder. Does it catch in your throat, *Johnny*?'

'Sticks and stones, Mrs Flynn. Like I say, successful intelligence officers look at the bigger picture.'

'Which is why I'm so glad Davy wasn't a *success*, as you term it.' My voice sinks several notches lower, to a schoolteacher growl as I close my eyes and imagine my matronly self, looming over an infantile Master Quinn in nursery school. 'DID YOU KILL HIM?'

'Someone had to do it!' he swipes, like a belligerent child, his eyes cutting away.

I slump further into the chair, while every cell and atom inside me deflates. That's it. I can't seek justice for Davy, but as I head to my own grave, I'll know in my heart who was responsible. It's not nearly enough, but it's something.

Quinn yanks me back into the room. 'We're wasting time, Mrs Flynn. I need assurances, of where and with whom you have logged this insurance policy with.'

My eyebrows rise, without my consent.

'Oh, did you think you were the first to use such a cunning plan?' he mocks. 'That lodging-a-copy-with-a-trusted-friend scam. Perhaps you're not aware that all those faithful comrades squeal in the end. Every single one of them. Believe me, I'll make sure they do.'

God, I want to slap him again. With a large brick, preferably. But he has that smarmy expression of the Gilda-bakes-cake story, and I strongly suspect he's bluffing again. He doesn't know what I have, and so far hasn't used threats against Frank as a cosh.

I lean forward and place my elbows on the table, a timely contortion on my face, caused mainly by a loo brush digging into my flesh. 'What I have, out there, will not only blow you to kingdom come, but will see the upper echelons of Leconfield House setting up shop on the moon.' Like Frank says, you might as well go the whole hog.

'Oh, yes? Prove it.'

I hold out my hands. 'How can I? Stuck here.'

Quinn gets up, spins towards the door, opens and sticks his head through the gap. Irritatingly, his words are muffled, but the tone is demanding. He closes the door, sits back down and smiles with immense satisfaction. If only I had that brick...

Within a minute, the door opens, and a second body moves in and sits beside Quinn.

'Brought your mummy to fight your own battles, have you Johnny?' I scoff. Given the scenario, I believe Frank might term that one 'burning all your own boats'. But hey, what have I got to lose? And it goes some way to masking my own shock, the volt of electricity that's just gone south towards my toes.

'A sense of humour, Mrs Flynn,' says Bea Baglan coolly. 'I feel it's good to have one in the circumstances.'

'I borrowed yours, though that didn't amount to much.'

She wavers not a millimetre, her dark strands of hair scraped and pinned into submission, leaving her face exposed and stark under the bare bulb, which has now started to flicker. Is that mere chance, or some MI5 lackey outside the door, fiddling with the electrics at intervals to further unseat me?

'What has Johnny here promised you, Bea?' I sneer with my stupid, runaway mouth. 'Are you finally going to rise up out of the basement and take your place among the big boys? The queen among kings? Because, personally, I wouldn't believe a word this little turd says.'

Quinn lurches violently off the chair and at me, swiftly brought to heel by her hand whipping out with the speed of a viper's tongue and thwarting his action. Her viper to his rattlesnake. Baglan's face remains rigid, but his flushes with frustration and fury, the toddler scolded and put in his place. Unwittingly, perhaps, but Bea Baglan has just whacked him with a very large, metaphorical piece of masonry. For all of a second, I find myself silently applauding her.

'Whatever the future holds, I am still Queen of the Registry,' she says bluntly. 'And you have committed the most odious of crimes in my books. Messing with my files. You stole covert government information, which is not only a criminal offence, but extremely impolite. I'd like it back. All of it.'

There's a decent stare-off, now the fuggy air has cleared a little, but in all honesty, I'm tiring of the stalemate. My chances of talking my way out of this one are miniscule, and waning by the second, so unless something changes here, they'll end up a big fat zero.

'Or?' I say, finally. 'Your boy here has mapped out my future nicely, and so I won't be inviting you all for Christmas. Sorry about that.'

She actually smiles! Lord forbid, the godmother of MI5's basement mafia cracks her granite flesh. I imagine a tectonic plate in far-off continent shifting in sympathy.

As swiftly as it came, the deep wrinkles around her mouth are pasted back in place. 'That's as may be, Mrs Flynn. I don't know about your exact fate, but your family remains safe, for now. Mother and daughter, I believe. They can have a long and, above all, untroubled life, if you give us what we want.'

A scornful laugh escapes. 'Would that I could believe you, *Bea*. What guarantees can you possibly give to a dead woman?'

'Trust,' she says.

One word. That single syllable is loaded with so much, delivered deadpan by the waxwork woman sitting opposite, her lips flatlined. Emotionless. And yet, I'm taken aback without knowing why, my own normally fairly acute radar now scuppered by fatigue and confusion. And fear. Something in the way she says it.

There's little else in my arsenal except sarcasm. 'You're saying I have to trust *you*, with my family. That's a comforting prospect.'

'Perhaps not, Mrs Flynn, but the fact is you have very few bargaining chips left.' Her eyes roll around the sealed room that's effectively my prison.

'Only the big prize,' I come back. Deadpan. 'The unexploded bomb. Were it to detonate in the media, it will be this government's very own Cuban Crisis.'

In the face of my threat, their silence speaks volumes. Maybe it wasn't such a bluff, after all?

'Let's assume for a minute that you agree to our request,' Baglan goes on. 'How would you want to defuse that bomb?'

'In person,' I say, judging that my chances of survival on this farm are about as good as those of the unsuspecting livestock outside. 'I get to see that my family are unharmed, or it doesn't happen.'

Quinn dares to shift in his chair, and she shoots him a sideways rebuke. 'Leave us,' she says, a mere ripple to her mouth.

Ooh, interesting, I think. Baglan is above Quinn in the chain of command here, age trumping his supposed charisma. The question remains: is she really the Queen Bee, or is there a king of the castle, staying out of sight?

With the petulance of a dismissed child, Quinn gets up and leaves. She watches him go, reaching down to a decent-size handbag that she arrived with. It causes a twinge of nostalgia for my own sack, since what she brings out is not insubstantial: a folded wad of newspaper, a small bottle of clear liquid, and a box of matches. All in all, I'm too perplexed to say anything. Cool as a cucumber, Bea Baglan separates individual sheets with her long, spindly fingers and screws each into a length, as if she's about to lay a fire in the grate. Except the one to her side is boarded up.

My chair shoots back at her next action, tipping the contents of the bottle over the pile of paper and picking up the matches. If our conversation was getting heated, this looks downright incendiary, what with the pungent odour of white spirit rising up from the table.

'What the...?' I hiss, though something – I don't know what exactly – makes me not cry out.

Much like Quinn, she silences me with one of those steely looks, gesturing for me to move further backwards. She sparks one match alight and drops it on the paper, stepping away smartly as flames shoot up and rapidly take hold. In one deft movement on the balls of her feet, she grabs the moth-eaten throw and feeds it to the hungry fire, careful to fan the flames rather than suffocate what is already a decent blaze, eating into the wood of the table. Smoke is billowing upwards and outwards by now, and yet I'm rooted to the spot, dumbstruck like some gormless idiot. I hadn't quite got my head around a clean shot execution, but ending my days amid an inferno is not in any plan, in the long or short term. For a good thirty seconds, she stands and watches it grow, devil-red reflected in her normally chilly eyes. Have I had it wrong all this time, and the ice queen is a closet arsonist and psychopath?

Smoke is rapidly filling the room, rising in line with the terror inside me. There's no time to ponder on precisely why, but does she really plan for us both to die in this windowless cell, in a derelict house and in the arse-end of nowhere?

It's then that Bea Baglan pulls out a further surprise. Casually pushing the table over and spilling the burning contents onto the wooden floor, she lunges at the door and opens it, creating a swift flash of orange as oxygen feeds the flames.

'HELP!' she shouts. 'The silly bitch has set the place on fire!'

Who? Me?

One of the heavy mob rushes in, but there's nothing to

smother the flames and no hope of doing so now, because the blaze has caught a scruffy rug and fire is snaking its way towards the sofa, the ancient contents of which are bound to be highly combustible. I'm fairly averse to all forms of dying, but burning and drowning have always been among my most feared, and yet, instead of running, I'm startled into a catatonic terror, rooted to a floor that's becoming just a tad warm through my soles. When Baglan yanks me towards the door by the arm, I follow like a lemming towards a cliff edge. By now, multiple bodies have barged past us into the room, attempting to beat back and contain the flames, except it works in reverse, and it's clear there's nothing anyone can do. And no fire brigade, not out here.

Quinn hurtles in, shocked and befuddled. 'What the fuck?' he yells, watching the flames climb like a monkey up the wooden window slats and hungrily lap at the ceiling.

'GET EVERYONE OUT!' Baglan screams in response. 'The whole place is going up.'

'But what about—' Quinn begins.

'JUST DO IT!'

Finally, the sheer heat and the flames licking just inches away jerk me out of this idiotic stupor, propelled into a state of utter panic, heart rate spiralling and sweat forming. Still, there's no escape, because Baglan's wiry fingers have a firm hold on my arm, even when I try to wrench away.

She tugs downwards, as you might do to a child if you want their undivided attention – or else. Her eyes, demonic against the bright conflagration, fix on mine. 'Trust me, Maggie,' she says, emphasising each word through reedy lips and gritted teeth.

What the hell does that mean? But in the midst of this

burning hellhole, what option do I have? Again. It could be the two halves of my brain playing tug-of-war: abject terror versus sheer bloody-mindedness bent on survival, but you know, I'm sort of apt to do just that. Trust her.

Please wake up, Maggie Flynn, from this shitty nightmare of gargantuan proportions.

Baglan shuffles us both into the hallway, the billowing smoke soon crowding my lungs. Against the roar and crackle of the blaze, the panic of half a dozen people and my coughing, her mouth moves close to my ear. 'The front door,' she hisses.

Now, I'm caught between petrified and confused. She appears to be trying to save me, having been the architect of this debacle. To what end? What *is* Bea Baglan's game?

This thought process takes all of a second, and happens – necessarily – as I'm shoved in a peasouper of smoke through the hallway. The open door is in sight, the light dying beyond it.

'Straight ahead,' she commands, with seemingly no concern for anyone else but me. A single cubbyhole snaps open in my spongy vortex, the one with a certain Soviet defector languishing in it.

'Yuri!' I shout at her. 'We have to get him out.' I'm flooded with images of his wife and children at a stark graveside somewhere in Russia, consumed with the same rage and bewilderment I felt over Davy. The why and the how, among a hundred other questions.

If he were here, Davy would not let that happen. Of that, I feel sure.

This time, it's me who tugs down on Baglan's upper limb. 'Upstairs. There's someone there.'

She looks back at what she's created, shaking her head, and I wonder if this level of self-made chaos shocks even her. 'There's no time.'

My alarm escalates further, because the previously chilly and impassive countenance of Miss Baglan is noticeably ruffled. Very much so. Then there's Davy coming at me from another cubbyhole. '*Yuri is a good man,*' he says into my ear, from his safe place in the earth's underbelly. My husband is very persistent. '*Good man, good man…*' his voice echoes.

This time, I take advantage of Baglan's attention on the door and wrench away from her grasp, stooping low to air that's only semi-lethal near the floor and sucking in a large lungful, then leaping for the stairs.

'Flynn!' she screams, but neither Baglan nor the bunion can stop the cocktail of adrenalin, need, duty and stupidity running through me, disappearing into thick, grey smoke that's billowing upwards. Just where I'm headed.

Thanks to the earlier blindfold, I remember which direction to go beyond the top stair: sharp left, then five steps to the room where I was held, a further four to the next door, which I only see because it's painted a vivid green.

'YURI!' I bellow.

Not wasting time with the handle, I launch my shoulder into the door (adrenalin also being a wonderful, delusory boost as to what you can achieve). THUNK. Once, twice, but the pain doesn't register, only the heat that's rising and the crackle of flames getting louder. The lock gives on my fourth attempt as I crash through the opening to find Yuri bent double and coughing near the window, having smashed the window glass in his own attempt to break free, though the steel bars remain rigid.

His eyes widen with obvious relief. 'Nova!' but he needs no instruction to follow me out, yanking a thin blanket from the bed and cloaking us both under it. From the top of the stairs and through the now black smoke, I make out an orange flicker of the encroaching fire. There are no words as we face each other and nod. Again, what's the alternative?

The cloak appears to act like some kind of Batman cape, because our movement down the stairs goes by in a blur; I barely register the steps before we're down on the ground, the house now a furnace as we hurl ourselves through the door and out, stumbling through the veil of smoke and towards a seam of untainted air – and straight into the hulk of a bullyboy.

'No, you fucking don't!' he growls, lunging at Yuri and making a grab for me. Yuri is firmly in his grasp, but his second swipe is less potent and I'm able to squirm away.

'Go, Nova, GO!' Yuri shouts, making himself a writhing handful of a captive.

But in my newfound superhero guise, I'm not about to give up on Yuri now, especially to the oaf who bullied me outside the toilet.

Toilet! I reach down, pull up my skirt and rip into the hole already forged in my tights. The brush handle makes a satisfying crack on the back of the oaf's head, and he lands with a thud, his grasp on Yuri instantly annulled.

'Over there – fields,' I pant to Yuri in shorthand. 'Woods beyond it, maybe?'

He scrambles up and nods. Behind us there is a fireball and chaos as we launch ourselves beyond its glow and into a dusky abyss. The rasp on the inside of my foot is agony, but the bunion can bloody well go to hell. We're a good hundred yards down the pitted driveway, peering for a way to vault to the fence and sprint across the grazing land, and... Jesus! What now?

From nowhere, headlights blaze out of the gloom, yards in front, two blinding circles of doom. Behind the white glare an engine purrs. Shit! The hovering Zephyr, a black predator lying in wait. My heart sinks and, beside me, Yuri stops in his tracks. Against the brightness, I see a sheen of sweat on his face, and the despondence of defeat. His rictus expression says: *We tried.* Behind the dazzle, a door opens and clunks shut.

'Magpie! For God's sake get in!'

Frank. Really? Unmistakably. Even the best mimic couldn't simulate his unique timbre.

In my befuddlement, and out of the twilight, he appears, in all his Frank glory. 'What the...?' I stutter.

'No time, Mags,' he says. 'Get in.'

Yuri follows my lead, beyond the light beams. Instead of the elongated Zephyr, there's a small and sturdy Morris Minor, engine now revving. The squat, bug-like car doesn't have the heft or speed of a large black sedan, but when it comes to escape vehicles, I'm not fussy. Frank gets in the front passenger side as Yuri and I bundle in the back.

'Let's get the hell out of here,' Frank commands to the driver.

The car lurches forward and makes a tight U-turn, accelerating at speed down the drive, as the blaze behind us lights up the car's inside mirror.

In its reflection are the waxwork, immobile and determined features of Miss Bea Baglan, firmly in the driving seat.

Twenty-Seven

20 May 1965

Baglan speeds away like the flames are licking at the Morris' backside, while inside it smells of leather and bonfires. And lingering fear. Yuri's wide eyes swing from the back window and the prospect of the Zephyr in hot pursuit, to the driver's seat, then back to me, as if searching for answers. I shrug, as much in the dark as he seems to be. Frank, yet again, is my saviour, but in what version of reality he's pairing up with the Registry Queen Bee, I'll never know. Neither a professional or personal connection is to be applauded in my books, her being a proven arsonist, with psychopathic tendencies still under consideration.

'Anything behind?' Frank says, in what sounds like his DI tone of old. Still, I'm a million miles from the cosiness of the Egg and the day's racing pages.

'No,' Yuri mutters.

'But why?' I cry. 'Are they letting us go for a reason?' I calculate: is there a dirty great roadblock up ahead, with firepower and little hope for all of us?

A second voice comes from the front, equally commanding. 'It must be because of Quinn,' Baglan says. 'I saw him on the ground, unconscious. There are five heavies in there, and one of them, plus Quinn, seemed to be under a beam as it fell. The last I saw – just after your *heroics*…' – she says this with clear disdain – '… was everyone focused on getting them both out, Quinn's body being hauled away.'

'Is he dead?' I project.

'Not clear,' she says, utterly void of emotion. 'But if he is, that piece of excrement deserves it.'

'So, why did you… do… that?' Words are hauled from my brain and then coughed up from my insides, a delayed reaction to the leaden fumes inside my lungs.

'Later,' she caps me off. 'Let's get somewhere safe first. Then we'll talk.'

The back of Frank's head dips in agreement. Since when did these two become such good buddies?

But I'm not about to be taken anywhere else unknown. Granted, I know *of* these people, but in this instant, I'm neither sure of their intentions, nor do I trust them. That's what a succession of blindfolds, secret safe houses and incarceration does to you.

'I need to go home. NOW,' I say. 'My family are in danger.'

'Not yet,' Baglan says, staccato style.

'Frank?' I appeal to his former self, the one who always has my back, the man who adores his cats and knows what it's like to lose your children, not to mention his current soft spot for Gilda.

'She's right, Mags,' he says, without turning his head to look at me. 'Quinn's lot are watching the house, and if we go anywhere near, we're all blown.'

'That's precisely why I need to go back!' I screech, too loud for the small confines of a Morris Minor.

Now, his head does whip around, and for the half-second while we drive out from under a canopy of trees and a sliver of light shows up his features, I glimpse the old Frank. His flared nostrils and wrinkled eyes tell me: *This is bad, Mags, but it's the best we can do.* With real words, he says: 'I've got our own lot watching Gilda and Libby too.'

'Who?'

'Ringo...'

'RINGO? Christ, Frank!' Trust comes to mind again. In my judgement, Ringo might be the reason we're having to hurtle through the English countryside in a mobile tin can.

'And Carlo,' he qualifies. 'But Ringo's all right. You've got him all wrong.'

'Have I?' But when he doesn't reply, I've little left to say. Of course, Frank and Baglan are right – MI5, or whichever subset Quinn heads up, will be watching my home, and I have to think of the bigger picture; the very realisation sticks in my throat, since it's what that bastard Quinn professed to do, right before he killed my husband. But there are three others in this car, one of whom risked what's left of his age-old career to rescue me, and one whom I risked my own life to save. The jury is still out on the other one.

Baglan's head finally swivels towards Frank as the gloom of the countryside gives way to the suburban landscape of Greater London, and we pass a sign for the 'Borough of Barnet'. 'We're almost there,' she says.

'Right-o.'

She draws up in a well-to-do street of detached houses, all

tended hedges and neat front gardens. Baglan turns off the engine. 'We're swapping cars. Just stay here for a moment.'

She gets out, walks up a short driveway to a single garage, unlocks it, and within a minute a smaller car emerges, that I recognise as a Vauxhall Viva, since Gilda drove one up until a couple of years ago. It's the same outline as the Zephyr, but a good half the size. Suffice to say, if we get into a chase with the MI5 bullyboys, a milk float has got a decent chance of outpacing the Viva's hairdryer of an engine. Baglan parks it on the road, urges us to make a swift transfer and then manoeuvres the Morris into the garage and closes the door. The whole switch takes less than three minutes, before Baglan is back in the driving seat.

'It's my aunt's,' she says by way of explanation. 'She's away, and it's untraceable to me.'

In the front seat, Frank sinks a little lower, already more relaxed. 'Let's go then. I don't know about you lot, but I need a large drink.'

The drive into central London takes less than half an hour, given it's a Thursday evening and past rush hour. Yuri hasn't said another word, slumped in his silence in the tiny back seat, his wide eyes drooping with the light drone of the engine and Baglan's driving, which I'm forced to admit, is seamless. I've no idea how long the poor man was kept at that derelict place, anxiety and interrogation leaving little room for sleep, and so he must be feeling either more relaxed in the back of the Viva, or entirely resigned to his future. Eventually, his head lolls to a definite slumber.

By contrast, I'm wide awake, high on adrenalin, with the brain cubbies opening and shutting at a pace, fulminating pictures of Gilda and Libby settling down to watch the evening television, naïve to predators outside the door, then images of that threat bashing into their sanctum and them becoming hostage to this whole bloody mess.

For the umpteenth time since hearing Yuri's definitive words, I turn the cosh on myself: *What the hell have got yourself into, Maggie Flynn?*

And everyone else.

The safe space turns out to be a large room in the Imperial Hotel, a vast modern, concrete edifice opposite Russell Square, and a stone's throw from the underground station. Baglan steers around the back and into a service entrance, parking behind a line of tall, conical industrial bins and shielding the Viva nicely. Almost as if she's arranged it, in advance.

Yuri stirs as we come to a halt, blinking himself awake, and we maintain a unified silence while Baglan leads us inside, crocodile-style, through a corridor packed with linen trolleys and into the noisy, bustling kitchen, nodding as she goes and parting the way like Moses. I feel anything but a disciple, the hair on the back of my neck at ninety degrees. In front of me, Frank follows in her wake, though he casts a doleful glance as we sweep by an open door leading to the shiny, twinkly bar.

Up two flights of the back stairs, room 214 is at the far end of the corridor, and so subject to no innocent passing traffic. Any footsteps going past the door are to be heeded and that's pure tradecraft on her part. Baglan unlocks the door and secures it behind us, with Frank beating a path to a bottle of whisky on the lone table and raiding the bathroom for a toothbrush glass. In a heartbeat, he's swigging down a large shot.

Whether he's exhausted, or been quickly institutionalised into planting himself automatically, Yuri sits on one of two twin beds. Baglan, meanwhile, is checking every light switch, lampshade or drawer, presumably for bugs. Finally, she turns and nods at Frank.

I take this as my cue. 'Right,' I launch at her. 'Will someone tell me what on earth is going on?'

'Sit down, Maggie,' she says, in a soft, near-demure voice, the shock of which almost makes me comply.

My legs, however, won't bend, stiffened by that lingering adrenalin. 'I might sit when I know whether *she* is friend or foe,' I say directly to Frank.

'Mags,' he tries to appease. 'Calm down. We're safe, for now. Just hear her out.'

'Are we, Frank? I'm not so sure, because not so long ago, the Queen of the Registry here tried to set me on fire.' My voice is strained and slightly hysterical, like that of one of two old harridan neighbours hissing over the back fence like cats.

Looking directly at me, Bea Baglan is all composure. 'I'm sorry about that, but it was necessary. I had to get you out of there, and create chaos at the same time.'

'I can think of better ways.' Now I've reverted to the petulant child.

'That's as may be,' she goes on, 'but I'm not sure you appreciate how close you and Yuri were to a full interrogation. For one so young, Quinn has a very extensive repertoire of methods. And everything was prepared in that barn alongside, for, let's say, a quick disposal.'

'Disposal' hits hard. It's Davy's fate, both of Libby's parents on a slab – kaput – and the finality creates a surge of nausea. 'All right,' I concede. 'I'm all ears.'

We sit opposite, Yuri and me on one bed, Baglan and Frank on the other. She reaches over to the phone and orders tea and sandwiches via room service, but mutters a particular name into the receiver, presumably someone she trusts. 'Trust' – that word popping out like a cuckoo in a clock and vanishing again. A discreet knock on the door produces a tray, the contents of which all except Baglan devour, as I realise just then how hungry I am.

My exhaustion, fear, suspicion, adrenalin and confusion give way to shock as the formidable Bea Baglan tells me, in a calm and measured voice, how she had known Davy – my Davy – for years, well before I did, in the war. 'We worked in SOE together,' she says. 'In France, Italy and North Africa.'

'How?' I'm struggling to picture her as a young woman, let alone in a beret, cycling between French and Italian resistance, beguiling her way to survival and victory.

'We were agents, in the days when we were proud to call ourselves such.'

A cubby door bursts open with the speed of a ballistic missile. 'Agent' tumbles out and the door snaps shut.

'What did he call you?' I ask bluntly.

She's slightly taken aback, but doesn't dodge the question. 'He never addressed me as Baglan. Always Bea.' The edges of her mouth curl upwards slightly, as if conjuring a fond memory. 'He called me Agent Bea, even after the war ended.'

The cubby swings open a third time, hurling out another realisation. *Trust AB*, Davy's locket message said, the words neon-lit behind my eyelids. 'Trust me,' she'd said, back in the burning house. And now, in a hotel room, with my loved ones under surveillance elsewhere, I'm being forced to put my faith in someone I so recently thought was the enemy, to fight against an organisation I imagined as my evergreen ally, and is now the fiendish adversary.

With typical Frank timing, he looks at me, plucking at my mind. 'It's true, Mags,' he nods. 'She is helping us. Right now, she's the only chance we've got.'

The sinews in my body fall away, and were it not for the tea and bread, I might have just folded onto the floor there and then.

Finally, Bea Baglan takes a swig from the whisky tumbler that Frank passes her, followed by a deep breath. Then she attempts to explain the circumstances of my husband's death.

In the typical post-war machismo world, Baglan had been rewarded for all her wartime sacrifice with a desk job at MI5; the old boys' network being what it was (and no chance of rising upwards), she propelled herself downwards to the Registry, where the old maxim of 'Knowledge is power' at least had some potential use. By then, she had already recommended Davy for a position at MI5, just months after he and I met.

'Did you see him over those years?' I ask, my swell of nausea beginning to turn a distinct shade of green. The older 'other woman' doesn't sit well alongside ham sandwiches.

Baglan shoots me a look: *I'm old enough to be his mother. Almost.* 'We met for lunch on occasion,' she says.

'To do what? Talk about old times and all that derring-do?'

The old Baglan look cuts me in two. 'Yes, sometimes.

We were colleagues – comrades. You don't forget that in a hurry.'

I look at Frank opposite and know she's right, feeling suitably chastised. 'Go on,' I say.

Being service employees, Davy did share some of his intelligence work with 'his' Agent Bea, using her as a sounding board, yet certain it would remain within the bowels of MI5.

'Back then, he could see the purpose of a security service,' Baglan says. 'He talked a lot about you, and Liberty, how he hated the deceit that his role involved. But he genuinely trusted that MI5's work would lead us all to a better world.' The clench of her jaw makes the tight flesh on her cheeks ripple, and there is a brief softness to her eyes, behind which there might be a tear forming. 'I know that for certain.'

Against every will driving me right now, I believe her. I also feel physically sick, but what she says rings true of Davy. 'Did he talk to you about his suspicions?' I ask.

'Not at first. He came to me about six months before he died, wanting to see anything I had on Congleton House. And Quinn. Obviously, I asked him why – it was risking my entire livelihood to expose files that he didn't have clearance for. Up until that point, he thought Slad might have been a weapons facility the Service was eager to keep under wraps. Highly immoral but not illegal.'

'What changed?'

He approached Quinn with his suspicions and was taken inside, witnessing the truth of it. I can only imagine that with Quinn's innate arrogance, he judged Davy as the kind of officer to see that ubiquitous bigger picture, and the benefits of a home-grown assassination squad, thinking that Davy would be drawn into the "programme", as they called it. They went to Slad just once together, and I know of two other occasions Davy travelled on his own, gathering evidence. That's when he told me, and I saw his horror, and how appalled he was.'

'Did you encourage him to go forward?' I asked. There's still a portion of me that would like to assign blame, in whichever direction – only natural in the grief process, so I've been told.

'I didn't *dis*courage him,' she says. 'But if you'd known Davy in the field, during the war, that wasn't something anyone could easily do. He was dogged. Once I'd located the dossier and read it myself, I was equally horrified. I thought Davy's moral stand was right. But he insisted I shouldn't do anything outside of Leconfield House – he needed me there, in situ, as his eyes and ears, and to keep tabs on who was pulling the files on a regular basis.'

'How was Davy planning to expose it?' The nausea inside me has turned to an ache, an active churning that I can't quell or control, but like that day at the mortuary, there is no stopping my need to know.

'Aside from me, he thought he couldn't trust anyone at Leconfield House, so the press was his only option. Remember, this was a particularly chilly part of the Cold War, and suspicion was rife inside MI5 and MI6. For safety's sake, it was best to keep any personal thoughts to yourself.'

'Although you knew about Quinn?' Frank cuts in.

She nods. 'Quinn is an arrogant arsehole, fancies himself as some suave double-dealer like Kim Philby, though he hasn't got half the brain. He makes the mistake of thinking everyone else inside MI5 has the ethics of Attila the Hun.'

'Who do you think tipped off Quinn about Davy's plans to upend the whole operation?'

Baglan moves her head from side to side, and her previously unshakable confidence seems to fall away. 'I wish I knew. But then, it was too late. Davy was dead.'

'And since then?' I challenge her. 'That was August '62, nearly three years ago. What have you been doing?'

For the first time, Baglan looks truly contrite, her thin face pained. 'What could I do, against the might of MI5 and Lord knows what else?' she argues. 'It's powerful and it has the ability to destroy lives, you know that all too well. I'd never heard anyone else talk about this "programme", and I had no one to turn to, no allies. For a while, I hoped they'd been frightened off by Davy's attempt and shut the whole thing down.'

Then, in a rare unguarded moment, Johnny Quinn caught Baglan with her nose in a top secret file after he'd requested it. 'I suspect that, even stuck in the basement, I was too high-profile within MI5 to be ghosted away,' she explains. 'My fellow Queens are a loyal bunch and they would have kicked up a stink if I simply disappeared. Quinn offered to "bring me in" to his rogue tribe. I had little choice, and at the time, I thought it was the best way of gathering evidence while I bided my time and waited.'

'Waited for what?' I say, incredulous.

For the first time – ever – she looks blindsided. 'For someone like you, Maggie,' she says pointedly, her black pupils pin-sharp. 'For someone to blow the dust off Davy's files. To care enough to go ferreting.'

Or for me to be sent – by a twist of fate – to babysit a Soviet defector.

We three turn towards Yuri then. In his exhaustion, he doesn't look as if he could blow out a candle in a gale right now. But he is the catalyst for us all being here, in a room in central London, beyond which a human travesty continues a little more than a hundred miles west in the sleepy Slad valley. It's unspoken, but we all know the job isn't yet done.

It is Yuri who speaks next, maybe because he's Soviet, or perhaps the outsider in our quartet, able to see beyond the combined outrage for our own British sovereign state. Probably because he's a spy. 'Who else requested the files?' he says.

'Pardon?' Baglan replies.

'You said you were tracking the file requests,' Yuri repeats. 'Can you guess how far up the chain this goes?'

'Yes.' Baglan casts around the room, then up at the light switch. Her fear is both palpable and disconcerting, the Queen stripped of her crown. My stomach bubbles.

'Well?' Frank nudges.

She bends into the circle. 'Rufus Garnett's office.'

Frank whistles. 'Fuck me! I always knew the old bastard was as bent as a two-bob note.'

The former DI Tanner is so busy being appalled that he misses Bea Baglan's next action, swallowing back her own disgust. But I don't. 'And who else?' I press her.

'The current Secretary of Defence has also shown significant interest.'

'Oh Jesus,' Frank murmurs. His eyes roll, no doubt watching his remaining happy life and retirement sink at speed down a very large plughole.

Twenty-Eight

20 May 1965

Despite the shock, and a seemingly insurmountable mountain to be scaled, we're all agreed. This needs finishing – for Davy, for those young innocents being schooled into murder and, well, because it's the right thing to do, full stop. The moral issue aside, the four of us are currently on the run and, personally, I can't see us tripping off to a remote cottage on Dartmoor and living happily ever after. One night at the Imperial is already pushing it.

Davy's initial plan stands firm, we decide: flushing out the filth with the aid of the great British press. I tell Frank about the hidden dossier buried in Highgate Cemetery, but it's now dark outside and the large gates will be padlocked. By the exchange of looks, no one fancies a spot of grave robbing by moonlight.

'That settles it, we need to find Eddie Markham,' Frank says, looking at Baglan.

'Tonight,' she says. 'I've never heard Quinn mention that

name, but he doesn't – didn't – tell me everything. He might already know about him.'

It's just gone seven p.m. but feels like midnight, and in that second I would give my right arm to lie down on the bright orange eiderdown (the shade of which would definitely appeal to Gilda) and close my eyes, as Yuri is now doing.

'It has to be Maggie and me,' Frank says. 'Markham is suspicious by nature, and he'll only give the dossier to us.'

'I'll drive,' Baglan agrees, then looks me up and down. 'I think a clean-up first, don't you? Jungle camouflage is not *de rigeur* on the city streets.'

Ah, the Ice Queen's normal service is resumed. And weirdly, it's quite comforting.

I'm often dismayed at my own reflection, but an unexpected shock awaits in the bathroom mirror. Scrubbing away the fire's soot-staining with cheap hotel soap, my skin is pale and lined under the stark white light, mouth sagging and eyes bloodshot. 'You're a sorry sight, Maggie Flynn.' The mirror spectre merely stares back and blinks with bewilderment, a look not suited to being a spy on the run. A wash and brush-up is all I can manage with the scant toiletries on offer, but I do feel better for it.

As I emerge, Yuri is sound asleep, and I wonder if this normally astute, alert and solid man has been given some kind of sedative by Quinn's boys to render him this weary. Frank is swigging again, this time from a tea cup. Baglan is nowhere to be seen, and that alarms me. 'Where is she?'

'She'll be back in a minute,' Frank reports, 'just gone to the car.'

'But will she be back?' My suspicions remain on a rollercoaster. 'Can we trust her, Frank? I mean, really?'

He guides me down onto the empty bed and puts his arm around my shoulder. 'I think we have to,' he says, in a soft voice. 'It was her that came and found me, told me what had happened. If it wasn't for Baglan, I wouldn't have had a clue where to find you. She saved you, Mags.'

'But could she be playing some kind of double game?' I look at him, and his crinkled face, smell the unique Frank combo of egg and cigarettes, and the whisky on his breath. 'I don't care about me, but I'm frightened for Gilda and Libby. She could so easily hold their fate in her hands.'

'She could,' he agrees. 'But I don't think so, Magpie. That's my gut feeling.'

'Your old inspector sensors?'

'Yeah, the ol' quiver-in-the-belly feeling, the bad one. I have to say, it's not there with Baglan. I think she's on our side.'

In the absence of anything else, and with my own gauge currently awry, it has to be good enough.

Baglan returns in minutes, clutching something that – along with Frank's absent tremor – restores my faith in her a little more. The beloved Poppins bag! Last wrenched from my hand as we entered the Zephyr outside Highgate Cemetery, I grab it with glee and forage for emergency moisturiser, a tiny lipstick and my array of bag lady hats. From out of nowhere, Agent Bea produces a stale-smelling blue jacket to hide my grubby ensemble and make me look less conspicuous. As ever, Frank has a flat cap stowed in his coat pocket, plus a thin-lensed pair of glasses. Quite what this oddly attired couple would be doing wandering around Fleet Street is anyone's guess; 007 gets to stride out of the sea and reveal a creaseless evening suit under his scuba gear, while I make do with a crocheted beret and the pong of mothballs. That's life. Real life.

Waking Yuri briefly, I tell him we're leaving, but not for long. His expression spills regret, perhaps that he's not in a fit state to do what he's trained for – to be a crack operative – but his pupils can't focus for long and he's soon drifting again.

'Let's go,' Baglan says with conviction. With a tiny spark of jealousy for their past connection suddenly ignited, I see what Davy must have glimpsed, in France and Italy all those years ago. The formidable Agent Bea in action.

By evening time, the offices of Britain's national newspaper are winding down for the day, the afternoon deadlines for the morrow's front pages having peaked in a frenzy, with the night news editors and skeleton staff taking control of the graveyard shift. Down in the basement, various presses are preparing to roll, rumbling and sending shivers through each building along Fleet Street.

'Are you sure he won't have left by now?' Baglan asks from the front seat of the Viva, parked opposite the entrance to the *Daily Express*, having driven around the block twice, on the look-out for Watchers of Quinn's clan.

'No, I'm not,' Frank replies, 'but short of trailing into every pub in a half-mile radius, this is the best place to start. I know he sometimes works late and rarely goes home. That's if he has a home.'

Judging by Eddie Markham's general dishevelment, it's a fair deduction.

We observe the entrance for all of ten minutes before Frank gets tetchy. 'Come on, Mags, he could be slumped over his desk in a drunken stupor for all we know, which means we'll be here all bloody night. It's time to cash in our insurance policy.' To Baglan, he simply says: 'Keep the engine running.'

She nods, the stern Baglan Registry visage back in place, but as we both exit the car, I'm sure I hear her utter: 'Be careful.' And it doesn't seem like an instruction.

Frank pulls out his best blarney for the night porter on reception; he's Markham's brother (I'm his wife, presumably), their sister is seriously ill and brother Ed can't be located at his flat. The porter nods knowingly, as if all too aware of Markham's nocturnal working habits. 'Let me ring upstairs, sir, and we'll try to find him.'

A single phone call puts Markham at his desk, though it takes some time for him to come to the phone. 'Eddie, I've some news for you,' Frank says into the receiver. 'Something best said face to face. Gillian's with me. Can we come up?'

Inebriated or not, Markham can't fail to understand the heavy emphasis in Frank's voice, and we're duly shown to the ancient lift. 'Fifth floor,' the porter says chirpily.

We both murmur a 'Thanks' and offer a weak smile, in line with our pseudo-distressed state. 'Did you spot the door to the back stairs?' Frank says as the lift door closes.

'Behind the reception desk, on the right,' I say.

'That's our exit point then.'

'Better to be safe than sorry, eh?'

'Yeah. Plus, I bloody hate lifts,' Frank grunts.

Markham is there as the doors swish open. Mercifully, he looks alert. Not so good is the mask of fury pasted across his pasty, fleshy features. 'What the hell are you doing here, Tanner?' he hisses, the day's tally of stale booze and coffee oozing from his mouth. 'I thought we agreed.'

'Sorry, but this is an emergency, Eddie,' Frank. 'We need access, and quick.'

Now, Markham's anger turns to concern – for his own safety. 'Do they know about me?'

'Not sure,' Frank says honestly. 'But it's best if we relieve you of it now. Just so you make it to your next drink.'

'Well, it's not here,' Markham replies flatly.

'What do you mean, not here?' For a street-savvy man, Frank seems genuinely perplexed. Exasperated, too, and for a second I see the toll this is taking on him, the drain on his already lined features. What me and my dangerous antics are doing to my dear friend and ally.

'You don't imagine I have a personal safe here, do you?' Markham blasts back in an urgent whisper. 'This is a newsroom, akin to a den of thieves when people go rummaging for a spare stapler. People here would sell their own granny for a front-page byline. You don't leave anything of value in your desk drawer.'

'So, where is it?' I press.

'At a friend's flat in north London. Crouch End.'

'Come on, then,' Frank chivvies. 'Let's go.'

'But I'm meeting someone for a drink,' Markham protests.

'Oh, I'm sorry, do we need to issue a written invitation for your sparkling company?' Frank's frustration manifests as heavy sarcasm. 'If it's that important, I'll buy you a damn bottle on the way.'

Markham appreciates the urgency then, grabs his mac and follows us out. 'You owe me, Tanner,' he grouches.

'Bill me later.'

Frank leads us down the service stairs, Markham behind and me in the rear, thankful that we're heading downwards, gravity just about propelling tired limbs and my will working to suppress a fresh grumbling from the bunion.

'Wait.' Frank stops, holds up a hand, and mines the background hum of the building for anything unusual, as we affect the posture of a line of waxworks. After thirty long seconds, he gestures a false alarm; from the back I watch Markham's lungs reinflate. On the ground floor, we come to a fire exit. 'Is this the back of the building?' Frank asks.

'The portal of shame,' Markham nods. 'A handy exit which avoids the top editorial brass, or the way out when you're fired.'

The door gives on a moderate shove, and Frank sticks his head out into a still warm evening. 'All clear,' he says.

As we walk out, the short, square lines of the Viva are easily seen to my left, its engine giving off a gentle throb. Is that good guesswork on Baglan's part? She was in the field for years with SOE, and can predict that even if you go in the front door, it's wise tradecraft to exit somewhere else. There's little time to reason, with Frank striding towards the car, head barely moving but I sense his focus is swinging side to side, sonar fully engaged. Markham totters behind, his pigeon steps evidence that he's well out of any comfort zone, despite being a hardened hack.

So far, so goo—

Oh Mags, you really shouldn't even think – let alone say – those things.

BAM!

Out of nowhere, my head parts company with my shoulders, a clunk hard into my neck and I go down, knees hitting the pavement first. In front, Frank's strangulated cry precedes his own crash to the floor, and I just see Markham's toes being dragged along the concrete and his pleading of 'Don't hurt me, don't hurt me!' before spangles cloud my vision and everything turns to molten lead.

'Maggie! MAGGIE!' My eyelids fight to rise, tethered as they are by hefty weights.

It's Frank's voice, but Baglan's face that I see first, her pointed nose almost to mine.

'Should we get her to a hospital?' Frank cries from behind.

'I'm all right,' I croak, stunned that my voice still works. It must mean I'm not dead. One arm just about functions, my fingers feeling for the ostrich egg that's nicely sprouting at the base of my skull. 'Pull me up a bit, will you?'

Sitting on the pavement, in a smelly back alleyway, I finally come to. 'Frank, are you hurt?'

'I'm fine, Mags. They must have judged an oldie like me needed less force to stay down. A sore shoulder, that's all. But I heard the crack they gave you.'

'You know what they say – no sense, no feeling,' I groan, plucking out a favourite idiom of Gilda's. Which, in itself, proves the brain cells are almost back to working order. 'And Markham?'

'Gone.' Baglan confirms what I already suspect.

'How did they know?' I question, hauling myself to standing with a good deal of help. 'And why were you waiting at the back?' Heavy with accusation, this is aimed directly at Agent Bea.

'I saw movement to the side of the building, and a car disappear to where the printer trucks go,' she says. 'It wasn't the Zephyr, though it seemed out of place, so I followed. I saw them hovering thirty seconds before you emerged, but by then it was too late. Two of them I recognised from the derelict house as Quinn's boys.'

'Did they see you, or the car?' Frank queries.

'I don't think so,' she says. 'They were too busy watching the back entrance.'

'Three candidates for the snitch who betrayed us then,' Frank punts. 'It's either the unwitting porter, Markham, or an inside job. The porter doesn't know us from Adam, and Markham looked genuinely scared. The third option, I think.'

Or a fourth, I ponder silently.

Disorientated, and in the dimness, I'm totally in the dark. Once I'm helped into the relative comfort of the Viva, I sink my head back and let the contents swirl for half a minute, mixed with a measure of self-pity.

Dragging myself back into the here and now, I deliberate. If Markham gives up the file (which present behaviour says he will, and fairly quickly), we have no bargaining chips. With or without Quinn, the drive behind the programme remains ruthless. And deadly.

The other option is the copy I binned outside the cemetery, though that's quite likely on a vast rubbish heap by now. That leaves the buried dossier, which means we're back to communing with the dead, and facing up to the resident vampire rumoured to haunt Highgate cemetery. In the pitch-dark. Oh joy. Frank and Baglan look duly sceptical.

I shrug, with that endless ruddy mantra: 'What choice do we have?'

Employing basic tradecraft means the journey north takes us much longer than expected, as Baglan weaves east and doubles back towards north-west London. Frank urges her to stop at a late-night pharmacy and hops out to buy me some much-needed aspirin and a lukewarm tea from a streetside vendor, and by the time we roll up at those Victorian gates – rendered more gothic by a moonlit glow – I'm partway to human again.

'Have you anything in the back?' Frank asks Baglan. 'A rope, or a tyre iron, perhaps?'

She shakes her head. 'It's my aunt's car, remember.'

'Too much to expect a lock-picking kit, I suppose,' he muses to himself, evidently with little hope.

'That I do have.'

'What?' His head spins towards Agent Bea.

'Call it a memento from the war,' she says coolly, reaching into her shoulder bag and pulling out a small leather pouch. 'They never asked for it back, and I didn't offer it.'

'And you know how to use it, I presume?' Frank's tone turns to admiration.

'Does a registry have files?' she quips, easing herself out of the car.

Looking at the height of the gates as we stand before them, me and my wearisome body are hugely relieved. Scaling any kind of heights has never been my forte. While Baglan and Frank move into the shadows and work on the large padlock and chains, I slide into the pee-pong phone box, with its overhead light flickering like a beacon.

With the insides of my head having been recently blended, I need to check on the note I left for Frank under the phone table, complete with a single hair of my own stuck into the gum. It's untouched by Quinn's posse, as far as I can tell, reminding me that I need to search for one Florence

Beecham, 'beloved wife and mother'. Shame her resting place doesn't have a grid reference. The rest is up to my shaken and stirred memory in retracing my steps... when was that? Only this afternoon? It feels like an entire life lived since then: kidnapped, interrogated and flushed from an inferno, escaped and battered. All in a dull day's work for a Watcher.

Like the opening credits to a horror film, the gates creak open eerily, with Frank wielding a torch from Agent Bea's glovebox, doubling as a weapon and illumination. 'You stay in the car,' he tells her. 'Hoot twice if you see anything suspicious, four if we need to get out fast.'

He turns to me. 'Ready, Magpie?'

Lord knows why, but I nod. Even as we slide through the gates, it's unclear which one of us is supposed to be Holmes or Watson. Crunching our way up the gravel walkway, I stop several times to get my bearings. Was it left or right at the crossing of paths? My head hurts with the blow, plus too much internal traffic vying for a parking space.

'This way,' I whisper with false confidence, Frank's torchlight focused down to our feet. Right on cue, an owl hoots its presence, courtesy of that horror film sound department.

I find myself counting steps, and though it's practically useless (since I didn't on my earlier visit), it does help to calm a wave of fresh anguish: what if I can't find it? Lives – plenty of them – rest on this. On Florence Beecham, but principally on me.

Under Frank's roving beam of light, the dirt mound of this morning's fresh burial appears, the location of which must have unconsciously lodged in me. I stop and sniff the air, less like Sherlock and more of a bloodhound.

'Mags?'

'This way.' It's easier then to retrace my steps, mimicking my farcical trailing of the hearse, on to the hideaway tree and... a twig snaps in the distance. My head whips up, pain zipping through my newly cultured egg. Frank is several paces behind, but to me, the disturbance seemed further away.

'Did you hear that?' I hiss.

'What?'

'A crack. A branch?'

Stock still, Frank cups a hand over his ear, like a bad actor decrying, 'Hark!' He shakes his head. 'Might be a night watchman. A fox, maybe.'

Hurrying onwards, I veer left then right, left again, as per my memory imprint, the torch beam combing over the silent dead in their forever beds. Through navigation or good fortune, the grave of dear Florence is suddenly in front of us. Instinctively, Frank and I stand for ten seconds, both turning a full circle, then drop down on our knees, scraping at the gravel with both hands. The envelope is easily uncovered, dusted off and stuffed in my bag.

'Let's get out of here,' Frank says, 'back the way we came.'

We turn in unison, only to see the way back is not so much barred, as occupied – by a heavy presence of what feels like more than one body, and a single, thin beam strafing the darkness. In the distance, the Viva's weedy horn is heard to parp four times.

'Shit!' he whispers. 'How in hell's name did they find us?'

'Follow me,' I say, borrowing another line from the bad film script, as if I have the foggiest idea which direction to go. Like so much of today, there's little option but to forge forward and away from peril. Frank flicks off the torch and we're running blind, with only the moon as guidance. Miraculously, I find myself hopping over graves and dodging around tombstones, bindweed and creepers pawing at my feet, amazed at what desperation can do for an injection of energy. The bunion daren't raise its head above the parapet of my leather shoe. Frank's heavy puffing is close behind, also running on the vapours of fear. Trailing us, are the strangled but ever closer voices of thugs: 'Over here,' 'To your right,' 'Cut them off,' 'Where are those bastards?'

There's no instinct but to head for an expanse of open night sky beyond the trees that promises escape. Until we hit a wall. Quite literally. The thud of my kneecap precedes my shoulder by a half-second into six feet plus of solid brickwork. 'Oooph!'

Suddenly, we're well past drama and into a comedy act, as there's a brief stand-off in debating who should give the other a 'leg-up'. I can't see myself pulling Frank's weight from the other side, but he insists I go first, my foot on his cradled hands as I'm levered to the top of the wall, the rough brick into my (well-padded) midriff, scrambling with my feet and then sitting scissor-like on the thin width, like a schoolboy urchin after a bout of scrumping. The bag comes at me next, hooked swiftly onto my shoulder, and then I'm reaching down into the gloom, relieved to find Frank's rough fingers, grasping and gripping at mine.

'Just leap!' I say in a hoarse whisper, an athleticism I don't normally associate with the former DI Tanner. But he does, his grey head bouncing towards me. And then his coarse flesh is gone, leaving me to clutch at nothing but air and empty hope.

'Got 'yer!' The gruff voice sneers over Frank's smothered

protests. In the half-light, I see and hear my beloved friend fight against a man who must be twice his size and strength.

'GO MAGPIE, JUST G—!' comes Frank's desperate cry, before his words are robbed by force.

Shit. *Sod that for a game of soldiers*, as Gilda is apt to say in her most belligerent of moods.

I do what spies do – naturally, and in a heartbeat. I assess. I see the single beam of light closing in, but still far enough away, shouts from the others in the distance, plus Frank is putting up enough of a struggle that the thug is not yet in control. Conclusion: there must be only one of them on him.

This time, there is no argument, only reflex. I see-saw one leg back over towards the cemetery side and land heavily on stony ground, sparking the bunion to painful protest.

But it has no dominion here. I don't think, just act. Using gut strength and the only weapon in my arsenal, I pinpoint the thug's heavy breath and swing the Poppins bag with every spare fibre in its handle, and in my being.

There's a decent whump on contact. 'UGGH!'

Mission accomplished as I hear the bullyboy go down like a sack of potatoes, then silence. Reaching blindly for Frank's hand once again, I help him to his feet.

'Bloody good aim, Mags,' he huffs.

With no time for congratulations or gallantry, I'm swiftly levering Frank up onto the wall, he teetering on top and tugging with his own reserves of strength at my hand. As my legs cycle frantically to gain purchase on the rough brick, I smell the sweat of fresh pursuers getting closer and see the torch beam sweep across the wall. Almost feel it comb over my backside too.

'*Mags!*' Frank hisses through gritted teeth, like a

weightlifter pulling energy from nowhere, and heaves at me one last time, causing my whole being to shoot like a circus act from a cannon, whereupon we both land in a heap on the side of the wall. The right side, luckily. Rising like a couple of old crocks, the two of us swivel and limp back towards the entrance, hoping to hell Baglan is still in situ, or making a loop around the block. Rather than stagger in plain sight, we creep back through undergrowth and fetid hedges, hugging the cemetery wall, the shouts of our pursuers audible across the wall divide and heading in a parallel route towards the entrance. The bunion is now shooting arrows of agony through my foot, but since I won't let Quinn, Garnett or the rest of MI5's rogues defeat us, a piece of my own flesh will not scuttle me for good.

Frank halts and crouches as the wall bends towards the entrance, moonlight catching the shiny black paint of a Zephyr parked at the entrance, but there's no one in the driver's seat, all of its occupants obviously on the hunt. Squinting to the left and right, and beyond into the shrubbery, I spot a portion of metal headlight poking through, in darkness. I blink. Is that...? Did it just flash?

'Frank?' I whisper.

'I saw it too,' he confirms. 'Must be Baglan. Take a chance?'

'Yep.'

Now I do feel like a cartoon spy as we creep, bent double, under a sliver of moon towards what we hope to God is the sanctuary of a Vauxhall Viva. Moving closer, I see it is her, and for all of our chequered past – plus my lingering suspicion – I have never been so glad to see the distinct, ostrich-like profile of Miss Beattie Baglan in my sights. Frank and I fall into the back seat, as she fires the engine and lurches away from the kerb, the whine of the Viva's hairdryer motor at full pitch, only switching on the headlamps as we swing at speed onto the main road.

'Did you get it?' Baglan shoots from the front.

'We're fine, thank you for asking,' I snap back.

'You're here, aren't you?' she's equally quick to reply.

What was I expecting? Sympathy and warm hugs from a woman who probably cheated death in wartime Europe more times than I've had hot dinners? 'Yes, we have it,' I tell her.

Frank is unkempt but upright, catching his breath. 'If they knew where to look for us, they probably know about the hotel, and Yuri.'

'But how?' I voice it, without wanting to think about the truth of it. A traitor in our midst. In the inner circle.

'Frank, did you tell Ringo about where you were, or why he needed to watch over Gilda and Libby?'

'No,' he attests. 'Nothing other than your house needed watching.'

Despite Frank's faith in her loyalty, my gaze swings to the back of Baglan's head, for the tell. The twitch. And yet, she's too good for that. Good enough, perhaps, to fool even Davy? There's nothing, her gaze directly on the road.

The bag and file are held close into my body; I'm determined not to let our precious booty go, something very sharp digging through the now torn, filthy material. In the exact moment that I reach in and burrow down to the bottom of its insides, a light bulb goes on in my head, cartoon-style. When I pull out the offending metal object a second later, it becomes reality.

'How the...?' Though it's battered, Frank knows instantly what we're looking at: the sides of a neat silver metal box bent and distorted, a small red light winking sporadically, like an overhead bulb on the blink. No wonder Quinn's man went down on one clout of the bag, his head clashing with its sharp corner. Result: the box is slowly dying but could still be transmitting.

'For fuck's sake, we've got a bloody tracker on us!' Frank exclaims. 'No wonder they found us.'

'Which explains why we've also got a tail,' Baglan says coolly, her voice not missing a beat.

Winding down the window, I wait for a break in the pedestrian pavement and hurl the box into a grassy patch. I'm instantly ricocheted back into my seat like a pilot hitting maximum G-force as Baglan shows exactly why she was (and is) Agent Bea, slamming down the gears like a pro racing driver, and we sail at speed down Highgate Hill, through Archway and on into central London. Traffic lights stream past, though it's hard to tell if they are red or green, plus the monolith of a London bus with its jaundiced yellow lighting, and at certain points I close my eyes, screw up my face and pray for a future.

'Can you see them?' she says.

'Still on us,' Frank reports, his knotty fingers holding on for dear life.

That's Baglan's prompt to take the next corner at considerable velocity, Frank and I flung into a corner of the seat in a heap. Behind us, the Zephyr's extended length and ungainly body struggles to keep up with several more twists and turns of the nippy Vauxhall – left, left and right again through residential back streets.

'I don't see them,' I shout over the squeal of the Viva's beleaguered engine. I daren't imagine the heat being generated under the car's bonnet.

'Let's just make sure,' she says, still seemingly unperturbed. With one final swing of the steering wheel and a yank on the handbrake, she spins us a good hundred and eighty degrees, shoots down into the entrance of an underground car park (at which point I swear that all four wheels leave the ground), swerves into a space and kills the engine, sinking down in her seat. Her measured breathing is just audible in the suspended air.

Silence. Echoes of a single door slamming shut. Eyes closed, my ears crawl the outside for noise of the Zephyr's engine, which I'm intimately familiar with.

'Think we lost them?' Frank ventures, his face pressed into the leather seat.

'Give it a few more minutes,' Baglan says from the front. 'Once they realise the tracker is gone for good, they'll head back to base.'

'Talking of which,' I say drily, 'where and how do you think they planted the tracker in the first place?'

Frank shoots his alarm at me.

'Presumably, you're looking at me when you toss that accusation,' Baglan says into the windscreen.

'And why would you think that?'

'Eyes in the back of my head,' Baglan counters with equal disdain. 'Didn't you know?'

She pauses before turning her head and shoulders towards me. 'Tell me, when did you and your bag part company, Mrs Flynn?'

Through the fog of this endless day, I cast back. It was

yanked from my grasp on being bundled into the Zephyr, then handed back by Baglan at the Imperial Hotel. It could have been her, but also…

'Quite,' she says, as if stalking my thoughts perfectly. 'It could also have been one of Quinn's boys, or Quinn himself. I'm not sure I would willingly risk my life on the racetrack of central London if I were the culprit.' Her eyes glint in the gloom of the car park. 'So, you see, Maggie, you might just have to trust me. For now, at least.'

I glare at Frank – for answers, reassurance, affirmation, or a sprinkling of his saviour fairy dust. He merely shrugs.

'We need to retrieve Yuri,' Baglan begins, officious again.

'What if they've already got him?' I pitch.

'Then he's already dead. But a tracker like that isn't sophisticated enough to pinpoint a single room at the Imperial. They would have had to knock on a lot of doors, and that might be his saving grace. And ours.'

The Viva's engine is hardly a purr as it limps back to its parking place behind the pong of the hotel bins, my heart heavy and sore throughout the entire journey. If Yuri is gone, after everything… I can barely bring myself to think it. Yes, he might have died in that fire, but he didn't. He lived, for his family. Only to… no, it can't end like that.

Parked up, Agent Bea exits the car and gestures for us to follow, walking us through the back kitchen again, where she's approached by what looks like the head chef. He whispers into her ear, she nodding, before we're all led down a short corridor. The door to a small office opens, revealing a man in pristine kitchen whites, though I might not trust this particular trainee cook with my stomach right now.

'Yuri!' I knock off his tall, crisp hat with an unapologetic hug, and for a second my relief threatens to spill over into tears. This whole thing started with Yuri, and so he must see it through.

'Nova, so good to see you.' His eyes shine from their tired sockets, his joy palpable in the strength of his grip on my arm.

'Did they come looking?' Baglan wants to know.

'Yes, though I was conscious enough by then to hear them approach – how is it you English put it? – like a herd of elephants, I think. They knocked on every door and, luckily for me, this hotel's drainpipes are very sturdy. Your good friend, Mario here, did the rest.'

'*Grazie mille*, Mario,' Baglan says, pumping the plump hand of the head chef. 'But I think now we'll get out of your kitchen, and your hair.'

We convene in the warm balm of the Viva's faux-leather seating. 'So, what do we do?' I say to myself, as much as the other three. By now, Garnett is likely to have Eddie Markham's copy of the file, and the element of surprise is lost. Plus, we're still on the run.

'Back to Fleet Street,' Frank pipes up with certainty.

'But Markham...?'

'It's not him we need. Someone else with skills.'

We all look to him, with bewilderment, and a certain amount of gratitude, that at least one of us has a plan.

Frank merely grins in the old Tanner style. 'And I know a man who can help.'

Of course he does.

Twenty-Nine

20 May 1965

With reluctance, we abandon the wrung-out Viva and opt for a taxi, which drops us outside the offices of a prominent national newspaper. Frank meets a man in the shadow of a back entrance, while I and Agents Bea and Yuri observe from a distance as whispered negotiations take place, a handshake securing the deal. From there, we're led – this time by Frank – into the heart of the building.

It's in a side office that I make a call to Vivien's flat, and pray that she's not out on a date at this time of the evening. She's in, and easily gives over the information we need.

'Be careful, Mags,' she says, as I prepare to ring off. 'These people, they will stop at nothing.'

'Nor will we,' I reply. Because, yet again, there's little choice but to finish this.

An hour later, a second taxi drops us at a pub on the corner of Jermyn Street. Frank, for all his bravado, is clearly in need of a pint as Dutch courage, and none of us have eaten since the Imperial, after which I must have run at least one marathon. At this time of night, the landlord at the Red Lion can stretch to several cheese baps, a pork pie and a jar of pickled eggs, but it tastes like a royal banquet.

'So how do we tackle this?' I sip at my tonic that I pretend is a double gin. 'Is it better to go in en masse, or discreetly, just two of us, with back-up outside?'

'Back-up for what?' Agent Bea argues. 'We have nothing else. It's this or bust.'

'Agreed,' Frank nods. 'Sometimes the simplest of tactics is best. In this case, safety in numbers. And the British stiff upper lip which – I can't believe I'm admitting this – might prove to be our saving grace.'

'Right then,' Bea Baglan says, putting down her empty glass, relieved of a single brandy in no time at all. 'Let's get this over with. Are we ready?'

Ready is not the label I'd apply to the rag-tag band of individuals who rise from the pub table; me in Baglan's donated jacket, the mothball smell replaced with a tang of cemetery undergrowth, and Frank's mac-and-flat-cap ensemble, looking like he's been dragged through the same hedge backwards. Yuri still smells of bonfires and – despite an intact work suit – even Baglan wouldn't pass muster at MI5's front desk now. Undeterred, we march resolutely along St James's and stand at the front steps of a pristine Regency building; White's is among the oldest of the 'private members' clubs in London, as formidable to me as the ski-slope stairs leading to the upper echelons of Leconfield House. From the street, you can smell pure Establishment.

Next to me, Frank feels for my hand and grips tight on

my fingers. 'Remember the bluster, Mags. Act important.' He turns his face to me and pushes out the special Tanner smile. 'We *are* important.'

'We'll huff and puff, and we'll blow their pompous house down, won't we, detective inspector?' I say it, squeezing down on his flesh as I do, though my level of faith is still to be decided.

Deep breath, Maggie. We're going to need it.

Frank is first to greet the concierge, standing at his desk that acts like a portcullis to his castle, a bastion of upper-class values. Seeing us, the displeasure on this sentry's face is mimicked in his voice: 'And what can we do for you. *Sir?*'

'Me?' Frank cranks up his Olivier from the first syllable. 'For myself, nothing, my good man. But for Sir Reginald Creed, whom I believe is a member of this fine institution, you can do a great deal.'

The hackles of the uniformed sentinel are instantly raised, but his daily duties in this club are all about absorbing rudeness, I imagine, and more often from the members themselves. His scepticism goes as far as raising his heavy eyebrows.

'Well?' Frank presses.

'There are certain rules in this club, sir.'

'But I'm wearing a tie,' Frank states, fingering the filthy material pulled from his pocket and loosely knitted around his neck. 'Not good enough?'

Sentinel coughs. 'It's the ladies, sir. The club doesn't permit—'

Standing next to me, an inch away, I feel the frisson of

electricity coming off Agent Bea's body. From the corner of my eye, her thin jaw clenches.

'It's true that two of my companions are women...' Frank interrupts.

Watch out, here comes the bluster.

'... females, I might add, who have done far more for this country than you ever could, or will. *Sonny*.'

Sentinel startles. He's far from young, but a good decade behind Frank. He glances at the entrance, on the steps of which is a burly suited doorman, the upmarket version of a nightclub bouncer.

'Don't even think about it, lad,' Frank says, moving towards a subtle tone of menace. 'I've got a Fleet Street photographer across the street, just ready to snap his exclusive – hard-working public servants expelled from a top London establishment. I believe that would be the newspaper headline. More than your job's worth.'

'More than my job's worth to let you in,' Sentinel snaps back, his accent slipping to somewhere just south of Portobello Road.

'Then, if you'll be so kind as to telephone inside, and relay a message to Sir Reginald, our esteemed Secretary of Defence.'

'And say what?'

Frank considers for a second. 'Tell him the Donkeys are here, transporting his file as precious cargo.'

We wait less than a minute before Frank's cryptic message has a miraculous effect. With extreme reluctance, Sentinel puts down the internal telephone and beckons us to follow. In the interior lobby it's all carved dark wood, high ceilings and a grand staircase dotted with Victorian portraits of eminent past members. All men, needless to say. I spot a former prime minister or two. Underfoot, the carpet is soft and sumptuous, and there's a hushed tone amid a gentle clink of glasses. Nothing 'smashing' or 'hip' in here, no mod London or the city's energetic youth pushing at society's boundaries, just fusty old men running the country, with age-old arrogance. I feel a frisson rising in line with Baglan's.

Just inside a second door, we encounter another prime example of this superiority. I've met Rufus Garnett only twice in my employment, when MI5's esteemed director-general addressed our intake of Watcher newcomers, and then at a boozy Christmas party. Both times, I cringed at his supercilious manner, the small man trying so desperately to fill the big shoes of his appointment, glad-handing and back-slapping with abandon. There's little bonhomie on show here, but I've no doubt he holds a deep contempt for the ruffians currently invading his world. Except that now, we have something he needs. Desperately. Enough that he might have to play nice.

'Tanner, isn't it?' He addresses Frank with gritted teeth, then nods at Agent Bea and me. 'Miss Baglan. Mrs Flynn.'

In the way he says my name, I'm utterly certain he knows all about Davy. Down to the last detail. He can't even look me in the eye.

'And you are…?' he asks Yuri. 'I don't believe we've met.'

'We have,' Yuri says with his most diplomatic smile. 'In East Berlin, once. I almost abducted you.' He proffers a hand. 'Nicolai Prokiev, KGB defector.'

'Ah, well, glad you're on the right side, at last,' Garnett stutters, limply taking Yuri's hand. Despite occupying MI5's top chair, he looks totally bewildered at having to engage with this pick'n'mix of the espionage world.

'What a coincidence you're here too, with Sir Reginald,' Frank smiles. 'Just a catch-up is it? Thankfully, it does save us all a lot of time and breath.'

Garnett coughs uncomfortably. 'There's a quiet room through here. The Secretary will join us in a minute, so if you'd just like—'

'I think not,' Frank says, forging towards a large fireplace in the vast library, where logs are crackling in the grate. 'This looks nice and cosy to me. And public.' On each side sit two leather wingback chairs, one of which is occupied by the Defence Secretary of our great British realm. As his very efficient personal assistant, Vivien knows her boss' itinerary down to the last minute, alongside his sexual foibles with fruit. Today, she's spot-on with his diary details.

Sir Reginald masks his alarm like a true politician. 'Gentlemen, and ladies,' he gestures. 'Please sit down.' The tiniest of nods signals his desire for Garnett not to make a fuss, then to the club's butler: 'Stevens, may we have some more chairs for our guests? And brandy all round, I think.' He smiles. Obsequiously, in my book. 'Always good to oil the wheels of negotiation, don't you think?'

I don't, but I could murder a brandy all the same.

Frank sits in one of the newly provided chairs, Baglan beside him, me, then Yuri to my right. Why does it feel like we're a class of school pupils let in for a peek, to see how the other half live?

Frank, though, is having none of it. He makes himself completely at home, just as if he were in the corner booth of the Blue Post, relishing a pint of bitter. 'So, gentlemen,' he begins, watching them eye the large, flat folder he's carrying under his arm.

As per the country's chief of defence, Sir Reginald seems to recognise a true council of war, and shunts himself forward in his chair, the scant wisps of his balding grey head backlit by the blaze.

'We know what you have,' he begins, in a tone that's anything but cosy. 'We've already seen your so-called evidence, and frankly, it's derisory, to say the very least. It will be simple enough for us to pass it off as entirely fabricated, a foolish attempt to smear this government by subversives bent on rocking the foundations of an elected Parliament.'

'Communists,' Garnett chimes in.

Frank merely nods. Heat from the fire pulses outwards and the crackle of wood is the only sound to fill our semi-circle of silence.

'So?' Garnett presses impatiently. His normally reddened face is slowly turning puce, and not just from the force of the blaze.

'Then, you have us beaten,' Frank says calmy. 'Clear as day.'

'What in the blazes is that supposed to mean?' Even Sir Reginald is getting hot under the collar, his arrogance twisting towards anger.

'It means you won't be in the least bit perturbed to see this on tomorrow morning's newsstands, will you?' Frank slips out the folder and opens it up. Inside, is a full-size proof of the *Daily Mail* front page, a fuzzy but unmistakable photograph of children at desks 'playing' with real weaponry, under a large headline in bold, black type: 'CHILD'S SPY SCHOOL UNMASKED IN BRITAIN', qualified beneath in smaller font: 'Russian-style secret facility for juvenile assassins. MoD implicated'.

'I would have gone with "infant assassins" myself,' Frank says. 'Undoubtedly, a better impact. But who am I to argue with Fleet Street? They are experts when it comes to exposing scandal. Look at poor old John Profumo.'

Garnett sits open-mouthed, sucking air like a goldfish in a bowl, while Sir Reginald's jaw swings side to side, his teeth undergoing a true grinding. I wager it's the picture which poses the biggest shock, Frank and I agreeing the most damning image was best kept out of our little dossier until the last minute, in case there was – God forbid – a mole in the very Secret Service protecting this country. Perhaps Kim Philby and his spy ring did do us one small favour after all: suspect everyone, trust very few. And don't show your ace card until the very end, or – in my case – tuck it within a very sturdy bra, hence holding back the negatives until the big reveal.

'You're bluffing,' Garnett barks. 'The *Mail* wouldn't dare publish that, not without warning us first.'

'And is that how our so-called free press works nowadays?' Baglan reinstates her regal crown, and the demeanour to go with it. 'Firmly in the pocket of the men who govern?'

Everyone sitting around the fire knows she's stating a fact, but like so much of the truth surrounding the British Establishment, you simply don't say it. Not cricket, eh?

'Perhaps you should ring the proprietor of this fine, upstanding newspaper personally,' Baglan goes on. 'If it is tomorrow's front page, then you can do your very best to stall it. Good luck, by the way, with averting the biggest press scoop this year. But if it is a bluff on our part, as you claim, you might have some explaining to do, and those wily old hacks will be picking up their notebooks and sniffing around before you can say Guy Burgess.' She says all this seemingly without drawing breath, and in the tone of Narnia's ice monarch. Even Creed looks fearful.

'When do you propose this to run?' he asks, voice like steel.

Frank makes a play of looking at his wristwatch. 'Ooh, copies should hit the newsstands tomorrow morning, about six a.m., I'd say. Which means it will go to press in less than two hours. That just about gives you time to ring ex-minister Profumo and hear what life is like in the political wilderness. Or...'

'Or what?' It's Garnett who leaps on the alternative, almost jumping from his seat.

'Our demands are met,' Frank says coolly.

Sir Reginald downs the last of his brandy, and looks for a moment as if he might throw the glass into the fire out of sheer, unbridled frustration. Instead, he places it carefully on a small side table and says, in a low growl: 'All right, how much do you want? As a group?'

Up until now, I've been watching this surreal game of ping-pong in silence, curbing my own fury. Now, it breaks free, and I vent. 'We don't want *money*,' I snarl without restraint. 'We want this to stop. For children not to be used as weapons, for you so-called protectors to have some bloody morals. To have a heart.' My voice rises up and over the wingback chairs, and there's a dissenting rustle of newspapers in response.

Rufus Garnett flashes me a hateful look. 'There's no room

for emotion in the world of true espionage, Mrs Flynn,' he spits. 'And you would know that if you were a true agent, rather than a minor observer.'

I have to physically restrain Frank then, his Donkey loyalty bubbling to the surface and his knees cracking as he goes to lunge, ready to throttle Garnett with his bare hands.

'It stops,' Frank demands. 'It stops now. Congleton House shuts down, and does not reopen in any form, at any time. And we want guarantees.'

'You don't have the leverage to demand that,' Creed tries.

'Don't we?' Frank holds up the very graphic mock-up again. 'I think the court of public opinion might have something to say about that. We also want immunity for all four of us, in writing, signed and sealed.'

'Listen, if you think you can come back into the MI5 fold after this—' Garnett tries.

'Why not?' Frank snaps. 'This country held onto Philby for years, even though you and MI6 strongly suspected he was a Soviet spy, the most dangerous mole this country has ever seen. MI6 even re-employed him, knowing the risk to public security. What's so different about us?'

Yuri nods emphatically, as a former KGB man very much in the loop.

But Garnett isn't a man to lose face willingly. 'Well, if you want to talk loyalty, perhaps you four musketeers ought to think about who betrayed your little endeavour in the first place. And who planted that tracker.'

His beady little eyes comb over each one of us, settling on me. Why me?

'Miss Baglan had every opportunity, and was in a perfect position,' Garnett goes on, goading mistrust in his slimy, foul manner. 'Then there's our Russian defector, here. Can you be sure he is who he claims to be, or working for us the whole time? After all, double-dealing has been his forte for many years. Are you sure he *really* knew your husband, Mrs Flynn?'

I swallow. My throat is suddenly parched. I imagined having those brain cubbies under control, but there's nothing like someone voicing thoughts deep within your psyche that you are desperately trying to repress. Now, Garnett is throwing petrol on a fire that's already raging. I don't want to think any of it, but I do. Or even contemplate what he says next.

'And Frank here,' he babbles on. 'Our reliable ex-copper – very quick to offer his help, almost too quick, I'd say. How do you think he hooked up with Miss Baglan and came running to your rescue, like a knight on a charger? Eh, Magpie?'

No. Not Frank. It couldn't be. Could it? The flames are leaping, the petrol creating a white-hot furnace.

'Mags.' Frank's voice is there in my ear, as he swaps places with Bea Baglan and shuffles in next to me. 'Don't listen, he's playing mind games. I would never do that to you. Never.'

I look into his crinkled Frank-face and I want to believe him. So much. But I'm so tired, and I just want to go home and ensure my mother and child are not damaged, or dead. For this day to end, and not to have to make decisions like this.

'He would say that, wouldn't he?' Garnett prods again. 'Tanner is an excellent liar, I'll give him that.'

Frank swivels, but instead of offering a fist to Garnett's

podgy features, his voice is as calm as a millpond. 'Maybe you want to tell Mrs Flynn all about your boy in the porn shop, eh Rufus? The one who's a dab hand with the cameras, but is a little too fond of a flutter on the horses, and who's got himself a large gambling debt. I followed him to the betting shop and watched him wager like an amateur. What did you do, Garnett, pay off the debt for him? Oh no, you'd string him along for a bit first, some good old-fashioned blackmail. Am I right?'

Garnett's nostrils flare, signalling Frank's theory is correct.

I shake my head, pushing away exhaustion and forcing reason to take hold. Terry. The cheeky chirpy chappy was, in fact, traitor Terry. I should have known it was too tempting. Stupid me. Only a twist of fate forced me to use a back-up in printing that crucial classroom image; oddly, the slimy but steadfast Bob emerges as an unlikely hero.

Deep down, though, I know who my friends are, and so did Davy. *Trust AB*. He would have trusted Frank, too, if he'd have known him. The four musketeers stand firm. All for one, and all that.

While Garnett is busy playing at spymaster, Creed sits silent, steepling his hands, elbows on his knees. Crucially, he hasn't dismissed Frank's demands out of hand. 'And suppose we agree to this,' he murmurs at last. 'What assurances do we have? Will we get the evidence, and the photographic negatives?'

'No,' Frank asserts. 'We'll keep an insurance policy safely under wraps.'

'What's to stop you bringing it out when something doesn't meet your approval in the future?' Creed pitches.

Frank swigs the last of his brandy and thumps it down

on the nearest surface, to renewed tutting from surrounding library dwellers. 'Trust,' he says emphatically. 'Loyalty and decency. I know those are fairly alien concepts to you boys, but perhaps you could try them on for size? Otherwise, these negotiations are at an end.'

Garnett gestures for someone behind to approach, and I feel the shadow of a large bullyboy looming. I tense my aching body, while my heart sags like a balloon. The bluff has failed. We'll be tossed out on our ear. Forcibly. To waiting cars outside. They'll separate us, different safe houses. Isolation and God knows what else.

'Do it,' Sir Reginald Creed hisses under his breath.

Garnett's crimson face swivels back. 'Sir? Surely, you're not giving in to these—'

'Do it, dammit!' Creed orders. 'Shut it down. It was a damned failure anyway, with that idiot Quinn overseeing it. He can't organise a piss-up in a brewery.' His granite face lifts towards Garnett. 'So, shut the bloody thing down. The PM won't stand for it should this get out. If there was still a torture rack in existence, we'd both be on it.'

He turns to Frank, a rictus smile worked into his mouth. 'I gather our business is concluded here?'

'Yes,' says Frank, though I sense he's slightly taken aback. 'We'll await proof of sale, as it were. Viable evidence of what we discussed, and the future of those children assured.'

All four of us make to rise, and although relief doesn't begin to describe my reaction, I haven't forgotten what's brought us here. Or who. The seething that's still inside me. 'I need more.'

Now, Creed's face turns to thunder, and we teeter on that iconic workhouse scene from *Oliver Twist*. '*More?*' he says.

'Minor to you, perhaps, but vital to me,' I say, ignoring reason, common sense and the thrashing inside my chest. 'My mother and child – you call off the dogs.'

He blinks, and coughs. 'It will be dealt with.'

'Now,' I say, standing firm in every way. 'I want to hear you say it.'

He exhales a lungful of exasperation and beckons the butler. 'Stevens, may I have the use of a phone, there's a good chap?'

We wait the minute or so as a telephone is brought and connected. In reaction to Creed's silent gesture, Garnett is forced to make the call. 'Stand down surveillance on Target Two Flynn,' he barks into the receiver. 'Immediately.' Then aims a sneer at me. 'Satisfied?'

'Not yet,' I say. 'There's still Quinn.'

Garnett's head whips around. 'What about Quinn? He's dead.'

'I don't believe he is, not in the way Sir Reginald just spoke about him. Which means I want him charged. Behind bars.'

'For what exactly?' Garnett spits.

'Murder. Cold-blooded murder. Of David James Flynn.'

Garnett pulls himself up and takes a step forward, his sour breath on me. 'Your husband died in carrying out his duties, Mrs Flynn, and his pension – your livelihood – reflects that. Let's not forget it.'

'Davy Flynn died because you and your lackey Quinn went rogue,' I rail, unable to contain my anger or my volume. 'Because you had ideas above your station, and because my husband had the humanity in him to know it was wrong. To do something, and then be killed by one of his own. That's not espionage, or tradecraft, or even simple betrayal. It's murder. Arrest Quinn, or the deal is off.'

Garnett stands his ground, chest puffed out, bristling in the face of my audacity. The sheer impudence of a mere Donkey. And a woman.

'Do what she says,' Creed orders, his patience lost entirely. 'Quinn is a loose cannon.' He gets up, walks forward and speaks directly to me for the first time. 'But you'll have to be satisfied with a closed court, Mrs Flynn. Quinn will be ably punished, but with no culpability on our part. That *is* spycraft, as I understand it. And it is also our final offer.'

Frank and I exchange looks. It's not his place to agree terms over Davy, but it is mine. For all four of us, for Libby and Gilda, it's the best justice I'm going to get for my husband.

'All right,' I say to the nation's Secretary of Defence.

And then I turn my back on him.

Thirty

20 May 1965

Tempted to run for the hills, the musketeers nonetheless manage to exit the library and walk with dignity through the doors of White's and out onto St James's, where the world seems not to have fallen off its axis one little bit. A sleek limousine drives by, followed by a bright red Mini blaring tinny transistor music, and a man nods as he walks past with his dog in tow.

We convene next to a phone box, and look in silence at each other. Frank, never short of words, seems dazed by our bizarre encounter. Yuri fidgets, hands in his pockets, and Bea Baglan's brow is knitted, face to the pavement.

Me? I'm equally speechless, drained of every syllable. Did that just happen? Four seemingly small cogs in the wheel of government, putting a large spanner in the works of said wheel?

'Well,' says Frank at last. 'What do we think of that? A success?'

Agent Bea's brow flattens, though her mouth is a straight

line. She looks dubious. 'It depends on what happens next,' she says, 'but you know, I think it was. We certainly spooked them.' And for the first time ever, in my presence at least, Bea Baglan issues a small laugh at her own pun, a sort of hoot, white teeth showing behind her thin lips. 'Quite apart from which, I haven't enjoyed myself so much in ages. Seeing Garnett's face was worth every penny of my pension.'

Having broken the ice, we remain at a loss; the anticlimactic feeling of achieving something that seemed unattainable, right up until the point where it wasn't. Is this how climbers feel when they reach the summit of Everest, and there's nothing up there but air, and the prospect of the descent? What do you actually *do* next?

My planned rendezvous with Grayling now defunct, we've all arranged to meet with Garnett at Leconfield House the following morning at ten a.m., to 'sort out details'. In the meantime…

'Drink?' Frank says, typically.

I shake my head. 'I need to get home, Frank. Make sure everything is all right.'

'Of course, Mags,' he says. 'And really, I should check my cats haven't abandoned me for next door's hearth.'

'Let's meet tomorrow, first thing,' Baglan suggests. 'Our own council of war before we go back into the lion's den.'

'Yuri?' I say. 'Have you a contact here, somewhere safe to stay tonight? You could always…'

'I'll find something,' he says, pulling up his face and offering a smile, though it's easy to spot the false bravado. Nothing to do with his skills as an agent, more weariness and what he's been through in past days. Contrary to popular opinion – and fans of Mr Fleming – even spies get tired.

'Come on,' Bea beckons to him. 'I've a spare room in my flat. You can sweep the place for bugs while I make a pot of tea.'

Still wary, still professionals, we move in a small pack towards the nearest tube station. Safety in numbers, as the very true saying goes.

'Miss Baglan, I've been wondering where on earth you learnt to drive like that?' Frank asks as we walk, his voice rich with admiration.

'North African desert,' she says smartly. 'Hooked up with the SAS in Cairo and they ferried me into the desert. The jeeps they used had some power in those engines. I had a rum old time screeching around the sand dunes.'

'Not quite north London in a Viva though, is it?' Frank argues.

'Same principle,' she says, the old matter-of-fact Registry Queen. 'Put your foot down, try not to hit anyone, or anything that has the power to derail you.'

And that, I muse silently, *is why my husband was happy to put his trust in you.*

Calabria Road is quiet as I make a tentative approach, no out-of-place vehicles (a Zephyr crucially), and no forms skulking behind the birch trees dotted along the pavement. My nose twitches, but detects nothing. Could it be that Creed and Garnett are true to their word? It's late by the time I walk up the garden path, very glad to see a cosy orange glow projecting from the living room, behind the not-so-subtle mandarin curtains.

'I'm home,' I sing into the empty hallway, as much for

me as anyone else; that if I say it, things might just be the same, unshaken, in their proper place, despite my unwise shenanigans of the past week or more.

'In here,' Gilda trills back. As I enter the front room, I see she's not alone, six or seven women of varying ages looking up from their texts. Of course, it's the third Thursday of the month – date for one mothership meeting or another.

'Some of you already know my wayward and hard-working daughter,' she announces to the gathering, with a tinge of reproach, but – I like to imagine – a soupcon of pride in the mix. 'Looks like you've had a long day, love?'

'You could say that.' Naturally, my eyes scan the vista. Incredibly, the psychedelic homage to Bridget Riley is actually something of a comfort. 'Everything all right, Gilda?'

'Yes, why wouldn't it be?'

Oh, no reason, other than the threat of your untimely kidnap and death.

I step behind her chair, bend and wrap my arms around a thin neck and sink a kiss into the top of her soft grey curls, smelling just what I need more than ever in that moment. Mother.

'Get on with you,' she laughs, batting me away playfully, and then to the group, 'She must be feeling guilty, I'll bet she forgot my promised bar of chocolate.'

'Sorry, yes I did.'

'Well make yourself useful, Mags, and put the kettle on. We're dry as a bone.'

'Of course. Is Libby upstairs?'

'Doing her homework, I hope,' Gilda says, head down and assuming control of the assembly.

Putting the kettle on to boil, I trudge upstairs, feeling every sinew of ache in my legs and back. I need a long soak in the bath. Before that, to see, talk to and appreciate my gorgeous daughter. If she'll let me.

'Hi Mum,' she says flatly as I enter the teenage den, more mandarin lighting and a hundred or more faces of pop icons staring from the walls, the looming lips of Mick Jagger in a permanent, copious pout.

'Hello darling. Have you had a good day? Finished your homework?'

She barely looks up from her copy of *Rave*, flicking nonchalantly through pages of nubile, hair-sprayed models in very short skirts. 'Yes, it's done.'

'What's wrong?' For a second, I regret the question. Some teenagers, I read in a magazine article recently, have an uncanny ability to sense disquiet, something about neurones in their changing brains, mother to daughter especially, the piece went on to explain. Has Libby sensed my unease, nay sheer terror, over the past few days? What have I done to upturn her fatherless, but otherwise happy, healthy adolescence? And do I have the energy to right my own wrongs?

'Nothing,' she grunts.

Except it's not nothing – I am enough of a mother to know that. 'Come on, what's up Libs? You can tell me.'

Brace yourself, Mags. Again.

She slams the magazine down and shuffles herself upwards to sitting on the bed. I lower myself beside her, adopting the pose of an exemplary listening parent.

'It's Denise at school,' she blurts.

'What about her? Is she being horrible to you?'

'No, it's not that,' Libby says, with irritation more than

distress. 'She was skipping around the classroom today, boasting about how she's got some.'

'Got what?' My mind goes into parental overdrive: drink, drugs, pills, uppers and downers, purple hearts. Things you hear about, contraband I see in Soho on a daily basis. The media – and London, apparently – is full of it.

'Tickets,' she says with disdain. 'Her mum knows someone, who works in the canteen at Abbey Road. She's got free passes for The Beatles.'

She slumps back into her pillow. Cross, not looking at me. *Shit! The bloody tickets.*

And yet, I'm almost smiling, though I wouldn't dare show such glee to my petulant, but very normal teenager, not while she's in this mood. What with Libby's disappointment, and Gilda's minor brush-off, all appears to be unchanged at 54 Calabria Road.

21 May 1965

My walk through Soho the next morning is both cheering and a little sad. Uplifting because nothing much has changed, and there's still what feels like the whole world in a microcosmos of its winding streets: scooters accelerating and leaving a puff of diesel in their wake, the street seller chat, and the heady aroma of good cappuccino, a cup of which I sink at Bar Italia before meeting the others. The downside being that I'm unlikely to have the luxury of this on my doorstep in the weeks to come. Whatever the outcome of yesterday or today, my Stable days are over, along with Frank's. No more end-of-day catch-ups over a pint at the Blue Post. Garnett and Creed will have us frozen out and sent to some hinterland of filing or admin, despite their promises. But that's life in the spy world. No one quite ever tells the truth, do they?

As I sip at an outside table, I ponder on whether I could return to my former life as a store detective. Without a doubt, I'd be in Libby's good books if I bagged a job at Mary Quant's Bazaar. But how would it feel, hemmed in for eight hours a day by four walls, racks of skimpy dresses and ostrich feathers? Caged, that's how. Perhaps I could join a private detective agency? Plenty of surveillance work there on cuckolding husbands and wives. Dull, but I would be out and about, using some part of my brain. I can't help my eyes instinctively tracking a woman moving at a pace along the pavement.

Twenties, lean to the point of skinny, legs up the armpits, black pumps to allow walking at speed, boutique houndstooth jacket over a Biba-esque dress and huge, over-the-shoulder leather bag, minimal make-up that complements her stunning, natural beauty and hair pulled back in a tail. Meets suede-jacketed man on corner, two kisses on either cheek. Very Jean Shrimpton. Model on her way to a job?

She turns as they go to walk off, her face in full view for the first time. If I'm not mistaken, it *is* the elfin Jean Shrimpton, clutching the hand of the man striding forward, who looks suspiciously like her current beau, the actor Terence Stamp.

I smile and swallow down the last dregs of coffee foam. *Still got it, Mags.*

*

Frank is already in situ at the Egg, racing pages open, looking for the world like nothing has occurred, in his best suit and freshly shaven, one cheek sporting the legacy of our skulk through Highgate's suburban undergrowth with a scratch or two.

'Morning,' he says, with far more cheer than he has any right to. 'Since you didn't ring, I assume everything's all right at home, with Libby and Gilda?'

'Fine,' I say, slipping into the booth opposite him. 'Untouched, and unaware. Seems it was a good bluff on Quinn's part after his visit. A master of the veiled threat is our Johnny.'

'Though not for much longer, we hope,' Frank says, signalling to the waitress for two teas. 'Did you sleep?'

'I think so. I mean, there were the dreams, of Creed and Garnett as spiny-toothed gremlins with devil eyes, the general stuff of nightmares, but I think I must have ignored them for a time. And you?'

'Like a baby,' he grins. 'Snuggled up to Blofeld and Bond.'

'The *Daily Mail* cover, has it melted away without any problem?' I ask.

'All sorted,' Frank reports. 'Nothing whatsoever to do with the news desk. I know one of the typesetters in the print room – told him it was a mock-up for a prank on a friend. He was more than happy to oblige for a small price.'

'Will you keep it? As insurance?'

'Going to frame it, Mags, and hang it in the toilet. It will remind me of our triumph.'

'And Eddie Markham, is he in one piece?'

'They ruffled his feathers, that's all. Whether he chooses to pursue it as a future story is up to him. But I think he might leave it a while.'

We pause and look at each other under the ridiculous ovoid surroundings, and I wonder if Frank is thinking the same thing, of the last time we were here, and what's happened since. And what's to come.

'Frank...' I begin, a distinct wobble in my voice.

'I know, Mags.' He reaches out a weathered hand and clutches at my fingers. 'I know.'

Enough said.

The arrival of Agents Bea and Yuri cuts into the moment, each looking rested and professional. From somewhere, Yuri has sprouted a new wardrobe of a black thin-weave polo neck and well-fitting trousers, with a tan suede jacket over the top – every inch CIA, I'd say. Baglan has gone for severe and austere, hair scraped back and a crisp black suit that signals she means business. I look at my own ensemble of blue trousers and white shirt that says I might just be about to go back to work loitering at a bus stop with my hidden Minox. If only.

'Morning, all,' Baglan says, and what with the smile she gives, and the golden glow of Egg ambience, I sense that she is a friend.

For a displaced man in a foreign country and an uncertain future, Yuri also seems strangely relaxed. 'What would you recommend here?'

'Well...' Frank, the expert on all things Egg, leans forward.

Breakfast ordered, we pow-wow.

'Any ideas on what we can expect?' Frank asks of Baglan. 'You know that old toad Garnett better than we do.'

'Difficult to say,' she begins, piercing the yolk of her recently arrived two poached on toast. 'Especially now. Have you seen today's *Daily Mirror*?'

Despite my ambling in Soho and past several newsstands, I haven't. She pulls out a copy from a copious handbag (the size of which sparks a good deal of envy in me, the handle to my own holdall having finally detached itself in protest this morning), and lays it on the table.

'DEFENCE CHIEF IN FRUITY SEX GAMES', the headline screams – a real one this time, on flimsy newsprint, with a whole paper behind it. 'Sir Reginald's private orgies with fruit cocktail revealed' it goes on, in thick black lettering.

'What? How?' I'm nonplussed, not by the revelations, since I know they've been tucked in Vivien's little black book for some time, but how they made it onto the front page of a national newspaper, a populist one read by many a British household, who'll presumably be tittering over their cornflakes as we speak.

Agent Bea looks unapologetic. 'They played dirty, and so I felt we should do a bit of smudging too,' she explains. 'I'm sorry to step on your toes, Maggie, but I know all about your good friend in the Ministry of Defence, and so I gave Mrs Remmers a call. She was very willing to help and "return the favour," as she put it.'

I sit, much like Garnett the night before, my mouth scooping in air. Frank simply looks on with renewed admiration.

'I'm aware I did this without the group's consent, but

it had to be prepared several days ago, discreetly. Garnett is no toad – he's much worse, an absolute snake, and if we walked in there today without collateral, we might not be arrested, but he will find some way to nullify his agreement. Without Sir Reginald Creed in support, his days are numbered, and he'll know it.'

'Do you think this will finish Creed in public office?' Yuri pipes up, between a mouthful of his omelette.

Baglan nods. 'All politicians since Profumo are terrified of something like this, and of more scandals to come out of the woodwork. They'll want him gone pronto. I wouldn't be surprised if he's drafting his resignation speech right now.'

'And Garnett?' Frank asks.

'Let's go and see, shall we?' she says, dabbing at her lipstick and getting up. 'Nice eggs, by the way. Can't think why I haven't come here before.'

'Always happy to stand you breakfast, Miss B,' Frank beams.

Amazingly, there's no sinister reception committee at the entrance to Leconfield House, and we're waved through without issue. Even Frank consents to riding in the rickety old lift, past the second floor – where we both feign a ritual wave to Hilda Grayling – and up to the top level. It's not as dusty as the second floor, and there are no flimsy partitions, but it's less ornate than I imagined, the air equally stagnant, as if they don't trust fresh particles to enter.

A secretary with a large bouffant greets us at the lift, leading us towards a green-painted door with Garnett's name on the front. 'He's ready for you,' she says.

We four pause. 'Are we ready?' Frank questions, and for a split second I see his future flash before his eyes. Judging by his expression, it's not lively and vibrant. Or very lengthy.

'All for one,' Baglan says, stepping forward, 'and one for all.'

Christ, she's had a sense of humour all this time.

He's sitting at a large desk, though not languidly, with elbows on the dark wooden surface. Crucially, he is not Rufus Garnett.

Tall, from the height of his visible torso, lean, angular face, greying hair – late forties – with piercing blue eyes, middling lips and a cleft in his chin. Looks comfortable in his own body. And the chair.

'Good morning, please come in,' he gestures, though doesn't get up, merely waves a hand towards the four seats placed at a curve in front of his desk. As we sit (again, that feeling of badly behaved pupils in front of the headmaster), he presses a button on his telephone. 'No calls, please, Natalie,' he says.

'Well, thank you for coming in,' he continues. 'For the purposes of anyone outside this room, my name is being kept under wraps for now, but you will discover soon enough that it's Guy Standing, though I trust you all to keep that to yourselves.'

Blimey, less than thirty seconds in and he's used the T word. To my left, I feel Frank prickle.

'Are we to assume that this is now your office?' Baglan says, softly, but to the point. In other words, are you the latest top dog?

'Mr Garnett has taken early retirement,' he says. 'As of this morning. And I am dealing with the issues thrown up by past days.'

Do I feel relief that Garnett has been ousted? Yes, and no. Reprieve in not having to deal with his double-dealing mendacity, but angry that he escapes the consequences of Congleton House, of the scores of lives he's corrupted. His only punishment might be a downgrading of his pension-fund and difficulty in pruning his roses. That doesn't amount to justice in my book. But then this is MI5, the so-called Secret Service; it will remain hush-hush, because that's the game.

'So?' Frank cuts in this time. 'How do we sort this mess out? For all of us.'

'Quietly and with the minimum of fuss,' Standing says unapologetically. 'No newspapers,' – he fingers a copy of the *Daily Mirror* lying to his side, though I catch a whisper of a smile on his lips – 'but with discussion.'

'And honesty?' I throw in.

'Yes, Mrs Flynn, with honesty. You have my word.'

'The word of a spy,' I say. Suddenly, my mouth is on a mission all of its own.

Now, Standing leans forward, clamps his hands and purses his lips. 'I can understand your reticence, Mrs Flynn,' he says. 'I was a spy, and I suppose, to all intents and purposes, I still am, though I fear I may not leave this desk for some time. I do, however, like to believe that even agents have morals and pure intent. Mine has only ever been to make our country a safer place, and to that end, I can only thank you for exposing what was, I promise you, not on this agency's wider agenda.'

'But how can that be?' I press. 'Garnett was head of MI5, and places like Congleton House don't run on a shoestring.'

'And you're quite right,' Standing concedes. Unlike Garnett though, he doesn't seem to have a blustering contempt for my indictment. 'Equally, Rufus didn't gain the top seat without a good deal of intelligence and guile, because that's exactly what governments demand of their spy bosses. With a few like-minded people and some clever accounting, it is perfectly possible to run operations—'

'Rogue operations,' Frank pushes in again.

'Yes, if you put it like that,' Standing agrees, 'though that won't ever appear in any document or transcripts of the detailed review that will follow, in private, of course. The best that we can offer you is our pledge – my pledge – to shut it down. And for those involved to be removed.'

'And the children? Those victims?' It's the first time Yuri has spoken, and it strikes me then he will have known Russian counterparts from Soviet spy schools, and worked alongside them. Maybe he was even one himself?

'They will have all the professional help they need to readjust,' Standing says.

'What proof will we have of that?' Bea Baglan says.

Standing unclasps his hands, and splays them outwards. 'Only my word, I'm afraid,' he says. 'And the fact that, should you go looking again, you won't find any evidence of moral wrongdoing.'

I note that he doesn't sweep it up into a category of general wrongdoing and underhand practices. But then, nations spying on one another is on shaky ethical ground, however you look at it. Which means everyone in this room is, too.

Do I trust him? My own radar has had several wires cut over recent weeks, but there are enough connections left for me to say... yes, I think I do. As I look at him, and the gentle wave of wrinkles on his forehead, he reminds me a little of Davy, and – had my husband lived and climbed the mystical career ladder of MI5 – he might be uttering the very same words now. Next to me, Frank's prickle is stilled. Good enough for me.

'And us?' Baglan picks up the mantle again. 'Will we be farmed out to retirement too?'

Now, Standing does affect some surprise, sitting upright. 'Only if it's a choice on your part,' he says. 'Personally, I feel you as a small group have achieved what this whole organisation failed to do. Plus, I will be making the prime minister aware of what your endeavours have done for this government. In consequence, we need people like yourselves. It's too early to make firm decisions now, but I'll be giving each of you a series of options going forward.'

'And does that include Yuri's family?' I ask. The conversation between a defector and a babysitting Watcher in that safe house has not left me, and it's important to have witnesses to Standing's promises. Let's not forget, we're sitting in the epicentre of duplicitous spies.

'Of course, every priority will be given to their safe transit westwards,' he assures. On my alternate side, Yuri's hand crawls towards mine and presses down.

Unlike Garnett's haughty dismissal the night before, it's a brief pause that signifies the meeting is at an end.

We rise, and this time Standing does too. 'Enjoy a few days off and we'll see each of you back here in due course,' he says. For a moment, I think he's even less scary than my bank manager. Baglan files out first, followed by Frank and Yuri, all in silence, possibly out of shock. All of us expected to be tossed out into the tundra, enduring a half-life in the shadows.

Guy Standing walks out from behind his vast desk and comes near. 'Mrs Flynn.'

'Yes?' Does the bank manager have a nasty surprise up his sleeve?

'I wanted to extend my condolences, about your husband.' He looks down at his large hands. 'I knew him a little. Not well, but our paths had crossed once or twice.'

Of course, the new head of MI5 might well be lying about that – he and Davy could have been total strangers, or intimate friends, but he is a spy, and so it's forgiven.

'Davy was a good man,' he goes on. 'One of the best.'

'He was. Thank you.'

He sniffs and extends one hand, which, when I take it, is firm and uncompromising, yet warm. 'And he would have been very proud. I do know that for sure.'

I turn to go, with a parting word from Standing: 'Is there anything else we can do for you in the meantime?'

Thirty-One

10 December 1965

While the chill of a British winter sets hard into the bones of the capital, temperatures inside the Hammersmith Odeon on this particular Friday evening are reaching volcanic proportions. Teenage girls are streaming into rows of seats and discarding coats and cardigans, fidgeting and squeaking in readiness for when they will no longer be able to hold back from the full-on hysterical scream. From my place up in a left-hand balcony, I'm just able to glimpse Libby and her best friend, Sally, in the stalls down below, agitating as the poor support bands go through their sets, largely ignored, the atmosphere brewing to almost boiling point in anticipation. She looks gorgeous in her new purple Quant dress, bought and paid for in Bazaar, rather than run up on Gilda's machine.

We're all waiting, myself included, with bated breath. Because when Guy Standing offered assistance in anything I needed, what else was I going to ask for? Something that perhaps only the nation's spy chief can ghost out of the ether. Not a pay rise, or a dream job, but end-of-the-rainbow stuff: those golden tickets.

From the moment they bounce onto the stage, mop-top to toe in black and John with his trademark peaked cap, the theatre erupts into a frenzy, the noise deafening and the screaming at a crescendo as the resounding guitar whine of 'I Feel Fine' kicks off the show. I smile, at my daughter up and out of her seat already, at these four lads who are young and enthralling, and how my life – in the great scheme of things – is pretty much 'fab'.

Ordinarily, I would have dragged Gilda here today, except that she's been in Tenerife for the past week – with Frank. The 'with' bit being anybody's guess, and who am I to ask? *Getting some winter sun*, she's scribbled in a postcard, and I don't doubt she is, some of the time. Of the four musketeers, Frank snapped up the retirement option, feeling his days running about London were numbered, though he opted to steer clear of his ex-wife and the Costa del Sol, deciding that Tenerife was the place to be for ex-pats. *Living the life of Riley, Mags*, his own brief missives say, *come and visit soon*. And I intend to. As soon as Libby breaks for her school holidays in a week or so, we'll both be flying out for Christmas, our first trip abroad as a family, to be greeted on the tarmac by a bronzed, sun-kissed Gilda. Smoothed over by love? With my beloved, though apt-to-be-prickly mother, it's better not to predict.

I'll be taking two weeks leave from my desk. Yes, that's right – my desk. Old, but solid and tangible, on the third floor of Leconfield House (and so well out of Hilda Grayling's sightline), it's an office that boasts only one partition, and thus qualifies as more than a cupboard. My job has a title that isn't quite 'Intelligence Officer', but as near as can be, and will lead 'upwards' in the none-too-distant future, Standing has been keen to assure. In every other way, our man in the top job has been true to his pledge. Yuri (I still can't get used to calling him Nicolai) and his family are settled somewhere in southern England – I don't know where exactly, and neither do I want to. But in the few times we've met in London over drinks at the Langham, he reports that his wife likes it here, her new washing machine especially, and the children already have a better command of English than their father. He feels safe, he tells me, though what that means in the world of a Soviet defector I may never know. About Davy, he remains tight-lipped – the conditions of his settlement, I can only guess. And he still calls me Nova.

Strangely, it's Baglan that's been gradually filling in those gaps. Agent Bea and I have struck up something of a friendship, and she is more than happy to reminisce over a good martini about her times chasing across Europe and Africa with the SOE, leaving me wide-eyed at the perilous scrapes of my then future husband, situations she very often hauled him out of. I owe her that, but also because those conversations are helping me to understand his desire to do something, and that need in him to do right. Absent or not, I understand my Davy in death, perhaps better than in life. I suppose it means I've made my peace with it, too.

It is also a bonus to have the ear of the Registry's top monarch, Agent Bea choosing to restake her claim on MI5's basement treasures, though I note she's often up and down in that cranky old lift to the top floor, in a 'consulting capacity', it's rumoured. Lord forbid those big boys should ever need a woman to sort them out. Not officially, anyway. Not yet.

And so, Maggie Flynn, 'Case Officer' – officially an MI5 operative – really is fine. Oddly enough.

The concert is almost at an end, the screams at fever pitch, the floor a jumping, bobbing sea of teeming teens, and the performers hoarse from trying to make themselves heard over the adolescent, screeching soundtrack. Paul McCartney announces the last song to hysterical tears and loud applause, and I fight to spy my own daughter down below, pawing at her wet cheeks and grinning widely. Her eye catches mine in one brief tear-stained second and, what is that I see? A glint, perhaps?

Above the cacophony of noise, a distinct voice cuts into my ear, the crystal-clear tone of my husband from beyond his grave. 'She loves you,' he says.

Yeah, yeah, yeah.

Author Note

UNSURPRISINGLY, I'm a huge fan of spy fiction, though my introduction to the murky arena of espionage did not come from reading the classic writers like Le Carre, but rather from television; as a child growing up in the 1970s, I was glued to re-runs of *The Avengers, The Saint, The Protectors* and *The Man From U.N.C.L.E*, among many other spy capers, plus our family's ritual cinema pilgrimage to catch the latest Bond film. Odd to say my first crush was on a puppet, but it *was* Captain Scarlett who captured my adolescent heart, and the prize toy in my collection was Mary Quant's own 'Havoc' doll, complete with a stylish black catsuit and plastic revolver.

Since the 1960s is among my favourite eras to write about, it's no shock that my own debut into the spy genre is set amid that gorgeous 'swinging' decade, in my birth city of London. But, given the youth seemed to have the monopoly in those years (and now being much, much older myself), I felt it was about time the middle-aged female spy claimed her moment in the spotlight.

As I continue to read my way through the classic catalogue of Len Deighton, Le Carre and Frederick Forsyth, I've had a ball creating Maggie Flynn, immersing myself in arguably the most vibrant period of the twentieth century – watching *The Ipcress File, Georgy Girl* and *Blow Up* became joyful research and never seemed like work.

There's a wealth of other resources that shape Maggie's world; Dominic Sandbrook's *White Heat* provided a political and cultural bedrock for the time, and Stella Rimington's autobiography *Open Secret* afforded a valuable insight into MI5's woefully late introduction of women into roles of responsibility, plus the practical layout of the old headquarters. Due to a chance encounter in a coffee shop (thanks Nick Tentis), I was piloted towards the best contemporary guide of the time in *Len Deighton's London Dossier*, giving me chapter and verse on shops, cafés, theatres and pubs of the mid '60s, some of which survive to this day. I can testify that Soho's Bar Italia serves good coffee, and the Regency Café in Pimlico still has Formica tables and a good breakfast. Sad to say, the Golden Egg chain is no longer with us, but I remember it well, the ovoid menus and being bathed in that distinct lighting. The Muswell Hill branch was my favourite.

As with each book, it's not just about what makes it onto the page; so many others shape, chivvy, publicise and sell the writer's wares. As ever, thanks to my own Agent Broo – Broo Doherty, from DHH Literary Agency – for understanding Maggie in a heartbeat. So, too, to Aria's editor Aubrie Artiano and her unbounding enthusiasm for all things *Mrs Spy*, plus the entire team at Aria, Head of Zeus and Bloomsbury. I appreciate every smidgen of effort made. And to copy editor Rhian McKay for rescuing my grammar, plus her quirky comments.

My support team of writer pals are unchanged and unbending – Sarah Steele, Mel Golding, Emma Flint, Hannah Dolby, Lorna (Elle) Cook, LP (Loraine) Fergusson and Jane Bailey – plus so many others. You prop me up, year round.

The dog walking, cocktail quaffing and knitting/maternity crews are such a huge part of my life: too many to name, but I am grateful to you all, every single day. You keep me sane. Rough Hands coffee shop in Stroud – you make sure I am ninety percent flat white.

As ever, I pay tribute to my biggest fan, my mum, Stella, and her impressive bouffant hair-do's I discovered amid the old family photos. This time, also to my late dad, Alan – he was never in the force, but he was a born and bred Londoner, and so when Frank Tanner blossomed in my mind, it was Dad's voice I heard in the dialogue: 'Right-o' being a case in point.

History – be it big or small – lives on the page.

About the Author

MANDY ROBOTHAM started her adult life as a journalist, only to become waylaid by children and birth. After twenty happy years as a midwife, she fulfilled a childhood dream of writing and publishing her first book. This is her second novel as M J Robotham, and she writes historical drama as Mandy Robotham – ably assisted by muse mutt, Basil – from her home in Stroud, Gloucestershire.